THE

DISENCHANTMENT

OF NARCISSA

TARVER

Also by Donna Birdwell

Not Knowing
(2019)
"...an expedition into a magical vision of reality."

EarthCycles, Book One:
Song of All Songs
(2020)
Winner of the SPR Silver Medal
"...an immersive and visceral vision of the future."

EarthCycles, Book Two:
Book of All Time
(2021)

EarthCycles, Book Three:
Beyond the Endless
(2022)

The Resistance:
Recall Chronicles 1 & 2
(2025)
"A vision of the future that's both harrowing and endlessly
entertaining." — Kirkus Reviews

THE DISENCHANTMENT OF NARCISSA TARVER

Donna Birdwell

Published by Wide World Home.
8944B Parker Ranch Circle
Austin, TX 78748 USA

donnadechenbirdwell.com

FIRST PRINTING – September 2025.

Publisher's Note: This is a work of fiction. Names, characters places, and incidents are either the product of the author's imagination or used fictitiously.

Birdwell, Donna
The Disenchantment of Narcissa Tarver
388 pp.
1. Historical Fiction – Fiction 2. American – Fiction
I. Donna Birdwell II. The Disenchantment of Narcissa Tarver
ISBN: 978-1-7355569-7-0

Library of Congress Control Number: 2025915208

I humbly dedicate this work
to the honor of
Isom,
Margaret,
Rebecca,
Priscilla,
and James,
and to their descendants,
wherever they
may have landed.

Cuimhnichibh air na daoine bho'n d'thainig sibh.
(Remember the people you came from.)
--Scottish Proverb

The struggle to understand is our only advantage
over this madness.
--Ta-Nehisi Coates,
Between the World and Me

PREFACE

This book is a work of fiction but the story it tells is true.

Most of the characters called Tarver in these pages are my own maternal grandmother's people. I have spent much of the past two years learning about the things my grandmother never told me.

Delving into ancestry.com and its treasure trove of documents, I applied skills learned in my research work as an anthropologist, specifically the skill of finding living, breathing communities of people in the dry pages of census records.

I dug through newspapers.com, where the words and deeds of some of my family members were laid out in painful black and white.

On two journeys to Mississippi, I visited the graves of many of the individuals who became characters in this book. I found the "big house" my great-great-grandfather started building before the Civil War. I also spent long hours in libraries and archives and museums.

In writing this book, I have tried to embody as much truth about the times as I could. My main character, Narcissa Tarver, is entirely fictional, as is her companion Julia and all of Julia's family. Characters who are real but significantly fictionalized have been given fictional names. Characters of historical significance appear as themselves.

I wrote this book because I was curious.

I'm publishing it because of what I learned.

Donna Birdwell, September 2025

Chapter One
A Beginning and an End

1909

Cissa should never have been born. She knew that for a fact. Her mother should have been beyond childbearing, but Cissa had come along anyway, and year after year she struggled to find some way to matter amid the sprawling family of Tarvers in the Mississippi countryside.

The Tarver who mattered most had always been her brother Duncan. Duncan, the golden boy who became a doctor like their father and then a politician. Duncan, whose name was in all the papers. In her mind, Cissa composed the headline for tomorrow's paper: SHERIFF DUNCAN TARVER DEAD.

Cissa stood at an open window in the dining room where the sullen summer breeze barely stirred the curtains. Her throat prickled with the dust stirred up by the feet of men and horses that crowded around her nephew Albert's house, the house that had been built for Duncan. There were fewer men there now, no more than a dozen compared to the scores who had escorted Duncan's body from Cowleton where he'd fallen, back here to Callander Road where he'd grown up.

Earlier, Cissa had walked down the road, approaching close enough to hear the men's words and to know they were not done cursing what had happened. She hadn't crossed over to join them. Watching now through the window, she easily picked out her brother Monroe, who stood half a head taller than most of the rest. Cissa was thankful they'd had the grace not to bring Duncan's broken body into their mother's house, the Tarver big house. The old woman's mind was fragile enough without having to take in the shock of what Cissa had glimpsed as they carried Duncan's body up the steps. The memory of it sent an icy shiver through her veins. She glanced toward the hall mirror, which she'd turned to face the wall as soon as she'd heard the news.

Cissa watched as Duncan's youngest son labored along the road and across the yard to her front door. Robby was at that uncertain age that teetered between youth and manhood. He entered without knocking. There was blood on his shirt and a feverish exhaustion in his eyes.

"Is that you, Duncan?" Mother spoke without turning around.

"No, Grandma, it's Rob." He frowned at Cissa and spoke in quiet tones. "Doesn't she know, Aunt Cissy?"

"I tried to tell her. But you know how she is. How are Lamar and Eli doing?" Cissa knew that two of Duncan's older sons had been wounded in the affray.

Rob nodded with downcast eyes. "Eli will be alright."

"And Lamar?"

Robby paused, fiddling with the hat he still held in his hands. "They say it'll be a miracle if Lamar makes it through the night."

"They have good doctors down there in Natchez," Cissa said. Her eyes locked briefly with Robby's, but the pain there was too much, and she looked away.

"Are you and Grandma going to be alright here by yourselves?" His hand went toward the pistol on his hip. His glance brushed Cissa's mangled right hand.

"I'm sure we'll be fine," Cissa said, bristling at this subtle reminder that even her family still considered her damaged hand a liability.

After a kiss for his grandmother that glanced off her cheek, Rob left.

Cissa watched him all the way back to Albert's house where men continued to disperse amid the creak of wagon wheels and saddles, the slap of reins, the rhythmic plod of hoofbeats on the earthen road. Cissa thought about the women tending to their tasks inside the house. Cleansing the deceased was a loathsome task at best, but when the body was as damaged as Duncan's was...

Monroe was the last man left on the porch; he sank down onto the steps. His shoulders slumped and then began moving rhythmically as he let his head fall toward his knees, grieving the loss of his brother. *Our brother,* Cissa thought.

She snapped the curtains closed against the scene. Before she could stop it, a burble of laughter escaped her throat. She knew it wasn't proper, but she couldn't help it. This all seemed so ludicrous.

Composing herself, she moved into the parlor where her mother sat in the big armchair, her head dropped forward, her hands folded in her lap. It was hard to tell if she was drowsing or merely praying. Cissa stood for a moment, her hand resting on the chair tidy behind Mother's head. Her finger traced the flowers embroidered there by Julia's expert hand. Her Julia.

Cissa took in a deep breath, wondering how Mother would bear up under this latest loss.

Chapter Two
Born to Wonder

1876 – 1883

Cissa had been a fragile wisp of a child with an unexpectedly lusty cry that wearied her mother. More often than not it had been her young nurse Julia—still a child herself—who had picked her up, bounced and jostled her, transmuting her wails into giggles.

As Cissa grew, there were untold hours of laughter-peppered clapping games with Julia and mud pies made from squishy black earth slapped between strong young fingers. "That be a nice one, Miss Cissa," Julia would say as she placed Cissa's creation on a sun-warmed stone to cook. Cissa felt most like herself when she was with Julia.

It was on a certain summer day heavy with sunshine and the scent of magnolias that Cissa made an important discovery: She found out where Julia lived. She'd never thought about Julia having a house of her own somewhere. Julia belonged to Cissa's house, though she didn't sleep there.

The two girls had followed Julia's little brother Benny through the forbidden canebrake and a stretch of scrub forest, arriving out of breath at a cluster of rough wooden cabins. Julia went straight to one of the cabins where a solid looking Negro woman sat on the steps, her folded hands resting on the flowered skirt that pulled tight across her knees.

When the woman saw them, warm laughter bubbled up, rising right out of her belly. There was an exchange of words between her and Julia—pleasant words in a back-and-forth that seemed to sort out a misunderstanding.

Cissa clung to Julia's hand. "Good morning," she said, edging closer to the Negro woman, uncertain how to behave in this unfamiliar place. She shifted from one foot to the other to relieve blisters that were forming because of wearing shoes without socks. She'd been wading barefoot in the creek and had left her socks behind.

"This here my Mama Zolene," Julia said.

"Pleased to meet you, Mrs. Zolene." Cissa smiled and held out her hand, irresistibly drawn by a desire to touch this substantial woman.

"Well ain't she the polite li'l thing." Zolene wiped her right hand on her skirt and then held it out toward Cissa, grasping the fingers of Cissa's proffered hand lightly in her own. "I know you be Miss Narcissa Tarver. I sees you time 'n again with my Julia up t' the big house."

Several youngsters edged closer, staring at Cissa with unabashed curiosity. They were all Negroes, all barefoot, all wearing simple shorts or dresses that bore evidence of untold hours of physical activity. Cissa felt taller under their gaze; she watched them with a wary eye and a furtive smile. She tucked a stray strand of fair hair behind a slightly sunburned ear, wondering if children with dark skin ever got freckles like she did.

Zolene turned toward the youngsters and scowled. She waved a hand, and they dispersed, though Cissa could still feel them looking at her from behind the cabins. She pulled her shoulders back and stood up straighter.

Cissa was unaccustomed to seeing so many Negroes in one place other than at the Presbyterian church when they held the afternoon service for coloreds. Once her family had been passing by and had stopped to listen to the singing and they had seen all the Negroes coming out when service was over. Now Cissa looked around the little community with mounting interest. "Do you live here, Julia?"

"Ever since the day she born." Zolene sounded as if that was some source of pride.

Something bright caught Cissa's eye. She pulled on Julia's arm and gestured toward the phenomenon. "What's that?" she whispered.

Zolene pulled her chin back in astonishment and, as if she were making an announcement to the whole community, said, "Chile ain't never seen no bottle tree!" And that warm laugh burbled up again. "Take her up close, Julia," she said, pointing her lips toward the tree.

Cissa had thought in that moment that the bottle tree might well be the most beautiful thing she had ever seen, glittering there in the sunshine pretty as a Christmas tree. Bottles of all colors adorned the ends of an old crape myrtle's branches, glinting green and blue and golden brown. Cissa approached with wonder, tilting her head side to side to catch each color in its best light. She reached her right hand toward a low branch and touched a blue bottle.

Julia grabbed her arm and jerked it away. "Don't touch, Miss Cissa." Julia glanced back at her mother. "Could be haints in there."

Cissa had heard of haints, though she wasn't certain what they were. She thought they might be something like ghosts. She knew they could cause trouble and sickness. She drew back her hand and tucked it behind her as she backed away from the tree. A prickle of fear settled in the palm of her bold right hand. The feeling didn't go away, even as Zolene bid them farewell. "You come back any time, Miss Narcissa. I be right pleased t' see you."

When Cissa couldn't be with Julia, she sometimes felt like she ceased to exist. Mother would look at her with surprise when she spoke, while Pop sometimes seemed to stare right through her. Her sister Matilda treated her like a doll that could be set on a shelf and ignored when she didn't feel like playing.

At times like these, Cissa would creep out of the house—a thing nobody seemed to mind—and run barefoot through soft patches of clover or squat in the edge of the creek, sorting pebbles and trying to catch tadpoles. The cats that lived in the barn were a frequent source of solitary comfort. There were moments when Cissa's heart smiled with a fierce joy as she stroked the silky black fur of the kitten Pop called Sambo, the one she herself had transformed from a wild thing into a gentle companion.

Cissa's birthdays were forgotten as often as not, but the year she turned six was different. Turning six meant she would soon be expected to attend school.

She had mixed feelings about school. On the one hand, she desperately wanted to learn to read and write. She often watched her father pore over newspapers, not noticing her as she sidled up close, staring at the lines of marks, wondering how they could hold Pop's attention so firmly. She also watched both Pop and Duncan write things on bits of paper that people carried away clutched like magic tokens certain to make them or their loved one well and healthy again. Clearly there was some power to reading and writing, and school was the place where Cissa would be initiated into its mysteries.

On the other hand, going to school would take her away from Julia. "I'll miss you awfully when I have to go to school every day," Cissa said, leaning with both elbows on the kitchen table, her chin resting on her two small fists. She was certain that Julia, too, would be desolate without her.

"You be learnin' so much you won't think t' remember me." Julia tossed her head, causing one of her many braids to fall over an eye. Cissa didn't believe her.

On the last Monday in October, when most of the cotton had been picked, ginned, baled, and hauled away, Cissa walked the half mile to the wooden building that housed the Mount Eden school. She made the journey in the company of Duncan's eldest children, Albert and Milly, and a neighbor girl who was almost eleven. It was Albert's second year and Cissa had tried asking him questions about what to expect. "Don't you know anything?" he answered and rolled his eyes before scurrying ahead as if he didn't want to be seen with three girls, two of whom were rank beginners.

A few of Cissa's schoolmates thought Milly Tarver and Albert Tarver were her sister and brother, which Cissa didn't mind. Both of her actual brothers—Monroe and Duncan—had been grown and married by the time Cissa was born; her sister Matilda had been almost fifteen. Other brothers and sisters were born who would have been closer to her age if they'd lived.

At school Cissa learned to write her letters with ease. She was captivated by the notion that these letters could be combined into words and then sentences and then whole stories. Her teacher Miss Armstrong praised her for the neatness of her work. "You have a graceful hand, Narcissa," she said. Cissa treasured that phrase—"a graceful hand."

Around the time school let out for cotton planting in March, Cissa began hearing talk of Matilda getting married. Mother became testy and bickered with Matilda more than usual. Cissa avoided them both.

She deduced from overheard conversations and quarrels that the fellow paying Matilda court was a young man of some importance. His father owned a shop in Marchelle, the county seat of Hinson County. The young man's name was Frances Henning, and he was well-mannered and polite, despite being a Methodist. He often brought little gifts for Matilda from his father's shop. He brought candies for Cissa.

Mother dug in her heels when Matilda declared her intention to move to Marchelle when she became Mrs. Henning. The town was almost twenty miles away, she pointed out, and Matilda was her only daughter. "Well, my only daughter who's any help," she said, giving little Cissa a baleful glance.

"Keep in mind that Matilda is twenty now and not getting any younger," Pop said. "We must think of her future. Besides, Monroe and Laura will still be here." Duncan with his wife Ada and their three children, had recently moved away from their house on Callander Road all the way to Cowleton, which was more than twenty miles away and in quite another direction.

"But Laura's got two little ones to look after and another on the way." Mother refused to be consoled.

Pop persisted. "You have Fannie coming in every day to do the cleaning and cooking and Julia looking after Narcissa."

Mother scoffed. "Every day? How would you know, Joseph? You're never here. That Fannie has more excuses every week. If this was the old times, we'd sell the girl and get somebody worth her salt."

"Well," Pop said, "if Fannie's become unreliable, how about we let her go as soon as the wedding's done and school starts up again. We can have that Julia girl start taking over the housekeeping. She must be nearing sixteen now, old enough to take on that responsibility. And there's really no need any longer for her to mind the child."

Cissa resented being called "the child," but she liked the idea of Julia still being at her house every day. When she shared the good news with Julia, she did not get the reaction she'd anticipated.

Julia scowled and folded her arms over her chest.

Cissa tried again. "You'll still be here every day when I get home from school, Julia. We'll have fun."

"Not so much fun, Miss. They be 'specting me to cook and clean, not just playmates with you no more."

Cissa walked away in a huff, offended that Julia was acting as if she didn't want to spend time together, as if maybe she didn't like Cissa anymore.

Donna Birdwell

The Tarver Family, 1880

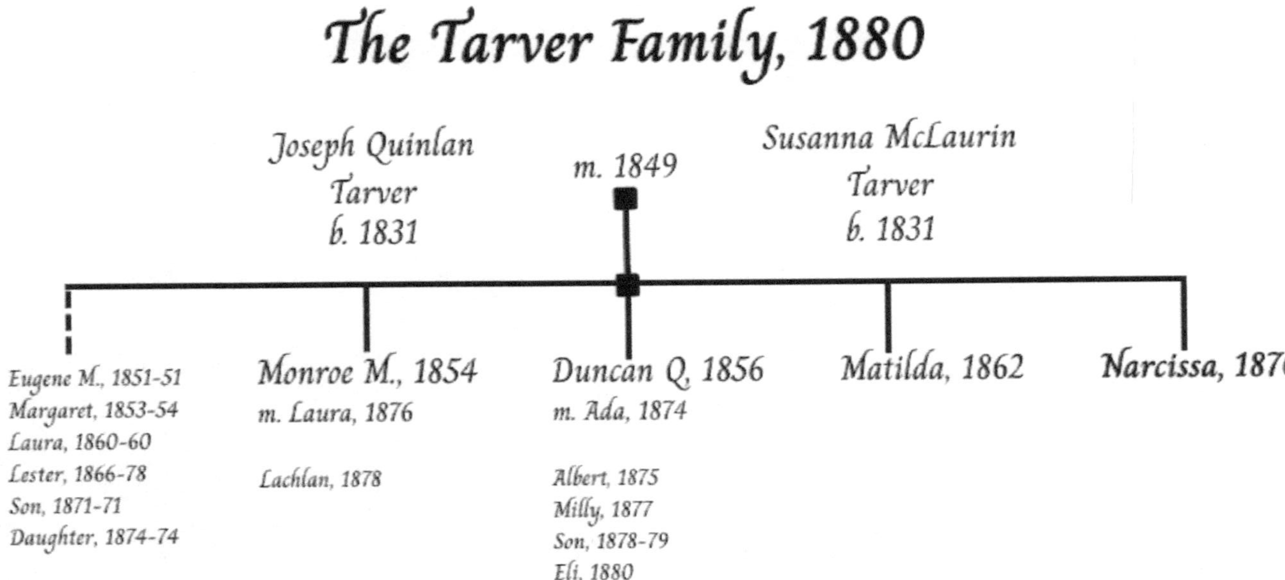

Donna Birdwell

Chapter Three
Along Came a Spider

Summer 1883

Julia continued as Cissa's companion through the summer, even as she began taking on other responsibilities. Cissa discovered that she rather liked the increased freedom from supervision. After summer term started, she spent more and more after-school time on her own, wandering barefoot around the yard and fussing with the cats in the barn.

"You leave Sambo alone!" Cissa threw an acorn at the pullet that was trying to steal the crust of bread she'd given to her little black cat. The chicken squawked, grabbed the bread in its beak, and scampered under the house. Cissa gave chase, crawling on hands and knees in the musty darkness as she scrambled after the offending fowl.

"Ouch!" There was a sudden pain in Cissa's right hand. "Julia! Julia!"

"You alright, Miss?" Julia's face drew into a concerned frown as she peered under the house.

"Something bit me." Cissa crawled toward Julia, forgetting the thieving pullet.

Julia reached for her and pulled her the last couple of feet out from under the house. "Show Julia," she said.

Cissa held up her right hand and pointed to the space between her index and middle fingers where a patch of red was beginning to show.

"Mmm-hmmm." Julia nodded sagely. "I puts a li'l soda on that there and you be right as rain. No cryin' now, Miss Cissa. It jus' a li'l ol' bug bite."

Cissa offered an apologetic glance toward Sambo. He looked hungry.

In the kitchen Julia found the tin of baking soda and dumped a liberal portion over Cissa's moistened hand, rubbing it into the space between her fingers.

"What's going on there?" Mother bustled into the kitchen. "Goodness, Julia, why in heaven's name have you dumped out all of our baking soda?" She looked as if she might strike Julia for her wastefulness, but Cissa began wailing and Mother quickly transferred her annoyance onto her, scolding her for crying over such a small nothing as an insect bite and then, as the story emerged further, for chasing the chicken and for feeding the flea-bitten barn cat that was supposed to earn his keep hunting mice. "Go on, now," she said. "Go sit in the bedroom and pray for forgiveness."

Cissa went to the bedroom that she shared with her sister. The only prayer she could think of was "Now I lay me down to sleep," which didn't seem helpful, so she sat by the window and stared out at the birds. She didn't feel sorry about feeding Sambo and she'd crawled up under the house many times before. What did she need forgiveness for anyway?

Despite the baking soda, the bite kept itching and within a couple of hours there was a sizable blister where whatever it was had sunk its fangs or stinger into Cissa's hand. She knew better than to make a fuss, so she bore her discomfort without complaint, even when the itching turned into a burning pain. It bothered her at school the next day, making writing difficult.

When she showed it to Julia a couple of days later, Julia advised her to go to her father. "He a proper white folks doctor. He gon' know how t' fix it."

"Don't you know anything to do?"

"Me, I lets my mama fix things. Mama Zolene know lots can help folks. But your pa, he don't take no store in nigger medicine. You bes' jus' ask him, Miss Cissa."

But Cissa didn't ask him, recalling several incidents in the past when she had shown her father a skinned knee or a cut finger only to be scolded, subjected to a medication that was more painful than the injury, and sent away with a lecture. "You must stop your whining, Narcissa. You need to learn to bear your little woes." This time Cissa resolved to be brave. She didn't let her father see her sore hand.

July came and Cissa's seventh birthday passed unremarkably. The spot between her fingers began to turn black. She wondered if the injury had anything to do with that blue bottle she'd touched at Julia's house or with whatever haint might have been inside the bottle. She tried saying a few belated prayers, but the wound got no better.

She still managed to keep it concealed in the folds of her dress whenever anyone other than Julia was around. She showed it to Sambo. He nudged his head against it and purred.

Cissa tried to convince herself that the spreading black spot meant her wound was healing, since the pain had been replaced by numbness. She kept thinking about the blue bottle. Then one day at breakfast, when she reached for the butter and almost dropped it, her father grabbed her hand and turned his full attention to it.

"What in the name of God Almighty happened here, Narcissa?" He was angry. Cissa had known he'd be angry. He made her get up and come around the table so he could examine her hand. And he made her tell him exactly what had happened and when. He didn't seem at all impressed by Cissa's fortitude in not whining about her small injury.

"Susanna, you and Matilda must not let this girl go galivanting around like some colored child. What we've got here," he said, "is gangrene. I never saw it more clearly even in the war hospitals. I'm afraid you've done it now, Narcissa."

She began to cry.

Cissa never remembered exactly what happened next except that there was more pain and blood than she'd ever experienced before in her entire short life. Her father did not believe in newfangled notions of using chloroform for surgeries, convinced that the pain itself was cathartic and, as he put it, salubrious. But he did see fit to administer a little bit of opium and a little more once the operation was complete, so Cissa slept a long while.

She awakened in the haze of a dream in which she felt very small, her sister Matilda's arms easily enfolding her entire body. In the dream, a group of men on horseback emerged out of darkness with torches blazing. There was shouting and raucous laughter. Cissa hadn't understood the words, but she'd understood the anger, and it terrified her. Matilda clutched little Cissa close as their father mounted up to join the riders. In her dream, some of the men were ghosts, their faces shrouded in the flickering torchlight. Cissa was certain that one of the ghosts was her brother Duncan. Mother was there somewhere, waving godspeed to the men as they galloped away. Cissa buried her face in her sister's neck as she yearned for Julia.

She blinked away the last vestiges of the dream and squinted, her eyes fixed on Julia's face, trying to stop the room from tilting and turning. Why was Julia here in the bedroom? And why did her right hand hurt so?

It did hurt. Tears came into her eyes with the awareness of just how much it hurt. She reached for it with her left hand, thinking to soothe the pain, but Julia grabbed her wrist.

"Leave it be, Miss Cissa," Julia said. "You jus' be still whiles I fetch Doc Tarver."

Cissa nodded and when Julia released her left hand, she did leave it lying still on her chest. She shook her head, trying to clear the cobwebs, and realized that her head hurt, too, though not as much as her hand. She raised the right hand up to have a look, to see what made it hurt so. She saw the bandage, stained with blood. And when she saw what had been done to her, saw the space where two fingers used to be, she screamed and sat bolt upright, holding the mutilated hand in front of her face as if it were some monstrous specter that she could frighten away by shrieking.

When Doctor Tarver entered the room, Cissa saw that it was not her father that Julia had brought, but her brother Duncan. "What did you do?" she screamed. "Where are my fingers?" Tears streamed down her face. "You have to put them back!" She was sure it was Duncan who had cut off her fingers. Pop would never do such a thing. She held her despoiled hand up toward her brother and sobbed.

"Now, now, baby sister," he said. "Don't upset yourself. What's done is done." He fumbled in his bag and pulled out a little bottle, which he handed to Julia. "Give her a spoonful of this every couple of hours, whenever she's awake. I'll wait for her to go back to sleep and return to put on a fresh bandage. She'll be well soon enough." Turning to Cissa, he said, "You see what happens to little girls who go crawling around where they shouldn't. There was a nigger boy over at Marston who died from a recluse spider bite like this. You're lucky you only lost a couple of fingers. It's time for you to start behaving like a proper little lady."

What he said didn't make Cissa feel any better. She looked up at Julia, who still held Cissa's left hand in hers. Julia patted the hand and began to sing.

Chapter Four
The Woman in the Forest

Fall 1883

Cissa missed the final week of the summer school term and, as August trudged toward September, she moped, spending long hours staring at her right hand, thinking maybe her fingers might be growing back. She nurtured a smoldering anger at Duncan for having ruined her hand. Whenever she thought about the blue bottle on the crape myrtle tree, she prayed a small prayer, even as her doubts grew as to whether Lord Jesus knew anything about how to protect people from haints. She grew fearful of insects and stopped walking barefoot in the yard.

Mother had at last made peace with Matilda's betrothal and the whole family was soon caught up in wedding preparations. Before Cissa's accident there had been talk of her being a flower girl, but that talk stopped. The wedding was set for late October, after the cotton would be sold, providing money to fund the celebration and to pay the shopkeepers for the cloth and other paraphernalia bought on credit or layaway.

One afternoon, when Cissa had been told several times to stay out from underfoot, and when Julia was busy polishing silver alongside Fannie, and when Cissa's nieces and nephews had all gone visiting elsewhere, Cissa went to the barn looking for Sambo. He wasn't there.

She wandered toward the path through the canebrake, which she now knew led to the community where Julia lived. Maybe Sambo had gone there. She thought about Zolene's warm laughter and how she'd said to Cissa, "Come back whenever you like." She had said that hadn't she? Cissa made up her mind to visit Zolene, to ask her if she'd seen her cat. Maybe she could also ask her about haints.

Cissa started off bravely enough, but somewhere along the path she missed a turn. Before long, she realized that she didn't know where she was. *Lost,* was the word that came into her mind, though she didn't want to admit it. She stood stock still there in the middle of the ill-defined path, uncertain whether to turn back or forge ahead. She couldn't decide to do either, so she plopped down on an old stump and began to cry.

Hearing a noise, she looked up and saw a stranger standing just a few paces away. The woman wore a loose-fitting long dress the color of earth, with faded embroidery along the hem and neckline. She wore a strand of red beads. Her straight gray hair was pulled into a long braid and her feet were enveloped in soft leather boots.

"You lost, little one?" the woman said, her eyes searching for Cissa's.

"I guess so." Cissa gulped, stifling a sob. She swiped her right sleeve across her face to dry her tears and then quickly hid her damaged hand behind a fold of her dress.

"Where you go?" The woman spoke in an odd way. She was dark, but she didn't look like a Negro.

Perhaps the woman's peculiarity should have frightened Cissa, but instead she felt drawn to it. The woman seemed at home here in the forest and her presence reassured Cissa. "I was going to visit Mrs. Zolene," she said.

"I take you. Come." The woman turned on her heel and strode off down the path.

Cissa scurried after her.

In fewer minutes than Cissa had expected, they arrived at the community where Zolene lived. The stranger stopped at the edge of the clearing and motioned toward Zolene's house. Cissa, feeling much relieved, turned to thank the woman, but she was gone.

Gone, too, was Cissa's desire to visit Zolene. She had a curious urge to turn back and follow the woman who had rescued her. More than anything, though, she wanted to be home where everything was familiar even though she so often felt unwelcome there. Once again, she stood mired in uncertainty. Finally she took a few hesitant steps toward Zolene's house. Julia's house. An old man spoke to her from the cabin next door.

"Julia ain't here, Miss Narcissa. She up at your place." The man's voice was deep and crusty. His face was shiny black, and his hair and beard were white as milk. He slouched in a straight chair pushed well back onto his porch.

"I was coming to see Mrs. Zolene," Cissa said.

"Miz Zolene ain't here neither," the man said.

"Oh. Well, would you please tell her I came to call?"

The old man chuckled. "Yes ma'am, Miss Narcissa. Fo' sure I tells Miz Zolene you come callin'." He leaned forward, craning his neck to look around the edge of the porch. He whistled.

A boy came running from behind one of the houses. A dog came, too. Cissa recognized the boy as Benny, Julia's little brother.

"You gwan take Miss Narcissa back up t' her house." The old man smiled and nodded at Cissa, then settled back into his chair. It creaked as he shifted his weight.

"Thank you…" Cissa hesitated. She wished she knew the man's name so she could say a proper thank you, but the name had not been offered. She scurried after Benny, who was already well down the path. Suddenly remembering her original mission, she called out to the boy to ask him about her black cat. He only laughed and hurried faster.

When Cissa got home, the only one who seemed to have noticed that she'd gone missing was Julia. "Where you be off to, Miss Cissa?" she said as she scrubbed away at a cooking pot.

Hesitantly, Cissa recounted her misadventure. She glanced over her shoulder several times to make sure no one else was listening.

"Oh." Julia scrubbed harder. "Mus' be Nubby find you. Mos' folks never sees Nubby. She keep t' her own self."

Cissa thought the strange name suited the strange woman. "Who's Nubby?"

"She Indian," Julia said. "Choctaw. My mama say when mos' Choctaw leave Miss'ippi to go up west, Nubby she stay behind."

"Where does she live?"

"Don't rightly know. Up in the forest, I reckon."

"We should go visit her sometime. So I can thank her for helping me when I was lost." Maybe she'd know something about Cissa's cat.

"Maybe we do that one day, Miss Cissa. Maybe we jus' do that."

Matilda's wedding went off splendidly, or so everyone said. Cissa found the whole affair tiresome. She had to wear a fancy blue dress with a waist. She'd been measured for it two months before, but it was now too tight across her stomach and shorter than it should have been. She was also forced to wear borrowed shoes that hurt her feet. Cissa's niece Betty was the flower girl. Cissa was nothing.

At the gathering that followed the ceremony, Cissa wandered from room to room. In the dining room, which also served as her father's study, the men talked about Democrats and Republicans. Cissa knew that the Tarvers were Democrats. Duncan talked the most and everyone listened when he spoke. He talked about the cotton harvest and prices and banks. Cissa wondered if "greenbacks" were some kind of frog. Duncan seemed to think they needed more of them. Albert perched on a windowsill, listening with a grave expression as if he understood what his father and the other men were talking about. Cissa tried to look grave, too, as she listened, but what they said made little sense to her. When Monroe noticed her there in the doorway he smiled beneath his bushy black mustache and Cissa smiled back. As she turned to leave the room, she saw her grownup cousin Cornelia standing behind her. "Politics," Cornelia sniffed as she took Cissa by the hand and led her away.

In the parlor, women talked about who'd been visiting whom around the county, who was being courted and likely next to marry, new babies, sick babies. One baby who had recently died, bless its little heart. When they started complaining about lazy colored help, Cissa kicked off her shoes and went outside. The grass felt cool under her stockinged feet.

Cissa liked the cake and the fruit punch, and she enjoyed running around with her nieces and nephews in the yard until she fell and muddied her new dress. She knew Mother would scold her for that, as well as for the green stains on her socks. She went to the barn and found that Sambo was back. He purred as Cissa stroked his sleek fur; she tried to imagine where he might have been all this time. She felt certain he'd been somewhere beyond the canebrake.

As a hubbub arose outside, Cissa crept out of the barn in time to see people tossing handfuls of rice at Matilda and her new husband Frank as they drove off to Marchelle in a buggy adorned with fluttering white ribbons. Mother had tears in her eyes, but Cissa felt happy. Sambo was back and she'd been promised Matilda's bed.

Chapter Five
Cissa's Left Hand

Winter 1883

Cissa reveled in having a proper bed of her own. Up until Matilda's departure, she'd slept on a raised pallet in a corner of the bedroom she shared with her sister. She vaguely recalled that once the girls' bedroom had been upstairs, just across from her brother Lester's bedroom. Cissa remembered clapping pat-a-cake with Lester, laughing with him when their hands missed. Lester had been almost twelve years old when he passed; Cissa had been just past two. Lester was spoken of in whispers if at all and Cissa understood that there had been something wrong with him. When she asked Julia about him, all Julia would say was that Lester had always been a sweet boy. "That chile hadn't got a ugly bone in his body," she said.

A few days before the winter term was due to begin, Cissa walked into the kitchen where Julia was working and announced: "I'm not going back to school." She said this as if it were a settled fact. How could she be expected to write her lessons with a useless right hand?

"Course you go back, Miss." Julia spoke with a ferocity that startled Cissa. "You already be readin' and learnin' numbers and sums."

Cissa was adamant. "I can't go, Julia. I can't write anymore. How can I write with half a hand?" She scowled as she tried to pick up a spoon between her thumb and ring finger.

"You jus' learn to write lef-hand," Julia said, vigorously rolling out the crust for pie. "I knows a few folks do things lef-hand. Cain't be so hard."

Cissa laid her two hands flat on the table and stared at them. The damaged right hand was still pink and tender where the index and middle fingers had been. She flexed the left hand and turned it over and back, studying it. "Do you think I could?"

"Course you can, Miss Cissa. Ifn you wants."

Cissa wasn't convinced, but she stopped whining. Julia offered her the trimmings off the pie crust and suggested she make a little pie of her own. It reminded her of making mud pies, but this pie Julia promised to put into the oven and cook along with the big pie for dinner. Cissa patted out the dough with her left hand.

That evening, by the waning sunlight at the table by the parlor window, Cissa gripped a pencil in her left hand and began laboriously tracing over the lines that were already written in her composition book. It was slow. Her lines were messy. Her hand cramped. But she began to think that maybe what Julia suggested was possible.

When the first day of school came, Cissa went. The other children stared at her hand as she knew they would; she tried not to care. She could still read her lines better than anyone else in her age group. When Miss Armstrong called students to come to the blackboard and work sums, she skipped over Cissa. Cissa didn't know whether to feel slighted or grateful. She knew she felt left out.

After school, Cissa sat down at the kitchen table with her school bag in her lap. "It was awful, Julia," she said, her voice soft and flat. "I don't think I can do school after all."

Julia looked away and slammed the baking sheet on the table. "You stop that talk, Miss Cissa. You jus' thank the Good Lord you be in school. Least ways one of us be learnin' her letters."

Cissa stared at Julia. "Oh," she said. That was the moment when Cissa understood that Julia working at her house every day meant Julia was not in school. She reached into her bag and drew out her lessons from the day. She smoothed a paper on which the teacher had written a line for her to practice writing. She held out the pencil for Julia.

After that, every afternoon, whenever Mother and Pop were about their own business, the two girls sat at the kitchen table for an hour or so while Cissa shared with Julia what she'd learned that day at school. Cissa was not a skilled teacher, but Julia was an eager learner.

Sometimes, as Julia wrote her letters and then words and sentences, Julia talked. "My uncle say they was tryin' to make it so's niggers and white folks could all sit in the same train cars and eatin' places all together, callin' it civil rights. But now we gots to be sep'rate. Uncle hear 'bout it down in Natchez. He say as how there be a big ol' meetin' of colored folks an' ever'body be jawin' 'bout it."

Cissa liked listening to Julia talk, even though she didn't always understand what she was talking about. She preferred hearing Julia sing.

As the weeks went by, Cissa became more capable with her left hand. At first her handwriting was barely legible but with continued effort it became merely odd. Miss Armstrong encouraged her and praised her efforts, even giving her a few exercises that she said might help. "We ordinarily use these exercises to help students who favor their left hand learn to use their right properly, but I guess they can work the other way around, too." Miss Armstrong chastised the other children when they made fun of Cissa for her disfigured hand, calling it a crawdad claw. Some of the boys made claw gestures at her anyway, whenever Miss Armstrong wasn't looking. Albert laughed at their antics.

As Christmas approached, Cissa begged for a doll. She had a wooden doll that a family friend had crafted in his wood shop, but its blank eyes and its mouth that formed something that wasn't quite a smile unnerved Cissa. Its body was hard and stiff, and its hair was painted on. Cissa had never given it a name. What she wanted was a doll with delicate hands and a porcelain face with glass eyes as blue as her own. She'd seen a doll like that in a shop in Marchelle when she'd gone there with her mother to visit Matilda. What she got instead—in addition to the usual stocking full of nuts and oranges—was a set of paper dolls with fiddly fancy dresses that she was supposed to cut out with scissors. When she saw them, she burst into tears and fled to the barn with the cats.

The days between Christmas and New Year's drug on for Cissa. The weather was cold and rainy, and Julia seemed to be always busy and eager to leave as soon as her work was done. Cissa fretted. She wished Sambo could come inside the house; it was cold in the barn. On the next to last day of the year Cissa was eating her morning oatmeal when she noticed Julia smiling at her from the kitchen door. "Come along in here when you done eatin', Miss Cissa. I gots somethin' t' show you."

Cissa slurped up the last of her oatmeal and hurried into the kitchen. There was a package on the table wrapped in castoff Christmas paper and tied with yellow yarn.

"That for you, Miss," Julia said.

Cissa's eyes went wide as she sat and began pulling off the string and then the paper. Julia had been given two new aprons and a head kerchief as a Christmas gift from the Tarvers along with some household items that they no longer needed. Cissa never expected anything from Julia.

A smile crept across Cissa's face as she saw what was inside the package.

"I know it ain't nice as the one you be hankerin' after, but she do have blue eyes and yella hair jus' like you," Julia said.

"Oh, Julia." Cissa got up from the table and hugged her companion, clutching the soft cloth doll in her left hand. The doll was plump with cotton, made of sturdy unbleached muslin, her face skillfully embroidered with round blue eyes and a little pink mouth that smiled. She had abundant yarn hair composed into more than a dozen tiny yellow braids. She wore a dress that Cissa knew had been made from the scraps of the dress she'd worn at Matilda's wedding. There was even a bit of lace around her neck. "Thank you, Julia." More than the doll itself, Cissa was moved by the fact that Julia had made it. She'd made it for Cissa.

Chapter Six
The Truth About Nubby

Spring 1884

The warm days of late March brought a bounty of azalea blossoms, a break from school, and the promise of spending more time with Julia. Cissa suggested that the two of them should go look for Nubby. Every time Cissa thought of Nubby, she felt a tug at her heart and a swirl in her mind as if there was something important about the woman that she needed to understand.

"I never did get to thank her properly for rescuing me when I got lost," Cissa said. "And Mrs. McNair at my Sunday School says we should always say 'thank you' to people who help us." She put on her most imploring face.

"Well, you ask Miz Tarver if she let me take you... somewheres." Julia raised her eyebrows and Cissa nodded.

She found her mother in the parlor with a bit of sewing in her lap. "Mother, may I go for a walk with Julia? Please? It's such a pretty day."

Susanna spoke without turning toward her daughter. "Yes, child. You may go."

Returning to the kitchen, Cissa announced, "Mother says we can go anywhere we please."

Julia packed up a couple of slices of molasses cake and the two girls set out on the path through the canebrake. "Mama know where Nubby keep herself," Julia said. "She take us."

But Zolene did not take them to Nubby. "Lord, chile, I ain't got time to go off on such foolishness," she said. "B'sides, ain't hard to find Nubby if'n you knows how to look." She explained to Julia that she should follow Chakchu Creek up to the big lightning oak and then turn up the side stream all the way to its source at a little rocky pond. "Then you jus' sets yourself down by that pond and waits. Nubby come soon enough."

"Is Nubby really her name?" Cissa found the name unbelievably odd.

"That's all I knowed her by," Zolene said. "But my Auntie, she know Nubby from back 'fore I's born and if I recollect rightly, she told that Nubby had a big Choctaw name. Auntie couldn't say it so she jus' call her Nubby."

Cissa wondered what a big Choctaw name might be like.

Her heart beat faster as she and Julia made their way along the creek, which was a running stream after the recent rains. She hoped Julia knew what a lightning oak was.

"That's it," Julia said, as if she'd read Cissa's mind. She pointed to a massive live oak festooned with beards of moss. The tree looked lopsided and on the ground beneath it lay a huge branch mantled in green and sprouting a few mushrooms. "See that black mark yonder?" Julia pointed high up to the place where the branch had apparently once been joined to the trunk. "Lightning done that. Come on, Miss Cissa. Up this-a-way."

The pond was larger and deeper than Cissa had imagined. The surface rippled where a spring spewed water, and far below that surface were roundish stones of many colors. Tiny fish and tadpoles flashed in the sunlight. The place was hemmed in by trees, one of which was even larger than the lightning oak, and one enormous stone.

Julia reached into the water with her hands and drank. Cissa followed her lead; the water was cool and refreshing. Julia opened the lunch bucket and offered Cissa a slice of cake. After Cissa had eaten, Julia ate, too. Then the two girls waited. They listened to a pair of cardinals chipping to one another in the trees. Every so often, they saw a flash of red as the male cardinal flew from branch to branch.

Cissa had begun to think that Nubby wasn't coming when she heard a scuffling of leaves from behind the stone and there she was. She held a long stick in her left hand like a walking cane.

"Hey, Nubby." Julia spoke first, her voice soft around the edges.

Nubby stood with her head cocked to one side, studying the two girls. Cissa wished that she'd brought a little thank-you gift for Nubby. Maybe a slice of cake or a few flowers from the patch out near the big cedar tree.

At last, Cissa broke the silence herself. "I came to thank you, Mrs. Nubby, for finding me and taking me to Mrs. Zolene that day." Nubby didn't respond. "You remember, don't you?" Cissa reached up and took the blue ribbon from her hair and held it out to Nubby. "This is for you. To say 'thank you' for helping me."

For a moment, Nubby made no move to accept the gift. "I know," she said. "Little gal lose herself." She smiled and held out her hand to receive Cissa's proffered ribbon. "Old ones like me, yes, we remember."

Cissa was expecting Nubby to say "thank you" for the gift, but she didn't. Instead, she reached into a pocket of her dress and held out her hand toward Cissa. "You keep this and maybe you don't get lost no more. Maybe you find your own way." She placed a round object into Cissa's hand.

Cissa stared. It was a wooden bead like the ones Nubby wore around her neck, stained red and decorated with a pattern of black dots. "Thank you," she said, but as she looked up she saw that Nubby was gone.

"You ready?" Julia said.

Cissa grinned and nodded. She clutched the bead in her hand, wishing she had a string so she could place it around her neck. She felt like dancing. "Sing to me, Julia," she said. And so Julia sang to her all the way home while Cissa danced.

When the girls entered the kitchen, they found Mother there amid a jumble of dishes and jars and tins. "There you are," she said. "I can't find anything around here." She banged a metal cup down on the table. "Where did you go off to anyway, Julia?" She didn't seem to remember having given Cissa permission to go for a walk.

"We jus'..."

Before Julia could finish her sentence, Cissa interrupted. "I asked her to take me somewhere, Mother. She took good care of me."

"And where did you have to go, young lady, that was so important that you had to drag Julia away from her work?"

Cissa was still bubbling with elation over her encounter with Nubby. "I had to go thank someone who helped me once. You always tell me to say 'thank you.' Mrs. McNair at Sunday School says so, too."

"That's very nice, Narcissa," Mother said, softening. "Who was it you had to thank? Maybe I should express my gratitude as well. Who?"

"It was..." Cissa hesitated, but then remembered how her pop always told her that she should never be afraid to tell the truth. "They say her name is Nubby. She's awfully nice, Mother."

"Nubby? That old Indian witch? Julia, you had no business taking this child off to see such a person as that. Heavens to Betsy, don't you know what she is?"

"She Choctaw, I think." Julia kept her eyes downcast.

"Whatever she calls herself, I know what my own mother called her. A witch. A witch and a bannee." Susanna turned toward Cissa. The look on her face frightened Cissa. "Your Granny Mag said she was a bannee. Her with her uncanny eye and her charmed beads."

Cissa stared, mystified. She'd heard of witches, but she had no idea what a bannee was. "A what?"

"Your Granny knew about bannees from the old country, and she said you could see one near a stream or a pond washing clothes, and they were always the clothes of someone who was about to die." Mother's eyes took on a haunted look and she clutched her hands together, shaking her head side to side. Her voice went soft and singsong. "A bannee woman is old, old, with one nostril, one tooth, feet webbed like a duck. She always knows who's about to die. Always." She grabbed Cissa's shoulders. "You must never go near anyone like that, Narcissa. Not ever again."

Cissa wanted to tell her mother that Nubby had two perfectly good nostrils and quite a few teeth in her mouth, though perhaps not a whole set, and feet that fit into ordinary-looking boots, but all she said was, "Yes, Mother."

Mother turned to leave, muttering to herself, but before she'd gone more than a dozen steps, she stopped and came back. "Now I remember what I was looking for," she said, and she focused her attention on Julia. Cissa snuck away to the porch, trying to imagine what a real bannee looked like and wondering if maybe they looked different in Mississippi from how they looked in Scotland and whether Nubby ever did any washing in the pond.

Days after these events, Cissa was still perplexed over the notion that her mother thought there was something bad about Nubby, who had been nothing but good to Cissa. She'd even given Cissa a gift, a bead that might be charmed. Cissa kept the bead well hidden. "Julia, do you think Nubby is what Mother said? A bannee?"

"Don't know nothin' 'bout no bannees, Miss Cissa." Julia continued dredging the chicken parts in flour for frying.

"A witch then?"

Julia dusted her hands together after placing the last piece of chicken into the bubbling grease. A cloud of flour made sunbeams in the light from the window.

"You bes' not be askin' me 'bout such things, Miss. Miz Tarver say it's true then mos' likely you gots to say so too."

Cissa frowned. Was something true just because Mother said so? She sat for a moment watching Julia turn the pieces of chicken in the fat.

Donna Birdwell

Chapter Seven
Being a Tarver

Summer - Fall 1884

The camp meeting at Rundle Springs in late summer of 1884 drew crowds from all the neighboring counties and beyond for several days of outdoor worship, socializing, and dinner on the grounds. Cissa looked forward to this break from her mundane routine, but the thing itself proved disappointing. The food brought in and shared by all the attendees was delicious, but it did little to make up for the interminable sermons inflicted on the crowds by a succession of pastors, each eager to demonstrate his superior familiarity with the word and the will of God. Cissa's interest was occasionally piqued by the conversations she overheard among grownups as she and her niece Milly wandered about trying to escape supervision. She heard her pop and Duncan talking about civil rights in a scoffing tone that contrasted sharply with what Cissa recalled of Julia's breathless recounting of civil rights discussed at some "big ol' meetin'" of colored folks down in Natchez.

"I'm thankful that Civil Rights Act finally got overturned," one man said. Those around him nodded and smiled. "Restoring rights to the states to organize our own affairs was the only sensible thing to do. We here in the South understand full well that the white man was born to command and I'm certain our Negroes know it, too."

"I have to say, I like the nigger better today than I did ten years ago," another man remarked. "He works better and is more respectful now that he's quit politics and settled down to his natural condition."

Pop nodded in agreement. "Most all of our Negroes around here are good natured, happy enough to depend on white folks."

Cissa certainly thought her Julia was good natured. Happy, too. And didn't she depend on Pop the same as Cissa did?

On the second and third days of the camp meeting, thunderstorms blew in, requiring worshippers to crowd together under leaky canopies for shelter most of the day.

"Cholera," Pop said a few days after the conclusion of the festivities. "Three more cases last night at one of the settlements down Chakchu Creek toward Marston." He ate his breakfast in haste as he'd already received a caller beckoning him to visit their ailing child some miles away. Cissa had heard the man explain that his daughter had bad diarrhea and pains in her legs.

Cissa clutched her belly and flexed her legs, finding nothing amiss.

Dr. Joseph Tarver was busy throughout August and September tending to patients all over the county, as both cholera and scarlet fever took their toll. One of Cissa's classmates died of scarlet fever and her two-year-old nephew Elmer, Duncan's next-to-youngest, died of cholera. There were many other deaths and many fresh graves at the Rundle Springs cemetery, but those were the two that hurt Cissa's heart the most.

"Get me the Bible, Narcissa," Mother said. "We need to make note of little Elmer's passing."

Cissa drug the big book out of its place in the sideboard and set it on her mother's lap. Susanna opened it not to the thick page between the Old and New Testaments where the immediate family were inscribed, but rather to a page in Psalms marked by a purple ribbon where separate sheets of paper held the names of Susanna and Joseph's grandchildren.

"Will there be a funeral for Elmer?" Cissa had attended the one for her classmate.

"The funeral's already been held," Mother said. "Not in the church, though. Just prayers by the graveside." Mother traced her finger down to where she'd written Elmer's name on the grandchild list only two years ago and entered the final date. She tucked the paper back into the place marked by the purple ribbon, but she didn't close the book. Cissa watched as she turned to the thick page that had all of the names of Cissa's brothers and sisters on it. Mother's finger paused at each entry that already had a date of death recorded. There were six of those.

Cissa leaned on the back of her mother's chair, studying the names. She noticed that some names given to Susanna and Joseph's children had also been given to their children's children.

"Who was baby Eugene named for?" Cissa asked, pointing at the entry for the first of her siblings who had died.

"For your father's Uncle Gene," Mother said.

"What about Margaret?" Hers was the next name on the list, another name with a death date attached.

"That's Maggie. She was named for my mother, your Granny Mag."

Cissa wondered if bannees ever washed baby clothes in their ponds and streams. She went on down the list, asking about each name. A web of family wove itself in her mind as she learned who was named for whom. She saw that middle names were important, too. Duncan's second name was Quinlan, after their father—Joseph Quinlan Tarver—and Monroe's second name was McLaurin, after Mother's family. "Your father's grandmother was a Quinlan," Mother explained.

"And what about me?" Cissa asked as they reached the final name, the one written below the last line on the page. "Who was I named for?" The two entries above hers simply read "Baby Boy" and "Baby Girl," with birth and death dates that were only a few days apart.

Mother swept her hand across the page. "I'd given up on namesakes by the time you came along. After all that had happened, we didn't know if you'd live or not. But I always did like those pretty yellow and white narcissus flowers that bloom in the early springtime. They don't last long, but they do look so pretty while they're here. I named you for those."

"Where did June come from?" Cissa needed to know about her middle name, too.

"Oh, that's when you were supposed to be born, or so I thought. You didn't come until July, of course."

Cissa wondered if she might have felt any different, being Narcissa July instead of Narcissa June.

Mother turned a few more pages in the Bible. Each page made a crispy sound as it sighed into place. Cissa could tell that her mother wasn't reading anything, just turning pages and remembering. As the spine of the book began to slip down between her knees, she closed the book and lifted it toward Cissa.

"Put it away, Cissy," she said. "Until next time."

Chapter Eight
In a Family Way

Winter 1884-85

After all of the sickness and death of late summer and early fall, Cissa was more than ready for school when it finally started up again in November. Miss Armstrong, who had somehow discerned that Cissa was sharing her lessons with Julia, started giving Cissa extra pieces of paper and even an occasional extra pencil. "So you can do more work at home," she said. But Cissa knew they were for Julia. Sometimes Miss Armstrong even let her take home one of the classroom textbooks overnight.

The cotton crop was good that year and Christmas was festive. Cissa received a new dress and a pair of shiny button-up shoes. Her niece Milly got a doll with a porcelain face, delicate hands, and blue glass eyes.

One particularly chilly day in February, Cissa arrived home from school to find her house empty and the fireplace going cold—no Mother, no Pop, no Julia. She ran back outside and looked up and down the road. She called to her six-year-old nephew Lachlan, who still stood at the front door of his own house. "Lachlan! Lachlan!" she yelled as she began running toward him.

Lachlan turned and waved. Cissa ran across the road and on down to her brother Monroe's house. There was a loud shout from inside and then a moan. "What's happening?" she said, feeling mildly alarmed. "Is Julia in there? Is Mother there?"

Lachlan nodded. "Grandma is in there with my mother," he said. "They won't let me inside. They said my baby brother is coming." Lachlan's eyes sparkled. He'd been hoping for a brother ever since he'd learned that his mother was in a family way. He liked his little sister Betty fine, but he thought a brother would be extra nice.

Cissa marched up to the front door and went inside. There was another shout, this time even louder, followed by a moan and a murmur of voices. Cissa tiptoed into the bedroom, where she saw her sister-in-law Laura propped up in the bed with her knees spread, her private parts on view for all to see. Cissa blushed, but she didn't turn away. Her mother was there, leaning over Laura, a hand on each knee, peering between Laura's legs. Laura's sister Ettie was also there, in addition to their neighbor, Mrs. Campbell.

"I want a doctor," Laura said. "Either one of them will do, just get him here. This baby wants to come."

"I'm sorry, Laura," Mother said. "Joseph is over Marchelle way today and Duncan is in Cowleton. I've sent word to both of them, but it will take time for either of them to get here. Meanwhile, I've sent Julia to fetch Zolene. You know she's delivered plenty of babies."

Laura let out another wail.

Cissa didn't know what to think. She'd watched a calf being born once, but the mother cow had never shouted and moaned like Laura was doing.

Nobody told Cissa to leave, so she stayed, crouched down just inside the doorway. She watched and listened. Soon Zolene bustled into the room. Cissa was surprised to see the three white women step aside to let the black woman take charge.

She watched wide-eyed as Zolene's fingers disappeared inside a space between Laura's legs. Zolene shook her head and sucked her teeth. She instructed Laura to lie back flat on the bed. Zolene began massaging Laura's huge belly. Laura complained, but she didn't yell. Zolene kept massaging and massaging. Every once in a while, Laura would let out another shout and Zolene would stop massaging. Then she'd start up again. Finally she nodded and, sticking her fingers inside Laura again, she said, "That's done it. Baby's head set right now. Next time them pains come, Miz Tarver, you just go ahead on and push."

There was more shouting and moaning as Cissa maintained her vigil by the doorway. Suddenly there was a different sort of yell and then the sound of a baby crying. Laura was crying, too. "Is it a boy?" she asked, rising up in the bed to try and see for herself. Cissa's mouth hung open in amazement as she marveled at how the baby had come right out of that space between Laura's legs. A whole new person.

"It's a pretty li'l gal, Miz Tarver," Zolene said. "Prettiest li'l thing I ever did see."

Cissa thought it was just about the ugliest thing she'd ever seen. It was covered in blood and goo and was all over purplish red with its face screwed into an awful frown. And it did cry so. Cissa stood up to get a better look.

"Narcissa June, what are you doing here?" Mother shouted, moving toward Cissa with her skirts held out as if to shield Cissa from what she'd already seen. "How long have you been there?"

"Since I got back from school," Cissa said.

Zolene laughed. "She have to learn sooner or later, Miz Tarver."

Susanna frowned. "Later would be preferred. The child is only eight years old."

Later that evening, Mother asked Cissa if she had any questions about what she'd seen. Cissa had so many questions, but in that moment, she could only think of one. "Does it really hurt so much?" she said.

During the school break for cotton planting that intervened between the end of winter term in March and the beginning of summer term in June, Cissa followed Miss Armstrong's advice and challenged herself with new tasks. She mended a tear in her everyday pinafore. She sewed a button on Pop's shirt. She experienced a quiet sense of triumph every time she accomplished something new with her left hand.

One afternoon, as Cissa and Julia sat at the kitchen table playing school while supper simmered on the stove, they overheard a conversation between Mother and Pop.

"I think the girl is in the family way," Mother said. "And if she is I need to know how far along she is and whether it will cause an interruption in her work."

Cissa looked up at Julia, her eyes wide.

Pop strode into the room and demanded that Julia stand up. "It's averred that you're pregnant, Julia. Come into the other room so I can examine you."

The pencil Julia had held fell to the floor as she rose to do as she was bid. She cast a woeful glance at Cissa as she left the room. Or perhaps the glance was directed at the schoolwork on the table.

Cissa picked up the pencil and stared at the tablet where she'd been showing Julia her seven-times tables. Cissa knew very little about women being in the family way. She knew that it meant their bellies would grow large and that eventually a baby would come out, like Laura's baby Janie had. Beyond that, all was mystery. How could her Julia have come to be in such a condition?

When Julia came back into the room, tucking in her shirtwaist and attempting to tie her apron with trembling hands, Cissa thought she saw tears in her eyes. Instead of sitting back down to resume the schoolwork, Julia went to the stove and began vigorously stirring the pot of stew.

"Are you alright, Julia? Are you really in a family way?"

"Yes, Miss Cissa."

Cissa frowned. "How does that happen?"

Julia laughed, but it wasn't the warm bubbling laugh like Zolene's that made Cissa's heart sing. It was a shrill, staccato sort of sound. "Don't you worry yo'self over that, Miss." She stopped laughing as her eyes fell on the tablet and pencils. "You jus' carry on with your schoolin' and don't worry none 'bout Julia. I still be here lookin' after you."

Cissa hoped that was true,

Chapter Nine
Learning Her Place

1885

As Julia's belly increased in size, she became more intent on her housekeeping chores and less inclined to spend time with Cissa. So Cissa was grateful when her niece Milly returned to Callander Road at the end of summer term. Milly was Duncan's eldest daughter, and their family had been living for some months in Cowleton, in Fulton County, the next county over from Hinson. Duncan continued to maintain the house in town, but Ada and the children moved back to Callander Road. Duncan spent many a night with his wife and children, returning often enough to keep a hand in the family farming enterprise, supervising laborers and sharecroppers alongside Monroe.

Cissa knew little about the farm work, but she could see that it was Monroe who seemed to take charge more than Duncan did and even more than their father, who often suffered from headaches and other minor maladies. Cissa occasionally saw her father massaging an elbow or a hip.

One day near the end of the cotton harvest, with the return to school just over the horizon, Cissa joined her nieces and nephews for a game of hide-and-go-seek at the big house, which had five rooms downstairs and two upstairs. There were lots of good places to hide.

Cissa chose the hall closet beneath the stairs, leaving the door ajar because otherwise it was disconcertingly dark inside. Through the crack, she could see across the hall into the parlor, where a group of ladies were gathered. Mother called it her sewing circle, but as far as Cissa could see, they did very little sewing. Mostly they talked.

"Duncan never was happy with that Armstrong woman," Ada said. She and Laura and Mrs. Campbell and two other ladies from the church were there in the parlor. Each had her sewing basket next to her and from time to time would do a bit of stitching. Ada's maid minded little Lamar while baby Janie slept in a basket next to Laura.

"Monroe wasn't exactly pleased to learn that Miss Armstrong had taught at a Negro school before coming here," Laura said. "I heard that she even boarded with a colored family." She sniffed with displeasure.

Mrs. Campbell spoke up. "My son over in Marchelle told me that he heard tell she been teaching from some books she claims were written by Negroes. Some fellow named Douglas? Sounds more like a Scotchman to me. Anyway, that ain't the kind of thing we want our Negroes being taught. And it's certainly not for our white children. Yankee teachers got no place here." She poked her sewing needle into her work and sat back, looking pleased with herself.

"Duncan helped them pick the new man and he's convinced the school will be much the better for the change. I have to admit, my boys complained often about Miss Armstrong, and we would have kept them in the Cowleton school this year if Duncan hadn't been able to get the new teacher."

Cissa sat in the dimness of the closet with a heavy heart. Whatever would she do without Miss Armstrong? She gave up on being discovered and crept out of the closet to go to the kitchen, seeking solace from Julia. She found Julia crouched over, gripping the back of a chair and making strange sounds. Lachlan and Eli and Betty were huddled under the table eating cookies.

"Julia? Are you alright?" Cissa tipped her head to one side and leaned over in an effort to see Julia's face.

Julia stood up, one hand still on the back of the chair, the other rubbing her own back as she breathed heavily.

"You gots to go tell your mama that Julia's time done come. Run on, now, Miss. You tell her that." Julia dropped into the chair, her knees wide apart.

Cissa scurried into the parlor where the ladies were tittering over some witticism. She tugged at her mother's sleeve and whispered, "Julia says to tell you that her time has done come."

Mother looked startled. "Oh," she said. She looked around at her guests. All eyes were on Susanna and Cissa. Nobody was sewing. "Well then. I... Well, let me just go see about this," she said. She looked toward her older guests and added, "It's her first child, you know. It could be a false alarm."

"Go on, Mother," Laura said. "Go see to Julia. I'll help our guests retrieve their things."

Cissa was sent home with Laura and her brood while Ada left her girl to help tend to Julia. The last thing Cissa heard before she left the house was Julia saying, "Yes ma'am, I'm for sure. No ma'am, I be fine walkin' to my mama's house," followed by a low moan. When Cissa went back home later that evening, she learned that Julia had given birth to a baby girl.

Cissa couldn't believe that her Julia was now a mother. She begged to go visit her and see the new baby, but they kept telling her, "Some other time, Narcissa." So she waited. And she learned that, for a while at least, she would have to make do without Julia around. Julia's younger sister Elsie was sent in her stead. It soon became apparent that Elsie was no cook, so Cissa had to endure hard biscuits and bland chicken stew and burnt pork chops and her mother's bad temper. Cissa missed Julia and fretted over the approaching start of the winter school term.

Cissa had no idea what to expect of the new teacher. All she knew about him was that his name was Mr. Warren and that he'd been more or less hand-picked by her brother Duncan. She also knew that Duncan had disliked Miss Armstrong, the teacher Cissa loved, so she had reason not to trust his judgment with respect to teachers.

On the first day of school in late October, Cissa slipped into her desk, her eyes fixed on Mr. Warren. He was almost as tall as Monroe, who was the tallest man she knew. He was thin but with a rounded belly. He had an angular face, greasy but still unruly pale hair, a thin blonde mustache, and eyebrows that were as close to curly as Cissa had ever seen. He held a wooden ruler in one hand and tapped the table with it as he watched the students gathering into the chilly, musty-smelling classroom. Cissa thought he looked almost as nervous as she was.

Cissa was predisposed to dislike the man and, as the days and then the weeks wore on, he did not disappoint. The very first day, when one of the students mentioned that Miss Armstrong had done something differently, Mr. Warren's icy gray eyes flashed and his voice dropped a full register as he replied, "This is Mr. Warren's classroom now. You will comply with *my* rules."

It didn't take long for Cissa to notice that Mr. Warren called on the boys far more frequently than the girls to answer questions, to read lines, or to work sums. He was particularly full of praise for Cissa's nephew Albert—Duncan's oldest boy.

Cissa was grateful when it came time for the school break at Christmas and New Year's. The only gift she received that year that she cared anything about was a little book of poems. The rest was just underwear and stockings and a few hair ribbons. She rather liked the green one.

School got a bit better when Mr. Warren started having them read poetry in class. Cissa didn't get to read aloud very often. Not like Albert did. On the day they were reading a poem that was one of Cissa's favorites, Mr. Warren waxed effusive in praise of Albert's reading when Cissa thought even Lachlan had read with more feeling.

She was still stewing over this, the unfairness of it, the knowledge that Mr. Warren favored Albert because of who his father was, when she arrived home to a pleasant surprise.

"Julia!" Cissa rushed to embrace her companion where she stood kneading dough in the kitchen. "I didn't know you were coming back today. But I'm so happy you're here. Did you bring your baby?"

"No, Miss Cissa, cain't bring no baby to work. And I only be back half-days for some more weeks. Miz Tarver gon' let me keep nursin' little Rosie a while more."

"Can't you bring her one time? Just so I can meet her? Rosie. You named her Rosie? She has a flower name, just like me." Cissa still had her arms wrapped around Julia's waist. Suddenly she stopped and backed away, her smile replaced by a more serious expression. "Did it hurt, Julia? When Rosie came out, I mean. Did she really come out from between your legs?"

"Not so bad, Miss Cissa. What you know 'bout birthin' babies anyway?"

So Cissa reminded Julia about having watched her sister-in-law Laura give birth to Janie. "She yelled an awful lot. Did you yell, Julia?"

"Time or two I reckon I did."

"Is she pretty, Julia? Does she have blue eyes like me?"

Julia laughed. "Lord, chile. You may know 'bout birthin' but not much 'bout babies. No, Miss Cissa, little Rosie be dark like me and her pa. Dark eyes. Nappy hair. That's how it be."

A few days later when Cissa arrived home from school, she found the kitchen buzzing with activity as Matilda, who was visiting for the day from Marchelle, cooed over Julia's baby. Zolene displayed her granddaughter in her arms as Julia beamed.

Cissa was overcome with excitement. "Can I hold her?" she said.

After a questioning glance toward Susanna, who frowned even as she nodded her approval, Zolene responded. "Course you can, Miss Narcissa. You just set down right there." Zolene placed little Rosie into Cissa's arms.

Cissa gazed with wonder at the baby's deep brown eyes and ran her hand over her soft hair. When Rosie grabbed her little finger, Cissa had to laugh. "I think she likes me," she said.

"How many grandbabies is this for you now, Zolene?" Matilda couldn't take her eyes off the cuddly brown bundle in Cissa's arms.

"I reckon that's fifteen now," Zolene said. She cast a wary glance toward Susanna. "Ones I knows about," she added. "Some my children been gone I don't know where."

Mother looked as if she was about to speak. Instead, she folded her arms across her chest and remained silent.

"Weren't you my nurse when I was a baby?" Matilda seemed unaware of Mother's discomfort.

"Yes, ma'am, Miz Henning. You was suckled in these ol' black arms 'longside my own li'l Abe."

"So your Abe is the same age as me? Does he still live here?"

Zolene glanced again toward Susanna and there was a sadness in her eyes as she said, "No, ma'am, Miz Henning. My Abe pass on same year he born."

Mother was now visibly perturbed. "Now, I don't see any need to be bringing up past unpleasantness. I have plenty of lost babies I could talk about, babies that needed milk when I had none and no one else would give it to them. But we should likely let Zolene take this baby on home so that Julia here can get on with her work. Come, Matilda, let's leave them alone now." Mother took Matilda by the hand and led her away like a child.

Cissa still held baby Rosie. "Is Mother mad?" she said.

"I think she be alright," Julia said as she took little Rosie from Cissa and placed her in Zolene's arms. She kissed the child gently on the forehead. Zolene did the same to Julia.

Chapter Ten
Life Lessons

1886

Without Miss Armstrong, school was a chore for Cissa, but at least Julia was back at her house. With no expectation of special help, Cissa struggled on her own to compensate for her disability. Reading and rhetoric were easy enough, and, although Mr. Warren disparaged her handwriting, the words Cissa wrote down were well chosen and occasionally received his grudging praise. Cissa also liked the geography lessons that Mr. Warren directed at the older students, but which Cissa heard anyway since they were all in the one room. She continued to share her lessons with Julia whenever she could.

One day, when Mr. Warren had given a particularly interesting lesson on the heathen tribes of Africa, where he said all the people were dark-skinned, thick-lipped, and nappy-haired, Cissa decided to borrow one of the books and take it home to show Julia. She was unaware that Mr. Warren was watching her.

"Narcissa," he said. "Why are you attempting to steal school property. You know that book is to be read in the classroom only."

"Miss Armstrong let me..." Cissa immediately regretted her mistake.

"Come up to my desk, Narcissa." Mr. Warren stood, slapping his palm with the wooden ruler.

Cissa felt all eyes on her and it was all she could do to contain the urge to run out the back door, but she did as she was told.

"Place your hand on the desk."

Without thinking, Cissa put her right hand out.

Mr. Warren tapped it with the ruler and when Cissa looked up at his face, she saw an expression that was somewhere between a scowl and a smirk. There were a couple of giggles from the back rows.

"Maybe the other hand in your case," he said. There was more snickering.

The ruler came down hard across the back of Cissa's left hand. Twice. Three times.

"Now maybe you will be more respectful of school property," Mr. Warren said.

Cissa was determined not to cry, but a couple of tears slid down her cheeks anyway and she found it impossible to concentrate on her work the rest of the day. She was grateful when Mr. Warren at last indicated that the day was finished. But then he said, "Narcissa Tarver, come up to my desk."

Cissa was petrified but managed to drag her unwilling feet up the aisle.

Mr. Warren handed her a folded piece of paper. "Give this to your father. And be certain that I will know if you fail to do so."

Cissa took the note in her throbbing left hand and tucked it into her pocket.

She walked home by herself, even though Milly and Albert and Lachlan kept looking back for her and dawdling so she could catch up. She didn't want to catch up. She didn't want to exist in that moment. She'd already received one punishment for her infraction. Why did she have to tell her father? And was it really an infraction? Miss Armstrong had always encouraged Cissa to share her lessons with Julia. Why wouldn't Mr. Warren let her do that?

When Cissa reached home, she was relieved to discover that her father was not there. Relief was short-lived, followed by another surge of nerves as she considered that maybe it would have been better to get this ordeal over with as quickly as possible.

Cissa pouted at the kitchen table while Julia worked. She wanted to tell her what had happened, but she didn't know where to begin. She thought back on the day, recalling Mr. Warren's presentation about the heathen Africans. "Mr. Warren says it's important for white people to tell Negroes how to vote and all. He says they're not smart enough to figure things out for themselves." She looked up at Julia, who still had her back turned. "Do you think that's true, Julia?"

Julia did not turn. "Don't matter what I think, Miss Cissa. All's that matter is what you think."

Cissa was taken aback. What *did* she think? No one had ever suggested before that what she thought might matter. "I think you're smart enough, Julia. But you're a girl and Mr. Warren says girls don't vote anyway."

Julia chuckled in that deep-throated way that reminded Cissa of Zolene. "You be right 'bout that, Miss Cissa."

Cissa thought she'd like to go visit Zolene and Rosie again soon and she said as much.

"You know Doc and Miz Tarver wouldn't like that," Julia said. "Besides, I don't live with Mama Zolene no more. I lives with Baxter. He my husband."

"Oh." Cissa knew that her sister Matilda had a husband now. She'd watched the wedding that made that happen. "You didn't invite me to your wedding."

"Well, it weren't no big to-do like Miz Matilda's."

"Tell me about it." Cissa leaned forward with her chin in her left palm.

"Not much to tell. Just me and Baxter and my folks and his folks and the pastor to make things all legal. We signed papers, just like Miz Matilda and Mr. Frank did."

"Was it Rev. Grafton?" He was the Presbyterian pastor in Rundle Springs. Cissa tried to remember when was the last time she'd heard Negro singing from the church there on a Sunday afternoon.

"No, Miss. We gots our own church now up at Cedar Hill. Our own colored pastor."

Cissa wasn't sure where Cedar Hill was. "Oh. Well, did the men stand around after and talk about politics and the women about courting and babies and all? And was there cake?"

Julia chuckled again. "There was all that, Miss Cissa, but the politics likely was some different. Cake was nice. Cake always nice."

Cissa was about to ask whether the cake had had white frosting with little flowers when she heard her father's heavy boots in the front hallway. Her words stuck in her throat. Maybe she could just run away. Surely nobody would miss her. Her hand closed around the little paper in her pocket.

Pop stuck his head around the door facing and asked, "Where is Susanna?"

"She gone to see Miz Laura, Doc Tarver, sir. She be back soon. I could go fetch her."

"No, never mind," Pop said. He nodded absently at Cissa as he moved toward the dining room where he kept his work space.

Cissa took a deep breath. She knew there was no way around this, no way to escape what must be done. Her father would be angry, but so would Mr. Warren be angry—maybe even angrier—if she didn't give her father the note. She had to do it.

She slid out of her chair and followed her father into the dining room. Without speaking, she laid the note on the desk in front of him.

"What's this?" He glanced at Cissa and then unfolded the note, picking up his spectacles and placing them on his nose. He read as Cissa began to tremble inside. Tears clutched at her throat.

Pop laid the note down and tapped it with his glasses. "Do you have anything to say for yourself, Narcissa?"

"I wasn't stealing," Cissa said. "Just borrowing the book until tomorrow."

"Borrowing. Now why ever would you want to do that?"

"Miss Armstrong used to let me bring books home to…to share."

"To share? With whom?"

Pop had told Cissa more than once that she must never be afraid to speak the truth, so she said, "With Julia. She can't go to school because she's working here but she likes learning stuff as much as I do, and I like talking to her about stuff." She hadn't meant to say nearly that much, but there it was. It couldn't make things any worse, could it?

"With Julia. The girl can read, can she?"

"Yes, sir."

"And write?"

"Yes, sir. Some. She especially likes reading about geography."

"Geography."

Pop didn't look as angry as Cissa had thought he might be. He drummed with his fingers on the desktop. She waited in breathless silence as he picked up the note and read it through again.

"Did Mr. Warren punish you, Narcissa?"

"Yes sir." She held out her left hand where bruises blossomed across the knuckles.

Pop nodded. "Well that's that then. I hope you've learned your lesson. I know you care about Julia, but you have to understand that you and she are different. Julia has already had more than enough schooling. What she's learning here in this house about cooking and cleaning is what she needs now. You must do the best you can in school, Narcissa, but you must also understand how the world works. And you must learn to abide by the rules. I will write a note of acknowledgment to Mr. Warren telling him that I've scolded you about your infraction and imposed upon you the need to be more compliant henceforward. You can take it to him tomorrow."

"Yes, sir." Cissa's heart was still beating fast, though now it was with relief rather than fear. She wasn't sure what all of her father's big words meant, but she did know that his belt was still firmly buckled around his waist and that was a good thing. Although she'd never experienced it or witnessed it, she knew that Pop was capable of administering a whipping. She'd seen Monroe whip Lachlan once and Monroe had said it was no more than what he'd gotten as a boy.

Later that evening, when Cissa was already tucked up in her bed supposedly sleeping, she heard her father discussing the school episode with her mother.

"She's a capable enough child in most of her schoolwork—penmanship aside—and she has a good heart," Pop said. "She will likely never amount to much. Her disability doesn't make her an attractive marriage prospect."

Mother sighed. "I know. No one would take her on as a schoolteacher, either. Who would want a teacher who can't write properly with her right hand?"

"Perhaps it's just as well. We should consider her a blessing for our elder years, Susanna. All the better if she never marries."

Cissa felt ashamed. Was that all she was good for? She was not a girl who dwelt much on daydreams about a future husband or children, but a future in which she was destined to nurse her parents in their old age left her feeling disheartened. *Why me?* she thought. But she knew why. She was the youngest and the last one left at home. Her older brothers and sister had lives of their own now, families of their own. Cissa had nothing.

Donna Birdwell

Chapter Eleven
A Secret World

1887

Cissa's sense of discouragement lingered, agitated by that niggling sense of "why me?" She tried to be the compliant and respectful child everyone wanted her to be, but she found it fit her no better than last year's school dresses. To avoid the discomfort of grownups' expectations, she learned to be invisible again, disappearing for hours at a time. She took walks down by the creek, played with the cats in the barn, or spied on squirrels and birds and chipmunks and dragonflies. Day by day, she strayed a little farther from home, but never too far. She remembered what it felt like to be lost.

At school, Cissa became a fluent reader, hungry for stories and unsatisfied by the content of her school texts. The only books in her house were the big family Bible and a shelf of volumes above her father's desk in the dining room. Cissa decided to explore those. Among the well-worn medical tomes she found a slim volume with an intriguing title: *The Secret Commonwealth of Elves, Fauns, and Faeries.* The book was bound in worn and faded leather and had a blossom of mildew on its back cover. Cissa sat down on the dining room floor and began to read.

Within a few pages, she learned that the shee or fairies were often called "the good people" though they could be very dangerous. According to Rev. Kirk, who had written the book, these beings were "of a middle nature betwixt man and angel" and they had "light changeable bodies, somewhat of the nature of a condensed cloud, and best seen in twilight."

Cissa shivered, remembering how Nubby had appeared out of nowhere and how Mother had called Nubby a bannee. Was Nubby one of these people? Was a bannee some kind of fairy?

Cissa did not put the book back on the shelf. Instead, she took it to her bedroom and continued reading. She read about how these fairy folk, with their "bodies of congealed air" were sometimes known to bake bread or use hammers. Might they also wash clothing in a stream or pond? The book didn't say.

The world described in this book felt very different from the mundane morality tales that filled Cissa's school texts. She was enchanted and terrified by turns. She read on, closing her eyes from time to time as she tried to envision the people and creatures and events she read about.

It wasn't until she'd had the book for almost a week that she bothered to look at the handwritten words inside the front cover. There in a childish scrawl she read "Duncan Tarver." Could this truly have been her brother Duncan's book when he was a child? Cissa often had a hard time believing that her brothers had ever been children at all. But there was Duncan's name right there in this book that was not about politics or medicine or any of the things she thought her brother cared about. As Cissa stared at the page, trying to imagine her brother reading about fairy folk in the "secret commonwealth," something else caught her eye. In a lower corner of the page near a water stain there was another name, written in blue ink that had faded into the yellowing paper. She tilted the page toward the light and squinted. "Margaret McLaurin" was the name.

Cissa frowned. She knew that McLaurin was her mother's family name, but Mother was Susanna, and her only sister was Abigail. Who was Margaret? And then she knew: Margaret was Mag. This had been Granny Mag's book.

Cissa, of course, never knew this grandmother. Granny Mag had died some ten years before Cissa was born. But Duncan and Monroe had known her, and they spoke of her from time to time. Cissa knew that Granny Mag had been born in Scotland and had married Cissa's grandfather in one of the Carolinas, though she could never remember which one. Both of her daughters—Susanna and Abigail—had been born in Mississippi. It was Granny Mag who had warned Mother about the bannees.

The book wasn't very long and a great deal of it was hard to understand. There were occasional strange words that Cissa found impossible to sound out. Cissa read the whole text anyway and then she read it again. The parts she liked best she read over and over, savoring the images they conjured in her mind, images of ethereal people, of birds and animals that were both more and less than they seemed.

Cissa searched her father's shelf for more books. She found one that contained a story called *Rob Roy*, written by someone called Walter Scott. But she left it where it was. It had an intimidating number of pages and wasn't half as appealing as the book about the commonwealth of fairies.

Cissa's long-standing fascination with watching cats and birds and other creatures took on new dimensions. She imagined that they were the subterranean creatures described in the book and that they were replete with magic. She told herself that when Sambo went missing, he had just gone through to the other realm for a time. She went over and over in her mind her encounter with Nubby at the pond by the big rock, increasingly convinced that Nubby was indeed some sort of fairy person. Sometimes she imagined Sambo sitting at Nubby's feet as the two of them shimmered midway between ordinary and otherwise. She began to think of the red bead with its black dots as a talisman and she took to wearing it on a string around her neck, carefully tucked inside her dress. She told herself this was to protect its magic, but of course it also kept it from being seen by her mother or anyone else. She spent more and more time by herself out of doors.

Cissa began spinning her own tales about magnolia fairies that lived in the tree next to the old summer kitchen and primrose fairies in the flowery patch beneath the big cedar. And down by the creek, there were whole battalions of frog fairies. More and more, Cissa immersed herself in an imaginary world in which she mattered, in which Narcissa June Tarver was the Queen of the Magnolia Fairies. She wrote some of these stories down in her composition book.

Cissa tried inducting her niece Milly into this world. "They fly up there and sip the nectar from the magnolia blossoms just like butterflies," Cissa explained. "And the frog fairies... Well, you have to be careful that you don't step on them when you wade in the creek. That makes them angry and when they're angry, you never know what they might do."

"Can you really see them?" Milly asked, her eyes wide with wonder.

"Of course." Cissa sniffed with disdain. "But perhaps you're not gifted with the second sight as I am. You'll just have to trust me."

And so Milly did, for a while. Each girl brought her doll to the games. Milly's was the lifelike china doll that she'd received from a great-aunt at Christmas. They called her Princess Winifred. Cissa had the rag doll Julia had made, now dingy with time and love. The doll's yellow braids had grown darker just as Cissa's own hair had done as she grew from a baby into a young girl. Both of the dolls, of course, could see the fairy folk as plain as anything. Cissa's doll was Princess Ursula Maryanne Virginia.

"Which frock should Princess Winifred wear to the dinner?" Milly said. Her doll had several different dresses, each one adorned with ruffles or lace or both. "I think the captain of the frog fairies likes the yellow one best."

Cissa sputtered. "Oh, Milly, it doesn't matter. The fairies don't care what color her dress is. They're made of *congealed air*!" Why did Milly always have to be reminded of such simple facts? "And the captain of the frog fairies has better things to do than notice what some silly pollywog princess is wearing. Heavens to Betsy, Milly, they have *powers!*"

Milly began to cry. She threw down her magic magnolia pod, jerked the magic kerchief from around her head and stormed off with Princess Winifred and all her frocks in tow.

After that, it was just Cissa and the fairies and Princess Ursula Maryanne Virginia. Cissa concentrated on managing the looming battle of magic between the magnolia brigade and the frog battalion. She often went back to the book about the secret commonwealth for added inspiration for her increasingly complex tales. She was studying that book on the steps in front of the house one day when her brother Duncan stopped by.

"What are you reading there, little sister?" he said. He tucked his newspaper under his arm and reached for the book.

Cissa let him take it without protest and without answering his question. After all, the book had once been his, hadn't it?

He began to chuckle. "Oh, my, I remember this. What a lot of nonsense!"

Cissa prickled at his insult but contained herself. "Did Granny Mag give it to you?" she asked.

"She did." Duncan grew more serious as he opened the book to the page on which his name and their grandmother's name appeared. "She said she brought it over from Scotland with her. She gave it to me not long before she died. I must have been about eight years old."

He turned a few pages, and his mustache couldn't hide his smile as a wistful look sparkled in his eyes.

"What was Granny Mag like?"

"She had a lot of stories." Duncan closed the book and shook his head. "All kinds of crazy tales from the old country about magical folk. Like it was some sort of invisible empire full of wizards and dragons." He gave Cissa a sidelong glance and then chortled as if he'd told some sort of joke. He sat down on the step next to her. "Such tales were fine when I was a child, but you have to grow up eventually and attend to serious matters based on facts. You have to join the real world." He put his arm around Cissa's shoulders. "How old are you now, Cissy?"

"Eleven."

Duncan gave her shoulders a slight squeeze. "I read a rather exciting book recently that's about a lost continent of Atlantis and it's more interesting than any fairy stories and has the decided advantage of being entirely true. Maybe I'll lend it to you one day." He closed the book and handed it back to Cissa. "Time to grow up, little sister." He patted her on the head as he proceeded up the steps and into the house.

Cissa sat with the closed book in her lap, feeling torn between her enchanted world and this thing Duncan called the real world. She didn't like being treated like a child. She'd rather be treated like the Queen of the Magnolia Fairies, but no one acknowledged her as that. No one in the real world.

Cissa wondered about the stories her grandmother had told to Monroe and Duncan and Matilda. She vaguely remembered hearing her sister begging Mother to "tell us one of Granny Mag's stories." More clearly she recalled her mother's response: "Those tales are best forgotten," she'd said. Cissa hadn't known what they were talking about at the time. Now she thought she had at least a glimmering of an idea.

Mother hasn't forgotten, she told herself. It was Mother, after all, who had told her that Nubby was a bannee and what Granny Mag had said about bannees, about how they had one tooth and one nostril and webbed feet like a duck. About how they were always washing clothes in a pond or stream and that the clothes were those of someone who was about to die. Cissa enjoyed the shiver that this image sent through her body.

The dining room window was open and Cissa listened as Duncan greeted their father.

"Well, Pop, I've done it. I've secured the nomination for Representative."

A chair scraped across the floor and Cissa knew Pop had pushed away from his desk to face Duncan. "Secured? Are you certain it's secure? I heard that Bloomfield is contesting some of the precinct results."

Duncan scoffed. "The party officials have signed off on it. I'm the district's Democratic candidate for the United States Congress." His voice shrilled with excitement. "Listen to what one of the Jackson papers wrote." There was a rustling of newsprint. "'After a contest both sharp and exciting, Dr. D. Q. Tarver received the nomination in Fulton County. Dr. Tarver comes of sterling ancestry, and though a young man, will prove an able foe of wrong and corruption.' What do you think about that, Pop?"

Cissa's heart swelled with pride. Her brother was someone of importance in the real world. She liked the statement about "sterling ancestry"; those were her ancestors, too.

Pop cleared his throat. "What do I think? I think you'd best take care not to let this make your head too big for your hat. You know I'm proud of you for representing us at the district Democratic convention. But now you're running a risk, beating out an incumbent the way you did by convincing those McManus Creek delegates to vote for you even though they'd bound themselves to vote for Bloomfield."

"It wasn't hard, Pop. You know we've got kin at McManus Creek."

Pop sighed loudly. "I'd rather hoped your involvement wouldn't go so far. Politics is a dangerous business, son. You see what happened to old Bloomfield. He's barely back on his feet from that gunshot wound. And we both know that affray was about the primary election. You're a doctor, Duncan. Just be a doctor and leave the politics aside. I've always felt I could be a better doctor by staying out of all the rivalries and factions that come from politics."

"Don't be so old-fashioned, Pop," Duncan said. Cissa heard the smile in his voice. "Lots of doctors are involved in politics. Reverends, too. I've always wondered why you didn't stand for office yourself. You know every voter in at least three counties, and most of them are beholden to you for some cure or for delivering their wives or comforting their old folks. Politics is a natural for a doctor."

Duncan paused and Cissa visualized him fiddling with his hat. She could almost hear her father drumming on the desk with his fingers.

"As for any danger…" Duncan laughed. "Well, doesn't that just make it more exciting? There's nothing quite like the thrill of being part of a crowd taking things into their own hands. I don't know why you've taken to avoiding such things. I remember a few times when you weren't so timid." A chair scraped again. "You know old Bloomfield's injuries will likely keep him from canvassing and give me an advantage. That fellow who shot him may have done me a big favor."

"You oughtn't to say things like that, Duncan. I saw too much bloodshed in the war to trust bullets to solve anything. And as for the excitement of the crowd…" Pop cleared his throat. "Well, sometimes they end up doing things they shouldn't. Nonetheless, you know I stand behind you, son. If you're determined to be a politician, you'll always have my support." Pop's voice was devoid of enthusiasm.

Cissa recalled times when she'd seen Duncan the center of attention at gatherings, whole groups of grown men hanging on his every word. How might it feel to have people listen to you so attentively when you spoke? Cissa, who could imagine fairies sipping nectar from magnolia blossoms, could not imagine such a thing.

Duncan bid their father farewell and left, bounding down the front steps with no further word for Cissa.

She watched as her brother swung up into his saddle and directed his horse toward Monroe's place, no doubt to share his good news there as well. Cissa stood up, straightened her skirt, and went inside the house. Entering her bedroom, she wrapped the book in an old headscarf and laid it in the top drawer of her bureau. Then she took Nubby's red bead from around her neck, laid it alongside the book, and closed the drawer.

Chapter Twelve
Something About Boys

1888

Cissa tried harder to be part of the real world, to figure out what it was and why it mattered. She paid closer attention to what grownups were doing, realizing that being a grownup was (whether she liked it or not) her eventual destiny.

Still hungry for stories, Cissa discovered that sometimes the newspapers her father and brothers brought into the house printed tales that continued from week to week. She began to follow these. She was drawn, too, to the occasional poem published among the news and gossip and the advertisements for patent medicines and farm equipment. Even more than the pleasing visual symmetry of the poems, she loved the way the words sounded. She began writing a few poems of her own.

Julia was in a family way again, which Cissa hadn't noticed at first because Julia's figure was now rounder than it had been before Rosie was born. She didn't ask when the baby was coming, not wanting to think about the absence of Julia that the event would necessitate. Thus, it came as something of a surprise to Cissa when, in mid-July, just after school one day, Elsie was back in the Tarvers' kitchen.

"Where's Julia?" Cissa asked, sounding somewhat peeved.

"She home with the new baby, Miss. Come jus' last night. Boy this time." Elsie said.

Cissa's heart sank, which she knew was not a proper reaction to such news. "Please give her my good wishes," she said. Surely that was a proper grownup thing to say.

Cissa tried to be happy about Julia's new baby but knowing that Julia would be away for some weeks or even months just when she herself was going to be stuck at home during cotton picking season made her grumpy. She spent her time reading whatever she could get her hands on, which was mostly newspapers. She watched for news of her brother's congressional race. She learned that

Bloomfield had managed to get his name on the ballot alongside Duncan's, contending that there were some shenanigans in voting procedures at the Democratic Party's district primary convention. That put two Democrats on the November ballot for the same seat. As best Cissa could tell, in the real world of southern Mississippi that was not a good thing.

Cissa continued writing, filling her composition book and tablets with little essays and stories. She discovered that she liked writing about things she observed in nature just as much as she had liked writing fairy stories. She showed some of her essays to Lachlan, who said he liked them. She also wrote more poems, which she didn't show to anyone, though she occasionally recited them to Sambo out in the barn.

The election was held just after school started up again, just after Ada gave birth to another son, whom Duncan named Quinlan. Duncan lost his contest with Bloomfield by about a hundred votes. Judging by a couple of conversations Cissa overheard between Duncan and Monroe and between Monroe and their father, she knew that Duncan was indignant about the loss, insisting that there had been chicanery.

"You know how it's done, Pop," Duncan said one day when Cissa was on the front porch with her tablet and pencil, working on a school essay. "They get their own people to run the polling places, count the ballots, and send in the returns. The other candidate doesn't stand a chance."

Cissa didn't like hearing her brother so angry.

"What's done is done," Pop said. "Make peace with it and move on." But there was fire in Duncan's eyes as he stomped away, closing the front door more forcefully than was polite.

"Albert!" he yelled, then muttered, "Where is that god damned boy anyway. He's never where he's wanted. Albert!"

"He left," Cissa said. "He said he was going hunting with some other boys."

He frowned at Cissa's tablet and pencil. "Well, if he comes by here, tell him he's wanted at home right away."

"Yes, sir." Cissa watched as Duncan mounted up and spurred his horse forward.

She turned her thoughts back to the essay she was writing for class. She felt like she always did her best work sitting here on the front porch, even on a chilly autumn day like this one. She was particularly proud of this essay. They'd been assigned to write something about nature, and Cissa was writing about watching a snake swallow a frog down by the creek. It had been a large frog, and her descriptions were vivid, using words like "devour" and "engorge" and "shriek." She read it through one more time. She'd just added a final sentence when she heard Albert and his cronies coming up the back path.

When Albert saw Cissa sitting on the steps writing in her tablet, he slapped his forehead and said, "Oh, criminy! I forgot we were supposed to write something for school." He reached for Cissa's tablet and wrested it from her hand.

"Your pop says you're wanted at home," Cissa said. "Right away." She held out her hand for Albert to give her the tablet back.

Instead, he tore out the pages she'd written on and said, "You won't mind if I borrow these. I don't even remember what we're supposed to write about." As Cissa attempted to protest, he waved her away. "I'll give your paper back to you tomorrow, Aunt Cissy. You said yourself that Pop needs me at home." And with a grin he was off, dangling Cissa's paper in one hand, carrying his shotgun and a dead squirrel in the other.

Cissa sat in stunned silence. Why were boys like this? She'd seen Albert take things before—candy from the store, a watermelon from a neighbor's field—but he'd never taken anything from her before, and certainly nothing like this. She looked down at her tablet, at the ragged edge where Albert had torn out the pages. *Crying won't help anything*, she told herself as she sat on the steps feeling helpless and violated and angry. Hot tears welled up.

<hr>

The next morning, Cissa ran to catch up with the other children on their way to school. She heard fragments of their conversation as she approached.

"Another sister," Lachlan sighed. "That's three now. I keep hoping for a brother."

Albert laughed. "I'll give you one of mine."

Cissa knew that her sister-in-law Laura had given birth yesterday, but she hadn't heard that it was a girl. Another niece for Cissa. She ticked through the list: Milly, Betty, Janie, Matilda's little Evelyn, and now this one.

As she caught up to Albert, Cissa grabbed him by the shirt sleeve. "Where's my paper, Albert. You said you'd give it back."

Albert shook her off. "I forgot," he said. "I left it at home. Sorry, Aunt Cissy." He didn't sound sorry.

"You forgot?" Cissa's voice shrilled with anger. How she wished she'd grabbed that paper back when he took it. It was a good paper. She'd spent a lot of time writing it while Albert had been out hunting squirrels. She'd been a fool to trust him. "You promised me," Cissa said. "You said you'd give it back."

"And so I shall. As soon as we get home this afternoon, I'll find it and give it back to you."

Cissa wanted to hit him. What was she supposed to do now? She didn't have a paper to turn in. She'd have to try and rewrite her essay quickly as soon as she reached school, working on it during spelling and arithmetic.

Mr. Warren assigned a lengthy set of multiplication problems for Cissa's group to work on while other students began reading aloud the essays they had written. Cissa hurried through the problems and then, with her tablet in her lap, wrote out what she could recall of her essay. Writing so hurriedly made her penmanship even worse than usual, as she prayed not to be called upon until she'd finished.

Suddenly the words that were being read caught her ear. It was Albert's voice, but the words were Cissa's. Her exact words. Cissa reeled with dizziness as the blood drained from her face. Albert hadn't just borrowed her paper; he was claiming it as his own. No doubt he'd simply copied it in his own handwriting. As he finished reading to murmurs of admiration and a smattering of applause, he turned and looked Cissa dead in the eyes as if to say, *Don't you dare.*

"Excellent work, Master Albert." Mr. Warren glowed with approval. "I would venture to predict that you have a great future as a statesman like your father."

The blood thundered in Cissa's ears as her face flushed hot. She struggled to calm herself, but her breath caught in her throat. She wouldn't cry. She couldn't. She'd done nothing wrong. Albert had stolen her essay and now he was being praised for it. Praised for her work.

A couple more boys were called upon to read next, giving Cissa a few more minutes to try and calm herself. A few more minutes to think what to do when she was called upon, to hope that they would run out of time before Mr. Warren got to Narcissa and they could all go out for recess.

"Narcissa Tarver. Please stand up and read your essay."

Cissa had to grip her tablet in both hands to steady herself. She had no choice but to read what she'd just written. Her voice was weak and tremulous as she began to read. About halfway through, someone snickered. Then someone else joined in.

"That will be enough, Narcissa." Mr. Warren stopped her before she was finished. "Your paper bears an uncanny resemblance to Albert's paper. Although it is not nearly so polished. You may sit down." Turning to the class, he continued. "I have told you all repeatedly that you must always do your own work and never copy your fellow students' work. Narcissa has disobeyed that rule. She will receive a failing mark on this assignment. It is my hope that she will learn a lesson from her failure."

Cissa was still standing, her anger unabated. When she spoke, her voice was so low that at first only the students nearest to her heard what she said. "I didn't copy."

"I said, 'Sit down,'" Mr. Warren's voice was stern.

Cissa remained standing and spoke again, this time with more force. "I didn't copy. That was my paper." She paused, aware that all eyes were on her. She had to tell the truth. "Albert copied my paper," she said.

A couple of the boys sitting next to Albert began to snicker. Mr. Warren gestured them into silence. "Narcissa, please do not compound your error by lying. Accept your punishment with grace, if you can." He cast an apologetic look toward Albert. "You have failed the assignment and that's the end of it. Now, class, please pass your papers to the front of the room to be placed on my desk."

Cissa sat. She tore the page on which she'd penned her hurriedly written essay out of the tablet. Then, holding the paper up so Mr. Warren could see it, she tore the paper in half, passing both halves to the student next to her.

When school let out for the day, Cissa lagged behind. She didn't want to walk home with the other residents of Callander Road. Milly turned around and walked back toward Cissa, falling into step beside her and placing a hand on Cissa's shoulder. "I believe you, Aunt Cissy," she said.

Cissa offered a wan smile. "Thanks, Milly," she said. "I'm going to go see Julia's new baby. Do you want to come?"

Milly took a step back and stopped. "Oh, I don't think we should, Aunt Cissy."

Cissa shrugged. "You go on with the others then. And if Mother asks, you can tell her where I've gone." Cissa had known Milly wouldn't come and she knew she shouldn't go either. But under the circumstances, doing something she shouldn't made her feel better.

Julia's house was tiny, but it was nicely whitewashed. There was a gray cat on the top step and the start of a bottle tree next to the porch. The cat scurried under the house as Cissa walked up the steps. She knocked and waited. There was no answer. Cissa was disappointed but thought that maybe Julia had gone to her mother's house. She wasn't ready to go home, so she turned toward the path that went to the colored community. She tried not to think about the unpleasantness of her day at school, but Mr. Warren's words kept resounding in her mind. He'd called Albert a future statesman. He called Cissa a failure.

As she neared the settlement, Cissa heard singing and clapping and laughter, and the sound of it made her smile. She thought that Julia and her friends and family must be having some kind of celebration, a celebration to which Cissa hadn't been invited. She hesitated for a moment, savoring the smell of roasting meat that wafted her way. Cissa figured that they probably wouldn't send her away, but she wasn't in the mood for celebrating. Reluctantly, she turned down the path that would lead her to the back of her own house.

The laughter that greeted Cissa as she emerged from the canebrake near Chakchu Creek sounded very different from the merriment of the colored community. These were boys' voices, loud and raucous. When the boys came into view, she guessed that they had been fishing and, from the look and smell of things, smoking cigarettes and imbibing somebody's pa's whisky. Cissa knew several of these boys from school and she knew they were not boys from the families Cissa's family interacted with.

"Will you look at that, Bobby!" one of the boys called out as another boy whistled. "It's Cissy, the little thief that claimed she wrote her cousin's paper. Whatcha gonna do now, Miss Fancy Pants—claim you wrote the Reverend's sermon?"

Another boy joined in. "I bet she thinks she wrote the whole Bible."

"I did write it!" Cissa quickly realized that the timing of her rejoinder was unfortunate as the boys collapsed into even more riotous laughter. "I did write the paper. And besides, he's not my cousin, he's my nephew."

"Aunt Cissy wrote the Bible!"

The boys collided into one another, drunk with derision and moonshine. They careened toward Cissa as she hastened her steps. One of them reached for her arm. She twisted away, but Bobby caught her around the waist.

"You leave me be, Robert Clark!" Fear grabbed Cissa even harder than Bobby did. "Let me go!"

Now there were three boys grabbing at her, holding her, pushing her back and forth between them. One of them, she couldn't tell who, put his hand over her breast and another lifted her skirt. Cissa tried to shout again, but her mouth was covered by somebody's hand and then by somebody's mouth that tasted of whisky. She pulled her right arm free and gave somebody a sound whack across the side of his face.

"Hey, now. No need to get ugly. We're just having a little fun. Gals are supposed to let boys have their fun."

"Let her go, Bobby," one of the boys said. "That's enough."

They let Cissa go, hurling a last few crude remarks at her as she lifted her torn skirt and fled. She didn't cry until after she'd sneaked into the house and into the bedroom. She didn't go to supper, claiming she didn't feel well. Her disheveled hair still smelled vaguely of cigarette smoke. She stayed in her room, struggling to mend her damaged skirt and wounded dignity.

Donna Birdwell

Chapter Thirteen
Looking for Answers

1888

Cissa lay awake most of the night, trying to sort out her tumult of emotions. Shame and anger wove together in about equal portions, leaving her confused. Was this something she should tell her parents about? Those boys who accosted her were some of the same ones who had mocked her at school, laughed along with Mr. Warren's ridicule of her. She didn't want to have to tell her parents about that. Also, she knew from experience that boys—even those boys—got away with things that Cissa felt had to be wrong. Her own nephew was getting away with the theft of her essay. Cissa's anger began to eclipse the shame.

After tossing for several restless hours, she got out of bed and, after lighting a candle, retrieved Nubby's red bead from the bureau drawer and hung it once again around her neck. She tried to remember the words Nubby had said when she gave her the bead.

She cradled the object in her left hand, supported by her damaged right, and let her anger burn up bright and strong—anger at the unfairness of it all, anger at her own sense of powerlessness. If only she could claim in this real world the power she'd imagined for herself as Queen of the Magnolia Fairies.

When she fell asleep at last, she was still clutching the red bead.

The next morning Cissa rose early. She tiptoed through the house and out the kitchen door, closing it softly behind her. The sun was not up yet, though the eastern horizon glowed a rosy orange. *Follow Chakchu Creek to the lightning oak.* Cissa was sure she could remember the way. She hadn't been to Nubby's pond since that day when she and Julia went there to thank Nubby for guiding Cissa to Zolene's house when she'd gotten lost.

Cissa felt lost again.

But this time it was a different sort of lost. It wasn't the terror she'd felt when she'd lost her way in the forest. Now she was just confused and there was no one to help her find her way, to find her place in this maddening real world. It was that kind of lost.

She walked through the dew-wet grass in the early dimness, following the path that Julia's daily trek had traced into the earth. As she approached the creek, a doe and a pair of fawns raised their heads, flicked their ears, and then continued drinking. Passing through the canebrake, she felt her breathing deepen. Birds began to twitter and flutter; a rabbit skittered across the path and into the shelter of a tangled dewberry vine.

This time of day, when troublemakers were yet sleeping, felt safe to Cissa. It felt like a time that belonged to people like Nubby. She walked as lightly as she could, listening to the birds and the breeze sighing through the branches.

When Cissa spotted the lightning oak, her confidence faltered. Up to this point, her excursion had felt like an adventure, a quest, but now that she felt assured she could reach Nubby's pond, she asked herself: *Why, Cissa? Why do you want to do this?* Would Nubby even be there? Would she be glad to see Cissa or annoyed at being disturbed so early? Maybe she wouldn't even remember the little girl she'd rescued so long ago.

Cissa didn't stop. She was certain that Nubby knew things, that Nubby held some secret power of a kind that Cissa wanted for herself. She continued past the lightning oak, and at last arrived at the pond. It looked smaller and shallower than she remembered it. There were weeds growing in the margins of its murky waters. Cissa sat down and leaned against one of the oak trees, the tallest and thickest one. She dug her fingers into the weedy grass and felt the earth soft and welcoming. She wished she'd brought something to eat, wished it was dewberry season. She wished that she knew where she was going. Not just the way to Nubby, but the way forward in this real world. Her way forward.

She waited. She turned toward every shuffling among the leaves, but it was always a squirrel or a chipmunk or a beetle. It wasn't Nubby. Something red on the far side of the pond caught her eye and she went around to investigate. It was a bit of cloth and Cissa tugged at it to free it from the muck. A yellow button suggested it had once been part of a shirt. Cissa had seen a red shirt once, among her father's things, though she'd never seen him wear it. Her heartbeat quickened as she recalled what her mother had said about Nubby, calling her a bannee, a witch who washed the clothes of someone who was about to die. Not Pop, though. His shirt had black buttons.

Cissa finally got up the nerve to look behind the big rock. She wasn't sure what she expected to find there, but all she found was more forest.

Nubby wasn't coming.

High up in the branches above her, a bird began to chant. At first Cissa thought it was a phoebe. No, maybe a chickadee. She listened, toying with the red wooden bead that hung around her neck, and suddenly Nubby's words came back to her, plain as anything: "You keep this and maybe you don't get lost no more. Maybe you find your own way."

Find your own way. But how was Cissa supposed to do that? Everything she did seemed to lead nowhere and end badly.

The bird kept up its chanting and singing. The themes of different birds tumbled into one another until at last there was the distinctive warble that assured Cissa this was a mockingbird. She thought about how good mockingbirds were at pretending to be other birds, but always, in the end, revealing their true identity as mockingbirds. Cissa looked up at the bird and smiled a quiet little smile. Then, with a sigh and the tiniest glimmer of hopefulness, she got up and headed home.

In the kitchen, she found a leftover biscuit and dribbled a little honey on it for her breakfast. She poured herself a glass of milk, wondering where Elsie had gone so early.

"There you are," Mother cried, her hands on her hips. "Wherever have you been young lady?"

So they'd missed her after all. Probably Elsie was looking for her. Should she tell Mother about those bad boys? About Albert stealing her paper? "I went out for a morning walk," Cissa said, "because I was upset." She'd start with that.

All at once, Mother lunged toward Cissa as, too late, Cissa realized she had forgotten to tuck Nubby's red bead back inside her blouse. Mother grabbed it and yanked.

"Ow!" The string cut into Cissa's neck as it broke.

"Where did you get this witch charm, Narcissa June? Don't you know what it is?" Mother's eyes were wild with fury as she held the bead between her fingers as if it were a hot coal. And then she did the unthinkable—she hurled the bead into the fire.

"Mother, no!" Cissa shrieked. Forgetting the cut on her neck, she sprang toward the stove and might well have plunged her hand into the fire to rescue her precious bead if Elsie had not appeared at that moment and pulled her away. Cissa fell into Elsie's arms, sobbing.

"I tried to warn you, Narcissa." Mother's voice seethed with disgust. "You don't know about such things as charms and witches, but I do." Her voice went low, almost a whisper, as if she were talking to herself. "They take babies."

Cissa pulled away from Elsie and glared at her mother. She couldn't bear to look at the fire where her bead was by now going up in flames and would soon turn to ash. She was tired of feeling sorry for her poor mother over the loss of her babies decades ago. She slammed the back door as she headed for the barn.

The day crept by for Cissa. She stroked Sambo for a while until he turned around and bit her before parading out of the barn with his tail waving. Any thoughts she'd had of confiding in her mother about her worries were gone. The tinge of hopefulness she'd found at Nubby's pond had also faded. She fumed and pouted and refused both dinner and supper. She slept very little.

The next morning dawned gray, threatening rain. Cissa dressed and went to breakfast. "Where's Mother?" she asked Elsie. *As if I care*, she thought.

"She gone to Miz Laura's place," Elsie said. "And Doc Tarver had early call." Elsie reached into the pocket of her apron and pulled out a small object, which she placed next to Cissa's plate.

Cissa's eyes went wide. "You found it!" She gazed up at Elsie, forgiving her in that moment for every burnt biscuit and lumpy gravy she'd ever made. She grabbed the bead in her left hand and clutched it to her chest. "Oh, Elsie, thank you!" And forgetting breakfast, Cissa dashed to her bedroom, determined to find a safe place to secure her bead. She felt that glimmer of hope igniting again. Surely this bead *was* charmed, but in a good way. It had survived being cast into the fire, hadn't it?

Her eyes fell upon the somewhat tattered rag doll Julia had made. It had come apart at one of its seams and Cissa had been meaning to try her hand at mending it. Yes, the bead just fit inside.

She plucked some cotton out of her pillow and stuffed it in around the bead. Then she worked with careful determination, holding the two sides of the seam together with her damaged right hand and stitching with her left. The seam was messy and irregular, but it would hold. Just to be extra safe, she stitched the doll's dress down over the seam. Then she hugged the doll once and tucked it next to her pillow. She felt as if she ought to say some words of protection over the doll and its new cargo, but all she could think of was, "Thank you, Nubby. Thank you, Julia. Thank you, Elsie." And then, with a smile, she added, "Thank you, Princess Ursula Maryanne Virginia."

Chapter Fourteen
Loss

Early 1889

The first week of the new year found Cissa pottering about the chilly house listening to Elsie banging pots and pans in the kitchen. The smell of burning fat drifted in the air. In the hallway, Cissa stopped in front of the big mirror. She could see her face in it easily now without standing on tiptoe. She recalled that when she was small the mirror had been nothing more than a bright spot high on the wall where colors moved and shifted for no apparent reason. She studied the face staring back at her now. The jaw was too square, the complexion too freckled, the hair too nondescript. She twirled a stray brownish strand, thinking of Milly's coppery curls and her creamy smooth skin.

It had been a month since Albert's theft of Cissa's essay. When she let herself think about it, it still rankled. She kept telling herself that at least she had Mr. Warren's word that it had been a good paper. If only Mr. Warren had believed her when she said it was hers. And as for the boys who had accosted her down by the creek—they were nothing to Cissa. She repeated it: *They're nothing to me.* She felt certain that if she'd tried to tell her parents about them she'd only have gotten the usual "boys will be boys" and a scolding for some transgressive behavior of her own.

Elsie had set the breakfast on the table, so Cissa wandered in and took her seat. Her mother joined her, still adjusting the waist of her dress over the corset she always wore. Cissa expected it wouldn't be long before Mother required her to wear one, too.

"When will Julia be back?" Cissa let the oatmeal drip from her spoon in gelatinous lumps. The only person Cissa knew with whom she could discuss her problems freely—the theft of her paper, the bad behavior of the boys who'd accosted her, her clandestine visit to Nubby's pond—was Julia. And Julia wasn't here.

"Julia is not coming back," Mother said.

"What? Why not?" Cissa felt her chest tighten. "Didn't you think she was good enough?" Her eyes angled up toward her mother with an accusing glare.

"Don't be impudent, young lady. The girl refused. But we'll find another girl. Maybe Elsie can stay." Mother's voice dropped to a low mumble. "You give these niggers a bit of schooling and they get too uppity to do kitchen work." Mother sniffed as Elsie plopped a basket of very brown biscuits onto the table.

Refused. The word stung Cissa's heart. Why would her Julia refuse to work for the Tarvers anymore? Had she gotten work somewhere else? Why ever would she do that? Cissa finished her breakfast and left the table feeling hungry. Or maybe that empty feeling was something else. Once upon a time, Julia had been the center of Cissa's universe. Then, for a time, she had surrounded herself with fairies and they'd made her feel like someone important. Nubby had somehow made her feel important, too, by giving her a charmed bead. Cissa had gone looking for Nubby and all she'd found was the unpleasant realization that if her life was ever going to get any better, she would have to do something about it herself. She just didn't know what that something might be. To make matters worse, her little black cat had been missing for weeks. And now her Julia was being taken from her. Maybe if Cissa talked to Julia, she could convince her to come back.

"I'm going to go by Ada and Milly's." That's what Cissa told her mother as she buttoned up her coat and prepared to leave the house. It wasn't really a lie, she told herself. She'd seen Ada and Milly leave earlier and she did intend to walk by their house on her way to Julia's.

This time when Cissa knocked on Julia's front door, it opened. "Miss Cissa!" Julia opened the door wide with a smile even wider, though she glanced over Cissa's shoulder as if checking to see if she was alone. She held an infant in her arms and little Rosie clung to her skirt. A fire burned in an iron stove at one end of the room, making the space warm and cozy.

"I came to meet your baby," Cissa said, figuring the discussion about why Julia didn't want to work for the Tarvers anymore could wait. And maybe a discussion about Nubby. And why Cissa had gone to look for Nubby.

"Well, he be hankerin' to meet you, too, Miss. He near six month old now." Julia pulled back the corner of the blanket that had covered the baby's face and turned him toward Cissa. "This here my son, Hiram. Hiram, meet Miss Narcissa Tarver." She thrust the baby toward Cissa.

"He's beautiful, Julia," Cissa said as she drew the baby to her bosom. And he was. His large dark eyes were fringed with the thickest eyelashes Cissa had ever seen. He found her eyes and offered a smile and a squeal that made her laugh.

When Cissa asked for a glass of water, Julia offered coffee instead. Cissa knew that it was considered improper for her to share food and drink in a Negro home, but the custom had never made much sense to Cissa. Besides, this was Julia. It was fine to drink the coffee she made in the Tarver kitchen.

Cissa and Julia spent a pleasant half hour drinking cups of chicory coffee and admiring Julia's children. Rosie held Cissa's soft white hand against her cheek. She counted the fingers on Cissa's left hand and then her right and then her own hand. She seemed fascinated but not in the least put off by Cissa's shortage of fingers.

"When do you think you'll be coming back to work?" Cissa refused to make it easy for Julia, determined to hear her decision in her own words. She'd already been away a good deal longer than she'd been after Rosie was born.

"Not coming back, Miss," Julia spoke with a quiet firmness as she adjusted baby Hiram at her breast.

"Oh, Julia, why not? You know I'll be lost without you." Cissa struggled for composure, feeling the tears rising in her throat.

"You near grown now, Miss Cissa. You don't need no nursemaid no more, that's certain."

"But Elsie doesn't cook nearly as well as you and...and she's just not you, Julia." Of course Cissa didn't need a nursemaid. She would be thirteen at her next birthday. What she did need was a friend. A single tear traced its way down her cheek as she drew little Rosie closer.

Julia tucked her breast away and wiped the milk from Hiram's face. "You know I care for you, Miss. Couldn't be no other way seein's how I been with you since you was jus' a tyke. But time come for me to make a life here with my own family." Julia got up and placed the sleeping baby in his basket. Rosie ran to be pulled up into her mother's lap. "My husband Baxter, he got this piece of land for our own place. This here house our own house. Our own farm. Ain't no big plantation, but we do fine plantin' for what we eat and some to sell. I plan on takin' in sewin' and earn my pennies here and there." Julia caressed Rosie's hair. "Baxter don't want me workin' outside no more."

"Plenty of other colored women work outside and I suppose some of them might have children, too. Maybe I could get Pop to pay you more."

"Not a question of pay, Miss. Your pa pay me what's fair, I reckon. We jus'... We works on our own account now, Baxter and me. For our own selves. And for Rosie and Hiram."

A couple more tears crept down Cissa's face and she whisked them away with her sleeve. Cissa tried to summon up some righteous anger against Julia, but if there was betrayal here, she couldn't put her finger on it. "Well, can I at least come visit you sometimes?"

"From my side, you always be welcome here, Miss Narcissa Tarver. Maybe you even meet Baxter one day. Baxter he be teachin' me more letters and numbers."

There it was. More of the education that Cissa's mother and father deemed unnecessary, even dangerous, for colored people. "Did Baxter go to school?"

"More'n me he did. His mama was on the Willow Creek plantation up above Marchelle. They taught all their niggers to read n' write. Set some of 'em free, too, long 'fore the jubilee. Mr. Chisholm Green, he be Baxter's uncle."

"Who?" Cissa thought the name sounded familiar, but she couldn't place it.

"Mr. Chisholm Green be sheriff of this here county. Used to be. Was in the gov'ment in Jackson, too."

"Really? And he's a Negro?" A discussion overheard between her brothers came back to Cissa. Something about a Negro sheriff who'd been troublesome, led astray by the wrong sort of white people. If the man was a troublemaker, why did Julia glow with such pride when she spoke of her husband's kinship with him?

The two sat in silence for a few moments. Cissa tried to think how to tell Julia about how Albert had stolen her essay or about how the boys at the creek had been so rude to her, but sitting here in Julia's warm cottage with its sparse furnishings and hand embroidered flowers tacked to the wall, she couldn't find the words.

"I went to see Nubby the other day," Cissa said at last. "But she wasn't there."

"No, Miss, I reckon she weren't. Miz Nubby dead, Miss Cissa."

"Oh." Cissa felt like the last bit of air had been drawn out of her. No more Julia and now no more Nubby either. She'd never even seen Nubby but twice, but the woman loomed in her experience as someone of significance. Someone important. Someone other people respected. Or feared. "What happened to her?"

"Don't nobody know. Uncle Jopher jus' find her dead up by the pond one day. They didn't rightly know how Choctaw deal with dead folks, but they did best they could. Wrapped her in a blanket and dug a good deep hole." Julia's voice went soft and her eyes took on a faraway look. "Bein' she was a conjure woman, they was determine to do right by her."

"Where?" Cissa wasn't entirely certain why she wanted to know, but she asked anyway. "Where did they bury her? Did they set a marker of some kind?"

"Don't think there's no marker. Old uncle say they put her 'neath the big oak, the tall thick one right there by the pond."

A shiver went up Cissa's spine as she realized that was exactly where she'd sat. The mockingbird's song came back to her with such clarity that she inadvertently glanced out the window.

"You alright, Miss?"

"I'm... Yes, I'm fine Julia. Just thinking about Nubby. And thinking I likely ought to get back home before Mother misses me." She thanked Julia for the coffee, promised to come again soon, and took her leave.

She didn't go back by the main road. Instead, she took the road that went up past the colored community and toward the canebrake by the creek. Cissa didn't think about any danger from errant schoolboys. She was thinking of Julia, thinking of Nubby, thinking of how she'd felt that day when she was lost and Nubby rescued her, thinking of the day that Nubby gave her the red bead with its mysterious black dots. She remembered how Julia had sung to her that day, how she'd felt like dancing. Now all of that was lost.

Something compelled Cissa to run, to run as fast as she could as tears came coursing down her face.

Heedless of bushes and roots and rocks, she ran, until her skirt snagged on something prickly and when she turned to pull it free her foot hit a root and she tumbled headfirst...

"Miss? You alright, Miss?"

Cissa opened her eyes to a dark face leaning near hers. She tried to speak, but only a weak moan came out. She blinked a few times, and the face came into focus, along with a searing pain in her left ankle that almost eclipsed the pain in her head. "What... What happened?" She tried to remember. She was going home. She was running.

"Can you sit up, Miss?" The man's face was drawn into a concerned frown. He kept his hands on his knees as he bent toward Cissa.

"I think so." Cissa rolled over on her side and held out a hand for the man to help her into a sitting position. He didn't take it. With a sharp cry of pain she achieved the position on her own.

"You think you be able to walk?"

Cissa reached toward her throbbing ankle and shook her head. The movement made her stomach turn and as she tried to look up toward the dark-faced man everything went bright and silent.

The next thing she heard was her mother's voice, shrill and unmistakable. "What have you done to my daughter?" she shrieked. "Put her down! Put her down this instant! Joseph! Joseph! This nigger has laid hands on our Narcissa!"

Then voices got mixed up all together, one on top of the next, Mother's voice, Pop's voice. Was that Duncan's voice? Cissa searched for the voice of the Negro who had rescued her but he either remained silent or had already gone away. She wanted to thank him.

"No, Pop. I told you, he never laid a hand on me," Cissa said.

"He most certainly did," Mother countered. "He had you bound up in those black arms like a... I don't know. You looked so helpless. So violated." Mother began to cry.

Cissa did her best to explain. She had to admit that her recollection was vague and that some pieces were missing. But she was certain that the colored man, whoever he was, had meant her no harm.

"Well, whatever it was that happened, it won't happen again," Pop said. "Your brothers are organizing the neighbors to hunt the nigger down. If he values his hide he'll leave this county and never show his face again."

Cissa gasped. *Hunt him down?* She tried to protest but, weakened by the medicine her father had given her for pain, she soon gave up trying to convince them that the only danger she'd been in was the result of a fall while on a reckless run through the woods. She let her mother undress her and wash her and pull the nightgown over her head. Her thoughts swam in disordered confusion as she lapsed into sleep.

Donna Birdwell

Chapter Fifteen
Stories

March 1889

The next morning Mother brought breakfast on a tray. Cissa sat toying with her egg and toast and listening to her parents talking outside the door.

"Did you see any bruising when you were washing her?" Pop asked.

"There were scrapes on her arms."

"Nothing under her skirt?"

"No."

"I see," Pop said.

Due to the injuries to Cissa's head and ankle, she was ordered to bed. Her father even forbade her to read, saying the strain on her eyes would be bad for her head. Mother read to her from some Bible tracts which put Cissa to sleep as effectively as any medicine. She remembered how Julia had comforted her after her fingers had been amputated. She missed the sound of Julia's voice, the sound of Julia singing.

Cissa couldn't stop thinking about the man who had carried her home after she fell. Who was he? She flicked through the images of colored people she knew by name, but none of them matched. His voice had been deep and resonant, and he'd spoken with a greater calm and confidence than Cissa was accustomed to hearing from Negroes.

Mother's prayer circle came for their regular meeting on Thursday. Cissa couldn't see into the room, but it sounded like a bigger group than usual. Cissa heard lots of "oh you poor thing" and "that precious child" and "so heartbreaking."

"You can't imagine the shock I felt," Mother said. "It was just awful. Fortunately, Joseph stopped him before..."

"I'm sure you heard about what happened last month over to Bentleys." That was old Mrs. Campbell's voice. "Poor woman.

Violated by some nigger brute her husband hired on to build a new barn."

"Happened up in Taloa County, too. There it was a young girl, just like your Narcissa." Cissa didn't recognize the voice. It sounded young and frightened.

"I can't talk about it." Susanna's voice wavered pathetically. "It's clear these niggers can't be trusted. I thank the Lord I have a husband and a strong son nearby to protect us."

"You remember what happened not more than ten years past when that bunch of niggers tried to take over Marchelle." Was that Mrs. McBride?

"Dreadful," Mrs. Campbell said. "The way they barricaded up there in the courthouse. But when our white boys brought out 'old Colfax' and shot off a couple rounds they skedaddled like a bunch of scared rabbits." She laughed.

"Yes," Susanna said, "my husband and sons were in Marchelle that day with the county Democratic Club. They told me the whole story." She sounded proud.

"What was the nigger's name that was leading that mess? The one that used to be sheriff? Niggers like that and the one that molested your Narcissa deserve to be shot." Mrs. Campbell said. "Yes, ma'am, hunted down and shot. Back in the day, our Ku Klux boys would've never stood for such things. Mark my words, these niggers still got their secret clubs that's plotting to kill all the white folks and take over. But my man and our eight sons ain't about to let that happen."

"Amen," someone said.

"Let's pray about it," Susanna said.

Each woman prayed in her turn for protection, mentioning those in special need who were sick or injured or misguided. Cissa's name was mentioned every time. She lay there in her bed with tears in her eyes, wondering how Mother's story of her accident had strayed so far from her recollection of it. Had she really been in the kind of danger they were talking about? Was she supposed to feel frightened? What she really felt was anger, but she couldn't have said who or what she was angry at.

⁂

Milly came to visit Cissa a few times while she was laid up, always working on some bit of embroidery as she sat next to Cissa's bed. "For my hope chest," she said. Cissa, who had no hope chest, complimented Milly's needlework, knowing it was a skill that she would never master. Not for the last time, Cissa silently cursed her damaged hand and the sequence of events that had caused it.

The only thing Cissa knew she was good at was words. She thought about the composition book where she had written her poems and stories. Maybe she'd try writing another poem. Some verses had been forming in her head about a little bird with a broken wing and she wanted to see how they looked on paper. Surely a little writing wouldn't do her head any harm.

She got out of bed and searched through her bureau drawer where she thought she'd stashed the composition book. It wasn't there. She searched among her stockings and body linen and still no composition book. However, as she searched, she noticed something uneven about the paper lining the drawer. She peeked underneath the paper and pulled out a couple of small books. She'd seen books like these in the shops in Marchelle. Her mother had always pulled her away when she tried to look at them. "Dime novels are trash, Narcissa. Not meant for nice girls like you."

But here were two dime novels right there in the drawer underneath her body linen. She was certain they must have belonged to Matilda, since this was her room, too, before it became exclusively Cissa's. If Matilda had read them, then surely they were acceptable for Cissa to read as well. Given the way Matilda had hidden them, however, Cissa figured she ought to be discrete.

Cissa climbed back into her bed and opened the first book, the one with a picture of a doe-eyed young woman with fair hair and a muscular young man poling a pirogue boat through the water: *Alice Wilde: The Raftsman's Daughter*. It wasn't until the light from the window began to fade and Cissa's head throbbed that she stopped reading.

⁂

The next time Milly came to visit, Cissa showed her the dime novels. Maybe Milly would like these stories better than she'd liked the fairy stories they'd acted out together when they were younger. Milly put down her sewing and picked up one of the books delicately, examining front and back covers but not looking inside. "Have you read them?" Her voice held a note of incredulity.

"I've read this one." Cissa pointed to the one with the picture of the muscular boatman on the cover. "Do you want to read it, too? Then we could talk about it. Sort of like a book club." She'd read something about a book club in the newspaper.

With hushed voices, so as not to be overheard by the grownups, Cissa read the first few pages to Milly and then Milly read the next few pages. Cissa had to prompt her on some of the harder words. By the time Ada called for Milly to go home, they were well into the story and Milly was captivated. "You can take it home with you if you like," Cissa said. Milly hesitated and then tucked the book inside her sewing basket, giving Cissa a wink as she left the room.

The next week Pop deemed Cissa's head injury sufficiently recovered so that her reading no longer had to be covert, although her choice of reading material still was. The injured ankle continued to keep her confined to the indoors. Whenever anyone else was around, she read tedious school books. When she was alone, she finished reading the second dime novel.

Her appetite for food almost equaled her appetite for stories and she wondered if Elsie's cooking had improved. But since meals were the only actual events of her days, it was possible that she mostly ate out of boredom.

"How is Julia doing?" Cissa asked Elsie one day as she dug into a second helping of bland chicken and dumplings.

"She good," Elsie said.

"Maybe I'll go visit her again as soon as Pop lets me leave the house."

"Then you bes' know she be back with Mama Zolene now."

The news startled Cissa. Julia's cottage had seemed so perfect, and she had looked so content. Why ever would she return to her mother's house?

"Are the babies alright?" Cissa thought maybe one of them had been ill.

Elsie nodded. "Little Rosie and Hiram be peart and fine, Miss." Elsie scurried back into the kitchen before Cissa could ask any more questions.

⁂

Milly became enamored with the dime novels Cissa had discovered. "Oh, Cissy," she sighed after having completed the first of the two books. The two girls rested on a settee that had been brought onto the front porch for Cissa's comfort. "Isn't it romantic? Didn't you love how the handsome rich man fell hopelessly in love with Alice?" She clutched the book to her bosom.

Cissa had been more inspired by the devotion that Alice's nanny had shown to her after her mother died. She'd also been intrigued by the school Alice had gone to in town and how it had turned her into a woman of sophistication.

"What are you girls doing out here?" Lachlan peered through the banisters at the end of the porch. Cissa and Milly had been so intent on their conversation that they hadn't noticed him approach.

"Just reading," Cissa said as she turned the books face down.

"Reading romance books." Milly tilted her head and gazed into the distance. "Books about love."

Lachlan came up the steps and reached for one of the books. "Where did you get these? Does Grandma know?"

"I found them in my bureau drawer," Cissa said. "I guess they must have been Tilly's."

"I've got a couple of books like these," Lachlan said. "Not romance books, though. Mine are about a fellow called Robin Hood and they're dashing good stories."

Cissa's eyes lit up. "Could I borrow one of them?"

Before summer term began, Cissa had read all of Lachlan's Robin Hood books and she was begging him to let her read a couple more books he'd borrowed from a cousin, books about frontier adventures in Texas. Cissa told Milly she could keep the two books she'd found in the bureau drawer.

The Tarver Family, 1890

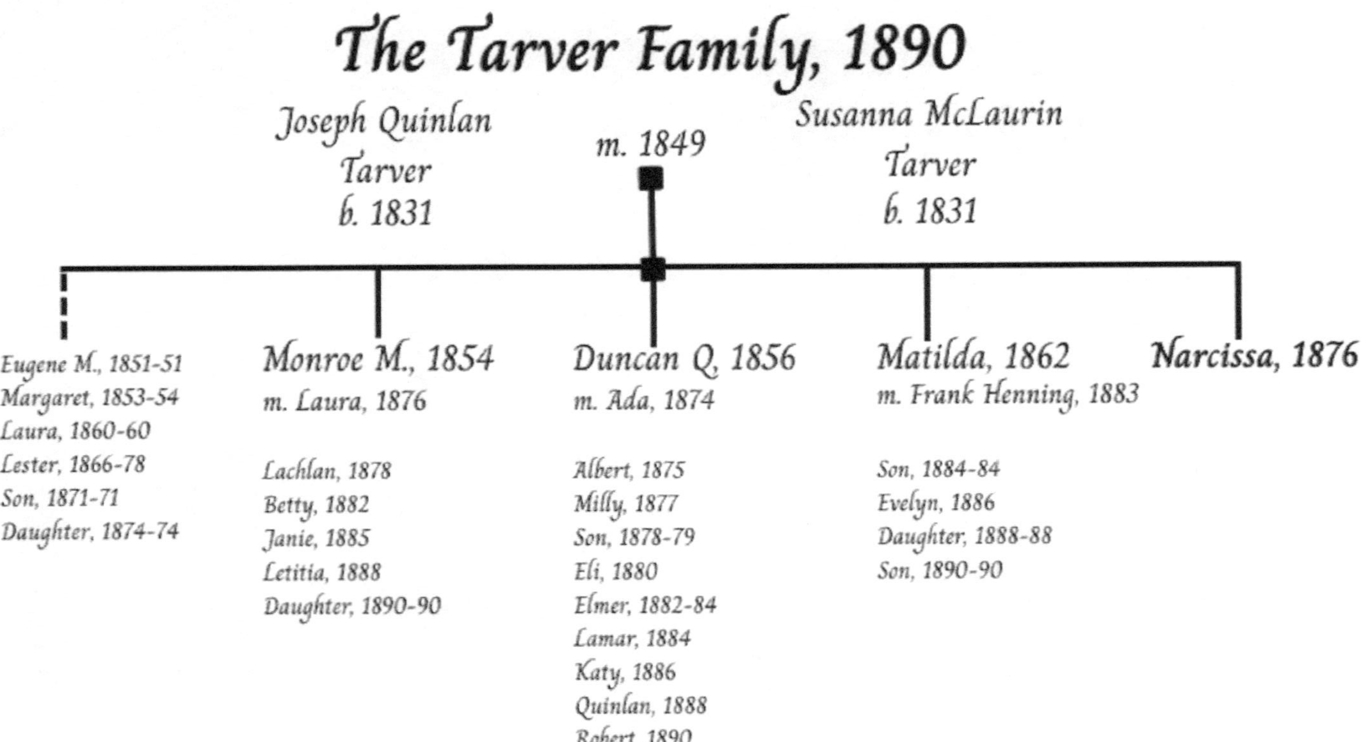

Donna Birdwell

Chapter Sixteen
Other Stories

1890

Pop sat in his favorite chair, a newspaper in his lap. His spectacles dangled from one hand and with the other he rubbed his eyes.

"Is everything alright, Pop?" Cissa said. She'd been at her brother Monroe's house to see her newest baby niece. Cissa hadn't liked the frown on Duncan's face as he held the whimpering infant in his hands. The baby seemed thin and hadn't wailed like little Janie had when she was born or howled like Letitia had when she was just new.

Pop looked up and shook his head. "It's just my eyes bothering me again. Come here and read the rest of this article to me, Narcissa." He held up the paper and pointed. "Start where it says, 'property qualification.'"

Cissa took the paper and settled herself on the end of the couch. She found the passage her father was interested in and began to read:

"Indeed, he was at heart in favor of both an educational and property qualification. He believed if his amendment were accepted it would cut off the votes of very few white people, and the colored people who would be permitted to vote would not materially interfere with the rule of intelligence. The calling of the convention..."

Cissa paused. "What is this about, Pop? What convention?"

"Constitutional convention. They're drawing up a new constitution for the state of Mississippi. Keep reading."

"And they're talking about who can vote?"

"Yes, they're trying to make sure that the government remains in the hands of the whites."

"Why?"

"Why?" Pop shook his head with a sigh. "Because that's the correct order of things, Narcissa. The good lord made the Negro race to be laborers and servants and it's wrong to burden them with responsibilities like voting. But the law of the land has unwisely given them the franchise, the exercise of which has created nothing but chaos and confusion in Mississippi and other states of the Confederacy. Our people at the convention are trying to set that right. Your mother's cousin Anse McLaurin is there working on it, you know."

"Oh," Cissa said, still not certain that her question had been answered.

"You needn't worry yourself about such things," Pop said. "You're just a child still. And a girl."

"I'm almost fourteen," Cissa said. She had no defense for the second charge.

Cissa continued reading, pausing from time to time as she tried to make sense of the words. She thought of her brother Duncan and what he might say about it all. She was certain that he would have something to say.

This was the beginning of a regular practice. Pop would receive a copy of the *Marchelle Advocate* or the *Fulton Gazette* or the *Beckport Journal,* and, after perusing the headlines, he would point out one or more articles for Cissa to read to him. He tolerated her occasional questions but rarely answered as fully as Cissa would have liked. She read several articles about something called the Farmers' Alliance. Cissa watched how her father reacted to the information in the articles; he would sometimes nod in agreement, sometimes frown. Sometimes he did both at once.

After they finished, Cissa would read other items for herself, columns about who was visiting whom in the neighboring towns and about upcoming church picnics and school events and gatherings of Confederate veterans. She saw the brief mention of the death of Laura's little daughter who had lived only a few weeks. She'd gone to Monroe's house for the prayers they said before they buried her. Her little body had looked so small, so insignificant. There was also an announcement of the birth of Duncan's son, Robert. That was five sons for him now, as well as two daughters. Monroe still had only Lachlan and three daughters.

In the *Marchelle Advocate,* Cissa read the weekly instalments of a mystery story. She also amused herself with perusing the advertisements for dresses and hats and sewing machines and typewriters and a medicine that promised relief for "female weakness."

Cissa read and reread information about the Blankenship Female College in Beckport, which offered a "Mistress of English Literature" degree. It boasted that among its graduates were the wives of some of the most influential men in the state.

The articles that Cissa read to her father made discussions that she later overheard between him and her brothers more intelligible. When Duncan waxed enthusiastic about the Farmers' Alliance, Cissa knew something about what it stood for, things like special warehouses for cotton so that farmers could hold out for better prices. Duncan had explained to Cissa that the Alliance was sort of like a labor union for farmers, a comparison that hadn't helped Cissa much, since she knew next to nothing about labor unions.

"It sounds as if the national Farmers' Alliance is on the verge of trying to create their own political party," Pop said. "Wouldn't it be unwise to allow such a thing that might divide the white vote here in Mississippi?"

"We're all still Democrats," Duncan countered. "We just want candidates to declare their support for Alliance issues like free coinage of silver and government regulations for railroads. Prohibitionists expect the same thing for their issues."

"Yes, and they're already organizing a Prohibition Party to put forward their own candidates," Pop said.

"With Democratic primaries getting so contentious," Monroe said, "maybe it would be easier if some of these folks did run their own primaries and put their own candidates on the general election ballot."

Every once in a while, Cissa would recall the day when she'd tried to ask Julia what she thought about Negroes voting and Julia had said that it didn't matter what she thought, only what Cissa thought. So sometimes Cissa asked herself, *What do you think about that, Narcissa Tarver?* She decided that she thought farmers working together to help each other was a good thing. As for prohibition, her confrontation with the boys down by the creek who had been drinking whisky led her to think whisky was a bad thing. She wasn't sure about free silver.

When school break came at the end of summer term, Cissa felt at loose ends. Milly had gone with her mother and Albert and their five younger siblings to visit relatives in Natchez. Other girls from school were also accompanying their mothers on lengthy visits to relatives in Natchez or down at the coast in Biloxi. One even bragged that her family was going to spend an entire month in New Orleans. Cissa's mother, on the other hand, never went anywhere during the fall break. So Cissa didn't go anywhere either.

Cissa had been meaning to pay another call on Julia and she thought this was as good a time as any. She started off down the road toward Julia's little cottage before she remembered that Julia didn't live there anymore. She was, according to her sister Elsie, with their mother Zolene now. Cissa altered her course, taking the path toward the colored community.

The way seemed more overgrown than Cissa remembered it. Narrower. Was this the spot where she'd felt lost and sat down to cry until Nubby showed up? Were these the tree roots she'd stumbled over that day when she sprained her ankle and concussed her head? Everything in the woods and canebrakes changed so fast it was hard to tell. Plants sprang up and then were chopped down or trodden down, only to spring up somewhere else.

As Cissa approached Zolene's house, she felt uneasy. The little community was too quiet. Two of the shacks were boarded up. The bottle tree looked dull and dusty. But the door and windows to Zolene's cabin were open wide and there was Zolene herself, shaking out a rag rug on the front porch.

"Hey, Mrs. Zolene," Cissa called out.

Zolene turned and when she saw Cissa she stopped beating the rug and called over her shoulder. "Julia, you gots company." She smiled at Cissa, but the smile looked tense and there was no sign of the warm bubbling laughter that had made Cissa feel so welcome in the past.

"Miss Cissa!" Julia's smile looked a bit strained, too, and as she passed by Zolene she muttered something that sounded to Cissa like, "Ain't her fault, Mama."

Cissa could see that Julia was in the family way again. And there was little Hiram, toddling along holding onto the back of her skirt.

"Come along up here and have a sit down, Miss Cissa," Julia said.

The two sat in chairs on opposite sides of the porch. Conversation came in brief questions and comments and long silences. Finally Cissa asked, "Why are you living here with Zolene now, Julia?"

Julia directed a sharp glance toward where Zolene sat inside the house shelling dried peas. "My Baxter he gone up north to Memphis looking for work," she said. "He didn't want me there at our house by my lonesome. 'Go stay with Zolene,' he say. So here I am." Julia rubbed her belly with one hand while the other clutched the back of little Hiram's dress.

Cissa offered her good wishes that Baxter would find work soon and earn enough money to come back to Callander Road and the little house he'd built for Julia. She was puzzled why Julia's husband would have left to find work since, according to Cissa's brothers, there was plenty of farm work here in Hinson County and never enough colored help.

"Thank you, Miss," Julia said. There was something flat and cool in the way she said it.

Cissa didn't stay long. Although Julia's and Zolene's words were as friendly as ever, there was something different that made Cissa uneasy. *Julia's likely feeling slighted because it's been so long since I paid her a call,* she thought. Maybe she could send Julia a present sometime. Something to let her know she hadn't been forgotten.

Donna Birdwell

Chapter Seventeen
How to Be Important

1891

Cissa watched as her mother climbed into Mrs. McBride's buggy, assisted by Mrs. McBride's colored servant. They were off to a meeting of the Hinson County chapter of the Confederate Memorial Association at one of the big old plantations near Marchelle. Mother had urged Cissa to accompany her, but Cissa had declined. She'd been to one of these meetings before and had felt out of place among a collection of women and girls who clearly thought themselves above the likes of the Tarvers who didn't even own a winter house in Natchez and thus did not participate in the rounds of holiday parties and festivities that still took place there.

Cissa heaved a sigh of relief and settled down on the couch for a quiet day of reading. Pop was out making medical calls, and in Mother's absence, Elsie had taken a day off, too, leaving a bowl of chicken salad for Cissa and her father's dinner.

Cissa was deep in the pages of her book when she heard footsteps on the porch. Before the door opened, she knew who it was. Duncan stepped into the dining room and then crossed the hallway into the parlor.

"Where's Pop?"

Cissa placed a scrap of paper inside her book to mark her place. "He's out on calls. No telling when he'll be back."

Duncan sank into Pop's big chair with a disappointed sigh. "I needed to talk to him." Duncan set his hat on his knee and then picked it up again.

"About your floater nomination?" Cissa had read to Pop about Duncan's contentious nomination for state floater representative from Burr and Fulton Counties in the papers.

Duncan looked up in surprise. "What do you know about that, little sister?"

"I know that Fulton County and Burr County are each backing their own man and that neither is giving in." She also knew that the

Burr candidate had carried that county with about three times the votes Duncan got. In Fulton County, the Burr candidate's name had somehow been left off the ballot, so all the votes went for Duncan. Voting was for delegates to the Democratic convention and each county got ten delegates.

Duncan chuckled. "I didn't know you were interested in politics."

"Why do we have floater representatives anyway?" she asked.

Duncan embarked on an explanation that sounded a lot like an arithmetic problem. Cissa was grateful when she saw her father's horse enter the yard.

"What brings you here, son?" Pop said as he hung his hat on the hall tree. "Did the floater convention finally reach a decision?"

The two men went into the dining room.

"What they've decided," Duncan said, "after at least two hundred ballots at the second convention, is that the Burr candidate and I have to battle it out on the November ballot."

Cissa fled to Lachlan's house to return a book. She found no one home except Monroe. He looked sweaty and tired. "Laura and the girls have gone to visit her sister for the day," he said. "And Lachlan's out checking on some of the sharecroppers."

"Oh." Cissa tried not to look disappointed. "I just wanted to return his book." She'd hoped to acquire another one.

"May I?" Monroe reached for the book and examined the cover. "You like reading these adventure stories, do you?" he said.

"Yes, I like them very much."

"I'm not sure it's good for you young people to read these kinds of stories. Give you ideas. Old Robin Hood was not exactly a law-abiding citizen." He grinned beneath his mustache.

"But he was always helpful," Cissa said.

"Maybe so, but he got away with things he likely shouldn't have. He sort of reminds me of our brother Duncan. That boy got away with everything when he was a child. Never seemed to get caught, though, no matter what he did. Lots of times he let me or one of our cousins take the blame for some mischief he'd dreamed up. I guess it prepared him for being a politician." Monroe chuckled. "I talk too much sometimes," he said. "Don't you go repeating what I say."

"Cissy!" The shout came from over near the barn.

"Your Aunt Cissy was just bringing your book back to you," Monroe said as his son bounded onto the porch. He handed the book to Cissa and disappeared into the house.

"My pop is getting me my own rifle on my birthday," Lachlan said as he tucked the book under his arm.

"Do you know how to shoot it?"

"Of course I do. He started teaching me to shoot when I was six. I have a shotgun, but a rifle will be better. Can you shoot?"

"No," Cissa said as she tried not to look at her damaged hand.

"I can teach you if you want to learn, Aunt Cissy."

Cissa almost laughed but she could see that Lachlan was dead serious. She surprised herself by saying, "Maybe."

Cissa didn't take Lachlan up on his offer right away. But after reading a couple of newspaper articles about a woman sharpshooter called Annie Oakley, Cissa decided to give it a try.

On a sunny afternoon in mid-November, shortly after Duncan Tarver narrowly won the floater seat in the Mississippi legislature, Lachlan led Cissa to a clearing beyond the pine stands. Targets had been set up some hundred yards away.

"Do you suppose Uncle Duncan will have to move to Jackson for his new job?" Lachlan asked.

"Pop said he'll just get a room there. Ada and the kids will still be here." Cissa felt some pride over her brother's victory. Duncan was an even more important person now.

Lachlan shouldered his shiny new rifle. "Hold it in your left hand like this," he said, "and then support it with your right."

"Do you shoot left-handed?" Cissa asked.

"I can. Pop says a real marksman has to be able to shoot both ways." Lachlan paused. "But just learning to do it one way or the other is good enough."

Cissa hated how people still altered what they wanted to say in deference to her injured hand. She wished they'd stop.

Lachlan placed the rifle in Cissa's hands. "How does that feel?" he asked.

"Heavy," Cissa said.

"You'll get used to it. Your hands get stronger." Next Lachlan laid a piece of old saddle blanket across Cissa's left shoulder and positioned the butt of the rifle against it. He adjusted her hands. "Now look down the barrel and sight what you want to hit. But before you pull the trigger, let me warn you: It's loud and it kicks, so brace yourself."

Cissa nodded. She had seen men—and a couple of women—shoot rifles plenty of times and she knew they were loud. She'd also seen how the rifle jerked back against the shooter's shoulder.

She aimed. She took a deep breath. She shot.

She almost fell backward. "Lord, Lachlan," she said, handing the rifle back to him and massaging her shoulder. "When you said it kicks, you weren't joshing!" She couldn't help laughing.

Cissa only shot the rifle three more times that day. She knew her shoulder was going to be sore. She didn't hit anything, at least nothing she was aiming at, but she felt elated. With Lachlan's rifle in her hands, she felt a certain power and that power felt like it was hers. It was a good feeling.

Chapter Eighteen
The Way of Women

Early 1892

When Milly missed a couple of days of school, all her brother Albert would say was that she was "feeling peakéd." An older girl whispered to Cissa that it was probably just that Milly had started her monthlies.

"Oh," Cissa said, having only a vague idea what her classmate was talking about. She knew it was something that only affected girls.

When she reached home, she asked her mother what a monthly was and if that could be why Milly had missed school.

Mother never took her eyes off her sewing. "Oh, little girl, you don't need to worry about such things yet."

Cissa started to mention the fact that she was a year older than her niece Milly, who seemed to be quite old enough to worry about such things. Had her mother even noticed that she now had breasts? Cissa merely said, "I think I'll go visit Milly and see how she's getting on."

But Cissa didn't go to Milly's house. Instead she went to see her sister-in-law Laura. She somehow felt that watching Laura give birth to Janie had established some kind of womanly bond between them.

"You should ask your mother," Laura said.

"I did. She wouldn't say. She thinks I'm still a child."

"Well, if you haven't begun your monthlies, you still are, in a way. But you do need to know what to expect. What are you now...fourteen?"

"Fifteen." Milly was fourteen.

"I wish I'd known about it when I was a girl, but my own mother passed when I was eleven and my stepmother never said a word to me about such things until the day it happened."

"Isn't Betty eleven now? Does she know?" Betty was Laura's eldest of her four daughters.

With a sigh, Laura said, "It's just when you... You bleed. Down there." She touched the front of her skirt. "So you fasten some rags to a belt to soak it up. And then you have to wash the rags. It lasts for a few days. Maybe a week. And it comes again every month."

Cissa was mildly horrified. "Bleed? Does it hurt?"

Laura laughed a little. "Not like a cut on your finger hurts. More like a headache. But in your belly. You'll know."

"And it happens every month? Why? Isn't there any way to stop it?"

"Getting married and having babies stops it for a time," Laura said. "But of course you needn't worry about getting married." She looked away. "Not yet anyway. And then eventually, when you're old, they say it stops altogether."

"How old were you when you married Monroe?" Cissa said.

"I was seventeen."

"And wasn't Mother seventeen when she married Pop?"

Laura nodded.

"I'll be sixteen in July." Cissa felt a heaviness in her belly as she considered how close she was approaching to what seemed to be marriageable age.

"My sister Ettie was already nineteen before she married," Laura said. "And your sister Tilly was twenty-one when she married Frank."

Cissa remembered how people had worried about Matilda being still unmarried as she celebrated her twentieth birthday, much less her twenty-first.

"Don't worry about it, Cissy. You needn't marry for quite a while yet, I'm sure. Your mother and pop need you to look after them and won't be eager to let you go."

Cissa did not find this encouraging. She couldn't help thinking it was all because of her lame hand. She'd heard old Mrs. Campbell talk about how unlucky it was to be left-handed, insisting that the left side belonged to the devil. Cissa also remembered how her parents had suggested that her damaged hand would make her unattractive as a wife. Mr. Warren had implied much the same thing. How was Cissa to find her place in this real world? She felt like a reject. And now she was going to have to endure these monthlies, whether she wanted to or not.

Cissa sighed. "Is Lachlan here?" She was ready to put her mounting annoyance aside in favor of a pleasant visit with her favorite nephew.

She found Lachlan sitting on the ground beneath the branches of a spreading live oak tree near the barn. It was midday and he was reading a book.

"Your mother said you were doing chores." Cissa leaned against the tree to get a better look at what her nephew was reading.

"Finished." Lachlan didn't take his eyes off the page. "Do you approve, Aunt Cissy?" He looked up at her with a playful grin.

"Where did you get that book?" It was a big volume with a fine leather binding.

Lachlan tucked a grass blade between the pages and closed the book. "It's from the library in Natchez."

This was the first Cissa had heard about this library, so she plied Lachlan with questions. She learned that it was a lending library where you paid a dollar and a half a month to borrow any book you wanted from their shelves and keep it for three weeks. "Where do you get the money to pay that much?"

Lachlan's cheeks grew a shade redder as he placed a hand protectively over the book. "Well, actually, it's not me that's a member. It's my friend Johnny who gets the books and then he lets me read them, too."

"Is that the fellow I've seen over at your house lately? The tow-headed one with the...with the chestnut mare?" Cissa had almost said something about the lad's pale mustache or his long legs and straight back and how he seemed one with the chestnut mare as he rode by Cissa's house on the way to Lachlan's.

"That's Johnny. His family lives up north of Rundle Springs, but he goes to school in Natchez."

"Boarding school?" Cissa had read about boarding schools in books and thought they sounded exciting. Most of the ones here in Mississippi were for boys. The only one she knew about that was for girls was the Blankenship Female College in Beckport.

"Yes," Lachlan said.

"What does he study?"

"The usual things. Literature. Geography. Rhetoric. Latin."

"Latin? Really?" In the novels Cissa had read, the most interesting characters always seemed to know Latin.

"He has to translate whole pages of writing in Latin. He says it's good preparation for being a doctor. His pop plans to send him to medical school over in Louisiana. At the university."

Cissa thought Johnny's family must be rich to have such grand plans for their son. Duncan was a doctor, but he'd learned his skills from their father, who had learned from a brother-in-law. "Do you ever wish you could go to boarding school?" she asked. "Or to university?"

Lachlan turned the book back and forth in his hands without opening it. "My pop says he needs me on the farm. I'm the only son and he counts on me." He clutched the book to his breast. "Four sisters now since Dee was born. Maybe I'll never have a brother."

Cissa knew what it felt like to be counted on for family responsibilities. "Do you think your friend Johnny would let me read any of the books from the library? Would you ask him?"

Lachlan lifted the book toward Cissa. "I've already finished this one. I'm sure Johnny won't mind if you read it, too. He'll be coming by on Saturday. Can you bring the book back to me by then?"

Cissa held the book gingerly. The title was *A Doctor of the Old School.* The author was Ian Maclaren. "Maclaren?" Cissa said. "Is that like McLaurin? Is he kin to us?"

"I suppose he could be," Lachlan said. "The stories take place in Scotland."

"Thanks, Lachlan. Yes, I'll bring it back by Saturday." Cissa was recalling a book she'd seen on her father's shelf, a book about Latin. She thought she might have a look at it.

Chapter Nineteen
Beyond School

Spring 1893

As the winter school term drew toward its close in the first week of March, Cissa grew irritable and short-tempered. She'd finally started her monthlies, and it wasn't quite as bad as she'd feared. Mostly it was annoying. It had prompted her mother to buy Cissa her first corset. That was annoying, too. Cissa refused to lace it up as tightly as Mother recommended. The most irritating thing of all, however, was the fact that Cissa would turn seventeen in July—too old for the Mount Eden School.

One day, as she and her father concluded their newspaper reading, Cissa broached a topic of her own. "Pop," she said. She'd thought about this for weeks and took a deep breath, determined to get her words right. "Pop, you know I'm a good student and therefore that I ought to continue my studies. I've read about the Blankenship Female College over in Beckport and I think that would be a good choice for me."

Pop rubbed his eyes and put his glasses back on. Cissa realized that he'd been dozing. This was not the most promising start for her important discussion.

"Blankenship." Pop said. He shook his head and chuckled. "Do you really think you're suited for studying music, Narcissa?"

Cissa recognized this as the kind of question that doesn't expect an answer and the color rose in her cheeks. "They also offer studies in literature," she said. "And they recently added science."

"I suppose you know about their tuition charges. And boarding costs."

Cissa did not know about these things. Their advertisements in the papers never mentioned tuition or board. "I could work to help pay for tuition. And I could live with your cousin Beulah," she said. Her father was not close with this cousin, but she was the only female relative Cissa knew about in Beckport.

"Narcissa, I appreciate your desire to further your education, but I'm afraid it is not in the cards for you."

"Duncan went to university." Cissa did not intend to give up so easily.

Pop chuckled. "Yes, your brother did attend two terms at the state university, and he came back with some highfalutin notions that the rest of us are still having to put up with. I was able to send him because it was Reconstruction time and there was a program offering free tuition and board."

"How come it was Duncan went to university and not Monroe. Monroe's older, shouldn't he have gone?"

"I needed Monroe here on the farm, Narcissa. Anyway, there's no free tuition now and with the price of cotton and the tariffs the way they are, I'm afraid Blankenship is totally out of the question for you. It's time for you to settle in here at home and be as helpful as you can to your mother."

There it was again. Narcissa Tarver's lot in life was to be nursemaid to her aging parents. She loved her mother and pop and wanted them to be happy. But what about her own happiness? Didn't that count for anything? She could see how education had helped her brother Duncan. He was a representative in the state government in Jackson and also president of the Fulton County suballiance of the state Farmers' Alliance. From discussions Cissa had overheard between Duncan and her father, she thought they must be doing important work. Why shouldn't Cissa do something important? How was she ever going to find her way?

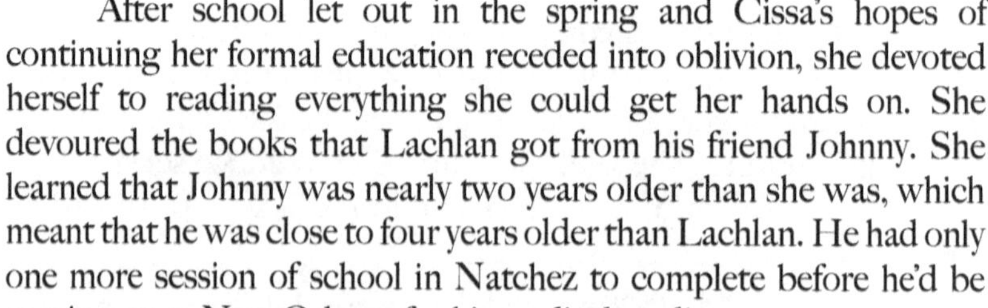

After school let out in the spring and Cissa's hopes of continuing her formal education receded into oblivion, she devoted herself to reading everything she could get her hands on. She devoured the books that Lachlan got from his friend Johnny. She learned that Johnny was nearly two years older than she was, which meant that he was close to four years older than Lachlan. He had only one more session of school in Natchez to complete before he'd be moving on to New Orleans for his medical studies.

The three often discussed the books they read, and Johnny welcomed Cissa's comments as much as Lachlan's. He even seemed to understand why she'd not finished reading *A Doctor of the Old*

School. She hadn't been able to get past the part where the doctor had to amputate someone's arm.

They sometimes collaborated in trying (and generally failing) to solve a mystery before Sherlock Holmes and Dr. Watson could. And after reading *Atlantis: The Antediluvian World*, they argued over the existence of that lost continent. Cissa found herself on the side of denying that such a continent as Atlantis had ever existed. She knew she was doing it to be contrary since her brother Duncan had once indicated that he believed Atlantis was real.

"Really," she said, "if Atlantis was so perfect, why are all the civilizations that grew out of it so different? And so...so fraught? I don't understand why Duncan thinks it's such a great book." Her cheeks pinked up with this unaccustomed assertiveness.

"Where do you think the Farmer's Alliance gets its ideas?" Johnny asked. "The Alliance folks love this Ignatius Donnelly who wrote about Atlantis. In fact, I'm told that he wrote the prologue to their most recent Peoples Party Platform."

Cissa went silent, thoughtful. "So the fellow who wrote this is a politician as well as a writer?" She found this intriguing.

Cissa began to think of Johnny as not just Lachlan's friend, but as her friend, too.

Johnny brought them one other book by Ignatius Donnelly, but Cissa never got around to reading it, having become immersed in another book, the one she'd found years ago on her father's bookshelf, the book called *Rob Roy*. It was a very long book and featured a young woman who was remarkably brave, even rebellious. Most of the story took place in Scotland and Cissa began to feel a sense of pride over her Scots heritage.

One day, after the three readers had been trying to decide whether Johnny should check out Mark Twain's latest book, Johnny said something unexpected. "My Uncle Martin asked me if I wanted to write some stories about this area for the Marchelle newspaper. He's the editor, you know."

Cissa had not known that. She read that paper every week, from front to back. How had she not known that her friend Johnny was related to the editor?

Johnny tossed aside the twig he'd been toying with. "I told him I wouldn't know what to write about. Besides, my school work keeps me too busy."

"He should get Cissa here to write," Lachlan said. "She's a good writer. And she knows all about what's happening around this area from all the ladies who come to Grandma's prayer meetings and sewing circle." The two boys laughed.

Cissa did, too. Her cheeks warmed. She was flattered that her nephew thought highly of her writing ability and was willing to say so in front of Johnny. She was unprepared for what came next.

"Would you do that?" Johnny said. "Uncle Martin told me he just wants a piece every week or two, sent in by Tuesday morning to put into the Wednesday paper or Thursday afternoon for the Saturday paper. I could recommend you."

Cissa knew that there had been very little in the *Marchelle Advocate* recently about anything happening in Rundle Springs or Callander. Not that much happened in these little communities anyway, but a lot of what she read about other places seemed no more momentous than what her family and their friends and neighbors were up to. "Would you do that?" Cissa echoed Johnny's question. And then she surprised herself by saying, "I could give you an essay or two that I've written if your uncle wants to see some of my work." She tried desperately to think of what to send. Maybe the description she'd written about the recent glass ball tournament. Everybody liked reading about shooting events and she knew how disappointed her brothers had been that the Marchelle paper hadn't mentioned it, especially since Monroe had done so well. Cissa had paid special attention, hoping to pick up tips on improving her own shooting.

"That would be grand," Johnny said.

Cissa retrieved the paper and, excited though she was about the notion of submitting something to a newspaper, she couldn't help remembering the last time an essay of hers had fallen into someone else's hands. *Johnny is not at all like Albert,* she told herself. *I can trust Johnny.*

A week later, Cissa was delighted to see her essay in print.

Chapter Twenty
The Real World: Whitecapping

Summer 1893

Every Tuesday and Thursday, Johnny picked up whatever Cissa had written for the *Marchelle Advocate*. She always had something, even if it was nothing more than a few comments on the weather or an amusing account of a neighbor's errant goat. Since it was cotton picking time, both Johnny and Lachlan were out of school and since neither of them was picking any cotton, Johnny spent a lot of his time at Lachlan's house.

Cissa told them about reading *Rob Roy*. "It's an exciting story, but the book belongs to my pop and I'm not sure he'd want me lending it out. I'm not even sure he'd like me reading it if he knew."

"I can check and see if they have it at the library," Johnny said. "I read a poem about that Rob Roy fellow recently. By Wordsworth? Yes, that was it. He said Rob Roy was like a Scottish Robin Hood. Maybe we should all read that book."

"Thanks," Cissa said. "Do you have any other recommendations?"

Johnny frowned. "There's a book called *Uncle Tom's Cabin* that some of the boys have talked about. Mainly because they don't like it."

"What's it about?" Lachlan asked.

"Slavery."

Cissa thought that sounded like a rather mundane topic. It was how things used to be, but it wasn't like that anymore. "What else do they have?"

Cissa continued reading to her father from the *Marchelle Advocate* and *Beckport Journal* and occasionally from other newspapers that came into his hands. He was particular about only reading avowed Democratic newspapers. "You can't trust what those other papers print," he said. Cissa had begun paying careful attention to the way the stories were written. She liked the stories that used exciting words that painted vivid scenes.

"Read me this one," Pop told Cissa one day, pointing to an article headed "Taloa Whitecaps."

Cissa read: "The present term of the Circuit Court in Taloa County is the first held since the outbreak of the peculiar crime in South Mississippi known as whitecapism." She paused. "Whitecapism?" she said. "What is that, Pop?" She'd heard the term before but had never fully understood what it referred to.

"Just keep reading." Pop sighed deeply and closed his eyes, leaning forward and clasping his hands between his knees.

Cissa continued. "Nine young white men, their ages running from twenty-one to thirty, were at this term indicted by the grand jury for cruelly and brutally beating a black man living on the place of R. Mullins. The Negro was one of the humblest and most industrious in the county. He weighs about one hundred ten pounds and is coal black. The trial developed some features of decided interest. The Negro's testimony was only corroborated by two colored women."

Cissa looked up at her father. "What was his name?" She looked back over the paragraph she'd just read. "They just call him a Negro. Surely he has a name."

Pop shrugged. "They don't name the defendants either. It's for their protection, I suppose. Just keep reading, Narcissa."

Cissa did. "The ringleader of the gang was the first man put on trial. He was indicted under a statute peculiar to this state, which makes the use of a cowhide whip or stick under a drawn pistol a felony and punishable by imprisonment in the penitentiary." Cissa paused briefly as she tried to visualize what that meant. She inhaled sharply and continued. "The Negro's testimony disclosed a case of unusual and revolting brutality. Some of the details are unfit to be put in print." Cissa paused again and glanced toward her father. His eyelids fluttered but remained closed.

She resumed reading. "He said he was visited at midnight by sixteen or eighteen men, and he was covered with scars. He fully identified the defendant who did not pretend that the Negro was guilty of any offense or had ever harmed him. The defense commenced by proving a complete alibi by his mother, father, and others. He also proved that the Negro's character for truth and veracity was bad."

"Wait," Cissa said. "So did this fellow beat the Negro or not?"

"That's what the trial is to decide, Narcissa."

"Oh," Cissa said. She continued: "The superintendent of public education of this county also testified for the defendant that the Negro had but recently told him that he was badly whipped, but that he did not know who did it." Cissa stopped reading

"But didn't he just identify the fellow in court?" She felt perplexed.

"Yes." Pop opened his eyes. "But maybe he lied."

"Or maybe the superintendent did?"

"Possibly. The jury must decide." Pop leaned back in his chair and tapped the arm with his spectacles.

"Who's the jury?" Cissa knew what a jury did, but she'd never understood who they were.

"Just ordinary citizens. I've served on juries a number of times."

"Will I have to serve on a jury when I'm older?"

"No, Narcissa. Women do not serve on juries."

Cissa wanted to ask "Why?" but then she thought better of it. She finished reading the article.

"The district attorney came back, however, with reputable testimony sustaining the character of the Negro and assaulting the character of the defendant's witnesses for truth and veracity. The trial grew hot. Defense lawyers sailed in with their usual vigor. The district attorney made a splendid prosecution, and the jury retired at about eight o'clock and were not out more than fifteen minutes when they returned with a verdict of guilty. It remains to be seen what the sentence of the court will be."

"So they believed the Negro," Cissa said.

"Or his lawyers. Thank you for reading that, Narcissa. That will be all for now."

Cissa kept her seat, reading through the article one more time to herself. *Which side was telling the truth?* she wondered. She thought the writeup could have used more details.

Cissa kept thinking about the story and about the Negro who was beaten. She was glad the man who did it was going to be punished. She thought again about the Negro who had rescued her when she'd been hurt and how he had been threatened with violence by her brothers. She remained convinced that he had done nothing wrong. Surely no one had harmed him, had they? They'd only threatened to do so. They just told him he should leave the county. She wondered if he'd actually left. She'd heard people talking about how a lot of Negroes were moving away.

It was a few weeks later that Cissa returned home from a visit with Lachlan and heard raised voices coming from the dining room.

"How do you know that?" Duncan was almost shouting. "My sources tell me that the grand jury were less than half of them good Democrats and only heard half the story before deciding to indict."

"And does their politics alter the evidence brought before them?" Pop's question was met with silence. He continued. "This whitecapping has got to stop before we lose all our hands." His tone was stern. "Those fellows set fire to a house with a whole family inside."

"I think what Duncan is saying, Pop, is that there were associates of his among the mob. Populists." Monroe stood facing his younger brother, his arms crossed.

"Maybe a few." Duncan spoke in more modulated tones. "But I understand why these men are so frustrated. Whether it's Taloa County or Burr or Fulton or even right here in Hinson, farmers are strained to their limit with debt, owing to unscrupulous merchants who lend at outrageous rates, steal our land, and then lure away our Negroes as well. That's what's got to stop."

"You're preaching to the choir, brother," Monroe said. "With last season's poor crop and dropping prices you know we had to go even deeper into debt to plant this spring. We might well end up losing more land. But is this kind of violence the way to solve the problem?"

"It won't solve the problem," Pop said. "But I guess it could have some effect on the worst of the unscrupulous merchants and labor agents. No, no, I'm not advocating violence, boys. But the labor problems and the debt just seem to get worse every year."

The newspaper left open on the parlor couch caught Cissa's eye. There was almost a full-page article headlined "Whitecap Anarchy Boldly Asserts Itself" and "Troops Called Out; Beckport Temporarily Becomes a Military Camp." Was this what Pop and her brothers were talking about? Wide-eyed, she began to read the article. She learned that there had been men in jail in Beckport charged with whitecapping and on Thursday a group of a hundred or more armed citizens had stormed into the town intent on freeing the captives. They'd been stopped by the Circuit Court Judge who had stepped out of the courthouse to confront them.

Cissa was entranced by the way this piece was written as much as by the information it conveyed. "No sooner had he stepped out than he was instantly covered by a pistol and three Winchesters in the hands of the members of the gang, and told if he advanced a step further, he would do so at the cost of his life." The words evoked the scene so vividly! The individual who wrote this article must have been right there in the middle of the action. And what exciting action it was. "The intrepid judge stood before the men who were thirsting for his blood like a lion at bay."

Cissa devoured every word of the story and although she was still uncertain as to why all of the things it documented had occurred, she was intrigued by the notion that whenever such incidents did occur, it was necessary for someone to be there to write about them. Could Cissa ever be such a someone? The thought sent a thrill through her veins. This real world was a pretty exciting place.

Chapter Twenty-One
It's Called Journalism

Fall 1893

Cissa slid into her chair at the breakfast table across from her mother, resolved to tolerate without complaint the usual lumpy oatmeal and biscuits that were too brown, still gooey in the middle, or both. She slipped her spoon into the oatmeal and found it unexpectedly smooth. Surprised, she lifted a corner of the napkin that covered the biscuits, revealing a basket full of the most perfectly fluffy and lightly browned biscuits she had seen since...well, since before Julia left. She leaned back and inclined her head toward the kitchen door. That figure bent over the stove was unmistakable. It was Julia.

"Mother," she whispered. "Julia's back."

Susanna stared at her from across the table. "Yes, Narcissa. Elsie is unavailable for a time. But Julia will only be here mornings. I'm afraid we're going to be on our own for supper." She darted a severe look toward Pop, who had just entered the dining room.

"Only until we finish the harvest," Pop said. "Then we'll find someone willing to work fulltime again."

After breakfast, Cissa carried her plate into the kitchen and set it on the table. "It's good to see you, Julia," she said.

"It's good to see you too, Miss Cissa." Julia continued with her work.

Cissa took a seat at the kitchen table and leaned forward on her elbows. "I hope you'll stay this time, Julia. You know I miss you something awful when you're not here."

Julia finally turned to face Cissa. She shook her head. "It's only for a while, Miss. You know I have little 'uns to look after."

"How are Rosie and Hiram doing?" Cissa asked. She wanted so much for everything to be as it once was between her and Julia.

"And Chisum," Julia said. "Chisum my baby boy. Rosie in school now and Hiram fixin' to start next term."

"And your husband? Did Baxter find good work up north? Has he come back?"

Julia turned back toward the stove and began stirring the stewpot with vigor. "Yes, ma'am. He got good work. But don't be asking when he comin' back 'cause you know he not comin' back." Julia's shoulders hunched together as she stirred. "I gots to get more onions," she said as she hurried out the back door toward the shed.

Cissa sat for a moment in confusion. Had Baxter left Julia for good? Julia was a good woman, one any Negro should surely be happy to have as his wife. Cissa rose from the table and returned to the dining room. She gathered her mother's dishes and took them to the kitchen. Julia had not returned.

Julia's reticence regarding conversation persisted. Cissa missed the talks they used to have but kept herself busy reading novels and studying Latin, utilizing the book she had discovered in her father's collection. She worked diligently, although frustrated by her inability to know how the words were pronounced. Finally, she asked Johnny for help. His visits had become shorter now that he was back in school. It was his final term before going away to the medical college.

"Where did you get this?" Johnny said as he flipped through the pages of the slim volume. "Are you really trying to learn Latin?"

"I'm trying, but I'm afraid I'm not making much progress." Cissa explained that the book was her father's, which Johnny likely could have guessed, given the book's focus on terminology pertinent to anatomy and medicine. After this, Johnny's visits always included a half hour or so helping Cissa with Latin. Lachlan was always there, too, which Cissa didn't mind at first.

Johnny's visits had become the highlight of Cissa's weeks. She loved the fact that he treated her like an equal, including her in conversations and never hesitating to debate points with her. He didn't even seem to mind that her hand was like a bizarre claw. Maybe Cissa's parents and Mr. Warren had been wrong about a boy never being interested in Cissa. Johnny seemed interested. Did he care that she couldn't do embroidery or play the piano? Cissa thought not. Johnny was going to be a medical doctor with a university certificate who could certainly afford to buy one of those new sewing machines and maybe even a gramophone. And surely he could pay other people to do chores his wife chose not to do.

That word made Cissa's heart beat faster. "Wife" was not a role she'd permitted herself to try on, even in her wildest imaginings. But maybe, just maybe, it was not out of the question.

The next Tuesday, Cissa watched eagerly for Johnny to ride by. She wasn't terribly proud of her latest contribution for the *Marchelle Advocate*. It was an article about an upcoming church sale of jams and pickles, which she'd tried to liven up with some colorful descriptions of the products. She'd also been entrusted with a letter that her brother Duncan wanted the *Advocate* to publish. The fact that Duncan had asked her to hand it over to Johnny to be transported to the editor of the paper left Cissa with an unaccustomed sense of importance.

As soon as she was certain that the chestnut mare coming around the bend was Johnny's horse, she darted back inside the house. She didn't want him to think she'd been sitting on the porch waiting for his arrival. She listened to the hoofbeats as they passed by and faded away toward Lachlan's house. She waited a few minutes and then gathered her two envelopes and made her way down the lane, trying not to walk too rapidly. She didn't want to arrive out of breath.

From a distance, Cissa watched Johnny tie up his horse to a low branch of the cedar tree on the far side of the house. He gave the horse an affectionate pat and headed toward the sugar shed out back where just yesterday Monroe had been making molasses. There was still a scent of it in the air. Cissa rounded the corner of the house and drew up short as she saw Johnny with his arm around Lachlan's shoulders. Lachlan leaned into the embrace as Johnny planted a kiss on the side of his face.

Cissa didn't know what to do. This felt like a scene from one of Milly's romance novels, but it was all wrong. Lachlan and Johnny were both boys. Cissa started to turn back but then she looked down at the envelopes in her hands. She had business to take care of. Shuffling her feet in the fallen leaves, she proceeded toward the two boys.

"Hey there," she called out.

Johnny took a step back and turned to give Cissa a wave and a smile. Lachlan briskly brushed the hair out of his face, letting a shock of it fall over the spot where Johnny had kissed him.

"Just in time," Johnny said, though Cissa thought her timing couldn't have been much worse. "I was telling Lachlan that I can't stay but a few minutes because my Uncle Martin has an important meeting to go to and wants me to help him set up the paper before he goes. What have you got, Cissa?"

Without a word, Cissa thrust the two envelopes into Johnny's hands. The one with "Rundle Springs & Callander" written in Cissa's backward-leaning script would be familiar to him. The one marked "To the Editor" brought a puzzled look to his face.

"What's this?"

Finding her voice at last, Cissa said, "It's something Duncan wants the *Advocate* to publish. He said it was important."

"Uncle Martin likes getting letters from politicians, especially if they're a bit controversial." He raised his eyebrows as he tapped the two unopened envelopes together.

"I didn't read it," Cissa said. She was well aware that some people found her brother's Populist ideas controversial.

Johnny shrugged. "By the way, Cissa," he said. "Uncle Martin wanted to know if you take shorthand."

Cissa had seen that word before in some advertisements in the newspaper. She wasn't sure what it was. "No," she said. "But I could learn."

Johnny grinned. "No doubt you could," he said. He reached into his pocket. "Shorthand or not, Uncle Martin said I was to give you this." He handed Cissa a wrinkled piece of paper—a dollar bill.

"What? For me?" She was at a loss for words. She hadn't expected to get paid for her little stories.

"He says a dollar a month from now on."

"But how will I get the stories to him now that you're going to be away at the university?"

Johnny explained that one of the farmers from Callander had taken a job at the cottonseed mill in Marchelle and rode in every weekday. "So if you can get your stories to Mr. Clay, he can bring them to Uncle Martin. I think he's some kind of distant cousin of ours."

"I can do that," Cissa said. Callander was little more than a mile up the road from her house, less if she cut across the fields. An easy walk in good weather and doable in bad. She tucked the dollar into her pocket.

Johnny held out his hand. "We've got a deal then."

Without thinking, Cissa stuck out her right hand to shake Johnny's. He didn't flinch. He clasped it as firmly and warmly as if it had been whole.

All the way home, tears stung at Cissa's eyes but refused to fall. Johnny both was and was not who she'd thought he was. She was torn between disappointment and delight. Her hopeful daydreams about Johnny evaporated. On the other hand—thanks to Johnny— she was now a paid writer. She tucked her right hand under her left elbow, savoring the memory of Johnny's earnest handshake.

Chapter Twenty-Two
Depression

Late 1893

The Tarvers' copy of the *Marchelle Advocate* was late arriving that Wednesday. Cissa was glad her father was away so that she could read it first, looking to see how her little contribution appeared in print. She was also eager to see if her brother's letter had been published.

She found her article on page four. It always pleased her to see her work in print, even though people outside the Rundle Springs and Callander area would never know it was hers. Sometimes she wished the newspaper would say who wrote an article.

Duncan's signed letter was on page two. She read the letter once and then read it again, still uncertain what it all meant. He lashed out at whitecappers who, he said, had been attacking cotton gins in the belief that shutting down gins would decrease the supply of cotton and thus push prices upward. Cissa knew her father and brothers were worried about the low price of cotton. "Suppose every gin in the Southern States was stopped, save Texas," Duncan wrote, "even then it would not affect the price of cotton. The convulsed condition of the finances of the world is the cause of this great depression." Cissa had seen other mentions of a "great depression." She knew that money in her own household was tight. Her mother had been insisting on mending stockings and altering clothes rather than buying anything new.

Cissa continued reading the letter. Instead of improving the price of cotton, Duncan wrote, "whitecapping absolutely destroys the value of our lands as a basis for credit" and "stops the further investment of money in our midst."

What intrigued Cissa most about Duncan's letter was the remedy he proposed. He said that the county sheriff should deputize two hundred or maybe five hundred men "known to be law-abiding citizens; let them organize with a system of secret signals" and assemble whenever one of them perceived trouble. It reminded Cissa of the activities of her imaginary magnolia brigade and frog battalion. She was fascinated.

Not long after this, Cissa learned that her brother Duncan was the president of something called the Farmers' Protective Union of Fulton County and that the Union was apparently avowed to do just what Duncan had proposed in his letter. Cissa was impressed. Her brother had power to make things happen in the real world. He was important.

Cissa, by comparison, felt crushingly unimportant. Despite her best efforts to write lively copy, her little contributions to the *Marchelle Advocate* felt boring and mundane. To make matters worse, Mother had begun insisting that she take more responsibility around the house now that they had only minimal hired help.

"You're going to cook more of our meals," Mother said. "Julia will teach you."

Cissa had little interest in cooking, but she was somewhat cheered by the prospect of spending time with Julia. At first Julia was all business, even scolding Cissa when she overworked the biscuit dough or burned the roux for the gravy. But in the aftermath of a particularly disastrous recipe in which Cissa had inadvertently added a half cup of salt instead of a half cup of sugar, both women collapsed in laughter. The lessons became more amicable.

As Christmas approached, the contents of the pantry dwindled. The cotton harvest had been adequate that fall, but the market had been a disaster. Cissa's father and brothers had long discussions about deflation and free silver and how the selling price for cotton was not even sufficient for them to break even. There was still meal from their own corn as well as dried beans and peas they had grown. Flour was down to a half dozen pounds in the bottom of the sack and the smokehouse held only a half dozen sausages and a single ham, which Pop insisted had to be kept in reserve for Christmas. Slaughtering another pig was out of the question, since the only pig they had left was a sow that would be dropping a litter of piglets soon. They killed whatever chickens they could spare without impacting their regular supply of eggs. There were still yams and potatoes and a few things canned in the summer. Cissa's brothers and nephews brought in an occasional water turkey or rabbit that they'd shot. Cissa gagged more than once as Julia showed her how to dress them. She had little problem with plucking the birds but cringed at skinning the rabbit.

And then it got worse. "I'm sorry, Julia, but unless you can work on credit until next summer, we're going to have to let you go altogether," Pop said one day.

Julia left.

Christmas was meager that year, and without Julia's culinary expertise the food was disappointing. Mother complained about Julia's disloyalty. "In the old days we never had to worry about the help leaving just because we were short of money for a season." Cissa knew she was talking about the slave days. As much as Cissa missed having Julia around, she was also glad that Julia wasn't obliged to work without getting paid.

For Christmas dinner there was the ham and sweet potatoes. There were canned green beans from the summer. There was cornbread and a modest pot of fresh pokeweed greens thanks to an unexpected run of warm weather. There was buttermilk pie and molasses cookies. There were no gifts.

The Tarver family gathered just the same, all the ladies dressed in their finest, which was mostly the same finery they'd worn the year before. Cissa wore a hand-me-down from Matilda, who wore a dress with an elevated waistline and a voluminous skirt that did little to hide her advancing pregnancy. Cissa hoped this baby would survive. Little Evelyn was now seven years old and eager for a sister or brother.

At the dinner table, no one complained about the simple rations. Matilda's husband Frank had brought a couple of bottles of wine from his father's shop, which they shared all around. Some of the ladies declined their share. Cissa drank hers, enjoying the warmth it kindled in her belly. They gave thanks for being together again and tried to be optimistic about the upcoming elections. Surely things would be better in 1894.

Chapter Twenty-Three
An Opportunity

1894

Meals improved around the Tarver household as spring fruits and vegetables came available. Weather held favorable for cotton planting, but Pop declared that, unless prices improved, a bumper crop would do them little good. In fact, he said, a good crop would likely only depress prices further by oversupplying the market. Nevertheless, in an act of desperate hope, Pop took out a small loan using the crop as collateral in order to alleviate the family's situation. They were once again able to hire help two days a week, albeit at reduced wages. Cissa had hoped Julia would come back, but instead they hired Elsie. With a dollar of the loan proceeds, Pop reinstated his annual subscription to the *Beckport Journal.*

Cissa received the *Marchelle Advocate* free of charge. She'd relayed another brief letter from her brother to the *Advocate*. In this letter he defended his vote in a joint session of the Mississippi legislature for Democrat Anselm McLaurin for U.S. Senator. The other candidate was Frank Burkitt of the People's Party. In his letter, Duncan asserted that his vote for McLaurin did not mean he was returning to the Democratic party. "I reserve the right to vote for my kinsman because he is a gentleman and statesman," he wrote. Duncan insisted that he himself remained a staunch Populist.

Cissa pondered her brother's actions. He argued so strongly for his Populist policies, but when family entered the picture, he sided with family. Cissa wanted to respect that, but she noticed that it was also the case that Anselm McLaurin appeared to be a far more formidable political force in Mississippi than Frank Burkitt. Was this about family or about power?

Cissa found herself drawn to the occasional article that discussed the possibility of letting women vote in elections. She mentioned one of the articles at the dinner table one day.

"Women have no need to be interfering in political affairs," Mother said, raising her chin as she glanced toward her husband. "I prefer to rest easy in the knowledge that my menfolk are taking care of me and voting in my best interest."

"But you always tell me what you think about things." There was a twinkle in Pop's eyes. "And I always listen. Maybe it would be easier if you could just vote your own mind." He smiled and patted Susanna's hand.

"Not easier for me," Mother said.

Cissa had begun to develop some ideas of her own about politics. Why shouldn't she be allowed to express them directly by voting? At the dinner table, however, she remained silent.

Pop's premonitions about the Farmer's Alliance starting their own political party were, Cissa soon discovered, quite prescient. In August of 1894 her brother Duncan was nominated as a candidate for the United States Congress by the District Seven People's Party. As far as Cissa could tell, almost all of Duncan's associates in the Famer's Alliance and Farmers' Protective Union were now Populists and pledged to vote for Duncan. He'd even managed to have his father appointed to a People's Party committee on resolutions for the district. The old man had not attended the party convention and was somewhat dismayed at this appointment.

For the next two months, Cissa saw little of Duncan as he was out canvassing in all nine counties of the district. She kept up with his activities by reading the papers. She knew that he was relying on members of the Farmers' Alliance to pull together crowds for his speeches. Letters written by Duncan appeared in a number of different newspapers, but the only paper that offered full throated support for his candidacy was the *Beckport Journal,* which advertised itself as the "Official Organ of the Farmers' Alliance of the Seventh Congressional District." The *Marchelle Advocate* remained steadfastly Democratic.

In the midst of all this, Cissa's nephew Albert—Duncan's eldest son—got married. He was nineteen years old, his bride barely eighteen. The wedding took place in Cowleton, where Duncan's family now planned to reside full time. It was a huge affair and Cissa got the feeling that it was as much a political event as a family one. She thought Albert looked a bit overwhelmed by it all. He and his wife Eva moved into Duncan's former residence on Callander Road.

One day in October Cissa answered a knock at the front door to find Mr. Clay's son Milton. Without a word, he handed Cissa an envelope and loped away, back down the road toward Callander. The message had Cissa's name on it, so she opened it and began reading.

"Who was that at the door?" Pop emerged from the dining room still holding his pen and a prescription pad.

Cissa had just finished reading her message and stood with her eyes wide and her jaw dropped. She closed her mouth but couldn't deter the huge grin that spread across her face. "It was Mr. Clay's boy, Milton," Cissa said.

Pop stood waiting for further explanation.

"Mr. Hodges at the *Advocate* wants me to write up something for the paper about Duncan's speech in Rundle Springs next Monday."

"No," Pop said, shaking his head vigorously for emphasis. "Absolutely not. I don't particularly relish you writing about the little goings-on amongst the church folks and ladies' clubs, though I've exercised forbearance. But a political event is not the kind of thing a young lady like you needs to get involved in."

Cissa's grin collapsed into a troubled frown. She was reasonably certain that a political event was precisely the kind of thing she needed to get involved in. How else was she to prove her worth as a journalist?

"Why, Pop?" she ventured. "There will be plenty of church folks and club ladies there, don't you think? And I won't exactly be involved. Just sitting there taking notes." She was already thinking of questions she could ask the attendees, but that didn't feel like anything she needed to share with her father. "It's my job. Mr. Hodges is counting on me."

Pop stood with his arms crossed looking Cissa up and down. Perhaps, Cissa thought, he was finally taking account of the fact that she wasn't a child anymore. Surely he remembered that she had turned eighteen in July. "Your job, you say?"

Cissa had never bothered to mention to her father that she was being paid for her contributions to the *Advocate* and he'd never asked why it was that she'd stopped asking him for money to buy her little necessities. "Yes, Pop. He pays me for my writing, you know." Of course he didn't know, but Cissa wanted it to seem unremarkable.

"He pays you. And how much is this pay?"

So Cissa told him. She didn't tell him she was saving up most of the money to either buy a typewriter or take shorthand lessons. She hadn't decided which to do first.

For an interminable few seconds, Pop stood looking down at the rug, swaying backward and forward in contemplation. "I will drive you to Rundle Springs for the event, then. And you will conduct yourself with decorum, Narcissa."

"Yes, sir." Cissa endeavored to look solemn and obedient, even as she brimmed with eager anticipation.

On the day of Duncan's speech Cissa wore her best blue dress, but without the matching hair bow. She wished for something more fashionable, more sophisticated. But, she reminded herself, this was only Rundle Springs, where people did not demand much in the way of fashion or sophistication. She managed to pin her hair up in a twist without use of ribbons.

Benches had been set up on the grounds of the Presbyterian Church for Duncan's event. When Cissa and her father arrived, there was already a small group of men chatting amiably under the trees. Cissa had to smile: Why had her pop been so worried? These were just the local folks out for a pleasant day of conversation and politicking. Cissa took a seat on the end of one of the benches near the front, feeling a bit like a schoolgirl again as she pulled out her notebook and pencil.

She watched. She scribbled a few notes. The little group of men grew larger, and a few ladies chatted among themselves, standing near their husbands. Cissa noticed another group forming toward the rear of the space, composed of men she didn't recognize. One of them had a crooked mustache and wore a plaid vest. Another wore the shiniest shoes Cissa had ever seen. She noted how these men spoke in low voices with occasional bursts of subdued laughter.

The crowd cheered as Duncan made his way to the platform that had been prepared for his speech. Cissa settled her notebook in her lap, pencil in hand. She was thankful that she had been reading her brother's published letters. Otherwise she might have had a difficult time following what he had to say. Every so often the men would cheer, and everyone would clap, nodding approvingly, which Cissa duly noted. Then suddenly, from the back row, someone shouted, "You Populists are ruining our state!" and another echoed,

"Yeah, get back to the Democrats where you belong!" Cissa turned and saw the man in the plaid vest standing and shaking a fist toward her brother.

"If the Democrats won't stand up for the good of the farmers, then we do what we must!" Duncan shouted, as the color rose in his face.

The man with the shiny shoes rose from his seat and stalked toward the platform as Duncan continued to speak. Cissa leaned away as he passed next to her, but not so far away as to miss the smell of whisky on his breath. "You're a traitor to the Democrats!" the man shouted, spittle flying from his lips. "Traitor! Traitor to your race!" He raised his hand and hurled something toward Duncan.

Cissa watched in horror as Duncan pulled a pistol from his waistband and pointed it at the man with the shiny shoes. "And you're a traitor to working farmers. Now get back to your damn seat or prepare to pay the price for your impudence." Duncan held the pistol pointed steadily at the man as he glanced toward the back of the crowd where two other men stood, shifting and fidgeting as if eager to make their departure, yet hesitant to do so with their companion under threat.

A couple of Duncan's supporters rushed the man with the shiny shoes and grabbed his arms, dragging him back toward his compatriots as Duncan tried to make light of the situation with a joke that Cissa did not understand. The crowd tittered nervously.

Cissa's hands shook as she recorded her observations. *A good journalist must be fearless, must never lose heart, must keep an eye on everything that happens and write it down.* She steadied herself and continued writing.

On the way home, Pop informed Cissa that she would not be attending any more political events. "I'm sorry I let you witness such a thing," he said.

Cissa was too busy writing her article in her head to pay him much mind.

When Cissa's account of Duncan's event appeared in the newspaper two days later, she was delighted to see that the editor had allocated it more than a full column. She read the piece with pride, wondering if maybe Mr. Hodges might start paying her a bit more if she could find more stories like this to contribute. She was especially pleased at the turns of phrase she'd used to evoke the excitement of the interchange between Duncan and the Democrats who had challenged him.

The front door slammed. "Narcissa June Tarver, you have something to answer for!" Duncan strode down the hallway and into the parlor where Cissa was still perusing the newspaper.

Cissa felt her insides clinch as she looked up at her brother, who seemed to fill the doorway with his rage.

"Yes, I know it was you. I know you've been writing little stories for the *Advocate*, but this is inexcusable. You could have written something supportive, but instead you waste nearly half a column going on about the scoundrels who disrupted my event." Duncan slammed his own copy of the paper down on the table in front of Cissa. "You apparently have never learned the importance of loyalty." His eyes burned with a fire that frightened Cissa.

"I...I only wrote the truth," she said. "I wrote what happened."

Duncan leaned toward her and banged his fist on the folded newspaper. "You betrayed your own, young woman. And you must never, ever do that again. We are family and family support one another. That is just how it is and I'm sorry it has taken you until now to learn it. Take this lesson to heart. Never forget." Duncan grabbed up his copy of the paper and shook it in Cissa's face. "Never!" He spun on his heel and strode back out the front door.

Cissa heard Duncan's horse whinny and snort in complaint as he slapped its flank roughly and cantered away.

Her heart felt as if it would gallop right out of her chest. There was a buzzing in her ears and her face burned from the inside. What had she done wrong?

Chapter Twenty-Four
A Question of Loyalties

1894-95

The day after Cissa's unpleasant encounter with Duncan, Pop called her into his office. He pulled one of the dining chairs around to face his desk. "Sit down, Narcissa."

Cissa sat. Her stomach fluttered in trepidation.

Pop leaned toward her, his hands clasped between his knees. "I heard what your brother said to you yesterday, Narcissa. I can't say that I blame him for being displeased with your report, though he may have approached you too harshly."

"I wrote what happened, Pop."

"Yes, I know. I was there, too." He paused and coughed, catching his breath in a wheezing sort of way.

"Are you alright, Pop?"

"Yes, yes. It's nothing." But Pop took another moment of quiet breathing before he resumed speaking. "You need to be careful with this little job you have," he said, getting to his point. "Don't let it consume too much of your time and effort. And don't let it distract you from your duties to the family. I'm not speaking only of Duncan. I'm speaking of your mother. She is not as strong as she once was, and she needs your care. I fear she will need it more going forward."

"Is she ill? Do you know something?"

"Not ill." Pop paused and took in another rasping breath. "Only old," he said. "It breaks my heart to see her this way." His gaze wandered away from Cissa and toward a framed wedding portrait on the wall. "She was so strong during the war, running our little plantation while I was off tending to sick and wounded soldiers. But it took something out of her. And then the loss of her babies. She seemed so surprised when you were born, and it looked as if you would live." His voice had taken on a dreamy quality, almost as if he'd forgotten that Cissa was there. "She had the two boys to look after and birthed two daughters before the war ended. One of those was your sister Matilda. The other..." He shook his head. "The servants were so restless in those days. They didn't know quite what an emancipation by the President of the United States of America meant for them here in the Confederacy. But most of our Negroes kept working. Those were hard days."

Cissa sat in silence, clutching her breath, afraid of interrupting this unusual outpouring from her father. He glanced toward Cissa and passed his hand across his face as if trying to brush away a fly. He leaned forward, staring at the rug.

"Your mother held on, of course, but it exhausted her. After the war, she swore she was finished, that the farm was now all my responsibility. She would manage the household, but she washed her hands of the farm. The loss of our servants hit her hard. And the loss of her status. She's a woman of quality, you know, and didn't know how to be poor. She's done her best to keep up appearances, to rear you and your brothers and sister to the life that should have been your birthright."

Cissa didn't know how to respond. Pop never went on like this, talking about family matters at such length and in such terms.

"Anyway," Pop said, looking up suddenly at Cissa. "What I want to tell you is that you need to keep family uppermost, and your mother's needs highest of all. I know what it's like being so much younger than the rest of the family. I was the last in mine and lost my father when I was six. I won't tell you not to go on with your newspaper writing. I can tell you enjoy it, and you appear to be good at it. And someday, when both of us are gone, you may need something to fall back on. But keep it in perspective, Narcissa. Your first duty is to your mother."

"And to you," Cissa said.

"As long as I'm around," he said with a smile. He reached out and patted Cissa's knee. "You're a good girl, Cissa. Now go see if your mother needs you for anything."

"Yes, Pop."

For the next week, Cissa attended her mother with heightened attentiveness, looking for subtle signs of illness or weakness. She was forgetful, of course, and capricious in her ways. In other words, the same as always. Cissa told herself that everything was fine and that she should stop worrying.

The near melee that had occurred at Duncan's canvass in Rundle Springs was repeated in several other towns as his contest for

Congress heated up. Cissa took note when Duncan took to carrying his pistol more visibly.

Cissa read reports of her brother's events with mounting interest, especially in the pages of the *Beckport Journal.* While the *Journal* reported with enthusiasm about the crowds gathering for People's Party events, the *Advocate* barely mentioned them. In the gubernatorial race, there were confrontations between Democrats and Populists all across Mississippi, as tempers flared, and political discord rose to a fever pitch. Duncan fumed about the lack of coverage of Populists in the *Marchelle Advocate.* Even the joint appearance in Marchelle of Democratic gubernatorial candidate Senator Anselm J. McLaurin and his long-time foe Populist Frank Burkitt received only a brief mention in advance. Their report after the fact was all about McLaurin. According to Duncan, it had been a rousing debate in which Burkitt had bested McLaurin on several points.

"May I quote you on that?" Cissa asked.

Duncan scowled. "Don't get impudent," he said. He pointed to an article in the *Advocate* that quoted the pessimistic views of Fulton County Sheriff Sam Cortman, who doubted that the Populists would have enough votes to take even that county. The paper reported that Cortman "has gone carefully over the registration rolls and says there is no question, but the Democrats have a majority."

Duncan scoffed. "So Cortman knows how everyone is going to vote, does he? You write for the *Advocate*, Cissy. I'll tell you what happened at my last event, and you write it up and send it to them."

"I don't think I should write about something if I wasn't there," Cissa said. She wanted to support her brother, but she also wanted to be a good journalist.

"Are you saying you don't trust your own kin to tell you what happened? I was there. I'm your brother. I'll tell you what happened, and it will be just the same as you being there yourself."

Cissa got out her notebook and wrote down exactly what Duncan told her to. When he read it and was satisfied that she'd gotten it right and that he was displaying himself in the most favorable light, he patted Cissa on the shoulder and said, "That should make the Democrats on the *Advocate* sit up and take notice. Send that in as soon as you can, little sister."

After Duncan left, Cissa recopied the account, toning down the language in a few places. As she made her way toward Callander to leave her contribution with Mr. Clay, she struggled with her conscience. Did other journalists do this? Did they write about things as if they'd been there when they hadn't? Her father's remonstrances about family loyalty kept her headed toward Callander. For better or worse, she would send this article to Mr. Hodges. Maybe no one would know who wrote it. *Mr. Hodges will know.*

When the next edition of the paper came out two days later, Cissa was pleased to see on the front page a headline reading "Democrat M. L. Anders and Populist D. Q. Tarver Debate Issues on the Stump." But when she began reading the article, she saw that this was not the account she had sent in. She groaned inwardly. Someone from the *Advocate* must have been there at the event. Someone who knew that Narcissa Tarver was *not* there.

Cissa was mortified. She also felt an inescapable ire rising in her chest. She wanted to scream. Why had she let Duncan talk her into this? What if Mr. Hodges decided he didn't want her working for the paper anymore? Should she send him an apology?

As she prepared supper that evening, she continued going over all the possible repercussions of her misstep. In her head, she wrote and rewrote her apology. Her mind was still awhirl as she sat down to eat the lima beans and cornbread she'd prepared.

"Your cornbread is better this time, Cissy," Pop said, as he crumbled it into his glass of buttermilk.

His kind words burst the dam of Cissa's remorse, and her tears began to flow. She fled from the table, hearing her father's voice: "What did I say?"

When a knock came on the front door the next morning, Cissa's heart leapt into her throat. It was Milton, Mr. Clay's son, and he had a note in his hand. Cissa sat in silence, waiting for Elsie to answer the door. But it was one of Elsie's days off. Cissa still didn't budge, watching as her mother shuffled toward the door, giving Cissa a hard look. She greeted the boy with diffidence and accepted the note.

Cissa watched Milton jog away toward Callander, knowing that meant he was not expecting a reply. She waited.

"It's for you, Narcissa." Mother laid the note on the table and gingerly settled herself into her customary chair.

"Thank you, Mother." Cissa picked up the note and went to her bedroom, where she placed it on the bureau next to the washing bowl. She sat on her bed for a moment, staring at the note. She reached for her doll and murmured under her breath, "Ursula Maryanne Virginia, please don't let this be the end." And then she felt foolish, praying for a doll's help.

She took a deep breath. *Just as well to get it over with, Cissa.*

The note was typed on a half sheet of paper. "Dear Miss Tarver," it read. "In future, please constrain your contributions to your immediate assignments and experiences." It was signed with Mr. Hodges' distinctive flourish.

Cissa focused on the word "future." She wasn't being let go. Her breath caught in her throat as she refused the tears of relief that wanted to come. *Journalists don't cry,* she told herself as she turned and winked at the doll she'd left face down on the bed.

Cissa continued reading accounts of her brother's campaign in every newspaper she could get her hands on. Whether she agreed with him or not, he was a person of some importance and that fascinated her. As far as she could tell, the *Beckport Journal* was still the only newspaper that had endorsed him. Duncan continued to sound optimistic whenever he passed through his parents' house.

"I'm confident of winning Fulton County by a big margin," Duncan announced, "and likely Chatah as well." It was a windy day and Cissa thought how appropriate it was that her brother's entry into the house had been accompanied by a sudden gust. She heard Pop murmur his approval from his study before joining Duncan in the hallway.

"What do you know about these cotton worms?" Pop asked. The two men entered the parlor, and Pop sank into the big chair. Duncan perched on the edge of the couch. Cissa kept her place at the little writing desk by a west window.

"Oh, that." Duncan shrugged. "I know they're out there and I've seen reports saying they stand to reduce our cotton crop by up to forty percent this year. But that's a good thing since a reduced harvest may be the only way to push prices up again."

"I suppose. As long as we make enough to cover our loan." Pop drummed on the arm of the chair with his fingers. "Son, I've been thinking that we ought to encourage the sharecroppers to diversify crops a bit more. Cotton is becoming downright unreliable." Pop looked worried.

"Anyway," Duncan said, "the only way I lose my race is if Cortman and his people engage in some sort of mischief. I was a Democrat long enough to know the kind of trickery they're capable of."

Cissa was at first amused and then annoyed at how her brother kept a conversation focused on himself. Was there really a danger of her family not earning enough from the cotton crop to repay a loan?

As election day neared, Duncan's mood darkened. "I know I have the votes of all the Alliance members," he said. "But I could use more support from the Colored Alliance as well."

"Why don't they support you?" Cissa asked.

Duncan snorted. "I'm sure they do," he said. "But most of them won't be voting. I said *Colored* Alliance, little sister. You know colored voters in most of the counties are few. Even fewer dare to vote any way other than how their employer tells them to."

On the day of the election, Cissa didn't see Duncan at all. Nor did she see him the day following. She learned that McLaurin had won the governor's race in an easy victory over his Populist opponent Burkitt. The gossip circulating about Duncan's race was that the election was close, but that the Democrats had pulled off that one as well. When the *Marchelle Advocate* arrived two days after the election, the figures were clear: Duncan had lost by a hundred votes. The People's Party declared its intention to contest the results.

"On what basis?" Pop asked, puffing wearily as he lowered himself into his favorite chair.

Cissa peered over the top of the newspaper she had been reading as she awaited her brother's answer.

"We're charging that our state voting laws conflict with federal law." Duncan sounded less than enthusiastic about this strategy. "At least that's what the state and national party leaders are saying in all the papers."

Cissa had been reading a news article, which argued snidely that Tarver was claiming that if all the ignorant Negroes in the district had been registered to vote, they would, in their ignorance, have voted for him. She wasn't certain they meant it as a joke.

Duncan continued, "Personally, I'm convinced there were enough registered voters to put me through, but Cortman and his gang kept them from showing up." He stomped back and forth, his hands clasped behind his back.

Pop sighed deeply and adjusted his position, extending one leg with a grimace. "Do you think the challenge will do any good?"

Duncan stopped pacing and turned to stare out the window. He shook his head and let out a vindictive sounding chuckle. "Likely not. It will go down as another election stolen from the only people who are trying to make things better for the decent folk of Mississippi."

Chapter Twenty-Five
The Landscape Shifts

1896-97

After her fiasco in submitting the story to the *Marchelle Advocate* about Duncan's event that she hadn't attended, Cissa stuck to writing about social activities and church gatherings. She didn't want to risk what little purchase she had on her budding career as a journalist. She noted when someone else wrote that Duncan's challenge of his Congressional election went nowhere in Washington. Duncan stopped talking about it, turning his attention toward the activities of his Farmers' Protective Union right here at home.

Cissa also kept busy developing her cooking skills, continually hoping for a word of approval from her mother.

"I think that girl has finally learned how to make proper biscuits," Mother said one day. "Where does Elsie keep herself, anyway? I hardly ever see her."

"I made the biscuits, Mother," Cissa said. "Elsie doesn't come on Fridays." Elsie had been back part time for going on two years and yet Mother could never remember which days she was there and which days she wasn't.

Mother furrowed her brow and buttered another biscuit.

Her forgetfulness was getting worse. As for Pop, he spent more time dozing in his chair than he used to and had fewer calls for his medical services. With the farm income still in the doldrums, Cissa knew that the family had been relying heavily on proceeds from Pop's medical practice. Even when he did make calls, he complained that it had become harder to collect from patients. In addition to all of this, ever since Duncan lost his election, Pop had stopped asking Cissa to read to him from the newspapers. Cissa fretted, trying to fend off her nagging sense that something was amiss.

Cissa looked up from her own newspaper reading, listening to her father's heavy footsteps in the hallway.

"Is anything wrong, Pop?" she rose from her seat on the couch as her father leaned against the door facing.

"Just feeling tired, Cissy. I'm going to go lie down for a bit until supper time."

Cissa thought he looked uncharacteristically pale. He'd had two consultations in a row, more than the usual demand on his time and energy.

"Will Mother be home soon?" Pop asked.

"I expect so. She's just down the road at Laura and Monroe's." Cissa folded the newspaper she'd been reading. "I could go and fetch her if you like."

"Oh, no need for that. I'll see you both at supper." He crossed over toward the bedroom with labored tread, closing the door gently but firmly behind him.

Cissa laid aside the paper, uncertain what to do. Should she go get her mother? *I'm sure he's fine*, she told herself. Mother would be home soon in any case. She went to the kitchen and began stoking the fire in the stove in preparation for heating the chicken and dumplings she'd prepared earlier. Her dumplings were getting better, though they still tended to be heavier than Julia's ever were. She was glad she had made the chicken and dumplings. They were Pop's favorite, though he always sprinkled them with a liberal amount of pepper. She thought she heard footsteps in the hall, but when she went to see if her father needed something or if her mother had returned, she found no one. As she passed the mirror, she thought she saw a figure reflected there, but when she looked, there was only her own face staring back at her. She tucked a stray strand of hair behind her ear.

Cissa got the fire burning steady and had placed the pot of food on the stove when at last she heard her mother coming up the front steps. She went to meet her in the hallway.

"Where's your father?" Susanna said, peering into the dining room toward Pop's desk.

"He's taking a nap. He said he was tired."

Mother glanced into the parlor. "In the bedroom?" She sounded surprised. Pop generally preferred to nap sitting up in his chair, disdaining the notion of sleeping in a bed during daylight hours.

"You can tell him that I've prepared chicken and dumplings for supper." Cissa watched as her mother made her way toward the bedroom she and Pop shared at the back corner of the house, the corner with one window facing south, another facing west, so that the room always caught the evening sunlight.

Cissa laid the table and set out the food. And then she waited. The clock over her father's desk ticked off the minutes. Had her mother fallen asleep, too? They were getting on in years and both seemed to doze off more readily than they used to. Pop had turned sixty-six at his last birthday and Mother would catch up to him in another month.

As the pot of food ceased steaming, Cissa grew concerned. *I'll just go check on them,* she told herself.

Cissa knocked softly on the bedroom door. There was no response. She knocked again. "Mother?" she said. "Supper is ready. Are you and Pop coming?" There was an inarticulate sound that Cissa wasn't certain constituted a response.

When she opened the door she saw her mother seated in a chair by the bedside, holding Pop's hand. Pop's eyes were closed, and his mouth was slightly open.

Cissa caught her breath and grasped the door facing as she felt the floor drop from under her. She knew. She didn't want to know, but she knew, and tears sprang to her eyes.

"Oh, Mother, is he...?" She couldn't say it.

Susanna turned slowly toward her daughter. Her face was drawn and her eyes blank. There were no tears in them. She shook her head, not letting go of her husband's hand.

Cissa had lost many family members over the years—little nieces and nephews, her brother Lester, elderly aunts and uncles— but she'd never been so close to death as she was in that moment, and she didn't know what to do with it.

Monroe reached the house ahead of Cissa, his long legs outpacing her exhausted limbs. She'd run all the way to his house and could barely put one foot in front of the other as she returned to the house where her father no longer lived.

Mother was still exactly where Cissa had left her. Monroe stood behind her, his hands on her shoulders, his head down.

"What are we to do?" Cissa whispered, not certain who she was speaking to.

Monroe turned to face her. "We'll do this together," he said. His eyes were moist and the lips beneath his mustache trembled ever so slightly, belying the strength in his voice. "Can you take Mother and get her a cup of coffee?"

Susanna submitted to her eldest son's direction, releasing Pop's hand at last and patting his shoulder as if he were only sleeping. Her face was expressionless as she accompanied her daughter into the parlor where her daughter-in-law Laura was waiting.

Cissa saw the supper growing cold on the table. She knew that no one could think of eating at that moment, but eventually they would need to consume something to sustain themselves. She covered the pot of food and set it in the pantry.

She took the kettle from the stove and poured it into the coffee pot with some chicory and a spoonful of real coffee from the tin that was kept for special occasions. She set the pot on a tray along with several cups and saucers and carried it into the parlor.

When Mother tried to pick up her cup of coffee, her hand shook so that she put it down again without tasting it. She folded her hands in her lap, staring straight ahead. "He should have given me some warning," she said. "What am I to do? He shouldn't just leave me like this."

As a single tear trickled down her mother's cheek, Cissa noticed how wrinkled that cheek had become, how white the hair was that framed her mother's face. *How has she become so old?* Cissa thought, and her heart ached for her mother's loss as well as for her own. How would they get along without Pop, who had always been their anchor, the mainstay of their family?

Cissa remembered how her father had spoken to her that day after Duncan had scolded her. Had he known then what was coming? All his talk about Cissa's duty to her mother and his reminiscences about how strong Susanna had been during the war. She felt certain that he'd been trying to prepare her for this moment.

Cissa wondered if the woman sitting there unable to lift a cup would be able to hold the family together in this new crisis. She looked as if she would need help to hold herself together. Cissa knelt down beside her and reached for the cup, placing it into her mother's hand, cradling that frail and wrinkled hand in her own to steady it. Susanna raised the cup to her lips and drank.

"It needs more sugar," she said. But she kept drinking, wrinkling her nose with every sip.

A special table was brought into the parlor where Joseph Tarver's body was laid out and the women of the family undertook to cleanse and dress him. Through it all, Mother moved like a ghost, barely there, reaching out occasionally to pat her husband's hand or shoulder or to arrange his sparse hair. Monroe set a chair next to Pop's head. He would sit there all night.

It was near midnight when Cissa finally put her mother to bed. Despite Monroe's presence, she ached with loneliness. Someone had turned the mirror in the hallway to face the wall and Cissa recalled what Mother had told her about this particular superstition. She was tempted to peek into the mirror to see if she could catch a glimpse of her father's spirit. Is that what she'd seen there earlier? She remembered back when she'd convinced Milly that she was possessed of the second sight. She'd almost convinced herself.

Before getting into bed, Cissa dragged her old doll out of the bureau drawer, hoping, perhaps, to somehow assuage the desolation of her father's absence. She clasped the figure to her breast, remembering when the tattered figure had been Princess Ursula Maryanne Virginia and Cissa had been the Queen of the Magnolia Fairies. Cissa thought of how safe she used to feel with Julia, who had stitched this doll especially for her. She thought of how the bead inside had come from the hand of the wild and mysterious Nubby out there in the forest.

She raised her head suddenly as the bedroom door opened. The dark figure standing there, outlined against the pale moonlight from the parlor windows, looked so small.

"I can't sleep in there, Cissy."

Cissa raised the corner of her sheet and scooted aside to make room for her mother.

Susanna lay down with a huge stuttering sigh and Cissa draped an arm over her, arranging the sheet to encompass them both. "It's alright, Mother." Tears welled in Cissa's eyes. "I'll take care of you."

Donna Birdwell

Chapter Twenty-Six
What Came Next

1897

The Presbyterian Church at Rundle Springs overflowed with mourners for the funeral of Joseph Quinlan Tarver. His coffin was borne into the sanctuary by his two sons, his two eldest grandsons, and two of his nephews from Fulton County. One of those nephews was the son of the physician to whom Pop had apprenticed. Mother held her head high and shed few tears, though she looked more fragile than ever in the black dress that always hung at the ready in her chifforobe.

Cissa herself was a bit astonished at how freely her own tears flowed. She and her father had never been what anyone would call close—Joseph Tarver was not demonstrative in his affection—but Cissa had trusted him more than she had trusted anyone else in her small world. In a dream last night, she'd seen her pop riding with a group of men on horseback, all of them carrying torches. She'd watched those torches recede into the darkness, staring wide-eyed until there was no light left.

Inside the church, Cissa sat next to her mother, resting her left hand over Mother's tightly clasped fingers.

The day went by in a whirl of eulogies and hymns and condolences and simple food made almost sacred by its offering at the Tarver family table. Cissa encountered cousins and second cousins and all kinds of Tarvers and McLaurins and other assorted kin, some of whom she swore she had never seen before. The obituary that appeared in the *Marchelle Advocate* and *Fulton Gazette* was composed by Cissa herself, with the aid of the family Bible and the good memory of her brother Monroe and a cousin from Fulton County. It was Monroe who had prompted her to add the information about their father's service as a deacon in the church and on the founding board of supervisors for the Mount Eden school. He also supplied the full names of their paternal grandparents, while the cousin insisted on noting that most of Joseph Tarver's eleven brothers and sisters had been born and lived in Fulton County, where most of their descendants still held property.

"So how did we end up here in Hinson County?" Cissa asked Monroe.

"Because this was where Mother's people lived—the McLaurins—and Mother inherited our land from them. It was divided between her and Aunt Abigail, since there were no surviving sons. Pop being by far the youngest in his family, there was nothing left for him on that side."

"So Pop was planting Mother's land? I always thought it was his."

"Most folks assume so," Monroe said, "and I think in Louisiana or Texas and maybe other states it would have been, but here in Mississippi property that comes to a married woman is still considered her property. Forever."

Cissa had never known any of her grandparents and had never thought to ask about things like land inheritance. She didn't ask now, but she assumed that since the land was Mother's that the farm would go on just as it had before Pop's passing, with Monroe and Duncan running things. She recalled what Pop had said about Mother having washed her hands of the farming business after the war.

Cissa hadn't put the information about the McLaurin land into her article. It felt like family business and not for publication. She just put it away in her memory.

Cissa once again slept on a raised pallet on the floor of her own bedroom, ceding the bed to her mother. The corner bedroom—Susanna and Joseph's room—was left closed and empty, with the curtains drawn and the bed draped in a dark purple spread.

Elsie had agreed to come in full-time for a few days to help out with the funeral preparations and the accommodation of out-of-town guests and hosting of visitors dropping by to offer condolences and covered dishes and baked goods. Duncan promised to cover Elsie's wages.

Susanna rose to the occasion, ordering Elsie about like the mistress of a grand house, commanding her to "tell the staff" to do such and such or get "one of the servants" to fulfill a task. She fussed at Cissa for spending too much time in the kitchen. "We have servants for that, Narcissa." But of course they didn't. They only had Elsie. It occurred to Cissa that her mother was somehow trying to relive her best years with her husband, years when they'd had a house full of servants and a thriving though modest plantation.

On the second day after the funeral, when the overnight guests had departed from the upstairs bedrooms, Cissa was startled to see that the woman bustling about the kitchen was not Elsie but Julia.

"Oh, Julia," she said, fighting back tears. "Its…I'm so glad to see you." She resisted the urge to hug Julia, instead inquiring about Elsie's wellbeing.

"Elsie be a mite peakéd today, Miss Cissa. How's you and Miz Tarver keepin'? I'm right sorry for your grief." As she spoke, Julia's hands kept busy with the breakfast preparations. She poured a cup of coffee for Cissa and set it on the table.

Julia's voice had deepened a bit with maturity, but it still held the power to wrap itself right around Cissa's heart and conjure a fluster of memories. Cissa grasped the warm cup in both hands and for a moment she was a child again, wanting to grab Julia's hand and run outside to play. Then she remembered where she was. When she was. "We're keeping well, I guess. We've been so busy. Not much time to think about what it's going to be like. You know. Without Pop."

"He live a long life, Miss. My pa he been gone a long time. Mama Zolene raise us up."

Cissa nodded, staring at Julia and trying to think how many brothers and sisters she had. "I guess I never knew your father."

"You wouldn't've. He serve up at McMaster place. Passed when you was no more'n a tyke."

Cissa stared into her coffee, into the dark liquid that obscured the little flowers she knew were painted in the bottom of the cup. There was so much she didn't know about Julia. Things like her losing her father when she was just young and being raised by her mother. A wave of something that was equal parts gratitude and grief swept over Cissa as she thought again about her own father. There were probably things she didn't know about him, too, and now it was too late to ask.

Later that day Cissa asked her mother, "Did you ever know Julia's father? Zolene's husband?"

"I don't think so," Mother said. "He wasn't one of ours."

The family conferred among themselves and decided that Milly's wedding should go ahead as planned only three weeks after

Joseph's funeral. Cissa was to stand as a bridesmaid along with Betty. Milly had insisted that both of her attendants should wear gloves and the ones she provided for Cissa had stuffing in the index and middle fingers of the right hand. Cissa found them ridiculous, as the two fake fingers tended to flop about. She said nothing, acknowledging with sadness that even her closest kin still found her deformity shameful, a thing to be hidden from view.

Cissa herself had mostly come to terms with her disfigured hand. She found comfort in the memory of how Julia's little Rosie had cradled and caressed her hand and how Johnny had clasped it warmly without his gaze straying from her eyes. Cissa found the lack of fingers less of a disability now, as she'd become competent in the kitchen and long since learned that her choice of words to write down was far more important than the aesthetics of her penmanship.

Cissa refused to entertain feelings of jealousy toward Milly. She couldn't keep such feelings from arising, but she could send them packing when they did emerge. In her heart she still nurtured the hope—or at least held space for the possibility—that someday someone might want to marry Narcissa Tarver. She was still friends with Johnny and from time to time received a letter from him. He was now in medical school in New Orleans and his letters were full of fascinating facts about what he was learning. Cissa spent hours composing her replies.

Milly's wedding took place in Cowleton, in the same Presbyterian church where Albert had married a few years before. Her ceremony was only a little less elaborate. Cissa gritted her teeth and wore the pink dress that Milly had mandated for her bridesmaids, even though pink was her least flattering color. Mother wore dark navy blue.

The celebration at Duncan's house afterward provided food and drink for a selection of the leading citizens of Fulton County. Several of those citizens were Baptists, so drink was nonalcoholic, although Cissa did notice how certain of the men would go outdoors and then return with their tumblers filled.

After the wedding, Cissa and her mother accompanied Matilda back to Marchelle for a week's stay. Matilda insisted it would be good for Mother to be away from the big house for a while, filled as it was with the lingering presence of her husband of nearly fifty years.

"No, I should go home," Mother had said, but she hadn't insisted, slipping instead into an attitude of meek compliance.

Cissa was grateful for the respite. The big house had felt bigger than ever, filled as it was with Pop's absence. The corner of the dining room where his desk rested was a lacuna in time that threatened to draw her into memory and nostalgia. His papers and other paraphernalia lay exactly as he'd left them. Cissa yearned to sit in his chair and reclaim what might be left of him there. Thus far, however, she lacked the courage.

Matilda insisted on Mother taking hers and Frank's own room, while they moved to a bed in the room with three-year-old Irwin. Ten-year-old Evelyn slept on a pallet to make room for Cissa. After the long buggy ride from Cowleton to Marchelle, Mother was ready to take a light supper and go straight to bed. "Did you take one of the pills Duncan gave you?" Cissa asked.

Mother nodded as she sank into the featherbed, her eyes already closing.

Cissa returned to the kitchen, where Matilda was finishing up the supper dishes. "Is she alright?" Matilda asked.

"I think so. I'm not sure she's fully grasped the loss of Pop, though. She's kept herself so busy first with the funeral and then getting ready for Milly's wedding."

"And what about you?"

Cissa's shoulders dropped as she drew in a long breath. "I'm alright." She wouldn't say how her future seemed to stretch out before her in an endless sameness that crumpled her soul like a piece of discarded paper.

"Well, while you're here, I'll take care of Mother, and you can take it easy for a bit." Matilda patted Cissa's hand.

Cissa's heart lightened a bit at the prospect.

After breakfast the next morning, Cissa announced that she was going for a walk. She headed straight for the office of the *Marchelle Advocate*, eager to meet face-to-face with her employer.

A smiling woman greeted her from behind a desk where a telephone sat proudly on one corner. "May I help you?" she said.

"Is Mr. Hodges in?" Cissa peered through an open door into the press room.

"No, I'm sorry." The woman sounded as if she meant it. "He's not expected for at least another half hour. May I tell him who called?"

Cissa tried not to show her disappointment. "Narcissa Tarver," she said.

"Oh, Miss Tarver." The woman smiled with evident delight. "I'm pleased to finally meet you. I'm Elizabeth Smith. But I'm called Liz."

Liz extended her right hand and reacted with only a small head tilt when Cissa grasped it warmly in her left. "I was sorry to hear about your father," Liz said.

Cissa nodded an acknowledgment. "Do you work here?" she said. *Well, of course she does, Cissa.* Her cheeks pinked a bit in embarrassment at her superfluous query.

"For six years now," Liz answered, sweeping Cissa's awkwardness aside with another smile. "In addition to minding the front desk, I'm also a copy editor, and may I say that your copy is some of the cleanest that we get. You're really quite a good writer, Miss Tarver."

"Cissa. I'm called Cissa. And thanks." Her cheeks turned a shade pinker.

Liz Smith offered a quick tour of the premises while they waited for Mr. Hodges. Cissa was fascinated by the racks of large type that had to be assembled back to front into headlines, as well as the huge rolls of newsprint and the big machine that did the actual printing. Liz pointed with pride to a complicated looking contraption with a chair pulled up in front of it. "This is our new linotype machine," she said. "It sets type by just punching those keys."

Cissa inhaled with pleasure the scent of printer's ink that she relished so much in each fresh edition of a newspaper. On a partially assembled page, she saw a headline about the revolution in Cuba. She also noticed banners for a couple of other newspapers besides the *Advocate.* "Why are those here?" she asked.

"Not every newspaper has its own printing facility," Liz said, "so they pay us to print their papers for them. These are just weeklies, and each comes out on a different day from our two editions. It keeps our printing staff busy."

Liz conducted Cissa back to the front office and offered her a cup of coffee. "Who else do you write for besides us?" Liz asked as she pulled a chair closer to her desk for Cissa.

"Oh, no one," Cissa said. "Only for the *Advocate.*"

"But you're such a capable writer. You know, the *Natchez Herald* is putting together a special edition soon that will have features on sporting activities all over the region and they're looking for more writers. You should apply to write something. I remember the piece you wrote on the glass ball tournament in Rundle Springs. Do you know Mr. Carson at the *Herald?*"

Cissa confessed that she did not know Mr. Carson, though she thought she recognized the name. "How would I get an article to him if I did write something?"

"Trains run between Marchelle and Natchez every day, so the mail is very timely. Sometimes we use the telephone to convey it to someone who knows shorthand."

"Do you know shorthand?" Cissa asked.

"I do, and it's a mighty handy skill to have in the newspaper business. Well, in any business really."

"I've been wanting to learn shorthand," Cissa said.

Liz opened a drawer in her desk and took out a well-worn paper bound booklet. She handed it to Cissa. "This and a lot of dedicated practice is all you need," she said. "If you work at it, you should master it in six months."

Cissa accepted the book with hesitation. "Are you sure?" she said. "I mean about the book. Are you sure you want to give it to me?"

"I've long since memorized the thing, Cissa. Yes, take the book and keep it."

Cissa expressed her gratitude and tucked the book into her purse. Learning something new and useful felt like exactly what she needed.

The two women continued chatting and Cissa began to feel so at ease with Liz that by the time Mr. Hodges returned, she was able to greet him and introduce herself with calm confidence.

"You really ought to write more material for us," Mr. Hodges said, reenforcing Liz's assessment. "Isn't that brother of yours running for office again now that his term in the legislature is finished?"

Cissa cringed. She'd gotten into enough trouble already trying to be a good reporter while also keeping her brother happy. "Yes," she said. "He's on the ballot for sheriff of Fulton."

"People's Party again?" Mr. Hodges made little attempt to hide his disdain for the Populists. "Do you suppose you could put together a piece for us on the lead-up? Let us know what Dr. Duncan Tarver is doing, what his points are? We try to give space to all parties."

Cissa took a deep breath. This sounded possible. "Yes, I'm sure I can do that," she said. "I'll speak to him."

Lachlan came down to Marchelle in a borrowed buggy to pick up his grandmother and aunt and ferry them back home. It was a day washed in sunshine, but Cissa felt a darkness closing around her heart as Lachlan turned onto Callander Road. She reminded herself about the book on shorthand she'd acquired from her new friend Liz. Is that what Liz was? A friend? Cissa wished she could have stayed in Marchelle, but as she gazed at her mother's frail, black-draped figure, she knew where her responsibilities lay.

It was later that evening that Cissa found her mother sobbing at the side of the bed where she hadn't slept since Pop's death. Cissa placed her hands on her mother's shoulders and bent down, kissing her lightly on the cheek before leaving her with the grief she'd bottled up for too long, and with a few of Cissa's tears in her white hair. That night Susanna returned to her own bed and long after dark Cissa heard her talking in a low soft voice. "I guess it probably came as much a surprise to you as it did to me," she said, "so maybe I shouldn't be mad at you for leaving me with no warning." The voice faltered. "I do miss you so."

Cissa stifled her own sobs with her pillow.

Chapter Twenty-Seven
Almost a War Correspondent

1897-98

Cissa's piece on Duncan's sheriff contest ran in the midweek edition of the *Marchelle Advocate* two weeks before the election. Cissa had quoted exactly what her brother wanted said and included a few remarks from his Democratic rival that she had gleaned from a broadside posted at the general store. Duncan was satisfied; Mr. Hodges was satisfied. Cissa was relieved.

When the election was held in early September, Duncan lost to his Democratic opponent by a mere twelve votes. Cissa felt certain that this time, under the circumstances, having so recently lost his father, Duncan would accept the result without protest. She was wrong.

In a spirited letter to the editor of the *Fulton Gazette*, Duncan insisted that he had lost votes "in part to chicanery, in part to fraud, in part to whisky, and in part to lies." He filed once again to contest the vote, engaging two lawyers to represent him. The case was heard before a jury in December and, although they conceded that there had been some irregularities in some of the precincts, they were not convinced that this had affected one candidate more than the other. The results of the election would stand. Cissa knew that this loss would not sit well with Duncan.

A few days after this decision was handed down, Cissa returned to the big house one afternoon to find Duncan seated at Pop's desk, busily sorting papers.

"Duncan," she said, anger flaring through her veins, "what are you doing?" Cissa had dusted the desk a few times, but she still hadn't had the heart to do anything further.

Duncan glanced up at her without stopping. "Since I'm taking over Pop's medical practice here in Hinson County, I've decided to use his desk. It's what he would have wanted."

Cissa didn't relish the notion of having Duncan in the house. She knew that Duncan and Monroe were also now fully in charge of the farm and there were probably records relating to that in Pop's desk as well. She took a deep breath and went on about her own chores. Her job was looking after Mother.

Cissa had long been aware of the ups and downs of family finance, but now she worried about how she and her mother would get along without the income from Pop's doctoring business. They were going to be entirely dependent on proceeds from the farm, and those had never regained the levels they'd achieved before the 1893 depression. Prices and weather had not been the best. Cissa figured they could make do with simple needs and Elsie as their sole household help, trusting Monroe and Duncan—mainly Monroe—to keep the farm going.

Whenever she could, Cissa worked on learning shorthand. She was intrigued by the new symbols for letters and word endings. She liked the flow of the script. As the new year approached, she spent at least a couple of hours every day working with the book Liz had given her. She made good progress.

She also read with voracious interest the developing news of a popular revolution in Cuba. Reports grew more alarming by the day. The stories were told in vibrant prose that held Cissa enthralled. She awaited each new installment with anticipation, finding these accounts even more thrilling than the serialized novels because this was real. Sometimes she transcribed passages into shorthand.

She asked her brothers what they thought about the situation.

"It's terrible," Duncan said. "People are dying in the streets from famine and disease with the Spaniards calling it their just deserts for engaging in insurrection. Did you know that in Kansas they've organized a group of volunteers ready to march to the aid of the revolutionaries? Troops in Texas have been ready to go for months." He paused and looked up into Monroe's face. "It's time we organized here in Mississippi."

Monroe demurred. "It sounds like President McKinley is trying to negotiate a peaceful solution," he said.

"But Cuba is not in some distant part of the world," Duncan countered. "It's not so very far from the mouth of our own Mississippi River. Do we really want Spain to continue exercising authority over shipments and commerce through Cuba?" Duncan was undeterred and Cissa soon came to understand that he was indeed working to gin up support for a Mississippi unit of volunteers.

Cissa's article on glass ball tournaments ran in the special edition of the *Natchez Herald* and in return for her work she received a subscription to the paper. They also printed her name as author of the piece. She continued writing about the small events in Rundle Springs and Callander and delivering them to Mr. Clay for the *Marchelle Advocate*. On a Tuesday in mid-February she arrived at the Clay farm to find a knot of men on the front porch conversing in excited voices.

"You can bet it was one of them Spanish bastards done it," one man exclaimed.

Cissa knew they must be talking about Cuba. She hurried closer, listening.

"Well, they don't know yet," Mr. Clay said. "All's the report said was that a ship called the Maine exploded and sank in the harbor there at Havana."

"Did that come in on the telegraph wire?" Cissa asked.

Several of the men looked at her with surprise. Mr. Clay nodded and said, "Yes, ma'am. It come on the wire for the news office. For sure it will be all over the next paper."

"Will there be a war?" Cissa couldn't hide her excitement. Oh, how she wished she could write about something as exciting as this. An American ship blown up in a foreign harbor where people were fighting and dying for their independence!

The general hubbub of the men's voices rose again, excluding Cissa by sheer volume. Some said that of course there would be a war while others argued that some kind of treaty with Spain would certainly prevent such a development.

It wasn't until August—four months after the US officially declared war against Spain—that Duncan and his son Eli were mustered into Company E of the Third Regiment of Mississippi Volunteers. Governor Anselm McLaurin commissioned Duncan at the rank of Lieutenant. Young Eli, being only eighteen, was a private. They were to serve under Captain Sam Cortman. Cissa recognized the name as that of the Democrat who had defeated Duncan for Congress a couple of years previous.

"Will you and Monroe go, too?" Cissa asked Lachlan. "You're older than Eli."

"I am," he said. "But Pop says two Tarver men at war is sufficient. And as for me, he says he needs me here on the farm. Only son, you know?"

"No you're not," Cissa said with a grin.

"True, but little Sammy and baby Joey are not terribly handy with a mule and plow yet, Aunt Cissy, and worthless ordering around the hired hands." A smile flashed across Lachlan's face.

"Is Albert going?" Albert was a full five years older than Eli.

"I doubt it. His wife is due to deliver soon, you know. Besides, Albert is Uncle Duncan's main help with the farm. And by 'help,' I mean he's the one who runs Uncle Duncan's share of the farm. He has to be here to supervise the cotton harvest."

At church on Sunday, Cissa assembled a full list of men who had joined the volunteers from the Rundle Springs area. She also collected statements from several family members. "So proud of our brave young men," one elder said. "May God protect and preserve our sons," said another. Cissa wrote it all down and put it into a story for the *Marchelle Advocate*.

Cissa followed the news about the war avidly. She was mesmerized by accounts of the work of a woman called Clara Barton who was providing aid to the starving mothers and orphans in Cuba through an organization of which she was president.

The *Beckport Journal* published a letter sent back by a Negro soldier about action he'd seen in the battle of Santiago de Cuba on July 1, in which several men died, and many were wounded. "After an hour's march," the soldier wrote, "we could hear the cannonading from our batteries." They marched on, soon encountering a white volunteer regiment pinned down as bullets from the Spanish flew all around. The black soldier finally detected the point of origin of most of the shots and gunned the sniper down from his treetop perch.

How Cissa wished she could write something about the war for the papers. It was what everyone wanted to read. Were Duncan and Eli in danger such as this? Cissa perused the letters Duncan had sent to Mother, hoping to find something exciting. Duncan, apparently, was still far from the fighting.

Mother held his latest letter in her lap, a look of deepest sorrow creasing her face.

"What is it, Mother?" After reading the other letters, Cissa couldn't imagine that there would be bad news.

"Oh, Maggie, Joseph's in such danger every day," she murmured, "out there among all those Yankees. I need him here at home."

"Mother, that letter's not from Pop. It's from Duncan. It's the war with Spain." It was the second time this week that her mother had called her Maggie. Cissa worried over her mother's increasingly frequent departures from reality. At times she seemed lost in time in her own private world.

Susanna gave her daughter a startled look and fanned herself with the envelope. "Of course," she said. "I know that. Will supper be ready soon?"

It was early afternoon, and they'd finished dinner not an hour before. "Not yet," Cissa said. "What would you like me to fix, Mother?"

"Maybe a soft-boiled egg with some crackers, Narcissa. I'm not very hungry. Pop will probably want his cornbread and buttermilk." She handed the letter to Cissa without another word.

Cissa took the letter into the dining room and sat down at her father's desk to read it. It occurred to her that her mother must have received letters from Pop during the war between the states; she wondered where Mother might have kept them. She also wondered if Duncan's experiences were quite as tranquil as he indicated in these letters to Mother. She decided to write her own letter to him asking for more details, suggesting that she could try to get it published in the newspaper.

When a reply finally came from Duncan, it held no first-hand reports of bullets flying or snipers shot out of trees, nor even any heart-wrenching observations of starving children. Nevertheless, Cissa thought she could craft his generalized remarks into an account worth publishing. She wouldn't pretend she was there; she would give Duncan due credit for the information.

Not only did Mr. Hodges publish Cissa's article in the *Marchelle Advocate*, but the story was also picked up and reprinted in the *Natchez Herald* and one of the Vicksburg papers. Mr. Hodges suggested that Cissa continue composing reports about the war, but before she could submit even one more, the war was over.

Cissa knew she should be joyful about the treaty with Spain, but she couldn't help feeling a twinge of regret that her career as a war correspondent had been nipped in the bud. Susanna, who had asked almost daily where Duncan was and could never quite understand what the current war was about, seemed relieved to know her son and grandson would soon be home safe and sound. "Did we win this time?" she asked.

Chapter Twenty-Eight
Broader Horizons

1899

With the war over, Cissa tried her hand at writing a couple of articles about modern methods of farming, based on some brochures published by the Farmers' Alliance. Duncan reported to her that he had begun employing some of the methods to good results. Cissa knew it was the farm hands, under Albert's supervision, or the sharecroppers who were doing the work, but she quoted her brother's claims, nonetheless. Between his medical practice and continuing political activity, Duncan rarely set foot in the fields. But he was always happy to get his name in the papers. He was particularly pleased when Cissa's story was picked up by the Natchez paper and even one in Jackson.

One day in midsummer, Mother sent Cissa to Monroe's to fetch another jar of molasses. Cissa sighed and said "Yes, Mother," feeling like a child again, being sent on a simple errand. At least it got her out of the house.

She found Lachlan coming out the front door, dressed in his work overalls. "Hey, Lachlan," she called out.

He smiled and waved, stopping on the porch to wait for her arrival. "What brings you out of the big house, Aunt Cissy?" he said.

"Being the errand girl," she replied with a grimace. "Mother wants more molasses. I think she's drinking the stuff these days."

"Come on around to the shed and I'll get you some."

The two walked side by side. Lachlan was only a few inches taller than Cissa, but it was all legs and Cissa had to hasten her step to keep pace with him. "How's Grandma?" he said.

Cissa hesitated. "She's as well as can be expected, I suppose. She forgets things." Cissa glanced across into Lachlan's concerned eyes. "She's called me Maggie several times lately. And I've heard her talking to Maggie, too. Asking her how she's doing in school. I'm pretty sure Maggie is one of her daughters who died as a baby."

Lachlan shot Cissa a troubled look.

"Sometimes I'm almost convinced Mother is speaking in tongues; she says such strange words that make no sense."

"Pop told me that he's heard her talking in the old Scotch-Irish language a couple of times lately. He said it was what Granny Mag spoke."

"That could be it."

They reached the shed and Lachlan climbed up to retrieve a jar with dark amber contents from a top shelf. "It's going to be molasses making time again soon," he said. "We'll probably take the rest of this into Natchez next time we go and sell it."

"I wish I could go with you to Natchez sometime," Cissa said. Then she laughed. "I guess I just wish I could go anywhere other than right here on Callander Road."

"We're going next Friday. Why don't you come along? I'm sure Betty would be willing to stay with Grandma for the day."

Cissa's eyes lit up as a tiny window of anticipation opened in her soul. "Friday? Are you sure? I'll ask Mother."

"And I'll ask my mother if she's willing to send Betty around to mind Grandma."

Cissa had two days to make ready for this unaccustomed outing. Elsie agreed to stay the entire day to see to Mother's needs, with Betty's help. Cissa had only been to Natchez once before, and that was when she was a small child. She'd seen everything from about waist high and tethered to her mother's hand. She expected it would look very different this time.

Mother had initially hesitated. "Oh, Narcissa, I'm not sure. Natchez is so filled with wickedness. Not a decent place for a nice young girl."

"Mother, I'll be twenty-three years old in a few weeks. And I'll be with Monroe and Lachlan." She paused. "I'm quite certain I'll be able to look out for myself."

"Well, just keep your wits about you. And don't go below the bluff."

Cissa had heard about what went on in Natchez below the bluff and, while it sounded exciting, it frightened her enough that she was reasonably certain she'd be able to obey her mother's directive. There was gambling and drinking and fighting and prostitution there. No, she wouldn't go below the bluff. At least, not without Lachlan or Monroe.

The day of Cissa's big journey began before sunrise and Cissa had assumed that they would be riding in the wagon all the way to Natchez, but when they reached Marchelle, Monroe reined in the mule at the railroad station. "How long has it been since you were on a train, little sister?" Monroe said with a grin.

"I've never been on a train." Cissa felt an odd mixture of shame for her inexperience and delight at the prospect of something new.

"Really? I guess that's what comes with being the last child, with only old people for company. Old people who never go anywhere." He held out a hand to help Cissa down from the wagon. "Lachlan, help me with our goods. Cissy, you can sit on that bench over there on the platform while we unload."

Cissa didn't sit. Instead, she walked back and forth along the platform, craning her neck to look for trains and studying the other people, imagining what business they might have in Natchez. No trains came through Rundle Springs or Callander, though when the winds were right Cissa could hear their distinctive whistle in the distance. For Cissa, trains were things in stories and in the columns of timetables printed in the newspapers.

Cissa cocked her head as she heard the whistle. She leaned over the edge of the platform, eager to catch a glimpse of the engine when at last it came into view. She watched, spellbound, as it grew larger and louder, stepping back as it came to a halt with a great clamor of puffing steam, clanking gears, and metal wheels screeching on metal rails.

Monroe led the way into one of the cars and Lachlan offered his hand as Cissa stepped up to follow him. With its rows of benches on either side of a central aisle, it made Cissa feel a bit like she was entering a school room, but without the desks. There was barely enough space on one bench for the three of them. Cissa sat happily squeezed up against the window with Lachlan by her side. She knew she was grinning like a schoolgirl, but she didn't care. This was even more excitement than she'd anticipated for her day's outing.

As the train picked up speed, the fields and pine forests whipping by her window made Cissa dizzy. Lachlan said they were likely going almost fifty miles an hour. The train made two brief stops along the way, at which nobody got off and several passengers got on.

When a Negro couple entered, they were quickly escorted to a different car by the conductor.

When the train slowed again, Lachlan nudged Cissa's shoulder. "This is it," he said. "We're coming into Natchez."

Cissa bobbed forward and back, trying to see out the windows on both sides of the car at once. They passed small houses and a sizeable lumber shed. "What's that big building?" Cissa pointed out the north window.

"That's the orphan asylum," Lachlan said. "Catholic, I think."

The next building of any size that they passed, Lachlan identified as a colored school. All of the people Cissa saw along the street and around the houses were Negroes.

A couple of minutes later, Lachlan said, "The big house up ahead is a girls' school. Stanton College."

Cissa's mouth fell open as she stared at the opulent mansion where young women could go to study…well, she didn't know what they studied, but she wished she could be among them.

As the train made its slow curve past several mills and warehouses, Cissa noticed people gathering their belongings, preparing to disembark. The engine crawled past a big freight depot and finally screeched to a halt next to a much smaller passenger depot.

Cissa stood to one side while Monroe and Lachlan unloaded their cargo. "I've got this, Lachlan," Monroe said. "You show Cissy around. I'll meet you for lunch later at McKinley's."

Lachlan led Cissa onto Franklin Street, pointing out a wholesale grocer's establishment on their left and a cotton textile mill on their right. The buildings were large brick structures, impressive for their sturdiness but not what anyone would call beautiful.

"What's that odor?" Cissa wrinkled her nose.

"Probably some combination of the coal yard where they fuel the trains and the cottonseed meal plant. You get used to it." Lachlan quickened his step toward a street congested with wagons pulled by an assortment of mules and oxen. "Most of this part of Franklin Street is where farmers and planters come to do business. Are you in the market for new harnesses or some seed corn, Aunt Cissy?"

Cissa shook her head with a laugh.

Lachlan took a right turn, promising that there would be a more interesting array of businesses on Main Street.

"Do you know where the newspaper office is?" Cissa asked. "The *Natchez Herald?*"

Lachlan furrowed his brow. "I seem to recall having noticed them somewhere. Maybe near..."

"There it is!" Cissa pointed down a side street to a sign hanging over a door with the name of the newspaper in bold black letters.

"Do you want to go there?"

Did she? Cissa wasn't sure as she noticed how fast her heart was beating and how her breath almost caught in her throat. "Maybe later. Show me more of the city first." She didn't want to look like a bemused country girl to the newspaper folks. She needed to get her bearings and get her feet on the ground.

They turned onto Main Street, where the wagons that had congested Franklin Street were replaced by buggies and coaches pulled by fine-looking horses. A cluster of men waited in front of a bank, chatting amiably.

"When do businesses open up?" Cissa asked as she peered down the street, searching for an answer to her own question.

"Honestly, whenever the proprietor and the clerks get there," Lachlan said. "But I think things along Main should be opening soon. Businesses on Franklin open much earlier."

Near the bank, the smell of fresh bread drifted from a shop where a variety of pastries and sweets were arrayed in the front window. Cissa watched with envy as customers exited with grease-stained paper sacks. She calculated how much money she had. Mother had given her six bits for her lunch and some shopping, but she'd also brought a dollar of the money she earned from her writing. Surely she could afford a few pennies for a cinnamon roll.

Cissa and Lachlan shared the roll as they wandered farther down the street. Cissa thought it was the most delicious thing she'd ever tasted, rich with cinnamon and dusted liberally with pure white sugar. A couple of barbers were doing a brisk early business. They passed a jeweler and a milliner and a shop selling sewing machines. Cissa stopped to study the machine in the window. She noted the price: forty dollars. Twice the price of a typewriter.

As they pressed on down the street, they were joined by more pedestrians. Cissa was surprised to see several Negroes among them, all well dressed and seeming at ease walking on a public street intermingled with white people.

A large brick structure loomed ahead of them that Cissa thought looked familiar. "What church is that?" she asked.

"St. Mary's," Lachlan said. "Catholic. They call it a cathedral. The Presbyterian Church is on Pearl, same street as your newspaper office."

They crossed the street and backtracked on the other side. More shops were open now and Cissa went inside a few, stopping just inside the doorway. The array of goods was overwhelming—shelves and shelves of boxes and things in glittering glass cases. The dresses touted at the dressmakers' shops made Cissa feel dowdy in her plain homemade attire. She reminded herself wryly that she wasn't exactly out of fashion, since her dress likely had never been considered fashionable even when it was new. She went into one of the dress shops and allowed herself to caress the fabrics. Some of them were exquisite.

As they approached Pearl Street on their return trek, Cissa noticed a mumble of voices. The mumble grew into a rumble. "Where do you suppose that noise is coming from?" she asked.

"I don't know," Lachlan said. "Let's go investigate."

There were reasons why Lachlan was Cissa's favorite nephew.

"The courthouse is down this way," he said. "Could be something going on over there."

But as they approached the courthouse with its regal columns and expansive green lawn, they could see where a crowd had gathered in front of a smaller building on the opposite side of the street.

"That's the jailhouse," Lachlan said.

Cissa's heart beat faster as she recalled the account she'd read about the riot at the jail in Taloa County, where armed men had come to free several of their compatriots who were being charged with whitecapping.

Cissa scanned the crowd. She saw no weapons. It was at this point that she realized almost all of the protesters were women. What *was* this about? She listened more intently to their chant. "Free Mary Maxwell! Women deserve to vote!" There were placards, too, with slogans about women's suffrage.

"Cissa!" There was a tug at her sleeve, and she turned to see the flushed face of Liz Smith, the woman from the *Marchelle Advocate.*

Cissa tried not to look startled. "How nice to see you, Liz," she said, as if Cissa Tarver encountering Liz Smith here in this crowd of protesters in Natchez was the most ordinary thing in the world. "Are you here to cover this for the *Advocate?*"

"Oh, heavens, no," Liz said. She sounded hoarse. She held up the placard that was in her left hand: "Votes for Women." She frowned. "I don't think Mr. Hodges would be pleased about my presence here."

Or mine? Cissa thought, stifling the thought that had begun to take shape in her mind about writing up this event for the *Advocate.* "Can you tell me why all of you are here in front of the jailhouse?" She could at least ask a few questions.

Before Liz could answer, Lachlan spoke. "Cissy, we should go." He looked decidedly uncomfortable.

After making introductions, Cissa said. "You go, Lachlan. I'll be fine here with my friend Liz. She knows her way around. I'll see you at the cafe. McKinley's, right?"

Lachlan's eyes darted back and forth, surveying the crowd. "Are you sure?"

As if in answer, Liz linked arms with Cissa. "I'll take good care of your sister, don't you worry."

Cissa didn't bother to remind Liz that Lachlan was her nephew, only agreeing to meet him at McKinley's Cafe in an hour. She could tell that Lachlan was ill at ease in the situation. Cissa was too, but she had no desire to leave.

As Lachlan disappeared toward the edge of the crowd, Liz explained to Cissa that Mary Maxwell was a well-known advocate for woman suffrage who had recently moved to Mississippi from Ohio. "Up there, women are allowed to vote for school supervisors and Mary had become accustomed to doing that. When an election came up here for school supervisors, she decided she was going to vote. When she wouldn't let go of the ballot she'd grabbed and wouldn't leave the polling place, they arrested her."

Cissa wasn't certain whether she found the woman's audacity horrifying or inspiring.

"Mary was a delegate at the state Women's Suffrage Association convention earlier this year up in Clarksdale. I heard her speak and she was very powerful."

"You were at the convention?" Cissa's friend Liz was full of surprises.

She nodded. "Shh, Mary's daughter is about to speak. Let's listen."

Cissa pulled a small notebook out of her purse and began to write down her observations, scribbling in shorthand. Liz glanced at her notebook and nodded in approval.

Cissa noted that there must be a hundred women present. At least seventy. Also a few men. She wrote down the messages she read from the signs. She listened to the speech and wrote a few quotes about women being of equal intelligence to men and often taxpayers, as well. "No one cares more than we do about the education of our children," the speaker said. Cissa noticed that there were several Negro women in the crowd. They weren't carrying placards, but they listened attentively to the speaker.

There were periodic bursts of cheers and applause throughout the speech, which concluded with a plea for the women to go peacefully about their business but to never forget the importance of winning the vote for all citizens. As the crowd broke up, Cissa tucked her notebook away.

"Did you get enough for your story?" Liz asked.

"Oh, I'm not planning to write it up. I just..." Cissa shrugged. "It's practice. Trying to train myself to notice things and to see what's important in any situation."

"That's commendable, Cissa. But I think you should write it up. You can send it to Mr. Hodges and tell him you just happened to be in town on other business—which I'm certain is true—and thought the paper could use a first-hand report."

"Do you think he might print it?"

"Either he will, or he won't. No harm in trying, Cissa. Where are you headed next? It's a bit too soon to meet that brother of yours at the cafe."

"He's my nephew," Cissa said. "I was hoping to go by the newspaper office."

"Capital idea. I'll go with you. I know some of the people there and can introduce you."

As they entered the premises of the *Natchez Herald,* Cissa took a deep breath, inhaling the reassuring scent of printer's ink.

"Good day, Mr. Carson." Liz approached the gentleman leaning over the print tray. She spoke with a confidence that Cissa envied.

"Miss Smith." Mr. Carson offered a friendly smile as he straightened up. His ink-smudged waistcoat pulled at the buttons across his ample midsection. "What brings you to our fair city today?"

Liz gave Cissa a furtive glance and merely said, "I've brought someone to meet you. This is Miss Narcissa Tarver. She wrote that piece for you about the glass ball tournaments in Hinson County, remember? And you ran a story she wrote about the war in Cuba."

"Ah, yes. Miss Tarver. You're a very decent writer. I believe we also ran a piece you wrote about modern farming. It's nice to meet a young writer with such diverse interests. Have you got any other stories for us?"

Cissa shook her head "no" even as Liz spoke up saying, "She could write up a story about the protest that just ended up by the jailhouse. She happened to be in town and heard the commotion and like a good reporter went to investigate."

Cissa couldn't speak. Why wouldn't Liz offer to write something herself? She knew more about the situation than Cissa did. Liz, however, did not want her employer to know she had come to Natchez to participate in a political demonstration for women's suffrage. Cissa was legitimately a bystander.

"Well, thank you, but there's no need for that. We sent one of our fellows up there as soon as we heard what was happening. I'm sure he'll do a decent writeup for us."

"Of course," Liz said. Her knitted eyebrows confessed doubts.

After a few more moments of pleasantries, Liz and Cissa left.

"You should write your story anyway, Cissa. Send it to Mr. Hodges of course, but also to Mr. Carson. Let him see the difference between what a man will write about our event and what a woman will write. Did you know that the president of the state Women's Suffrage Association is the editor of a newspaper up in Clarksdale?"

Cissa did write up an account of the women's suffrage protest and Mr. Hodges did run it in the *Marchelle Advocate,* although he cut almost half of what she wrote, making the event sound rather insignificant. Much to her surprise, Mr. Carson ran her account in its entirety in the *Natchez Herald,* word for word as she'd written it, under the headline "Lady Visiting From the Country Witnesses Protest." A couple of days later she received a note of congratulations from Liz: "You see? Mr. Carson may be a bit old-fashioned, but he can recognize worthy journalism when he sees it."

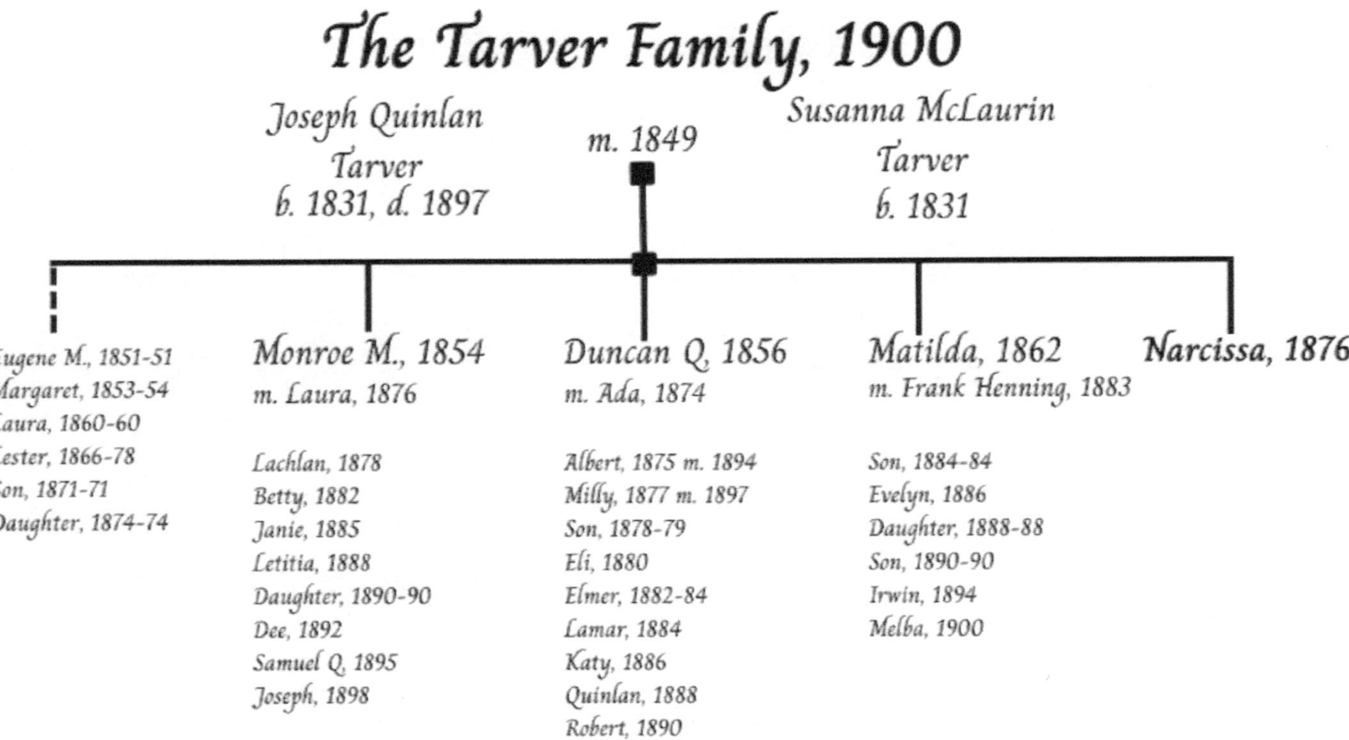
The Tarver Family, 1900
Joseph Quinlan Tarver
b. 1831, d. 1897
m. 1849
Susanna McLaurin Tarver
b. 1831
Eugene M., 1851-51
Margaret, 1853-54
Laura, 1860-60
Lester, 1866-78
Son, 1871-71
Daughter, 1874-74
Monroe M., 1854
m. Laura, 1876
Lachlan, 1878
Betty, 1882
Janie, 1885
Letitia, 1888
Daughter, 1890-90
Dee, 1892
Samuel Q., 1895
Joseph, 1898
Duncan Q., 1856
m. Ada, 1874
Albert, 1875 m. 1894
Milly, 1877 m. 1897
Son, 1878-79
Eli, 1880
Elmer, 1882-84
Lamar, 1884
Katy, 1886
Quinlan, 1888
Robert, 1890
Matilda, 1862
m. Frank Henning, 1883
Son, 1884-84
Evelyn, 1886
Daughter, 1888-88
Son, 1890-90
Irwin, 1894
Melba, 1900
Narcissa, 1876

Chapter Twenty-Nine
New Century, Dark Times

1900

On the first of January 1900, Cissa felt that something momentous had happened. The Nineteenth Century had ended, and they were now commencing the Twentieth Century. Several newspaper articles declared that in fact the old century wouldn't end until 1900 finished, with 1901 being the opening year of the new century. Cissa understood the logic but continued to feel that there was something exceptional about this January 1, 1900.

The feeling didn't last. On the second of January, Cissa dropped off another routine contribution for Mr. Clay to convey for the Wednesday edition of the *Marchelle Advocate.* She returned down Callander Road, walking heedlessly while musing over what she might write about next. There was so little going on in her small orbit, centered as it was on home, Rundle Springs, and Callander. How she longed to return to Natchez or even Marchelle.

She looked up and saw, in the distance, a woman walking toward her. The woman was wearing a dress of a fashionable cut. *Unusual for a Negro,* Cissa thought. With a start, Cissa realized that the woman was Julia, and for the merest moment she wanted to run to her, to put her arms around her and be enfolded in the familiar security of Julia's strong soft arms. But those arms belonged to others now.

Cissa picked up her pace. How long had it been since she'd seen Julia? A torrent of emotions stirred in Cissa's heart; remembered affection twisted up with memories of those days when she'd been convinced that Julia no longer cared about her. Could those be Julia's children walking on either side of her, the tall boy and the bonny little girl?

"Julia!" Cissa called out as she came nearer.

Julia greeted her with a smile but did not offer the hug for which Cissa hungered. "Miss Cissa," she said. "How are you keeping?"

"Oh, I'm fine," Cissa said. "You're looking well." Julia looked older and there was something about her eyes that had changed. They always used to look so deep and soft. Now they looked shuttered, wary. "I love your dress, Julia." The dress was almost identical to one Cissa had seen in a shop window in Natchez.

"This here one of my frocks I make," Julia said, stroking the skirt proudly. "I sews for lots of folks these days. Folks brings me cloth and a dollar and I stitch up whatever they like. Seems as how I gots a knack for cuttin' and fittin' and stitchin'. And now I got my sewin' machine, work go easy."

"That's wonderful, Julia." Cissa suppressed the twinge of jealousy that accompanied the news of Julia's sewing machine. She wondered if "folks" included "white folks." She could almost feel the texture of the cloth she had coveted from the Natchez shop. "How are the children? Rosie must be, what, twelve or thirteen now? And is that Hiram there with you?"

"All my chil'ren peart and fine, Miss Cissa. Rosie fifteen now and this here Chisum. Hiram at home with his sister. The little 'un here be Isabella. She near five." Julia patted her belly. "There be one more come January."

"That soon?" Cissa admired the artful construction of Julia's dress even more, the clever way it disguised her advancing pregnancy. "And how is your husband?" Cissa knew enough about pregnancy to figure Julia's husband must be back.

Julia averted her gaze, staring down the road toward Callander, her likely destination. "He keepin' well. Come for a visit now and again. Cain't leave his good work."

"Is he still in Memphis?"

"No, ma'am. He in Tulsa now. Up in Oklahoma. He work in a bank."

An image arose in Cissa's mind of a Negro pushing a broom inside a bank building.

Julia continued, "He say what he do is called 'teller.' He handle lots of money." She raised her chin a bit higher.

"Oh," Cissa said. "That sounds very important." Her mental image tried to readjust itself, but it was difficult. How could a colored man be a bank teller?

The two women talked a few minutes more. Julia never met Cissa's eyes again as she kept edging in the direction of Callander.

"Well, I won't keep you further, Julia." Cissa said, "I'm sure you have somewhere to be." Cissa laughed. "Unlike me. I'm just going home to tend Mother and stir up something for supper. It's just that it's so good to see you. And your precious children." Julia hadn't asked about Susanna or anyone else in Cissa's family. "I'm ever so happy to hear about your sewing business. Maybe I could bring you something one day and you could stitch up a dress for me."

"For white folks, mostly I goes to them to take measures and such," Julia said. "Come now, Isabella," she called to her little daughter who crouched in the grass watching a chipmunk. "It was nice to see you, Miss."

And then Julia was gone.

Cissa continued homeward, looking over her shoulder a couple of times, noting Julia's purposeful stride and how it contrasted with her own hesitant meandering.

Duncan's visits to the big house had become a regular thing as he sought to keep his medical practice and political influence active in Hinson County as well as in Fulton County where he lived. Cissa tried to make peace with the fact that Pop's desk was now Duncan's. His political gatherings were generally accompanied by the aroma of cigars, a habit he had taken up ever since his foray to Cuba in the war with Spain. Cissa could also tell what business her brother was about when he brought one of his sons: If it was Lamar, the business was medicine, but if it was Eli, it would be politics. Today it was Eli who had accompanied him.

Cissa busied herself dusting the furniture in the parlor. Mother had gone back to her bedroom, which she did sometimes, just to sit on the bed and stare out the back window toward the big cedar tree that was so often swaddled in wildflowers.

The conversation from the dining room caught Cissa's ear.

"I hear they finally set loose the fellows they been holding in the jail down there in Chahtah these two months. You know, the ones took care of the nigger what shot old man Preston."

The voice sounded vaguely familiar and Cissa tried to recall if she had seen this person when he entered her brother's study. Thinking she could take this opportunity to practice her shorthand, she picked up her notebook.

"Of course they did," Duncan answered. "No self-respecting white man would vote to indict his fellow citizen for trying to protect his own."

There was a shuffling of feet followed by Eli's voice. "So if those men didn't hang the fellow who shot Preston, who did?"

Duncan chuckled. "Nobody said they didn't do it, Eli. Only that there was insufficient evidence brought before the grand jury. No evidence, no indictment."

Cissa frowned at her brother's breezy manner. He'd served as a legislator before. And wasn't his Farmers' Protective Union supposed to be about upholding the law? Cissa continued her notetaking.

"There's more rumblings about that nigger society they been organizing down around Vandy. Something's coming, mark my word."

Cissa still couldn't place the voice. She kept writing, listening more intently now.

"All the more reason why we have to be organized ourselves in order to push back on such nonsense," Duncan said. "Eliminate the troublemakers before they get off the ground."

"My pa recollects what happened over at Willow Creek back when he was just a young'un. Slaves burnt that plantation house down to the ground with that little gal inside. Such things could happen again."

After Duncan escorted his two friends from the office, he entered the parlor and saw Cissa's notebook on the table. He picked it up. "What's this scribbling?" There was a jeer in his tone.

"I was just practicing my shorthand," Cissa said, holding out her hand to receive the notebook.

"And what did you write down?" Duncan's tone had changed.

"I like to practice writing down what I hear. It's nothing," she said.

"You wrote down what we said? That's what all this means? Read it to me." He handed the notebook back to Cissa.

She read a few lines.

"Stop," Duncan said. "That's enough. Now give me those pages." He scowled. "And in future refrain from writing down my private conversations."

Cissa resented his demand but told herself that if all she was doing was practicing, then the practice had already been accomplished and she didn't need to keep the notes. "Of course," she said. She gave him the pages.

Duncan went back into the dining room. A moment later Eli came out to request coffee for his father. He accompanied Cissa to the kitchen.

On the kitchen table was Cissa's latest copy of the *Marchelle Advocate*, laying open to a story on page two that had drawn Cissa's attention. It was flagged by a headline about a lynching in Chahtah County. When Eli picked up the paper, Cissa asked, "Is that what your pop and the other men were talking about?"

"Among other things," Eli said. His voice was mild and almost soothing. Such a contrast to his father's voice. He turned a page. "Did you read this story about the eclipse coming up next week? They say the moon will cross in front of the sun and we'll be under its shadow for a few minutes. I think that sounds awfully exciting. It's happening early in the morning."

Cissa thought Eli sounded more animated talking about this eclipse than he did when discussing politics and it made her smile. "I'm always up early, so do you think I should take a peek?"

"Definitely, Aunt Cissy. It's a truly rare thing."

Cissa poured two cups of coffee and after Eli left the kitchen with them she poured one for herself and sat down to read her paper. She found the article about the eclipse. It did, indeed, sound like an inspiring phenomenon.

She turned back to the article about the lynching in Chahtah. As Duncan's associate had said, the twelve men who had been held on charges of lynching had been released after the grand jury declared there was insufficient evidence to indict them.

It seemed to Cissa that cases of whitecapping and lynching were becoming far too common. She had been haunted for days after reading of a case in one of the northern counties in which three Negroes—a mother along with her son and daughter—had been beaten and hung in connection with a murder involving the consumption of illicit whisky at a blind tiger establishment. Later on, someone completely unconnected to the three had been convicted of the murder. As far as Cissa could tell, those who had done the lynching were never punished. No one seemed to care that three innocent Negroes had been brutally killed for a crime they didn't commit. Cissa had had a terrifying dream about this case in which the three Negroes hanged were Zolene and Julia and her brother Benny. Thinking of it again made her shudder.

She turned the page and saw a couple of short articles about the question of women's suffrage. One of them was a brief report stating that the general assembly of the Presbyterian Church had refused to offer support for the cause, despite a plea sent to them by Susan B. Anthony. Cissa had run across that name before. She knew that several states had already granted the vote to women in all elections except federal ones. Some articles—even a few written by women—argued that voting was too burdensome for women, since it would distract them from their primary responsibilities as wives and mothers.

But what about those of us who are fully adult but neither wife nor mother? Cissa thought. She had turned twenty-four at her last birthday. Unlike Matilda's case, no one seem concerned by the fact that Narcissa was now entering her mid-twenties with no prospect of marriage. Her nephew Eli—four years her junior—was courting a girl from Fulton County and expected to announce his engagement any day.

On Tuesday evening Cissa prepared a piece of smoked glass, which the paper had said would be necessary if she wished to view the solar eclipse without damaging her eyes. On Wednesday morning she went outdoors early, while Mother was still abed.

The sun rose clear, and the birds twittered and chirped in their morning chorus. Cissa's mind flitted to the dawn walk she'd taken searching for Nubby. She remembered feeling safe in the certainty that this time of day belonged to people like Nubby.

Just as the day became bright, it began to darken again, even though there were few clouds in the sky. Cissa walked down the steps and into the yard. She looked through her smoked glass toward the sun and saw how a piece of its disk had disappeared. Remembering what she'd read, she tried to imagine this as the edge of the moon and the darkness she was experiencing as its shadow. After a while, the birds fell silent and somewhere in the distance a dog barked. As the morning grew darker and quieter Cissa was moved to tears, filled with an oppressive sadness as the day's beginning was overwhelmed by darkness. She looked again at the sun through the dark glass and saw only a bare sliver of brightness. But then, as she sat there on the front steps with tears on her face, it began to grow light again. Shortly, the birds resumed their chatter. A rooster crowed. Cissa took a deep breath and went indoors to make breakfast.

Chapter Thirty
Almost a Real Journalist

1901

"Message for Cissa Tarver!" Milton had taken to announcing communiques from Mr. Hodges by shouting at the front door. Cissa found it amusing. Mother did not.

"Why does that boy shout like that?" she grumbled. "He needs to knock politely like a proper young gentleman."

Cissa ignored her, opening the door to accept the note Milton held in his hand. "Thanks, Milton. Will you be waiting for a reply?"

"Yes, ma'am. My pop says it's urgent and Cousin Martin wants a reply right away." The boy did enjoy sounding important.

Cissa invited him to come in while she read the message, but he said he preferred waiting on the porch.

"Such a lot of commotion," Mother fussed.

Cissa assured her that everything was alright. If Mother had it her way, there would never be anything happening at the Tarver place ever. Cissa stood by the window and opened the envelope.

"Dear Miss Tarver," she read. "I would like for you to come to Marchelle and cover an important trial at the County Courthouse on Tuesday next. This could be accomplished in a day if you can arrive early and stay late enough to complete your account. Please reply forthwith. You will of course be compensated. Sincerely, Martin Hodges."

Cissa was incredulous. She was finally being asked to cover a story like a real reporter, a real journalist. She glanced across the room to where Mother sat with knitting in her lap that had progressed little over the past week. Cissa must think how to present this to her mother. She knew she could not offer Mr. Hodges a response without first considering Mother.

"I'm going to dash down to Monroe's for a few minutes," Cissa said. "Can I get you anything before I go?"

"No, dear. I'm fine." Mother picked up her knitting and then laid it back down again.

Cissa hoped that one of Monroe and Laura's older girls would be able to stay with Mother for a day or two. At first Laura, who was hugely pregnant, demurred. But Betty, Janie, and Letty insisted that among them, they would be more than able to look after everyone—their mother, their younger siblings, and their grandmother. In fact, they seemed excited about the prospect of such grownup responsibility and happy to help their Aunt Cissy who was going to visit Aunt Tilly in Marchelle.

Rushing back home, Cissa took a moment on the front porch to catch her breath and steel her nerves.

Entering the parlor, she settled herself casually onto the end of the couch nearest her mother's chair and explained her plan. "Betty says she would be happy to stay here with you until I get back." She took a deep breath and waited.

"Oh," Mother said. "Something for the paper. Betty would be here? She's such a dear child. She makes nice biscuits, doesn't she?"

"Very nice biscuits, Mother. Better than mine. I'm certain you and she will enjoy your time together."

"Yes, I'm glad Betty wants to come stay with us a day or two."

"Well, I won't be here, Mother. Just you and Betty. I'll be in Marchelle."

"With Matilda. Oh, it's nice that you've decided to visit her. You should get out more."

Cissa decided to take this as an agreement and, kissing her mother on the cheek, she hurried to the study to dash off a quick note for Mr. Hodges.

Although the trial in Marchelle was a good opportunity for Cissa to prove the worth of her shorthand, it was not as exciting as she had hoped it might be—a dispute over a land deed that affected plans to construct a new school. "Why couldn't you have covered it?" Cissa asked her friend Liz as the two women sat in the office eating sandwiches during the lunch break from the trial.

"I've given notice," Liz said.

Cissa almost choked on her bite of sandwich. "What? Why? But you love it here."

"I do. You know I do." Liz blinked furiously. "Did you know I was engaged to be married?"

Cissa had not known. She tried to recall if Liz had ever even mentioned a man in her life.

"Well, I am engaged," Liz continued. "My fiancé Bill has been in Texas getting set up in business. But now things are getting on well and he's sending for me."

"And you'll go?" Cissa's view of Liz Smith was shaken. Liz was her model of an independent woman, employed on her own account. She was even an activist of sorts for women's suffrage.

"Yes," Liz said. "Oh, I know what you must think, that I'm abandoning a promising career in favor of a life as housewife and mother. But it's not like that. You'd have to know Bill. He's in favor of women's suffrage, too. And the business that he's starting up is a small printing and publishing establishment. We'll be working together. Yes, of course I'll also be expected to be a housewife and I suppose that someday we'll have children, but..."

Cissa didn't know whether to be angry at Liz or sorry for her. Or was she perhaps envious that Liz might be able to combine a job she loved with a husband and family? "Well, I will certainly miss you. Where will you be going in Texas?"

"San Antonio. It's way over in the interior of the state. Bill says it has a lot of possibility."

Mr. Hodges walked in the front door and, surveying the two women's somewhat emotional countenances, he stopped. "So I suppose Liz has told you about her plans? Has she told you about mine?"

"No, I'm leaving that to you," Liz said.

Cissa turned toward Mr. Hodges expectantly.

"I want to offer you Liz's job, Miss Tarver," Mr. Hodges said.

Cissa was stunned. "You...me?" She was embarrassed by the pathetic squeak in her voice.

"I realize you will need to consult with your family before giving me an answer," he said. "The pay would be a little less than what Liz has been receiving; she's been rewarded for her years of experience. But we can discuss all the details later."

"I'm flattered," Cissa said, trying not to sound as flustered as she felt. The sparkle in her eyes and the insistent smile on her face left little doubt as to what her answer would be if the decision were solely up to her. But it wasn't. "How soon will you need to know?"

Mr. Hodges indicated that he was willing to give her a week to decide. "That's when Liz will be leaving us, and I really can't get along without the kind of help and support she provides. And the kind of help I know you'd provide."

When Cissa returned to the courthouse to cover the final hours of the trial, it was difficult for her to maintain her focus. *What will Mother say? Would Betty be able to move in and care for Mother? Could Matilda provide a place for me at her house?* She forced herself to write more notes than usual, not trusting her memory.

After writing up her story, Cissa lingered at the *Advocate* office, pressing Liz for more details of her day-to-day activities. Liz explained about copy editing and proofreading. She found a printed sheet of standard proofreader's marks to give to Cissa. "This is what you'll use in marking up copy that comes in before giving it to the typesetters. Though sometimes you may want to do a full rewrite. Yes, some of it is that bad." Liz laughed. "Have you ever used a typewriter?"

Cissa shook her head and held up her damaged right hand. "I've never tried," she said, "though I've often wished to."

"There's this new system called touch typing that is very fast, but most people manage to type using just two or three fingers. I'm sure you'll be able to figure it out. Just a matter of learning where the keys are and learning how to strike them just so."

Cissa glanced up at the clock on the wall. "Oh, dear. My sister will be wondering what's become of me." She rose and reached out her left hand to bid Liz goodbye, but Liz drew her into an embrace. "Will I see you again before you leave?" Cissa asked, feeling unexpectedly distressed about being parted from her friend Liz.

"Likely not," Liz said, releasing her embrace but keeping both of Cissa's hands in hers. "But we can write." She turned and reached for a pencil and, in the margins of the paper containing proofreader's marks she wrote down her address in San Antonio.

"And how shall I address you," Cissa said, "given that you're about to be married?"

A brief frown flitted across Liz's face. "I suppose the appropriate form will be 'Mrs. William Benson'," she said. She held the paper out to Cissa. "Promise you'll write?"

"I promise," Cissa said.

"Wherever have you been?" Matilda scolded as Cissa entered the front hallway. "I'd begun to think you'd left for home without telling me!"

"I'm sorry, I got tied up at the newspaper office."

"Newspaper," Matilda scoffed, though her tone was not entirely convincing. "I didn't think they'd claim you for the entire day. Was it an exciting trial, then?"

"The trial was rather mundane." Cissa took a deep breath. "But it was an exciting day, nonetheless. Mr. Hodges has offered me a regular job at the paper."

"Really?" Matilda's tone was dubious, but her smile betrayed the possibility that she might be proud of her younger sister. "You must tell me all about this."

So Cissa did, offering all the details she knew over her plate of cold supper. "Do you think Mother will agree?" she said at last as she put down her fork and placed her refolded napkin next to her empty plate.

"Oh, Cissy, I wish she would!" Matilda leaned on her elbows across the table, her chin in her hands. "I'd love to have you live here with us. You could be such a help with the children." She lay her hand on her expanding waistline.

Cissa couldn't suppress a slight smirk. Was she to be thought of as no more than a family caretaker no matter where she went? This was not, however, the time to argue that point. "You know it's what I want to do," she said. "Let's hope that Mother has got on well with Betty and Betty with her. That could be a good arrangement, don't you think?"

⁂

With Matilda's husband Frank's assistance, Cissa was able to get a conveyance back to Callander early the next morning. As she walked the final mile home, she went over and over in her mind the things she might say to her mother. *It's a wonderful opportunity. I would learn so many useful skills.* She didn't think those arguments were likely to sway her mother in the least. What she really wanted to say was, *I need to get away from here, get out on my own, find out what I'm capable of.* But she knew she couldn't say that.

As Cissa approached Monroe's house, with her own now visible in the distance, she saw Betty on the porch, signaling to her. "Aunt Cissy!" Her voice was faint but clear.

Cissa's heart skipped a beat. Why was Betty here and not with Mother? She quickened her steps, almost running. Betty ran to meet her. "What's happened?" Cissa asked. "Is Mother alright?"

"Grandma's fine," Betty said. "She's inside. It's my mother who's not well." Tears welled up as she continued. "She started having pains yesterday and then fits. The baby came but..." She shook her head.

"Oh, Betty, I'm so sorry." Cissa hurried up the steps alongside Betty. She'd recognized Duncan's horse tied up on the big live oak. "What does Duncan say?"

Betty let out a strangled sob. "He said Mother could have died. I was so scared, Aunt Cissy." She turned toward Cissa with her big watery eyes and Cissa could do no other than draw the girl into an embrace.

Duncan stared daggers at Cissa as she entered the house, her arm around Betty's shoulders. "Fine daughter you are," he said, "running off and leaving Mother like that when Betty was needed here with her own mother."

"We couldn't have known Mother would come to her time so soon." Lachlan said. "Mother agreed for Betty to go and stay with Grandma. I was here to go for you and Janie stayed with Mother. I'm not sure what would have gone differently if Cissa had been here, Uncle Duncan."

"It's the principle of the thing, Lachlan." Duncan spoke in his stump-speech tone—authoritative, allowing no quarter for disagreement. "Cissa's place was with Mother, not running off to some little job that would have been better performed by a man anyway. Lachlan, pull the cart around and take your grandmother and Cissy home where they belong. Laura needs peace and quiet."

Cissa was genuinely sad for Laura and the loss of her baby, but her heart was also breaking over the knowledge of how this episode would stymie any hope of her taking the job at the *Advocate*. She did as she was told and swallowed down her despair.

Chapter Thirty-One
Life Goes on Around Her

1901-02

A reply came on Friday from Mr. Hodges to Cissa's note declining his job offer. She focused on two sentences: "Your talents will be difficult to match." And "I will continue to offer you assignments." She clutched the note in her fist, clutching too at her heart that pounded with all the frustration she could not voice as she made her way out the kitchen door, past the shed, around the barn, and down toward the creek.

Cissa had wanted that job. She had to acknowledge this to herself. She had wanted it very much. In fact, she still wanted it. Or something like it. Even in childhood, she had never felt more trapped than she did in this moment. She recalled her impulse to run away when she was ten and had gotten in trouble for trying to borrow a school book to take home for Julia. It happened again a couple of years later when she'd been admonished for claiming as her own the essay that Albert had stolen from her. Now she felt as if her whole future was being snatched away.

Cissa loved her mother. Of course she did. And she felt guilty for having abandoned her to Betty's care when she went to cover the trial in Marchelle. She kept telling herself there was no way she could have known that Laura would fall ill the way she had. Her intellectual conviction of this truth was undermined by the echo of her brother Duncan's words: "Cissa's place was here with Mother." And even more distant, but still clear in her mind, his admonition when she'd written exactly what happened at his canvass speech instead of the flattering account he'd desired: "You betrayed your own, and you must never do that again. We are family and family support one another."

Do they? Cissa asked herself, searching for instances in which anyone in her family had come forward to support her. Well, there was Lachlan, of course. He was loyal. Lachlan was the one who had recommended Cissa to Johnny's uncle as a good writer. He'd even spoken up for Cissa in the face of Duncan's harsh words on Wednesday. But mostly, she acknowledged, it was the young who were expected to support their elders and women who must support their men. Cissa was both young and a woman.

Cissa crumpled the note paper between her hands and was on the verge of tossing it into the creek. But then she stopped. Mr. Hodges had said nice things about her in that note. He still wanted her to work for the paper. He might even offer her more assignments. If such assignments entailed travel to Marchelle or beyond, Cissa was doubtful that she'd be able to accept them. And, oh, how she wanted to be able to be a real reporter, traveling about and writing exciting stories that people read with avid interest.

She smoothed the paper out and folded it in quarters, tucking it into her bosom. She'd have to write to Liz, to let her know the sad news.

When she reached the house, Cissa found her mother standing in the kitchen doorway, holding it open wide as she mumbled something in what Cissa was now convinced had to be the old Scotch-Irish tongue.

"Let's go back inside, Mother." Cissa guided Susanna away from the dangerous back steps that had no railing. "Are you feeling poorly?"

Susanna uttered another unintelligible phrase and then looked up into her daughter's face with a start. "I... Poor Laura," she said. She stopped and leaned against a kitchen chair, swaying precariously as she clung to it. "It's the shee, Narcissa. They come for the babies."

Cissa recognized that word from the book she'd read about the commonwealth of fairies. She knew it referred to a type of Scottish magical folk. "No, Mother, Duncan said the baby was positioned poorly and then Laura had convulsions. It wasn't the shee."

Mother shook her head as a sigh stuttered from her throat. "Poor Laura," she said again. "And poor Maggie and Eugene..."

With a start, Cissa realized that the Laura her mother meant was not her daughter-in-law, or not *only* her daughter-in-law. It was also the little daughter Laura she had lost so soon after the loss of her first daughter, Maggie. Eugene was another of her lost babies, her firstborn. Cissa felt the need to do something to settle her mother back into reality, back into the here and now. "Sit down, Mother, and I'll get Elsie to make you some lemonade."

Cissa did write to Liz. And all through the summer and into the fall of 1902, Cissa carried on her correspondence with Liz Smith who was now officially Mrs. Captain William Benson. "Captain" because her husband had received a commission in the war against Spain. Liz found that appellation amusing. "Why should I be called 'Captain'?" she wrote. "I never served in the military."

Liz told Cissa she must begin keeping a string book of all her published articles. "You're worth more than Mr. Hodges is paying you," she wrote. "You should ask for more, but you need to have evidence of how much of what he prints is your work."

Cissa told Liz all about how Monroe and Laura kept trying to find a wife for Lachlan and how it never seemed to work out. She told Liz a little bit about their friend Johnny and hoped that Liz might understand why it was that Lachlan, approaching the age of twenty-four, was steadfastly disinterested in finding a bride. Lachlan's younger sister Betty, on the other hand, now had a beau and everyone expected that to culminate in marriage. Betty had just turned twenty.

Liz confessed to Cissa that her husband's business was not on such firm ground as she'd been led to believe. "We've ended up mostly printing advertising bills, but since our font inventory is limited, those don't look as good as we'd like them to."

Cissa expressed her sympathy and tried to reassure Liz that things would get better, though of course she had no grounds for such a prediction. All she had was that inexplicable glimmer of hope that refused to be extinguished in her own heart. Liz's confession, nonetheless, made Cissa want to reciprocate, so she told Liz that her nephew Albert's marriage seemed to be on rocky ground. She was uncertain how much detail to put into writing.

Albert's wife Eva had given birth to four sons in rapid succession, and she now suffered from various complaints that kept her in bed for days at a time. Albert grew surly, accusing his wife of being lazy and neglecting both husband and children. It had come to a head recently when Eva turned up at Laura and Monroe's house with a black eye and a sprained wrist. Laura said there were also marks on her back and buttocks that looked like the marks of a belt.

"Duncan was too easy on that boy when he was young and this is what it's come to," Monroe fumed. "Duncan would let him get away with murder." Cissa recalled Albert's theft of her essay and before that his theft of candy from the local shop and a melon from a neighbor's field. In every instance, he gleefully denied that he'd done anything wrong.

Cissa continued her diligent reading of the newspapers. There were more reports of whitecapping attacks on Negro homesteaders and laborers. There were several court cases that Cissa would have found far more exciting than the land dispute she'd covered for the *Marchelle Advocate.* The *Fulton Gazette* observed that "the county is threatened with an epidemic of crime in which guns and pistols are very much in evidence." The article went on to note that "an unusually large number of criminal cases now being disposed of by the Mississippi courts reach their final adjustment at the end of a grass rope."

There were also many column inches devoted to a dispute in Fulton County between Sheriff Newell (who had defeated Duncan in the last election) and the county treasurer Felix Cortman over some funds that Newell claimed he turned over to Cortman but which the treasurer swore he never received. The amount was something in excess of two thousand dollars.

"Why?" Cissa asked Duncan one day when he had joined them for a dinner of not quite burned pork chops and only slightly lumpy mashed potatoes. "Why does this case of the missing funds down in Fulton not get resolved? They keep sending it up the chain of courts time after time. Didn't the treasurer already make good on the sum that Sheriff Newell claimed was missing?"

Duncan chuckled. "It's not about the money anymore, little sister. Neither man wants his good name sullied by accusations of theft or fraud. But I'll tell you, people have pretty much picked sides and decided whose story they believe."

"Don't they just want to know the truth?"

"They want to know who wins and who to ally themselves with." And that was all Duncan had to say on the matter, taking the opportunity of having an attentive listener to launch into complaints about the dire labor situation. "I tell you, we're going to be hard pressed to have enough hands to bring in the cotton crop this year."

Cissa took another helping of potatoes for herself and passed the bowl to her mother. "If that's so," she said, "then why are these whitecappers threatening Negroes all the time? Isn't that why so many of them are leaving the area?"

"Lots of them are being lured away by agents sent from some of the Delta plantations." Duncan scowled as he helped himself to another pork chop and more potatoes. "And as for the whitecappers, well the intention is..." Duncan paused as he sawed at his pork chop. "I believe the intention is only to put the Negroes in their place, not to scare them off altogether. Negroes have been leaving for years now, little sister. Once they get a bit of education they get discontented with their proper place in society and go off somewhere thinking they can do better. I think most of them eventually come back. I would say 'sadder but wiser,' but wisdom is probably not a quality available to Negroes. So I'll just say they return more resigned to their lot in life. Although..." He frowned.

"Although what?" Cissa couldn't help thinking about Julia's husband and how he'd gone north looking for work. According to Julia, he did not intend to come back. Not to stay, anyway.

"Ah, there are always a few troublemakers, trying to organize Negro secret societies and the like. Of course, that has to be scotched before it can do any real harm. Law and proper order must be maintained." Duncan stared at the ceiling for a moment and then leaned forward toward Cissa. "We're starting up a new organization down in Fulton County, Cissy. A Farmers' League. I want you to write up something about it for the Marchelle paper."

Cissa cringed. Would she be allowed to write what she wanted or only what Duncan wanted? What she said was: "Of course. What can you tell me about it? Is this related to the Farmers' Protective Union?" That was the organization Duncan had formed back before Pop died.

"Oh, this is much more significant. I'll give you a copy of our declaration of purpose and the text of a resolution we passed. And I'll tell you that there were some six hundred men at our first meeting, including all of Fulton County's leading citizens. They made me president." His chin lifted slightly as he said this. "I think we've got a system set up that will bring much better order to our county. We're applying for a charter from the state."

After Duncan left, Cissa sat at her father's desk and perused the materials he'd left her. The avowed motto—"Unity and Charity"—was certainly appealing. That was their first stated purpose. The second was "to elevate mankind mentally, morally and financially." She continued reading: "Third: To perfect a better system of upholding civil officers in maintaining law and order. Fourth: To exert our powers to secure harmony among all mankind and to promote the interests of the laboring classes. Fifth: To harmonize racial differences, to suppress riotous conduct and to adopt a better system for controlling labor."

Cissa read through the purposes again. These all sounded high-minded and noble, though only peripherally related to farming. It sounded as if Duncan might truly be making an effort to improve conditions rather than—as Cissa generally believed motivated him—to promote himself. The organization's single resolution was this: "Resolved: That we will not tolerate or countenance any violations of the law, or any hoodlumism of any kind…" If Duncan had been there, Cissa would have pressed him to explain how his organization with its six hundred members meant to do that, but he wasn't there so she simply quoted the resolution in its entirety and placed her article in an envelope to convey to Mr. Clay the next day. It would be in Mr. Hodges' hands for publication in the Saturday paper.

When the Beckport paper arrived on Friday, Cissa was mildly annoyed to see that they had already published the information about the Fulton County Farmers' League. Their account, however, included an editorial caveat. The editor indicated that they would be fully in support of the Farmers' League "if the above was the real animus and object of the organization." However, the piece continued, "there is strong circumstantial evidence tending to show that this so-called Farmers' League, which comes before the public in such fair and seductive guise, is largely responsible for, and some of its members actually engaged in the reign of lawlessness now prevailing in portions of these counties." The editor charged that the citizens who had formed the organization were themselves the likely perpetrators of the very acts they claimed to condemn.

Cissa frowned as she read the passage again. Could this be true? Could Duncan and this organization of which he was president be engaged in such activities? She knew the editor was talking about whitecapping, about the recent round of threats to Negroes, especially those who worked for merchants and those who were trying to establish their own farms outside the purview of white farmers and planters. She'd heard from Monroe that several black farmers had been beaten, and one house burned. And there was that mysterious death of a young black man in Fulton County that they'd been unable to pin on anyone.

Chapter Thirty-Two
An Incident on Callander Road

1902

A few days after Cissa's article about Duncan's Farmers' League appeared in the *Marchelle Advocate*, Lachlan slipped into her house in the early morning with a warning. "There was an incident here on Callander Road last night," he said. "My pop wanted me to give you this." Lachlan laid a pistol on the table in front of Cissa. "I know you've never shot a handgun, but at least it could work to scare someone off if they threatened you."

Cissa stared blankly at the weapon. "An incident?" Her mind was still trying to grasp the situation, which appeared to be dire enough to recommend the use of firearms. "What kind of incident? Who would threaten me and Mother?"

"All I know is that there was an incident just up the road here. Shots were fired into a house, and there may have been injuries."

Cissa had so many questions. Up the road where, exactly? Who did the shooting? Whom did they injure? But what she asked was, "Was it whitecappers?" Her heart sank, thinking of the colored community "just up the road" where Zolene lived. Where Julia lived.

Lachlan glanced over his shoulder, out the window in the direction of Julia's place. "It sounded like whitecap work," he said. "Pop says the Negroes may try to strike back. He says they've been getting plenty riled up lately. I'll let you know if we hear anything more."

Cissa's mind reeled backward to a time when Julia had been the center of her universe. Was she alright? Surely Julia and her kin, her community, were no threat to Cissa. But who had been hurt?

Whatever had happened, Julia would know.

Cissa picked up the pistol. "Show me how to use it," she said.

Lachlan took some bullets from his pocket and showed Cissa how to load the gun. Then he showed her how to hold it in her left hand and support it with her right. "If you fire it, it's going to kick back pretty hard, so brace yourself. And don't fire unless you have to."

Cissa tried to imagine what circumstances would constitute having to fire a pistol at someone. Or at least toward them. She took a deep breath and laid the pistol back on the table.

"You probably won't want to let Grandma see that you have it," Lachlan said.

Cissa had never seen her mother with a firearm, but surely she'd had some kind of weapon during the war when Pop was away tending to injured soldiers and avoiding Yankees.

"Pop was saying that it would be a good idea for you and Grandma to come and stay with us for a few days. Until things settle down. I wasn't sure how you'd feel about that." He stepped back from the table where the pistol lay.

Ordinarily Cissa might have resisted the implication that she couldn't take care of herself. But this was also about Mother. And it might suit Cissa's own purposes. "Maybe that would be best," she said.

"Do you want to come now? I've got the wagon out front."

"Take Mother now. I'll gather up some of our things and come down a little later. Yes, yes, I'll be careful."

Susanna asked no questions and did as she was bid. As soon as she was bundled into the wagon, Cissa went back inside the house, but instead of preparing a bag for their stay at Monroe's she sat down at her father's desk to prepare herself for what she knew she needed to do.

After taking a few deep breaths to calm her racing heart and murmuring some unaccustomed words of entreaty to the Almighty, she rose to go. After a moment's hesitation, she tucked Lachlan's pistol into her purse. *Just in case,* she told herself. She couldn't help recalling that day when Lachlan had first showed her how to shoot, the feeling of power she'd had with that rifle in her hands. *It's different when all of a sudden everybody's carrying a gun,* she thought as she donned coat and scarf and went out through the kitchen door.

She wouldn't take the main road. She didn't want to be seen. She'd take the old path by the creek and through the canebrake. Elsie had told her weeks ago that Julia and her children were back in their own house, so Cissa made her way there with rapid strides. Before long she found herself standing on Julia's front porch. The boards across the front windows caused her a moment's hesitation. Had Julia moved again? But, no, there were sounds from inside the cabin. The sounds stopped when Cissa knocked. A second knock was met with what felt like even deeper silence.

"Julia?" she called out softly. "Julia, it's me. Cissa. Are you there?"

The door opened and a hand emerged, pulling Cissa roughly inside the cabin.

"What you doin' here, Miss Cissa?" Julia hissed.

Cissa glanced around the darkened cabin and saw Zolene bending over a bed in the corner. Hiram and the younger children sat huddled together nearby. Cissa's hand went over her mouth. "Oh, Julia, not you! And Rosie?" She hurried to the bedside where she saw the young woman, her left shoulder covered in a bloody cloth. Cissa fell to her knees in tears.

Julia stood over Cissa, her arms crossed. "You got no business bein' here, Narcissa Tarver."

Cissa had never seen Julia so angry. "I'd heard someone had been hurt and I was afraid..."

"*You* was afraid? You?" A bitter laugh sputtered from Julia's lips.

"I was afraid those ruffians might have attacked you," Cissa said, rising to her feet and bristling slightly at Julia's tone. "And it seems I was right. I'm so sorry, Julia."

"Don't tell me you don't know who them ruffians be, Miss Cissa. Don't you try and tell me you don't know what your own brother Duncan be up to. He and his mob all up in this, Miss Cissa. Can't say as he the one shot my Rosie, but I bet you he know who did."

Cissa's knees disengaged, and she sank back to the floor. "But...his League is supposed to be about keeping law and order, not about doing things like this." She thought about the article she'd written for the Marchelle paper. Was the *Beckport Journal* editor right? Was Duncan's Farmers' League merely a cover for whitecapping, for terrorizing Negro families? She looked up at Julia, halfway hoping the woman might offer her a hand or a chair but she didn't.

"Law for them, not for us," Julia said, forcing her words between clenched teeth. "And order they want is order that keep black folk sunk to the bottom. They gives the orders and we takes 'em."

Cissa tried to compose herself, tried to deny the tears that wanted to fall. Why had she come here where she clearly wasn't wanted?

At that moment the back door of the cabin opened, and a man stepped inside with an armload of firewood. Cissa looked up into the man's face and the two stared at one another in stunned silence.

"It's you," Cissa whispered. "You're the man who brought me home when I fell. Are you...?" Her head jerked toward Julia, her mind spinning almost as it had that day when she'd hit her head.

"Yes, Miss Cissa. This my Baxter. This my husband your brothers sent away from his family. But he don't forget us. Baxter, he don't scare easy. He come back. He keep comin' home and we keep workin', makin' our place." She reached out her hand to Baxter as he finished stacking the wood next to the stove.

Baxter's eyes were like nothing Cissa had ever seen—a cold, controlled anger that burned into her very soul. She felt exposed and vulnerable, aware of a power in this man even while she knew he would not use it to harm her. How had she not known that it was Baxter who had rescued her that day? Maybe she hadn't wanted to know, hadn't wanted to believe that the man who had been ordered away after offering kindness was none other than her beloved Julia's husband?

Cissa struggled to her feet and, smoothing her skirt, looked around at the little black family as if seeing them for the first time. "I'm so sorry," she said. It was all she could think of to say. She stared at Baxter, this tall, strong, very black man with intelligent, hateful eyes and a pistol strapped to his hip.

"You probably shouldn't be here," Baxter said.

Cissa remembered that voice. So calm. So confident. "I'm sure it's alright," she said. "I can go where I please."

"Sure you can." Julia harrumphed, crossing her arms over her bosom. "White gal go wherever she please. Black folk get ordered go here go there, don't go there."

Julia's anger cut Cissa to the core. But she knew Julia was right. Cissa was accustomed to going where she pleased. But this was Julia's house. And Baxter's. If they said she shouldn't be here, shouldn't she respect that? Didn't they have a right to say who was in their own house?

"I'll go," Cissa said. "Is Rosie going to be alright? Is there anything you need?"

Zolene turned to answer. She looked exhausted. "She bad hurt, Miss Narcissa. She could use some lead sugar to stop this bleeding. And some opium for the pain. But we cain't call no white doctor."

"I can get that for you," Cissa said. "Duncan keeps some of his medicines there at the house. I know both of those. I'll go get it and bring it back."

"Mama, we don't need nothing from white folk. Let her be." Julia's voice fairly seethed with rage.

"For Rosie, Julia. We does what we has to for Rosie." Zolene's voice was soft but firm.

"It would be better for us to send someone to fetch it," Baxter said. "Chisum can go." Turning to the child and resting a hand on his shoulder, he said. "You just follow Miss Cissa up to her house, son. Keep well back. Don't go inside. She'll bring the medicine to the barn." He glanced up toward Cissa, who nodded her assent.

Fighting back tears, Cissa voiced her wishes for Rosie's recovery and took her leave. On the way home through the back pathways, she let the tears stream down her face unrestrained, her thoughts and feelings a chaotic tumble. There was remorse, and there was anguish over Julia's wrath. Whatever friendship might once have existed between Cissa and Julia was gone now and Cissa's heart was breaking.

Only once did she allow herself to glance over her shoulder to see that Chisum was there. She should have known—did know—that the child would be following his father's instructions. And she got the distinct feeling that he did it not out of fear or blind obedience, but out of trust and devotion. Maybe that was what loyalty was like.

"Where you going, boy?" A voice broke through the forest calm and Cissa spun around. A young white man was pointing a pistol at Chisum.

A prickling rage swept through Cissa so suddenly that it took her a moment to realize that she was now holding Lachlan's pistol in her own hands and pointing it at the young white man. "You leave him alone," she shouted, her voice erupting with a force she'd never known she possessed.

The white man turned his pistol toward Cissa and for an interminable moment the two stood facing one another with drawn weapons. "Narcissa?" the man said. He let his own gun drop to his side. "What are you doing out here?" His face contorted in a sneer. "This boy belong to you?"

Cissa kept her own pistol pointed toward the white man. "He belongs to no one but his family. Now you get on your way and leave the both of us alone."

The man laughed and, after holstering his pistol, held up both of his hands. "Only because it's you, Miss Tarver. But you tell these niggers they best behave themselves." He turned to go and then turned again toward Cissa, one hand still on his gun. "And you best mind your own self."

After the man was gone, Cissa dropped her pistol back inside her purse. Chisum had never moved from the spot where he'd been accosted. He stared at Cissa and then nodded, as if giving her permission to proceed.

As they continued down the path, Cissa's blood thrummed in her head as her spirit dropped to a place that knew no tears. This young boy's house had been riddled with bullets, his sister shot, and now he'd been threatened on a lonely pathway for no reason at all. She kept hearing the white man's voice in her head. She knew that voice. Her blood ran cold as she realized where she'd heard it: She'd heard it in Duncan's office, in her own home.

As for herself and her rash behavior, Cissa acknowledged that her white skin had been her salvation. And maybe the fact that she was a woman. If she'd been a Negro with a drawn pistol—man or woman—she'd have been dead now. She was absolutely certain that was true. If she'd been a white man... Well, she wasn't sure.

Cissa located the medicines Zolene had mentioned. She sat down at the desk and, with trembling hand, penned a brief note to Julia, promising to get whatever was needed for Rosie's recovery, telling her to leave notes in the woodbox by the old summer kitchen. Or she could send word with Elsie. She didn't mention the threat to Chisum. That was his story to tell. It was the first time Cissa had ever written a note to Julia. She took the medicines and the note to the barn and handed them over to Chisum. He accepted them with a nod and took off at a run for home. Cissa stood watching him, fearful for his safety. Then she noticed how he left the path and broke into the brush. He knew his way. Even at his tender age, he knew how to evade white men with guns. If he hadn't been trying to follow Cissa, it's likely he'd never have been noticed.

By the time Cissa reached the kitchen door, she was shaking uncontrollably. She poured a glass of water and gulped it down. She knew she had to pull herself together and get to Monroe's house before they sent out a posse to search for her. As she gathered up a few belongings to pack into a bag for her mother and herself, she brooded over how to explain her tardiness to Monroe. Should she tell him the truth about where she'd been, what she'd done? About what had happened? Or should she fabricate a lie? She wasn't comfortable with lying, but perhaps it was sometimes necessary. She focused on this instead of the greater dilemma of whether her brother Duncan was a whitecapper, whether it was indeed his men (surely not himself) who had shot multiple times into Julia's cabin, wounding Rosie, terrifying all of Julia's children, and infuriating Julia herself. She was certain that the man who confronted Chisum on the path was one of Duncan's friends. Cissa was still undecided as she made her way with leaden steps down the road toward her brother's house.

She slowed her pace even more when she recognized Duncan's horse tied up to the big oak tree in the front yard. Her heart raced as the anger she had tried to ignore surfaced with full fury. Why was Duncan here? She steeled herself and marched up the front steps, suitcase in hand.

"There you are," Laura said. "We were about to send Lachlan down to see about you."

Lachlan stepped forward with a half-smile and took the suitcase from Cissa's hand. It wasn't heavy. Just their night clothes, a change of body linen, and a few toiletries. It would have been even lighter if not for the pistol.

"What took you so long?" Duncan scolded. "You know it's dangerous out there."

She wanted to ask whose fault that might be, but she restrained herself. "It's not dangerous for me," she said, knowing from immediate experience that this was true. "It seems to be the Negroes who are in danger."

Duncan snorted and then chuckled. "Well, you're right about that, little sister."

Cissa's face reddened and her hands closed into fists. "You think that's funny?" she said. "You think it's funny that our Julia's daughter was shot and could have been killed?" Her voice got louder. "You find that amusing? I should write it all up for the papers and let them know exactly what your so-called Farmers' League is all about."

The slap came fast and hard, sending Cissa reeling backward, clutching her left cheek. "How dare you," Duncan snarled. "You have no idea what we're trying to do."

Cissa's cheek burned, and her jaw ached, but her mouth still worked. "I know what you *say* you're trying to do. But I have eyes and can see what's really happening."

As Duncan raised his hand to strike again, Monroe grabbed his arm. "Calm down, brother," he said. "There's no need for this. Cissy is obviously upset about Julia's girl being hurt. I'm sure she didn't mean what she said."

Cissa's eyes flashed fire but she kept her mouth shut, glaring at Duncan, whose right arm was still in Monroe's firm grip.

Duncan shook himself free. "Just remember who you are, young lady," he said. "The Tarver family sticks together. We've no need for any nigger lovers causing trouble."

If not for Laura's hands squeezing Cissa's shoulders, she might have said more as Duncan stormed out the front door. Then she caught sight of her mother seated across the room, staring in confused disbelief as tears glittered in her eyes. Cissa released the tension in her arms and shoulders and felt a lump rise in her throat. "Why is he like that?" she said.

No one answered.

"How do you know it was Julia's girl who got hurt?" Monroe asked.

Cissa realized that the moment for offering any of the plausible lies she'd formulated on her walk was long past. Truth would have to do. "Because I went to Julia's house to see if she and her family were alright."

"You went...?" Monroe's voice rose in anger and then he stopped himself. After a brief pause he simply asked. "And how is the girl doing?"

"She got hurt pretty bad, but Zolene is there looking after her." There was no way Cissa was going to say anything about the medicine. She also wasn't inclined to mention the episode on the pathway. "Why would those men shoot at Julia's house anyway? She's just a nice colored woman who happens to be a good seamstress."

"And who happens to be married to one of the worst Negro troublemakers in three counties." Monroe shook his head. "Didn't you know that?"

"Baxter? But he talks...educated. And you know he's the one who brought me home when I was injured, don't you?"

"I know. I didn't know at the time what he was to Julia. But Mother was so upset and Duncan felt like we had to do something. It's just too bad he didn't stay gone."

"How could he, when he has a wife and family here on Callander Road?"

Monroe said nothing, though his eyes strayed toward his two young sons playing in the corner.

"Do you want something to eat?" Laura asked. Her voice was soft and intimate. She still had one hand on Cissa's shoulder. "It's past dinnertime."

"No thanks," Cissa said. "I'm not hungry. But I would like to borrow a pen and some paper." She ignored the alarmed look that passed between Laura and Monroe.

Donna Birdwell

Chapter Thirty-Three
Brotherly Troubles

1902-03

Cissa wrote up her story about what had happened to Rosie, though she didn't name any names. She included a reference to hearsay about a lone young Negro boy being threatened by a pistol-toting white hoodlum. Before the rest of the household was up, she was on her way to Callander where she handed over her envelope to Mr. Clay.

"Make sure Mr. Hodges gets this," she said. "It's important."

Mr. Clay gave Cissa a puzzled look. She realized she must look a mess, with uncombed hair and half-buttoned shoes.

"I'll get it to him," he said.

As soon as she turned back toward Monroe's house, Cissa was seized with dread. What would Duncan say when the story ran? *I don't care*, Cissa told herself. She had written only what she knew to be true. She hadn't used names, neither Julia's nor her brother's. She hadn't mentioned the Farmers' League either, since she had no firm evidence that they were the ones who had caused harm to Julia's family. And she'd reported the incident with the young boy as local gossip. Mr. Hodges might very well excise that part for want of evidence. She hoped he wouldn't.

She had just taken off her coat when Lachlan came in with a newspaper. "There's something in the *Fulton Gazette* you should read, Aunt Cissy." He placed the open paper on the table and pointed to a headline: "Dr. Tarver Resigns - Will Not Be a Party to the Whitecap Lawlessness in This and Other Counties - Is Ready to Take a Hand in Stamping It Out."

"What?" Cissa picked up the paper and sat down. "Duncan said this?"

"Apparently," Lachlan said. "It's a letter he wrote. Maybe knowing it was your Julia's daughter got hurt in that shooting made him stop and think."

"No, he must have written this letter days ago for it to be in this edition of the paper," Cissa said. She began to read. The letter did seem to say just what the headline advertised. Duncan roundly condemned whitecapping as "unjust to the merchant who earned the plantation by the sweat of his brow or who inherited the land." It was also, he wrote, "an outrage on the farmer" and "a violation of the law and damaging to public interests." There was no mention of the suffering inflicted on Negro families.

The letter mentioned the rumors that had been circulating some months previous about "Negro preparations for war on the whites" and explained that the Farmers' League had been organized in response to just such threats. Cissa had heard these fears discussed, but she hadn't connected them to her brother's Farmers' League. Duncan concluded his letter by stating his belief that "the Negro, like the mule, is a necessary evil and should be treated right so long as he behaves himself." Cissa scowled, thinking of Julia and Baxter and their children and how decidedly un-mule-like they were.

There was a postscript to Duncan's letter calling for citizens to join in a mass meeting to be held on the first Saturday in January and declaring his formal resignation from the presidency of the Farmers' League.

Cissa didn't know what to think. She recognized the letter as a political piece, designed to appeal to the merchants and farmers and other good citizens and clearly not aimed at "nigger lovers" like herself. Is that what she was? Just because she held fond feelings for Julia and her family and gratitude toward the man who had rescued her when she'd been injured and helpless?

If Duncan was genuinely trying to distance himself from the whitecapping, perhaps Cissa ought to support him. Perhaps she shouldn't have sent her article to the *Advocate*. But didn't people need to know about what had happened to Rosie, regardless of who did it? Cissa's cheek stung as she recalled Duncan's reaction to her accusation that his Farmers' League might have been the ones responsible. And then Julia's words came back to her: "We don't need nothing from white folk." Quite possibly Julia herself would be angry at Cissa for writing the story.

Cissa expelled a huge sigh of frustration. It was all so confusing.

When the account of the shooting appeared in the *Marchelle Advocate* on Wednesday Cissa recognized that the story was not the one she had written. The reference to a lone young Negro boy being threatened at gunpoint was still there, but it looked like someone else had rewritten her material to incorporate information about a similar incident in Fulton County, just across the border from Hinson. She relaxed a bit, knowing that If Duncan asked her if she'd written this piece, she could truthfully answer that she had not.

It was decided that Cissa and Susanna would stay on at Monroe's through Christmas, for their own safety. In her heart, Cissa scoffed at this. Her encounter with the gun-toting white fellow had assured her that she was in no personal danger. She was also reasonably confident that she was under no threat from Baxter and whatever associates of his might live in the area. Why did men always try to make women feel more vulnerable and fearful than they needed to be?

Cissa went back to the big house on the next day that Elsie was due to work, meaning to tell her to come work at Monroe's house instead, but Elsie didn't show up. Cissa was not surprised. After what happened to Julia, Elsie might never come to work for the Tarvers again.

Cissa lamented the big house standing vacant while she and her mother endured the cramped quarters at Monroe's already overcrowded house, but she didn't argue. With Laura and her daughters working in the kitchen, there was little for Cissa to do other than read the papers.

Christmas passed with minimal festivity. There were small gifts for the children but none for the adults. Lachlan called Cissa aside and showed her a fine new book that had come for him in the mail from Johnny. "It's the latest Sherlock Holmes story," he said. The title was *The Hound of the Baskervilles.* He promised to let Cissa read it when he'd done with it.

Then with a mischievous grin he handed a wrapped package to Cissa. "Johnny sent you a gift, too, but I was selfish and wanted to show you mine first."

"You rascal," Cissa said as she gave her nephew a playful slap on the hand. She could tell the gift was a book and she tore away the paper to see what book it might be. The title was *Lady Rose's*

Daughter, by Mrs. Humphrey Ward. "I believe I've heard of Mrs. Ward," Cissa said, thinking to herself that this was perhaps the best Christmas gift she'd ever received.

Christmas dinner was ample. They'd prepared for Duncan and his family to join them, but Duncan decided they would spend Christmas in Cowleton instead, holding a big dinner for relatives and friends in Fulton County. Duncan sent a box of sweets for the children and a bottle of brandy for the grownups.

Two days after Christmas, Cissa and Susanna went back to their own house. Elsie showed up for work as if she had known when they'd return. Everyone acted as if nothing had changed. Whenever Cissa asked after Rosie, Elsie answered, "She alright, Miss," and offered no details.

Cissa continued to check the wood box next to the shed every day to see if there might be a message from Julia, but it wasn't until the last Thursday of the year that one finally appeared. "Miss Narcissa Tarver," it read. "Zolene says that Rosie will recover. Thank you." That was all. The handwriting was fluid and elegant, much nicer than Cissa would have expected of Julia, and she wondered if perhaps Baxter had written the note. Cissa was relieved, of course, to know that Rosie was going to be alright, but she had hoped for a few more words from Julia.

When an issue of the *Fulton Gazette* arrived on the front steps the next day, Cissa claimed it. She settled onto the couch in the parlor and began paging through, reading little more than headlines. One headline stopped her. "Dr. Tarver Reconsiders," it read. "He Writes a Second Letter Saying the Farmers' League Will be Expurgated and Exonerate Itself."

With some trepidation, Cissa began reading the text of her brother's new letter: "Since my last week's communication regarding the whitecappers in this county, my mind has undergone a complete change." Cissa threw the paper down in exasperation. What was Duncan up to now? She'd held out some lingering hope that he might finally dissociate himself from the Farmers' League and its alleged involvement with whitecapping. Now this? Clearly, someone had gotten hold of him and persuaded him to change his mind. Again. She didn't know who that might have been, but if all the members of the Farmers' League were indeed oath-bound, as the Beckport paper recently reported, that meant Duncan was as obligated to support the organization as anyone else. *What manner of monster have you created, Duncan?* Cissa wondered if it might be the kind of monster that would devour its creator.

Cissa picked up the paper again and read on. "Such an organization as the Farmers' League, represented by over six hundred good men and some of the very best the county affords, after the expurgation and reorganization that will follow the receipt of our charter, will present the best police force for law and order that could be procured." He wrote further, "I do not intend for the Farmers' League to be branded as whitecappers because of the action of a few turbulent men." He again disavowed "night meetings" and reiterated the open invitation to a "full meeting" on the third day of January on the grounds of the Cowleton courthouse.

Later that day while Cissa was visiting with Laura, Duncan dropped by. He studiously ignored Cissa. He'd come to invite Monroe to accompany him on a trip to Jackson the following week to meet with the governor. "We're going to invite him to the January gathering of the citizenry in Cowleton and we could do with a show of support from Hinson County as well," he said. "I need you there with me to make the point."

Monroe was scraping the inside of his pipe, and he continued his task without looking at his younger brother. "Except for the incident at Julia's place, Hinson has been mostly spared from whitecap activity. Besides, I doubt that my traveling with you to Jackson would be of much value." He tapped the debris from his pipe into an ashtray.

"I'm the better judge of that," Duncan said. "But if you don't want to go..."

"I've got a farm to run."

"And a grown son."

Monroe packed tobacco into his pipe and reached for the matches.

Duncan picked up his hat and left.

The governor didn't come to the meeting in Cowleton on the third of January. Instead, Duncan received a letter from the attorney general denying the Farmers' League's charter application. Cissa learned about this as she learned about so many things, by eavesdropping on conversations occurring in her father's old office between Duncan and a couple of his associates, while cigar smoke hung heavy in the air.

"The attorney general says that our proposing to enforce the law is in violation of the constitution?" The speaker's voice rose as if questioning the attorney general's declaration, or perhaps his sanity. "How can upholding the law ever be illegal? Makes no sense."

Cissa heard some angry foot shuffling and chairs scraping across the wood floor as all three men no doubt endeavored to examine the letter. She was seated in the parlor and leaned forward to get a better view, trying to identify the man who spoke.

"Well," a second voice interjected, "he states here that 'the courts and offices are created for this purpose, and similar power cannot be delegated by a charter.' I don't see why it isn't our inherent right as citizens to enforce the law. It's a God-given right. What do you propose we do now, Duncan?"

"It would seem," Duncan replied, sounding more thoughtful than usual, "that our only course is to withdraw the application for charter."

"Disband the League?" The voice sounded incredulous.

There was a low chuckle that Cissa knew came from Duncan. "Of course not," he said. "And let us be sure to remind all of our members to bear in mind their sworn obligations."

Murmurs of approval greeted his statement.

Cissa flapped her newspaper in consternation. Apparently, these men cared not a whit about any charter. They had an oath binding them to one another. For them, that was enough.

❦

Cissa was not at all surprised when, a few months later, Duncan announced that he was once again running for sheriff of Fulton County.

"He's sure to be elected this time," Lachlan told Cissa. "My pop says that no one who took the Farmers' League oath would dare to vote against him."

"I keep hearing about that oath," Cissa said. "What do you know about it?"

"Well, I've not taken it, so I can't be sure. But I do know it's a blood oath. Penalty of death for any League member who violates it."

Cissa scowled. The *Beckport Journal* had suggested as much. She was grateful that Lachlan was not bound by such an oath.

When the Democratic primary election was held in mid-August, Duncan handily defeated his opponent Gordon Cortman, winning the nomination for sheriff and making it a foregone conclusion that he would be elected in November. Now that the Populists had faded away, the Democrats won more easily than ever. Cissa also noted that "Cousin Anse" McLaurin won the Democratic nomination for U. S. Senate and James K. Vardaman became the apparent governor elect.

Meanwhile, Cissa honed her writing skills and tried to distance herself from her brother's politics by penning a series of stories about ordinary citizens who were adept at some craft or another. She wrote about the blacksmith's fancy gates and the saddler's custom leather holsters and messenger bags. She wanted to write a story about Julia's skillful dressmaking, but when she sent a note to Julia proposing such an article, she received no response.

Cissa managed to extract from Elsie the information that Baxter had gone back to Tulsa. Elsie added that Julia and the children had moved back in with Zolene, leaving Julia's own cottage—the one on hers and Baxter's land—vacant. Cissa took a walk one day near the little house and thought she saw a wisp of smoke coming from the chimney. But in addition to the boards across the windows, there were now boards across the front door. She walked away without knocking.

Donna Birdwell

Chapter Thirty-Four
A Turning Point

1904

Cissa was not surprised when, shortly after Duncan was installed as sheriff of Fulton County, he announced that he had selected "twenty good men" from each supervisor's beat in the county who were ready to "ferret out the law breakers and to punish them severely." At least, that is what one of the Jackson newspapers reported when Duncan went to the state capitol to visit Governor Vardaman. Cissa suspected that these were likely the same men who were captains and their teams in the Farmers' League. She read a brief report in the Fulton paper noting that former Fulton County Sheriff Newell—the one who had been in the long-running battle with Felix Cortman over mishandling of county funds—had purchased a plantation in Louisiana where he and his family intended to settle. Cissa took this to mean that the dispute, which had gone three times to the state Supreme Court, was now over and that Newell had lost.

Several newspapers, meanwhile, reported more episodes of whitecap violence, with houses shot up or set ablaze and threatening notices posted. Cissa wondered if the "law and order fund" that Sheriff Tarver announced for hiring detectives might contain the same dollars that had been under his care as financial officer of the Farmers' League. She tried to ask Monroe about this, but he just shook his head and said, "Best not to ask, Cissy."

Another thing Duncan did after becoming Sheriff was to install a telephone at his mother's house. Cissa's house. Now that he was a duly elected law enforcement official, he seemed to have put his disagreement with Cissa behind him. Perhaps he assumed that his authority over her was now beyond question. Cissa avoided saying anything that might disabuse him of such a notion.

Duncan said that the telephone was so that he and Lamar could more easily reach their patients and be reached by them whenever they were in Hinson County, but Cissa suspected, once again, that it had more to do with politicking than doctoring. Duncan explained to Cissa how to answer the implement politely and take messages. He also showed her how to make calls herself.

"Pick up the mouthpiece and jiggle this thing here," Duncan said. "Then you wait for an operator to answer. When she comes on, you give her the number you want to call and wait for her to connect you. Perfectly simple, really."

Cissa was pleased by the notion that she might use the instrument to communicate with the *Marchelle Advocate*. The news office had had their own telephone for quite a while now, but with none within her own reach, Cissa had had no opportunity to ring them. Cissa was more willing to put up with having Duncan around if it meant she had access to a telephone.

It had been several weeks since Cissa had received a letter from her friend Liz in Texas, so she was delighted when she saw Liz's name on the return address of a letter that arrived on her doorstep in mid-June. She'd known that Liz was pregnant, and she'd been concerned about her well-being. She tore open the envelope.

As she read, her eyes grew wide. She smiled. She frowned. "Twins?" she whispered in disbelief. "Oh my."

"I've no time for work at all now," Liz wrote. "The babies are fine and healthy—a boy and a girl—but I can't say the same for myself. Feeding and tending them exhausts me and we're not yet in a financial position to hire help, especially without my shoulder to the wheel alongside Bill and without the business that came our way during the political canvasses. We will soldier on. Bill has ideas of starting up a small newspaper of his own, but that must await a more opportune time."

Cissa was still sitting on the front porch with the letter in her lap when she saw Lachlan coming along the road on his sorrel horse. He pulled up and dismounted in front of her house. "Hey, Aunt Cissy," he called.

It was a pleasant late summer afternoon and Cissa invited him to sit with her on the porch. Lachlan told her that he'd been delivering some of the last of the present season's molasses to the general store up the road. "Pop would have preferred taking it to Natchez. Better prices there. But he says we always end up spending more than we take in when we go to Natchez." Lachlan laughed and then lapsed into silence, his gaze directed back down the road from where he'd come.

Cissa told him about her letter from Liz and about the twins. She didn't say how sad it made her that Liz was no longer able to do her writing or work toward votes for women.

"Twins. There haven't been any twins around here for some time now." He fidgeted in the straight wooden chair. "Johnny's coming 'round this weekend, Aunt Cissy, and he wants you to join us. Maybe after lunch on Saturday?"

"I'd like that," Cissa said, trying to ignore how her heartbeat accelerated with the mention of Johnny. "How's Johnny doing? Isn't he about finished with his medical course?"

"Mmm-hmm. He finishes at the end of this year. I think he's trying to decide where he wants to set up his practice."

"Won't he set up near his home? Near his folks?"

"I don't know." Lachlan leaned forward in his chair and poked with the toe of his boot at a spot where the paint was flaking away from the boards. "I guess maybe he'll tell us that when he's here. He said he had some news."

For the next two days, Cissa tried hard not to think about what Johnny's news might be, but the more she tried not to think about it, the more she thought about it. Was he intending to move far away? Or was he perhaps wanting to stay in Hinson County? Maybe forge even stronger ties to the county by marrying a local woman. *No, I can't think anything so foolish,* Cissa chided herself. She knew Johnny's strongest tie was to Lachlan.

On Saturday morning after the breakfast things were cleared away, Duncan arrived with a couple of his cronies. His visits to his office at the Tarver big house were becoming more frequent, and the visits rarely seemed to have anything to do with doctoring. Cissa slipped into the parlor and, after greeting her mother, sat down to listen and pretend to read.

"This is certainly not what I'd been led to expect with our 'great white chief in the governor's office." The man spoke in a haughty voice.

"They deny our charter for our Farmers' League, but then they give full support to that upstart Law and Order League over in Burr County." That was Duncan.

There was the sound of a match striking, followed shortly by the aroma of cigar smoke.

"I never thought they'd convict those fellows in Burr." Though Cissa couldn't see this man's face, she could hear the exasperation in his voice. He sounded young and maybe a little frightened.

"They wouldn't let nobody from the Burr Farmers' League on the jury. But somebody must of told who they was. Somebody who forgot they oath." The man laughed, a rough-sounding noise.

No one else laughed.

"They say that the governor's Pinkerton detective is poking about in Fulton County now." The younger man sounded tentative, as if he hoped what he said might not be true.

"You know what this is really about, boys, don't you?" Duncan's voice was low and hard. "That detective is under orders from my own sworn enemies—political as well as personal enemies. They'll stop at nothing to bring me down."

"Don't you fret, Doc Tarver. Boys here in Fulton and Hinson, we know our sworn duty. We ain't fixing to go weak like those Burr fellows. That detective fixing to come up empty here."

A detective! Cissa thought things might be getting more interesting down in Fulton County.

It was nearing noon when Cissa saw Johnny ride by. She waited until after she'd eaten her own lunch and seen to her mother's repose in the parlor with her sewing and prayer book. "I'm going down to Monroe's for a while, Mother," she said. "I won't be gone long."

"Thank Laura for that cake she sent," Mother said.

"I will, Mother." Cissa knew that the cake her mother meant had been received and consumed to the last crumb more than a week ago.

When Cissa arrived at her brother's house, she found much of the family still gathered at the dining table, though the plates and bowls were mostly empty. "Lachlan and his friend have gone out back, Cissy," Laura said as she wiped the hands of her smallest son. "They said you should join them."

Cissa saw Johnny and Lachlan before they saw her. They stood in a close embrace, Lachlan's head nestled in the crook of Johnny's neck as Johnny caressed his cheek, raised his chin. Cissa stood riveted in place and watched as they kissed. It wasn't a quick kiss on the side of the face like the one Cissa had seen before. This time their lips met and lingered. Cissa watched, aware of her heartbeat thundering in her ears, aware of the heat rising in her temples. She unclenched her fists and took a deep breath, stepping back behind the corner of the house just before Lachlan glanced in her direction. The two men parted and sat down on a bench next to the sugar shed. They were still holding hands.

"Hey, there," Cissa called as she approached, trying to sound casual and cheerful in spite of her internal turmoil.

Johnny rose to his feet and extended his hands. "It's so good to see you again, Cissa. You're looking well." He grasped both of Cissa's hands firmly, warmly in his.

"You, too, Johnny," Cissa said, wondering what he would think of the high color in her face. He pulled up a stool for himself and said, "You sit there next to your...nephew? I can never remember how you two are related." He smiled in a way that was so engaging Cissa had to smile back.

She relaxed a bit. How could there be room in her heart for jealousy when she cared about both of these men so deeply? "I've been his Aunt Cissy since I was two years old," she said.

"What did you think of the book I sent you?" Johnny asked. The three embarked on a lively discussion of that book as well as the one Johnny had sent to Lachlan, which Cissa had also read. When they lapsed into silence for a moment, Lachlan looked up at Johnny and said, "I need to go check on the horses. I'll be back in a few minutes."

Cissa caught her breath. This felt like a ploy to give Johnny some time alone with her. As Lachlan walked away, Johnny abandoned the stool and moved to the bench next to Cissa.

"Lachlan said he told you earlier that I've been trying to decide where to set up my practice once I graduate."

Cissa nodded.

"I've still not reached a decision on that. However..." Johnny took a deep breath. "My parents are insisting that a family physician needs to be a married man. They're pressuring me to take a wife."

Cissa risked a glance up into Johnny's face. He was frowning, his eyes half-closed.

"In fact," Johnny went on, "they've selected a bride for me and are planning to announce our engagement this fall."

The news swept over Cissa like a basin of cold water, leaving her mute. How could he marry this girl when it was clear he loved Lachlan?

He reached for Cissa's hand. "She's a nice girl, Cissa. Pretty enough and my folks say she's gifted in all the social graces that will make her a good doctor's wife. But I'd rather have someone like you. You're prettier and smarter by a long shot. I care about you quite a lot, Narcissa Tarver. And I figure I ought to have a say in this matter, so..." He stopped and took a breath. He still wasn't looking at Cissa. "Would you be willing to be my wife?"

There it was. This was the moment Cissa had longed for, a proposal from a handsome and successful man who had long since won her heart.

Why did it feel so wrong?

"What about Lachlan?" Cissa gave Johnny's hand a squeeze and then released it. She looked up into his face as it collapsed into profound sadness. Tears rimmed his eyes.

"You know that's impossible," he said. "At least this way we'd all be family." His gaze drifted away and, by the longing in his eyes, Cissa knew he was looking at Lachlan.

"I can't," she said. "I can't marry you, Johnny. You know I love you, but I can't be your wife. Marry the girl your parents picked for you if you must. Be happy if you can. And..." Cissa caught her breath and swallowed hard. "And know that you will always have people on Callander Road who love you."

Johnny reached over and put an arm around Cissa's shoulders, a gesture she accepted as brotherly. "Can we always be friends, then, Cissa? Will you forgive me for being as I am?"

"Of course, Johnny." The words came out flat. Cissa desperately willed them to be the truth.

Cissa looked up and saw Lachlan watching from the doorway of the barn, his arms folded, his head down.

Cissa returned home with a heavy heart. She'd just refused a proposal of marriage from the man she loved. Should she have accepted? Surely Johnny would have permitted—no, encouraged—his wife to continue working. There was also the fact that marrying Johnny would have extracted her from the ongoing turmoil of the Tarver family. But she always would have known who Johnny's heart truly belonged to. She didn't understand it, but she could see it was true. No, she wouldn't have been happy married to Johnny.

I'm getting too old to expect any proposal of marriage, Cissa told herself. She'd turned twenty-eight at her birthday a few weeks back. So many of her nieces and nephews were married now—Betty last year and Lamar a few months ago. Janie had recently announced her own engagement and had asked Cissa to stand as her matron of honor. Little Janie! Cissa had watched Janie being born and now she was to be married. She would have two dates by her name in the family Bible. Cissa still had only the one, only the date of her birth.

That night Cissa cried herself to sleep.

Chapter Thirty-Five
A Detective in Fulton County

1905

"Well, of course I'll go if I'm needed," Cissa said, feeling a bit guilty for trying to sound altruistic about spending a week in Cowleton instead of in the boring dullness of her own home on Callander Road. Duncan's wife Ada was ill and since Cissa was the only adult woman in the family with no husband or children to be responsible for, she was nominated to provide care. *And whose fault is that?* she asked herself. Was she to spend the rest of her life second-guessing her refusal of Johnny's proposal?

It was agreed that Mother would stay at Monroe's house while Cissa was away. Letitia, Monroe's eldest at home now that Janie was married, had seemed almost eager to have her grandmother there for a week or so.

Cissa wasn't looking forward to the caregiving or to being in her brother Duncan's company. She was leery of his political activity, suppressing her displeasure in the name of family loyalty. At least Duncan would be out of town for the first few days on sheriff business in Jackson.

What Cissa did look forward to was being in Cowleton, the seat of Fulton County where there were far more newsworthy events happening than what took place on Callander Road. Whitecappers were once again on the move, and she was intrigued by the possibility that the Pinkerton detective who had pursued whitecappers so successfully in Burr County might be on the prowl in Fulton. A little excitement might help her forget her broken heart. At the very least it would break the endless cycle of sameness from which she'd begun to feel she might never escape. She made a quick call to Mr. Hodges at the *Marchelle Advocate* to inform him of her plans and offer her services as a correspondent. She doubted that her sister-in-law was so ill as to require constant care.

Lamar came to pick Cissa up in his father's buggy. On the journey, she plied him with questions about his mother's condition.

He was surprisingly reticent. Lamar was apprenticing as a physician and Cissa would have expected him to offer at least a few medical insights.

Upon arriving at Duncan's house—a house bigger than the Tarver "big house" on Callander Road—Cissa went immediately to Ada's bedside.

"Cissy, there was really no need, though I am glad you're here." Ada's words were a bit slurred, and she looked more ill than Cissa had anticipated.

"I'm glad to be able to offer some support," Cissa said. "How are you feeling?" She took a seat in the chair next to Ada's bed and eyed the array of medicines on the side table.

"Maybe a bit better," Ada said. "Though I often say that and then by evening I feel myself slipping away again. I haven't been myself ever since my fall back in November."

Cissa hadn't heard about such an accident and pressed for more details.

"Oh, it was nothing," Ada said, turning her face toward the wall. "I don't even recall exactly how it happened. Duncan says I must have slipped on some grease on the kitchen floor. Anyway, I fell against the table and broke a couple of ribs. Knocked my head. And there were bruises on my wrists." Her voice trailed off as she gazed absently out the window, clutching her left wrist. "Poor Duncan," she said at last. "He works so hard for the good of the people and gets nothing but trouble for it." Her gaze came back to Cissa's face. Her eyes had an unnatural glitter.

"Don't you worry about him," Cissa said briskly as she began picking up the little bottles and vials one by one. "Let's just worry about getting you back on your feet and feeling peart again." She didn't recognize all of the medications, but one of them that she did recognize was laudanum.

Cissa had never stayed overnight at Duncan's house before, having always arrived with family and returned home on the same day. Unlike Monroe's house, which had been full of little girls, Duncan's house had been full of boys. His three eldest—Albert, Eli, and Lamar—were now married, as were his daughters Milly and Katy, both of whom were expecting. The two youngest boys—Quin and Rob—were now sixteen and fifteen and still in school. When they were home, they squabbled incessantly, but they were often away until late in the evening.

Duncan had left a note for Cissa, indicating that their maid Inez came in every day but Sunday and would be doing all of the cooking and cleaning. Cissa need do no more than tend to Ada and supervise Inez and pick up Ada's medication refills from the pharmacy.

⁕ —— ⁕

"I'm here to pick up some medicines for Mrs. Duncan Tarver," Cissa said.

"You're the sister?" The pharmacist barely looked at Cissa. "Doc said you'd be coming." He fumbled around under the counter and then handed her a brown paper bag.

"Thank you." She tucked the parcel into her purse. Ada had indicated that no payment would be necessary as Duncan ran a regular account with the pharmacy. As Cissa turned to go she noticed a man who seemed to be watching her intently.

The man approached her. "You're Doctor Tarver's sister?" he said. "I understand you write for the newspapers." He extended his hand. "I'm Hector Davis. Do you have a minute?"

Cissa recognized the name, and it made her catch her breath and keep both hands to herself. This was the Pinkerton detective. Cissa recognized the opportunity that was presenting itself to her. She could interview the locally famous (or infamous) detective and send an exclusive to Mr. Hodges at the *Advocate*. She also recognized the personal peril of such a course of action. Her left cheek tingled as she recalled her brother's capacity for anger and violence. Duncan would never forgive her for even shaking hands with the Pinkerton man, much less engaging in conversation with him. "I'm afraid I don't," she said.

"Perhaps another time, then," Hector Davis said, offering an engaging smile.

Cissa watched him walk away. He was a handsome gentleman with strong features and bright dark eyes, the kind that never miss a detail. Well-dressed but not ostentatious. His shoes were polished but worn down a bit at the heels. A conversation with him surely would have been entertaining and perhaps enlightening.

Leaving the drugstore, Cissa crossed the street to the offices of the *Fulton Gazette*, intending to pick up a copy of their latest edition.

The smell of newsprint as she entered the premises reminded her of the life she could have been part of if she'd been able to take the job at the *Advocate* when it was offered. That was more than three years ago. And now she'd just passed on an opportunity to do an exclusive interview that might well have been picked up in the Natchez paper and maybe even in Jackson. She squared her shoulders, wondering if she'd made the right choice.

"May I help you?" The young man behind the counter looked no older than Duncan's boy Robby.

"Just a copy of today's paper," Cissa said as she pulled her coin purse from the neck of her shirtwaist. She glanced around the office. There was an older man behind a desk and another man tying twine around stacks of printed papers. She guessed that the man at the desk might be the editor. Cortman? Yes, that was it. Sam Cortman. Cissa had cultivaated a habit of always looking at the names of editors and other staff listed in a newspaper. She also knew that this Sam Cortman had once been county sheriff and had served in the state legislature. He was an important figure in the sprawling Cortman family, which had built the imposing building on Main Street that bore their name.

"Hot off the presses," the young man said as he slapped a newspaper down in front of Cissa.

"Anything in it about that Pinkerton detective poking around town?" Cissa asked this in a voice loud enough to carry to the man at the desk. His head jerked up at the name "Pinkerton." He rose and ambled toward the counter.

"What makes you think we've got a detective here in town, ma'am?" The man rocked back on his heels with his arms folded across his belly.

"He introduced himself to me over at the drugstore," Cissa said, using her most innocuous tone. "Well, I guess it was him. Davis, right? Hector Davis?"

"Why would he introduce himself to you like that?" The man frowned, swaying backwards and forwards as he stared at Cissa.

"I'm sure I couldn't say," she answered. She extended her left hand to the gentleman. "I'm Cissa. Narcissa Tarver. And you are?"

He grasped her hand and shook vigorously. "I'm Sam Cortman, Miss Tarver. Editor in chief of the *Fulton Gazette.* Are you the young lady who writes for the *Marchelle Advocate?*"

"Why, yes I am," Cissa said. "I'm just in town for a few days. At my brother's house."

"And your brother is Sheriff Tarver. But how did Davis...? Never mind. Who knows how these detectives know what they know. I hear he's a good one. Thanks for the news tip, Miss Tarver. We knew Davis was in the county but hadn't found him in town yet. By the way, you might find the story on page two there of some interest."

Cissa nodded, picked up her newspaper and left. If she couldn't interview Detective Davis, maybe she could at least take some satisfaction in being a source of a hot news tip for the *Fulton Gazette.* It didn't feel very satisfying. She was eager to pass on the information to Mr. Hodges as well, but she decided she could spend a few more pennies and get a cup of coffee at the café. Ada would be fine for another half hour. As Cissa crossed the street again, she saw Sam Cortman heading for the drugstore. She could have told him that Detective Davis was no longer there. She'd seen him leave, though she hadn't seen which way he went.

At the café, Cissa sat at a table near the back where she could watch the comings and goings without being obvious herself. She ordered a coffee and settled down to read her newspaper. The front page carried a report on yet another incident of whitecapping in which shots were fired into another Negro homesteader's cabin. *Just like Baxter and Julia,* she thought wryly. She returned to the words "shots were fired." *As if shots just materialize out of thin air,* she thought. *Who fired the shots? And who were the homesteaders whose home was attacked?* The article didn't say. There was also no mention of the Pinkerton man.

On page two she found a reprint of a story from the *Natchez Herald,* based on an interview their reporter had conducted with Duncan in Jackson earlier in the week. It was headlined "Sheriff of Fulton County Discusses Whitecapism—County Almost Free of Lawlessness." Of course Duncan would try to put the most positive face on things. The reporter quoted Duncan as indicating that the whitecap outrages in Fulton County were "an outgrowth or survival of the famous Ku Klux Klan of reconstruction days," an observation, Cissa thought, that was undoubtedly true. Was Duncan also right in indicating that the element was isolated in a small portion of the county up around McManus Creek?

When Cissa read Duncan's contention that there had been "no whitecapper troubles in Fulton County for a year or so" and that "conditions are now permanently peaceful," she turned back to the article on page one and sighed. Duncan also had told the *Herald* reporter that in the most recent circuit court session at Cowleton, the grand jury after a thorough investigation, had "failed to find any evidence on which to base charges against alleged whitecappers." The reporter confirmed that Detective Davis was now in Fulton County "laying the foundations for his investigations."

Cissa was so absorbed in her reading that she failed to notice until the last moment a couple of men approaching with apparent intent to occupy a booth near her table. One of the men was Hector Davis. Cissa ducked behind her newspaper as the two men slid into the booth. Mr. Davis, fortunately, took the spot that placed his back toward Cissa.

"You can't tell me anything more than that?" Davis used a cajoling tone. "You know I won't put your name in my report if you don't intend to testify."

"That's all I can tell you." The second man spoke in softer tones than Detective Davis and kept his head down, his hat pulled low. "But you go talk to Jewel. He's mad enough he might... Well, I don't know for sure he'd testify. You have to ask him."

"Jewel, eh?" And then both voices grew so soft that Cissa couldn't pick up any more of the conversation.

The man who was not Hector Davis got up and walked out, pulling his hat even lower over his eyes. Cissa tried to memorize a description. Average height, slightly stocky build. Dark hair with a good haircut and a well-trimmed mustache. He wore a suit jacket with work pants and there was mud on the backs of his Sunday shoes. The bulge at the back of his jacket probably meant he was carrying a pistol. She wished she'd been able to get a better look at his face.

After drinking her coffee, Cissa knew that she needed to get back to Ada. But she didn't want to leave until after Detective Davis left. Well, she could, but if she did he would be sure to recognize her.

"Are you ready to order lunch?" the waitress asked Mr. Davis.

Much to Cissa's relief, he said, "No, I may come back later for a sandwich, honey, but that's all for now. Here's for the two coffees. And a little extra for you."

As Detective Davis rose to leave he turned toward Cissa, who once again sheltered behind her newspaper. "Miss Tarver?" he said.

Cissa groaned inwardly as she laid her paper on the table and tried to smile. "Mr. Davis," she said.

With a hand on the back of the chair across from her, he said, "Do you mind?" and then, without waiting for her to respond, took a seat.

Cissa glanced around the room as her heart began to pound. At the moment, she and Hector Davis were the only patrons. The waitress was slouched behind the counter with a dime novel.

"I suppose you heard what we were talking about." Davis gave Cissa a conspiratorial grin.

"Some of it." Cissa knew this man was a professional at interrogation; she needed to keep her guard up. It was not an easy thing to do with a man whose smile was so engaging. He seemed so open and genuine. Without meaning to, Cissa smiled back. "It sounds like you're making some headway," she said.

Davis leaned forward with his folded arms on the table. "Some," he said. "But I've heard something about a case up in Hinson County that I haven't been able to get anyone to talk about. Somewhere on Callander Road?"

"Is that so?" Cissa's breath caught in her throat. She knew he was talking about what happened at Julia's place. She thought again about the incident she'd just read about and her dissatisfaction with how it was reported. She took a deep breath. "But you're making good progress here in Fulton. Is there anything you can tell me about that?"

Davis chuckled as he sat up straighter. He began to drum with his fingers on the table, a gesture that reminded Cissa of her pop.

"I can tell you," he said, "that I've already got several witnesses who have given sworn statements, and I expect to have a lot more before the end of the week. You can tell that to your newspaper." He grinned at Cissa and raised his eyebrows.

Cissa nodded. She took a deep breath and began to speak in a voice that was barely above a whisper. "The incident on Callander Road was at the home of Baxter Green and his wife Julia. Their daughter Rosie was seriously injured. I believe Mr. and Mrs. Green have now moved." It was the simple truth. Cissa had written about it for the *Advocate*, although that article had not printed any names.

There was no need for her to say that Julia and the children had simply moved in with her mother, Zolene.

"How seriously was the daughter injured?" The lines between Davis's thick eyebrows deepened. His voice had a reassuring timbre.

"It was a bullet to her left shoulder that tore a gaping wound. Without the proper medicine, she might well have bled to death," Cissa said.

Davis reached into his jacket pocket and pulled out a small card. "Here is where you can get in touch with me in future," he said. "Thank you for your help."

"Likewise," Cissa said as she accepted the little card. She held it in her hand as she watched him stride out of the café.

What have I done? Cissa thought as he disappeared from view. She'd expected to feel nervous and frightened for speaking to this man whom her volatile brother considered to be an agent of his enemies. Instead she felt elated. Duncan didn't need to know about this.

Cissa composed her article in her mind as she walked home. It wasn't much, but it was more than she could have hoped for. She was relieved to find that Ada was sleeping. The only other person in the house was Inez, who was busy in the kitchen. Cissa went immediately to the telephone and called her story in to Mr. Hodges at the *Marchelle Advocate.*

"Well done, Miss Tarver," he said. "We'll get this into our next edition."

As she hung up, Cissa grinned and tapped her hands together, applauding herself. Mr. Cortman might suspect who had scooped the *Gazette* on this, but no one else would know, since her name would thankfully not be attached to the story. As for Duncan...Well, she wouldn't say a word to him at all unless he asked. And hopefully he wouldn't ask.

Late that afternoon, Duncan arrived home, looking disheveled and disgruntled from his long journey back from Jackson. Eli had picked him up at the train station in Vandy and now followed him into the house, lugging his suitcase and briefcase. Duncan greeted Cissa with a nod.

"How's Ada doing?" he asked. "Are you giving her all the medicines?" Duncan scowled at the two bottles Cissa had brought back from the drugstore that were still sitting on the dining table.

"Yes," Cissa said. She didn't mention that she'd cut the laudanum in half this morning, convinced that Duncan had been using it to keep his wife docile. She doubted whether it was necessary for any other purpose. "Although you know, now that I'm here, I was thinking that maybe we could cut back on the laudanum. I can watch her and if she seems in too much pain we can step it up again."

"So you're a physician now?" Duncan scoffed. "Go ahead, though. Do as you like. Tell Ada I'll be in to see her later. I'll be in the office until supper. Seven o'clock, as usual. Something light."

"I'll tell Inez." Cissa bristled. Couldn't her brother even go in and greet his ailing wife?

Cissa was in the kitchen with Inez, discussing meal plans for the next few days, when Duncan came in holding a couple of sheets of paper and a pencil. "Read this over for me, Cissy," he said as he laid the pages and pencil on the table. "I'm about blind with exhaustion, but I want to get this letter over to the *Gazette* right away. I'm going in to see Ada now."

Of course, Duncan, I'd be happy to do as you ask. But of course he hadn't asked; he'd just issued an order. With a bitter sigh, Cissa sat down at the table to read. "Mr. Editor," the piece began, "Why does Governor Vardaman see fit to send his detective to Fulton County, where whitecapper activity does not exist?"

Cissa thought again about the front page article in the *Gazette* and about her conversation with the state's detective. She read on. It didn't take long to pick up on Duncan's defensive tone as he pointed out that he was "the chief executive officer of Fulton County" and "chairman of the law and order committee, composed of one hundred of the best citizens of this county, of which I enclose to you a list." Was he talking about his Farmers' League? Duncan's political organizations seemed to shift and change like the weather. Cissa felt certain that the Law and Order League she'd read about recently was something separate, something that in fact opposed the more ruthless activities of the Farmers' League. She looked at the final page of Duncan's work; it was a lengthy list of names, in which certain surnames recurred.

"If I am not a criminal," Duncan wrote, "then I should be entrusted with the management of every movement tending to the suppression of crime set on foot by any legally constituted authority." Cissa frowned but did not lift her pencil. "If I am a criminal, then

Governor Vardaman should remove me from office and place therein some man who is capable and competent to manage the hoodlums of Cowleton and command the fear and respect of the criminals of Fulton County. So long as I am sheriff, by the eternal, I will be sheriff."

Cissa sat up straighter, her eyes widening over her brother's strong language. It was not consistently the clearest language, but it was certainly strong. He went on to note that no member of this "law and order committee," of which he claimed to be chairman, had ever indicated to him the desire to employ any "special agent or detective." He also claimed that he had received no notice of any "lawless action by organized outlaws" during his time in office.

Cissa's eyes grew wider when she read the next words: "I am ready at all times to support and aid Governor Vardaman in any and all efforts to maintain law and order, even if it should call for that sacrifice of that dearest of all things to mankind, my life. I will positively tolerate no outlawry, nor will I tolerate any violation of law by Detective Davis or his band of disgruntled politicians and personal enemies of mine."

Cissa cringed. For whatever reasons, Duncan's ire against Detective Davis was escalating. Surely that anger was misplaced. Davis seemed like a trustworthy sort who was only trying to get to the truth.

In the letter, Duncan asserted that people of Fulton County should require that the governor pay their expenses if they were called to go to Jackson to speak with the detective. "If Davis is a detective, let him come to Fulton County and dig up the evidence. If he is a cur and coward, as I believe him to be, then let him stay at Jackson and write for people to meet him there." *Oh, if he only knew,* Cissa thought. But clearly Duncan did not know that Davis was already present right here in Cowleton.

"Mr. Editor," Duncan continued, "my personal and political enemies are at the bottom of this, and I defy them." He went on to make thinly veiled accusations toward particular individuals. The implication was that they were people who had not joined his Farmers' League. "Aye, sneaking scoundrels! They did not show up, they are my enemies." Duncan concluded his diatribe with the words, "I will be sheriff, or I will be nothing."

Cissa looked up to see Duncan watching her from the doorway. His shoulders were stooped with weariness, but his eyes flashed with the anger of his prose. Cissa struggled to remain calm.

"Well?" he said.

"Duncan, are you sure you want to say all of this? You know it's going to make people even angrier."

He grabbed up the papers. "I didn't ask for your opinion," he said. "I just wanted to make sure all the words were spelled correctly and that the commas and things were in the right places."

"I fixed a few of those," Cissa said. "You're a strong writer." She couldn't tell him he was a good writer, since some of his sentences were altogether awkward. She also couldn't tell him his ideas were anything other than repugnant to her.

Duncan's letter appeared in the next issue of the *Fulton Gazette*, which did not reach Cissa's hands until nearing midday. Duncan had left early, saying he would take breakfast at the café. Cissa did not leave the house, sticking close to her duties of tending to Ada.

There were a couple of bad days for Ada as Cissa adhered strictly to her program of reducing and then eliminating her sister-in-law's intake of laudanum. It galled her to think that her brother had kept his wife on the drug for his own convenience. Cissa noticed how Ada shrank into herself whenever Duncan was around; she began to wonder about the circumstances of her sister-in-law's fall.

Gradually, Ada seemed to be more herself again.

Duncan was another matter. The spring court session was due to convene in Cowleton in a few months, and he grumbled over their declared intention to take up Governor Vardaman's whitecapping agenda. The governor had successfully pursued whitecappers in Burr County last year, and several of those men—including at least one member of the Burr Farmers' League— were now serving time in prison. Worse, the same detective who had brought those men to justice was now right here in Cowleton. Duncan had learned about that (though not from Cissa) and he fumed about it. Duncan's associates had been thoroughly convinced that Vardaman, with all his rhetoric of white supremacy, would never punish its defenders. They'd called him their "great white chief." Cissa understood that they now felt betrayed.

Duncan paced about the house like a caged animal.

"What do you think the grand jury will do this session?" Cissa asked Duncan over supper one day. Inez had begged for a day off and Cissa had made a pork burgoo, which she considered one of her best meals. At least it was the least likely to go wrong.

"We're trying to get them to postpone the session." Duncan prodded at a piece of meat on his plate and scowled.

"On what grounds?"

Duncan snorted. "Don't let your newspaper scribblings go to your head, little sister." He put the piece of meat in his mouth and after a moment of vigorous chewing swallowed loudly. "It's planting season. Most anyone who would be placed on the grand jury is engaged in farming and they need to be at their own business, not the governor's and his lapdog detective's."

"But isn't the court session always held this time of year?"

Duncan glared and did not respond.

The next morning, Cissa got up to find Ada in the kitchen supervising Inez over breakfast preparations. "It's good to see you looking peart again, Ada," Cissa said. "Has Duncan already gone out?"

"He left early to go to Natchez," Ada replied.

When Inez went into the dining room to lay the table, Cissa approached her sister-in-law and, placing a hand on her arm, spoke as softly as she could. "I have to ask you, Ada. Did you really fall last month? Or were you pushed?"

Ada shook off Cissa's hand and turned away. After a moment's silence, she looked back into Cissa's face. "He'd never done anything like that before, Cissy." She spoke in hushed tones. "It's just that he's been so wrought up lately over the political mess." Ada's face was tense and drawn. "A man can only take so much."

"Or a woman?" Cissa simmered with anger against her brother.

"Leave it alone," Ada said. "We'll get through this. I'm thankful to you for coming to look after me, but it's probably better you go home now."

Chapter Thirty-Six
Loyalties Challenged

February - April 1905

Cissa arrived home with a heavy heart, thinking of Ada and how the poor woman had to put up with Duncan every day. Cissa was surprised when Letitia met her on the front porch. She was supposed to be helping to look after Mother at Monroe's house. "Is everything alright? Is Mother here?" Cissa asked after thanking Quinlan for bringing her suitcase from the wagon.

"Grandma kept insisting on coming home," Letty said. The girl paused just outside the front door and spoke in a low voice. "Is she always this forgetful, Aunt Cissy? I don't know how many times I had to tell her that you were helping look after Aunt Ada in Cowleton."

Cissa shoved aside the twinge of guilt for having left her aged mother. "That sounds about normal for her," she said. "I know it's distressing."

Letty took the suitcase from Cissa's hand and held the door for her to enter. "Does she often wander off?" Letty asked.

"What? Why, no, she's never done that. Did she? Tell me what happened."

Letitia explained that one day after everyone at her house had been busy in the kitchen, she'd gone into the sitting room to bring her grandmother a cup of sassafras tea and found her missing. "We looked everywhere for her, all over the house and around the property. We called and called. Oh, Aunt Cissy, I was so frightened." The girl grasped both elbows as she fought back tears.

"But you found her." Cissa thought about how cold it had been lately; her mother had truly been in danger.

"Yes, she'd walked all the way back here by herself. I found her in a dark corner of the shed, mumbling something about hiding from the Yankees. It was all I could do to persuade her it was safe to go back inside the house. She was so cold, Aunt Cissy. Since we knew you were coming back today, we didn't bother to take her back down to our house. We just bundled her into some blankets and lit the fire."

Cissa's sense of guilt mushroomed. She put her arm around her young niece's shoulders. "I'm so sorry you had to deal with that. Let's go tell her I'm home now and then you can go back to your own house and get some rest."

Before departing, Letty inquired after her Aunt Ada and Cissa assured her that all was well in Ada and Duncan's household. She knew that wasn't the truth, but it was what Letty needed to hear. Cissa berated herself for succumbing to the lies and half-truths families told in order to keep up appearances.

Letitia was already on the front steps when she stopped and turned back. "I almost forgot," she said. "A package came for you while you were gone. I put it on the hall table."

When Cissa picked up the little package, her heart gladdened to see that it was from Johnny. He sometimes sent postcards or letters, but a package was special. She laid it back on the table and went into the parlor to see her mother.

Susanna tilted her head toward Cissa with a blank look. "Maggie, could you pick up my yarn for me. It dropped on the floor, and I don't want that puppy to get it."

Cissa took a deep breath to steady herself before answering. "Of course, Mother." She picked up the yarn and laid it in Susanna's lap. "Would you like a glass of warm milk? It's turned chilly out there again."

"Has it?" Mother clutched the ball of yarn with both hands. "Yes, milk would be nice. Take some to your father, too." She picked up her knitting and squinted at the tangled strands of yarn.

Cissa said nothing. There was no point arguing with her mother when she made mistakes like this. She usually came back around after a while.

Cissa found the jug of milk and poured some into a pan. *How has Mother gone down so much in just a week?* she thought. *Or has she been slipping away so slowly that I hadn't noticed?* She would have to keep a closer eye on her mother to make sure she didn't wander off again.

When the milk was about to simmer, Cissa poured it into a tumbler and took it into the parlor, cradled in a soft blue napkin.

"How nice," Mother said. "Thank you, Narcissa." She took the glass in both hands and sipped. The ball of yarn was on the floor again. Cissa picked it up.

In the hallway, she picked up her little package from Johnny. At the kitchen table with her own glass of milk, Cissa undid the twine and wrappings, revealing a sturdy little box, blue with gold embossed flourishes and a hinged lid. Inside the box was a fountain pen and a note. The note read, "Dear Cissa. I'm told these are the latest thing for serious writing and thought you should have one. I also wanted to let you know that I am now engaged to the lady of my parents' choosing. I remain forever your friend, Johnny."

Cissa felt her bottom lip tremble as she whisked away a tear. *Dear Johnny,* she thought. This could all have been so very different.

The pen was a sleek and shiny black with a gold nib and when she held it in her hand it felt perfectly balanced. There was a little lever on the side that would fill the barrel with ink. There would be no more dipping her pen every line or two, usually just as she'd thought of a whole string of good words she wanted to write down. It was a thoughtful gift, an indication that Johnny understood what was important to Cissa. She knew she would think of him every time she used the pen. She went immediately to fill it with ink and write a note of thanks.

As she unpacked her suitcase that evening, Cissa found the little card that Mr. Davis had given her. It read "Hector Davis, Pinkerton Detective Agency" and then a post office address in Jackson. Recalling her brief conversation with the man sent a prickle of excitement along her arms. She tucked the card into a bureau drawer between the doll that Julia had made, the one harboring Nubby's red bead, and the book about the commonwealth of fairies.

Mother seemed more settled now that Cissa was back home. At least she didn't wander off. But it hurt Cissa's heart every time her mother named one of her lost babies or spoke of Pop as if he were still here, still part of their daily life. Somewhere in Susanna's mind he would always be present.

Shortly after her return, Cissa received a copy of the *Natchez Herald* that mentioned her brother's visit to that city. The article referenced the letter he had published in the *Fulton Gazette*, the one Cissa had suggested might make people angry. Apparently it had, as his interview with the *Herald* included firm insistence that he most certainly did not consider Governor Vardaman an enemy. "The truth of the matter is," the article declared, "Sheriff Tarver and Governor

Vardaman are warm personal friends." It also quoted Duncan as saying that he had no objections to Vardaman sending Detective Davis to Fulton County to investigate whitecapping. This, Cissa knew, was not true. The article concluded by stating that Sheriff Tarver "looks to be a man of iron nerve and courage. He is a quiet, easy spoken gentleman." *Except when he's not,* Cissa thought.

Cissa enlisted Elsie's help in keeping a close watch on Mother, explaining how she had wandered off. "How is Rosie doing?" Cissa asked.

"Good, miss. She good." Elsie offered no details.

The weather grew erratic, gray and sunny in turn. Then in mid-February cold rain turned overnight to sleet and ice and snow. Giant icicles hung from the eaves of the house and both front and back steps became treacherous. Branches laden with ice dipped low and finally cracked and crashed to the ground, punctuating the gray-ceilinged, white-blanketed silence that enveloped Callander Road for days. Only the mailman managed to make it through, and when he delivered the papers, Cissa learned that telephone and telegraph lines were down all through the south, as well as electrical lines for the places that had electricity. It wasn't supposed to get this cold in southern Mississippi, even in February. Cissa's sense of isolation, of everything being frozen in time, made the frigid days almost unbearable.

When the thaw finally came, it was as if winter had spent itself; the last week of February was almost springlike. Cissa longed for some renascence for herself as well. She looked for every excuse to leave the house, to break free if only for an hour or two from her responsibilities to home and Mother. She went to the little general store up the road toward Rundle Springs in search of baking soda or washing soap or writing paper. While she was there she always took some time to peruse the newspapers on the counter. The storekeeper Mr. Barnes subscribed to several papers—one from Jackson as well as all the local papers. These kept patrons entertained and were later used to wrap parcels. At home, Cissa still received both the *Marchelle Advocate* and the *Natchez Herald* gratis. She had also taken out a year's subscription to the *Fulton Gazette* while she was visiting in Cowleton. At a dollar or more a year, she couldn't afford more than that.

In one of the first issues of the *Gazette* that arrived (a day late) at the Tarver house, Cissa was dismayed to read that there had been yet another incident of whitecapping in Fulton County. This time the residence of some Negro homesteaders had been set ablaze. There had also been another mass meeting of citizens at the Cowleton courthouse. In the lead-up to this meeting, Duncan had tried to imply that it would be in support of his Farmers' League. Instead it marked the clear divergence of the Fulton County Law and Order League from any association it might have been assumed to have with Duncan's group.

At the mass meeting, Duncan had given a speech, the text of which was published in full by the *Gazette.* In the speech, Duncan encouraged cooperation with Detective Davis's investigation, though he also pled with the citizens to bring to him personally any evidence they might have about individuals who might be engaged in whitecapping. He avoided saying it outright, but Cissa readily inferred that he meant for folks to bring information to him instead of to the detective. Duncan offered a hundred dollars reward for information brought to him that led to conviction. *An unlikely outcome,* Cissa thought with some bitterness. With loyal public support, Duncan said, "I will need no detective to put down the outlaw."

The *Gazette* article also cited the text of a notice that had been sent to a Negro homesteader: "We, the citizens of Fulton County have decided that you can move out of Fulton County. If you don't you know what is the penalty. Death is the penalty. We have decided this, if you don't move we will kill you if we haft to git you between the plow handles. Now you can move or let it alone, but we intend to carry out our plan." According to the *Gazette,* the notice was accompanied by a threatening illustration, which the paper did not reproduce. In his speech, Duncan had condemned the author of such a notice as a "lawless coward" seeking to "incite renewed interest and excitement in an unnecessary investigation" at the behest of Duncan's own "personal and political enemies."

Cissa wondered how the obvious tension with this new Law and Order League would impact Duncan's ability to carry out his obligations as county sheriff.

A few days later, Cissa received a letter. The handwriting on the envelope was unfamiliar and there was no return address. The postmark was from the station at McManus Creek. With mounting curiosity, Cissa opened the letter, her eyes going immediately to the signature: It was from Hector Davis. She dropped the letter onto her father's desk and stared at it as she wiped her palms, which suddenly felt very moist, on her skirt.

"Dear Miss Tarver," the letter read. "As your kinsman has recently stated in an open meeting as well as in the press that he no longer objects to having a detective operating in Fulton County, I was wondering if perhaps I could speak with you again. I will be in Callander Tuesday next so perhaps we might meet when you go to drop off your news."

Cissa was horrified. And flattered. And confused. Surely Davis ought to know that Duncan didn't mean what he said about welcoming a detective in Fulton. And how did he know where she would be next Tuesday? *He's a detective, Cissa. He knows things.* She tucked the letter back inside the envelope and into the pocket of her apron.

That week, Cissa went to Callander on Monday afternoon to drop off her contribution for the Wednesday edition of the *Marchelle Advocate* with Mr. Clay's wife. She told herself that encouraging further encounters with Detective Davis would be asking for trouble. All the way back home she kept looking over her shoulder, half expecting to see him there on the road and feeling a twinge of disappointment that he'd been so easily evaded. She wondered what he might have been ready to share with her about his investigations. She wondered what he might have wanted to ask of her.

Around the middle of March, Cissa learned that an "executive committee" of the new Law and Order League had been called to Jackson to meet with Governor Vardaman. "Do you know what's going on?" Cissa asked Lachlan one day after he'd finished stacking firewood inside the kitchen door.

Lachlan tipped his hat back to brush the perspiration from his brow. "Not really," he said. "But the last time Uncle Duncan was visiting with Pop it sounded like he's convinced that the committee is going to demand his removal as sheriff."

"Really? But didn't they adopt Duncan's points at their meeting? I thought he wanted them to ask that the detective be withdrawn." Try as she might, Cissa could make little sense out of who Duncan's friends were and who he considered enemies. She picked up a couple of sticks to stoke the kitchen stove.

"That may be what Uncle Duncan wants, but... All I know is what he said to Pop."

Over the next week Cissa read conflicting reports in several different newspapers, some stating that there was going to be a request for Duncan's removal, others strongly denying any such intention. Near the end of the month, she encountered a letter that Duncan had sent to a number of different papers. It ran in the *Natchez Herald* under a startling headline: "TARVER WROTH - Sheriff of Fulton County Replies to His Critics - His Statement Is Salty - Asserting That He Has Not Been Treated Right Dr. Tarver Scores Law and Order League - Is Ready for His Enemies - Declares He Has Some Good Guns and That He Is Endowed With the Law of Self-Defense."

Oh, Duncan, Cissa thought. *What now?*

The letter began as a firm but restrained statement of Duncan's role in the origin and activities of the Farmers' League and was clearly an effort to distance himself from the most outrageous actions attributed to the group, which, he argued, was organized on the grounds of the courthouse and in broad daylight. He didn't mention where subsequent meetings were held, although it was widely believed that they met at midnight on a sandbar of the river far from town. He also didn't mention the Attorney General's refusal to grant the charter the Farmers' League had sought. He did point out that there had been "no organized outlawry for two years; all quiet, county at peace." Cissa knew that saying such a thing in print didn't make it true, but she read on. In spite of such peace, Duncan wrote, "the Yankee must come down to cast his insinuations upon the officers of the law."

He doesn't talk like a Yankee, Cissa thought. Recalling Hector Davis's voice also brought to her mind his genial smile and inquisitive dark eyes.

Duncan's saltiest wrath was directed toward the Law and Order Executive Committee, whose legitimacy he questioned. Cissa read with heightened interest her brother's review of the members of said Executive Committee. One of them, he charged, "cannot write his name legibly, nor can he write anything else" and has a brother who is a "fugitive from justice" on a charge of murder. Another lost a recent election to a "friend and relative" of Duncan's. A third was identified as the brother of the man Duncan defeated for the sheriff's office, a man whom Duncan had pursued on gambling and illegal whisky charges. He went on down the list, making a special point of how these men had been unable to win the votes of their fellow citizens when they ran for office, in contrast, of course, to Duncan himself.

If these weren't his enemies already, Cissa thought, *they are now*. Nobody liked seeing their family's dirty laundry aired in public like that. Were Duncan's allegations even true? And how many of the allegations he cited stemmed directly from efforts of the sheriff's office?

Finally Duncan came to Detective Hector Davis. He spoke of "Davis's glib witness, who says six hundred men took an oath to kill all obnoxious Negroes. There never has been in the history of our county a Negro killed by whitecaps" though he admitted that "one killing resembled it years ago." Cissa could think of several incidents to which he might be referring.

Toward the end of his lengthy missive, Duncan referenced his service in the war against Spain. "I have some good guns," he wrote, "and nature endowed me with its first law—self-defense. The names of my sneaking enemies are written down in red ink, so when I am gone my friends may know who they are." He concluded by vowing to continue his work as sheriff, running down "hoodlums, gamblers and other criminals."

Cissa spent much of the afternoon that day thumbing through the papers at the store. Duncan's letter was carried in several, but none had more sensational headlines than those in the *Natchez Herald*. Cissa struggled to understand what was going on in her brother's world, which was, for better or worse, her world, too. Where one paper made light of the whitecapping and praised Duncan's work as sheriff and in the Farmers' League (or his former organization, the Farmers' Protective Union), the next insinuated that he and all of his associates might soon be indicted for the very acts that the organizations publicly decried. The Law and Order League and its Executive Committee took pains to distance themselves from Sheriff Tarver and his Farmers' League despite Duncan's pretensions that they were somehow allies.

If Duncan is innocent of wrongdoing, Cissa thought, *why is he so intent on keeping the detective from doing his work?* Hector Davis was only interested in uncovering the truth, wasn't he? Perhaps it was that truth that Duncan feared. If so, where did that leave Cissa?

The editor of the *Beckport Journal*—who had been one of the leaders in pursuing whitecappers in Burr County—implied in an abstrusely worded piece that he was in communication with an "insider" from Fulton County who knew the whole ghastly truth about whitecapping there. Perhaps this "insider" was one of the men who had given Davis the sworn statements he'd mentioned to Cissa. Maybe it was Jewel, whoever he was.

If Cissa had had the gumption to go to Callander on Tuesday rather than Monday and had met again with Davis, she might have known the answers to these questions. And maybe more. Hector Davis was one person who Cissa felt convinced was devoted to uncovering the truth about these things. Cissa, too, wanted to know the truth. But her hands were tied by her obligations to her family, a fact that she found increasingly burdensome. Like it or not, she was tied to her volatile brother, whose behavior was becoming increasingly erratic and capricious as he struggled to maintain his authority and influence.

Cissa continued turning these things over in her mind as she walked home with her packet of baking powder. Taking a shortcut across a field, she noticed several horses tied up behind Albert's house. One of the horses was Duncan's.

"Aunt Cissy!" It was Albert's wife Eva, standing on the back steps and waving furiously. She signaled for Cissa to join her.

Cissa waved back and turned her steps toward the house.

"Duncan wants to see you," Eva said, as soon as Cissa was close enough to be addressed in a normal voice. She sounded a bit breathless.

Cissa's heart lurched into her throat. She tried to think what she might have done this time to offend her brother. Had he somehow learned of her communication with Hector Davis?

When Cissa entered the parlor, she found Duncan in the company of Monroe and two other men she had seen meeting with Duncan at the big house. Her heart skittered with unwelcome timidity while her brain brimmed with questions arising from the materials she'd just been reading. "You wanted to see me?" she said.

"Sit down, Narcissa," Duncan said, motioning for one of his colleagues to clear a space for her on the couch.

Cissa perched and waited.

"I was just mentioning to these gentlemen the fact that my sister knows shorthand. That's true, is it not Narcissa?'

Cissa was unaccustomed to being treated with such formality by her brother. It almost felt like respect. "Yes," she said. "I've become fairly accomplished in the skill."

"Good. Then I will need you to come down to Cowleton in a few weeks to take notes for me when the grand jury convenes to hear what Vardaman's Pinkerton scoundrel has dredged up." He paused, waiting for the three other men to nod their approval. "You will not write anything for any newspapers, just write up observations for my own records. I'm tired of being deceived by people who say one thing happened or was said when in fact it was something else altogether. You won't be able to sit in the grand jury room, of course, but you can write down everything you see and hear in open court and as people come and go. Mother will also come and stay with us in Cowleton for the duration."

This was unexpected. What was also unexpected was how excited Cissa felt. Yes, she was being ordered (not asked) to assist her brother, but it meant she would be on hand for what she knew was going to be an important and newsworthy event.

"If I'm there, Duncan, I will need to be able to submit something to the *Advocate.* They pay me to write for them, you know."

Duncan bristled visibly at Cissa's assertiveness. "So you're asking me to pay you? You're not willing to do this out of family loyalty?"

"No," Cissa said, shaking her head vigorously as she struggled to keep her voice steady and strong. "That's not what I meant. I'm not asking you to pay me. I'm asking you to allow me to comply with the expectations of those who do pay me. Surely you shouldn't mind me writing a little piece or two for the *Advocate.*"

"I don't see what would be wrong with that," one of the men said. "Hodges says she writes good stories."

Cissa knew Duncan must be thinking about the piece she'd written years ago about his canvass speech in Rundle Springs. She hadn't written anything that wasn't the truth, but she understood now that there were times when Duncan found the truth distressing.

"She won't write anything unflattering to you, I'm sure," Monroe said, directing a sharp look at Cissa.

"Probably just a sidebar piece, describing the general temper of things and activities outside the court," Cissa said, already formulating in her head the kinds of questions she would like to ask people. The questions she'd like to ask Hector Davis. Surely he would be there.

"Alright, then," Duncan said at last. "But keep in mind that your first obligation will be to stick by me and document the things I indicate to you."

"Of course," Cissa said. "I can do that."

A few days later, Cissa learned that the proceedings against whitecappers would not be held in Cowleton after all. Instead, they were moving to the state capitol and would be held in conjunction with the convening of a federal grand jury. Duncan informed her that it would be necessary for her to travel with him to Jackson.

Donna Birdwell

Chapter Thirty-Seven
Important Work in Jackson

May 1905

Jackson loomed in Cissa's mind as a great city where important people went to do important things. And now Narcissa Tarver was going. She had mixed feelings about her reasons for going: Her brother was sheriff of a county in the crosshairs of the governor's crusade against whitecapping, and many people seemed to think he himself might be guilty of that very crime. But she also was being thrust into the midst of something about which there would be stories in all the papers. Maybe some of those stories could be hers.

Duncan made arrangements for Cissa to stay with a cousin in Jackson, since staying at the Norvelle Hotel, a place that would be teeming with political men of all stripes, was out of the question. Cissa did not know this cousin, although Duncan assured her that they had met some years ago at a wedding and that the cousin had a daughter around Cissa's age. "Cousin Virginia is Cousin Anse's niece," he said. Being a close relative of former Governor and once again Senator Anselm McLaurin meant she was a woman who mattered.

"Eli will accompany you whenever an escort is necessary, Cissy," Duncan said and Cissa didn't argue. She didn't particularly like the idea of needing an escort, but she would be a stranger to Jackson and Eli knew his way around. Eli was four years younger than Cissa and had always seemed to her to be quiet and reserved, not the best suited for the political future for which Duncan seemed to be preparing him. "Eli will see to it that you are where I need you to be when I need you be there. Do you understand?"

"Yes, of course, Duncan." Cissa offered a smile to Eli. Her nephew didn't look any more thrilled than she was about his assignment as her escort.

Duncan reached into his pocket and pulled out a roll of bills. He peeled off several and handed them to Cissa. "Get yourself a new dress or something. Whatever it takes for you to look presentable in the company of city folks."

Cissa immediately thought of Julia. "I'm sure I can get Julia to sew something for me."

Duncan huffed. "You will not," he said. "No sister of mine will be seen going around Jackson in nigger attire. Go to Natchez if you must but try to get something decent."

Cissa restrained her desire to defend Julia, to tell Duncan that Julia was as good as any seamstress in the city. A visit to Natchez would be nice.

The train arrived at Jackson's Union Station in the afternoon of the last day of April and it was filled with men from Fulton County. Cissa had scribbled notes during the journey as she tried to ascertain which men were coming to defend accused whitecappers and which to assure that they were duly punished. As the train disgorged its passengers onto the platform, Cissa stared around in amazement at the network of tracks that ran through the station. She'd seen the station in Marston where two rail lines intersected and the several lines in Natchez, but never anything like this. She wondered where the various lines might lead.

"This way," Eli said as he nudged her elbow to guide her through the crowd. He carried her suitcase in one hand and his own in the other. They passed through a well-appointed waiting room posted with a sign saying "Whites Only" and past a cafe where the aromas of spicy fried things reminded Cissa that she had not eaten the lunch she'd packed for herself.

Outside there were carriages and buggies and, much to Cissa's amazement, a horseless motor car. In the center of the street a trolley waited.

"Not that one," Eli said as he set the two suitcases down on the boardwalk. "We have to wait for the Number Four. This is the Number Three. It's a new car and supposed to be very fine. It goes up to the new capitol building."

Cissa watched as Duncan and two of his companions crowded onto the Number Three. From what Cissa could see, it did look fine. It was paneled inside in dark wood and equipped with plush chairs. The beveled glass windows glistened in the late afternoon sun.

The Number Four, which Eli assisted Cissa in boarding, was shabby by comparison, though still nicer than the little horsedrawn trolley that plied the main streets of Natchez. Eli paid their fare. The car jerked into motion and Cissa watched as a panorama of buildings and people slid by her window. Almost all of the people Cissa saw were white, with only the occasional Negro trailing behind a white man or woman, clearly in service. They passed shops and a couple of banks. It seemed to Cissa that all the buildings were constructed of yellow brick or whitish stone. The roads were paved with red brick.

"That's the federal courthouse just over there," Eli said, pointing in the direction of a stately structure visible down a side street.

"That's impressive," Cissa said, trying to envision herself entering the building amid a press of important people.

"Oh, not the big stone building with the dome and all the columns," Eli said with a grin. "That's the county courthouse. The federal building is the red brick next to it."

The red brick building was not nearly so imposing. It had columns—two small ones on either side of the main door—but they looked almost like an architectural afterthought. The base of the building was shrouded in vines.

Soon the trolley curved onto a residential street lined with mansions set well back from the road amid manicured lawns and gardens. The car stopped a couple of times to let people off and on. Then Eli pulled a cord to indicate to the driver that he intended to get off at the next stop.

Cissa caught her breath as the scent of magnolias filled her senses. "Does Cousin Virginia live in one of these houses?" she asked.

"No," Eli said. "She's on the next street over."

On Jefferson Street the houses were smaller and set on less expansive pieces of ground, but they were still larger and far more elegant than Cissa's "big house" on Callander Road. In front of one of them, Eli set down one of the bags to open a low gate that looked to Cissa more decorative than functional. "She knows we're coming, right?" Cissa said, trying not to feel like the country girl she knew she was.

"Of course." Eli strode up the front walk with Cissa a step behind. Before they'd reached the porch the front door opened to reveal a smiling uniformed Negro maid.

"Miz Virginia waiting for you in the parlor," she said. "Come this way."

Eli handed Cissa's bag to the maid and set his own on the floor next to the hall tree. They followed the maid into the parlor.

Cousin Virginia—with her buxom figure, round face, and soft blue eyes—did look vaguely familiar to Cissa. She welcomed her country cousins with open arms, a huge smile, and a tray loaded with sandwiches and glasses of tea. There were chunks of ice in the tea. She introduced them to her daughter Annabelle, who was sixteen. So much for Cissa being in the company of someone "near her age." Sometimes it seemed to her that men assumed all unmarried women were adolescents. After little more than a half hour of pleasant conversation, Eli departed, indicating that he would return early the next morning to collect his aunt.

Cissa found herself alone with two cousins she barely knew— Virginia and Annabelle—and an attentive black maid who was called Hattie. A gentleman had paused briefly in the parlor doorway, scowling at the assembled ladies before continuing down the hall. Cissa assumed he was Virginia's husband George.

Annabelle seemed uncertain whether to be in awe of her cousin who was, Virginia said, serving as secretary to her brother who was a former legislator and now a county sheriff, or to hold her in disdain, coming as she did from the country and a rough part of the country at that. Mostly Annabelle flitted about trying to impress Cissa with her city sophistication.

Hattie led Cissa upstairs to her room and offered to help her unpack, an offer that Cissa declined. "I'll be fine, thank you, Hattie," Cissa said.

Alone at last, Cissa plopped down on the featherbed and sank into its softness. Her body was exhausted, but her mind raced. She was in Jackson, and she was going to cover an important story. *Yes, but it's a story that might well bring shame to my entire family.* She closed her eyes and took a deep breath.

By the time Eli arrived the next morning, Cissa, outfitted in her new frock (which she had bought in Marchelle, not Natchez), was enjoying a second cup of milky coffee on the side terrace with Cousin Virginia. She was grateful for Eli's arrival as she'd run out of topics of conversation. She could only tolerate so many expressions of sympathy over her damaged hand and insincere assurances that she would eventually find a good man and marry and have children, as if that was the only thing that would make her existence worthwhile. She was eager to get out and do something that made her feel competent and useful, if not quite important.

The press of people inside the courthouse was intimidating, but Eli—thankfully a tall young man—was able to spot his father and led Cissa over to where Duncan was deep in conversation with some associates. Despite the early hour and open windows, it was already uncomfortably warm inside the building.

"There you are," Duncan said, placing an impatient hand on Eli's shoulder and drawing him into the circle. "This is my son Eli. Anything you can say to me, you can say in front of him." Duncan's eyes narrowed as he glanced toward Cissa. Then he gestured toward her. "This is my sister Narcissa. She's here to take notes for us."

Cissa pulled out her notebook and pencil. Duncan turned back toward his companions.

Addressing Eli, but in a clear voice that carried, Duncan said, "It appears that the grand jury is not going to be content with the sixteen indictments already scheduled for arraignment. They're gunning for more. And they're not just looking at people they think are directly involved in actions intended to shoo folks off their lands. From what I hear, they're open to arguments of complicity. And there's no telling how far they might be able to go with twaddle like that."

Complicity. Cissa wrote the word a second time in her shorthand script. Did that mean that anyone who even knew about whitecapping activities and didn't try to stop it might be indicted? Perspiration blossomed at her hairline and in her armpits. She glanced around the room. There was another gaggle of men circled up on the opposite side of the hallway and among its number she recognized two faces. One of them was Gordon Cortman, the man Duncan had defeated for sheriff. The other was Detective Hector Davis. He was the one who appeared to be the center of attention. Cissa assumed the remainder of those in the circle were the members of what was billing itself as the Fulton County Law and Order Executive Committee. *Enemies,* she thought. *These are the ones Duncan sees as his enemies.*

Cissa spotted a bench closer to the enemy gathering and quietly shifted to it, tilting her head down, though not quickly enough to prevent Hector Davis from catching her eye and offering what almost looked like a smile. Cissa sat and listened.

"How many indictments do you think they'll hand down?" one of the men asked.

Davis rocked back on his heels, gazing at the ceiling as he turned ever so slightly in Cissa's direction. "If they accept all our evidence, probably hundreds. Maybe a thousand."

Cissa's heart skipped a beat as she continued her notetaking. She doubted there were as many as a thousand white men in all of Fulton County. Could they really indict so many? Surely not Duncan, though. He's the sheriff. Duly elected by the people of the county.

"How can they not accept the evidence?" Another man spoke. "I'm sure we're on the right side of history here. Vardaman may not care about niggers' rights any more than we do, but he's bound and determined to put an end to lawlessness and these whitecappers are a lawless bunch. We're here to defend the law."

Cissa frowned, trying to understand why these men were Duncan's enemies. They seemed to be intent on stopping the kind of activity that had injured Julia's daughter and who knows how many others. *Whose side are you on, Cissa Tarver?* She cast a furtive glance toward her brother's circle on the opposite side of the room and kept writing. Hector Davis had just indicated that he carried with him signed confessions from more than two dozen men.

"They are here and ready to testify," he said. "Ready to name names and quote chapter and verse."

"But now they're going to have to say all that under oath," another man said. "And you know sometimes that oath makes people forgetful."

"Especially when someone's taken a different oath that carries a death sentence if they break it." A murmur ran through the group.

"If we can get enough of them to tell the truth," Hector Davis said with a frown, "then the scales tilt in our direction and they'll know they have nothing to fear."

Cissa turned her attention toward a set of doors at the end of the hallway that had just swung open. The crowd pressed in that direction and Duncan signaled to Cissa to move that way as well.

Cissa entered the courtroom and found a seat near the back. She felt the pulse in her temples surge as a man at the front of the room declared the opening of the regular May session of the U.S. Fifth Circuit Court for the Southern District of Mississippi, Judge Henry Clay Niles presiding.

The first order of business was the empaneling of a grand jury, the selection of which, Cissa had to assume, had been decided ahead of time since it only took a few minutes to read out the list of names. As twenty-one men stepped forward to take their oaths, Cissa noticed that two of them were Negroes. The only man Cissa recognized was Gordon Cortman.

After swearing in the grand jurors, Judge Niles commenced his charge to them as Cissa took notes.

"There are parts of our illustrious state," the judge began, "in which lawlessness runs unchecked, and government homesteaders are intimidated by bands of men working in the dark of night. How foolish it is," he continued, "to send missionaries to foreign lands when there is such a splendid field of operation at home among men who join oathbound organizations, openly declare themselves against law and order, and try to live in a community among themselves and governed by their own will and caprice, riding up and down the public highways at night and shooting promiscuously into churches, schoolhouses and at signboards and raising hell generally." He insisted that such behavior had nothing to recommend it, and "is a sowing of seeds that will produce a harvest of ruin and desolation."

Cissa wrote it all down. As she glanced around the courtroom, she noticed that Hector Davis had taken a seat just across the aisle from her. And he was looking at her. She quickly turned her eyes back to her notepad, but not before seeing Davis raise his eyebrows and nod in apparent approval of her activity. She took a deep breath and continued listening.

The judge had moved on to speak about other cases that were likely to be presented to the grand jury. He spoke at some length of peonage in which Negroes were held in virtual slavery by indebtedness. He deplored such situations, declaring that slavery was "one of the most mournful chapters in American history." In our enlightened age, he said, no form of it should be tolerated.

Judge Niles also issued a strong warning to those "who hang around court rooms during the session for the purpose of finding out what is going on in the grand jury rooms, or who infest the hotels and boarding houses and try to influence some weak petit juror in his decision." In the performance of their duties, the judge said, jurors "should have no friends to conceal nor enemies to punish." Cissa squirmed, knowing that she fully intended to be one of those persons hanging around trying to find out what was going on. The judge hadn't said that such persons were breaking any law.

After the judge concluded his charge to the grand jury, observers were excused from the room and the jury went away to begin its work. Duncan approached Cissa and guided her into a side hallway, accompanied by Eli. "Well?" Duncan said.

Cissa pulled out her notes. "You were there so I won't review what the judge said."

"Yes, yes. What about earlier? I saw you over near where Cortman and that infernal Pinkerton were holding court."

"They sounded fairly confident about their witnesses," Cissa said as she scanned her notes. "They're looking for a lot more indictments. Hundreds, Davis said."

Duncan's eyes smoldered. "We'll see about that," he said. "I want you to stay here in the hallway and let me know who goes into the jury chamber. Descriptions if you can't pick up names. And note down the time they go in and when they come out." He nodded toward the large clock on the wall, which had just clicked another minute forward.

Cissa clutched her notebook to her breast. "But didn't the judge caution against such things?"

Duncan chuckled. "Well, he may not like it, but everybody does it. And all you'll be doing is taking notes. Eli will come get you for lunch when they recess."

Cissa found a seat and prepared to do as her brother had instructed. She was nervous about it, the judge's strong words continuing to echo in her mind. *I'm only taking notes,* she told herself. Yes, but to what use did Duncan intend to put those notes? To what use might she put them herself?

Cissa settled down to observe. She wasn't the only one seated in the hallway. There were a couple of well-dressed men sitting well apart from one another, heads down, feet shuffling nervously. Were these witnesses? A couple of younger men lounged nearby, chatting casually. At the very end of the bench was a Negro woman who sat erect, her head held high, her gaze fixed on the only window.

Occupying a chair across the hall from Cissa and closest to the door into the jury room was Detective Davis. In her notes, Cissa described him as looking alert and confident. He held a large grip sack overflowing with documents, which he took with him on his repeated visits to the grand jury, in between visits of other individuals. Unlike the witnesses, Hector Davis maintained his demeanor of ease, clearly in his element here in this charged judicial proceeding. Cissa felt as nervous as the witnesses looked, especially when she noticed Hector Davis looking at her and noticing her looking at him. *Of course I'm looking at you,* she thought. *You're the most important man in the room and I need to know what you're up to.*

Between jotting down notes, Cissa composed a little piece that she was determined to submit to the *Advocate.* Mr. Hodges had said she should go to the Western Union office and send by telegraph any information she might glean from her presence at the courthouse. He would cover her costs. When Eli came to collect her for lunch, she insisted she wasn't hungry, that she only wanted to take a little walk and stretch her legs. "Do you know where the Western Union office is?" she asked.

Eli gave her a sly grin. "Determined, are you?" He led her outside and pointed down the street. "Head this way toward the old capitol building and you'll see their offices there on the right. It's catty-corner across from the Baptist Church. You can't miss it. Oh, and there's a bakery next door. Just in case you decide you are hungry after all."

Cissa headed in the direction Eli had indicated, relieved to be outdoors and away from the crowded and overheated courthouse. She had just spotted the Western Union sign when she heard a quiet voice behind her. "Miss Tarver!" She turned. It was Detective Davis.

She turned back around quickly. She slowed her steps but didn't stop. What was Davis up to? He should know that Cissa Tarver, currently serving as secretary to Sheriff Duncan Tarver, should not be seen in public conversing with the Pinkerton detective who was in the employ of people Duncan called enemies. When Cissa glanced around again, she saw Davis jerk his head in the direction of a side street.

Cissa looked down at the notebook in her hand. It held the story she had written up for the *Marchelle Advocate*. What else might she be able to include in her story if she spent a few minutes in conversation with Hector Davis? With a furtive glance over her shoulder and a pounding heart she altered course, following Davis down the side street. He entered a door with a placard for a law office. Cissa followed. There was no one at the desk.

Even though it was cooler inside than on the street, Cissa perspired profusely.

Davis gestured toward a bench. "I thought you might like a little something extra for that story you're about to file," he said. "How would you like to say that an unnamed but highly reliable source assured you that there is every indication that witnesses are standing firm in their testimony to the grand jury?" He waited a moment.

"Oh," Cissa said, realizing what Davis was offering. She opened her pad as he repeated the words more slowly.

"...every indication that witnesses are standing firm in their testimony to the grand jury."

When Cissa looked up after recording his words verbatim, she noticed that he was looking at her damaged hand.

"You're very quick with that shorthand, Miss Tarver. Are you naturally left-handed?" There was no pity in his voice, only curiosity.

"No," Cissa said. "I learned to write with my left after a childhood injury. It was a spider bite that went to gangrene." Why was she offering these personal details to a man she barely knew?

"I admire you for not letting a little thing like that hold you back," he said. "You seem to be a good newswoman."

For the first time, Cissa offered Hector Davis a heartfelt smile. "Thank you," she said. And then she surprised herself by asking, "Are you really a Yankee?"

"Yankee? Me?" Hector Davis chuckled as his eyes sought a far corner of the room. "No, I was born and raised in Tennessee. My folks were from Virginia." He paused. "I guess the Pinkertons got a bad name here in the South when some of them worked as spies for the Union during the war."

Cissa hadn't known that about the Pinkertons. She wasn't sure why something they'd done more than fifty years ago should be relevant today. "I'd best get on down to the Western Union," Cissa said.

"Of course." Davis stood up and extended a hand to Cissa, who rose without taking it. "Don't worry," he said with a grin. "I've got some work to do here so I'll stay a while. No one is going to see us together."

After Cissa had relayed her story to Mr. Hodges, she reflected on her brief conversation with Detective Davis. She was grateful for his quote. Even though it had to be anonymous, she thought it might mean her story would merit a slightly larger headline. But why had he offered it? And then she recalled the conversation she'd overheard earlier. No doubt what Davis had told Cissa was something he wanted the remaining witnesses to hear to encourage *them* to stand firm in *their* testimony. *Be careful, Narcissa Tarver. This man may be using you for his own ends.* She recalled how Duncan had used her reporting to get what he wanted into the paper. She'd vowed not to let that happen again, to listen to her gut or better angels or whatever it was. She needed to keep her wits about her.

Chapter Thirty-Eight
"Worst Possible"

May 3-4, 1905

On Monday evening, Cissa handed over to Eli the transcriptions in longhand of all the notes she had taken during the day, omitting the information Hector Davis had shared with her in private. On Tuesday, she continued documenting the comings and goings outside the grand jury room. She noted the time on the clock for each entry and departure. She learned from overheard conversations that something called "demurrers" and "pleas in abatement" were being filed with respect to the sixteen whitecapping indictments that had been handed down in a previous court session. She watched Hector Davis intently but had no further conversations with him. Her submission to the *Marchelle Advocate* was brief.

"What are demurrers and pleas of abatement?" she asked Eli on Tuesday evening as she handed over her next batch of transcribed notes.

"Legal mumbo-jumbo," Eli said. "Basically it just means they're trying to get the cases dismissed or at least delayed for some reason or another. Generally because of some flaw in the charges or who's making them or on what grounds."

Later that evening, Cissa sat in her room reading the account of the day printed in the pages of Jackson's evening daily paper. There was little there that she didn't already know. The paper's description of the Fulton County citizens in attendance at court annoyed her: "In personal appearance a majority are not pleasing to behold. They are typical residents of the backwoods, rough and uncouth in appearance." She reflected on her brother's consistently dapper style and his insistence that she herself be well dressed. The paper was not wrong about some of the others.

Near the main article Cissa found a small piece that drew her interest: It was about the Cortman family of Fulton County, and she could see that it was an attempt to distance two family members—Gordon (who was on the grand jury) and Phillip (who was an officer of the Law and Order Committee)—from Felix, who was currently serving in the state legislature. Felix was also the treasurer who had been involved in the infamous controversy over missing Fulton County funds. *So much for family loyalty*, she thought. She wondered where the boundary lay. When was loyalty stretched too far?

Cissa had just picked up a magazine she'd found on the bedside table when she heard a knock on her door. "Come in," she called.

The door opened to reveal Annabelle holding a small tray with a glass of milk and some cookies.

"Why, thank you, Annabelle." Cissa was surprised to see her young cousin instead of Hattie.

"I thought I'd bring it to you myself this evening," Annabelle said as she continued holding the tray. "I'm going roller skating with some friends tomorrow evening and Mother says I should invite you to come along. She said you ought to have some fun while you're here in the city."

Cissa suppressed a smile, feeling certain that this was not the way Cousin Virginia had expected her message to be delivered. "That's kind of you," she said, "but I'm sure I'll need to stay here to transcribe my notes. Do you go roller skating often?"

"Oh, yes. It's quite the thing now. They play all the latest tunes on the gramophone, and we skate round and round." Annabelle dropped her chin and looked up at Cissa with a mischievous grin. "We even hold hands with a boy sometimes." She giggled.

Cissa almost wanted to go, thinking how diverting it would be to watch groups of young people enjoying themselves. She doubted she'd have the courage to try skating. Then she pictured herself, the lonely spinster sitting on the side watching, and she was glad she had an excuse for staying in.

<hr>

When Cissa arrived at the courthouse on Wednesday morning, she sensed an elevated tension in the air. There were fewer observers in the hallway outside the grand jury room. Detective Davis breezed past and, without looking right or left, entered the room. Cissa took note. He came out barely ten minutes later and, with a casual nod toward Cissa, strolled down the hallway and out of sight.

"What do you think is happening?" Cissa asked of the man sitting nearest to her. He was a young man with disturbingly erect posture and an annoying habit of foot-tapping.

"I'm guessing that they've reached their decisions," he said. "Get ready for some fireworks."

After another half hour in which nothing happened, the doors to the jury room opened and stayed that way. The jurors were not there.

"Let's go," the foot-tapper said. "They'll be in the main courtroom ready to hand over something to Judge Niles."

Cissa's heart beat fast as she made her way into the courtroom, which was soon full to overflowing. She claimed a spot off to one side where she could see the judge clearly. She could also see where Duncan sat near the front of the room. She couldn't see Eli, though she knew he was there somewhere.

A bailiff stood and banged a staff on the floor and shouted in a loud voice for order. He had to do it a couple of times before the room finally quieted. "The U.S. Fifth Circuit Court of the Southern District of Mississippi is now in session, Judge Henry Clay Niles presiding."

"Has the clerk of the court received the grand jury's decisions?" the judge asked.

"I have, your honor." Stepping forward, the clerk handed the judge a sheaf of papers.

Judge Niles studied the papers, looking over each of the pages twice and never raising his eyes to look at either jurors or anyone else in the courtroom. Cissa could not read the expression on his face. She spotted Detective Davis seated just behind the grand jurors near the front of the room. She couldn't see his face.

At last Judge Niles nodded and cleared his throat. "The grand jury has issued..." He thumbed back through the stack of papers. "We have six true bills." He picked up the paper from the top of the stack and adjusted his spectacles. "For the crime of conspiracy to intimidate government homesteaders, the following individuals are indicted: Duncan Q. Tarver..."

Cissa gasped as a clamor erupted in the courtroom. If further names were read, Cissa didn't hear them.

Indicted! They'd indicted Duncan!

"Order! Order!" The judge banged his gavel.

There was no order.

"Clear the courtroom," the judge commanded.

As Cissa was unceremoniously pressed toward the exit with the rest of the throng, she caught her brother's eye only briefly. Was he smiling? Someone came forward and placed him in handcuffs, and Cissa watched in horror as Duncan was escorted from the courtroom through a different door.

Stunned, Cissa stood in the hallway, unable to move or even think.

"Aunt Cissa!"

She craned her neck in the direction of Eli's voice. There he was, looking almost as panicked as Cissa felt. "What has happened?" she said as her nephew stepped nearer.

"Worst possible," Eli said. "Let's go over here where we can talk." He guided Cissa down a hallway and into an alcove away from the crowd. After glancing down the hall to make certain they were alone, he reached into his pocket and handed a wad of bills to Cissa. "Pop said if it came to this I was to give you money and send you home. I'm on the list, too, Aunt Cissy. As well as Albert and Uncle Monroe."

"Monroe?" Cissa couldn't believe it. "But he never... He's not even from Fulton County."

"I know. I hear they mean to send federal marshals to round up the whole lot. They'll probably have me in cuffs before I can leave the building. Aunt Cissy, there were six true bills issued, and each one had at least fifty names. They've gone after everybody who has ever been associated with Pop's Farmer's League. But we'll fight it. I'm sure we haven't done half the things they say. It was just a few bad apples got carried away. Anyway, Pop wants you back home safe. Things could get rough around here and he says Granddad would never forgive us if anything happened to you."

This invocation of her father's care almost undid Cissa. She accepted the money and tried to focus as Eli gave her detailed instructions of which train to catch and when. "I'll try to send word to Lachlan to meet you at the Marston station, but if he doesn't make it, change for the Marchelle train and you can go to Aunt Tilly's."

When Cissa arrived at Cousin Virginia's house she was met at the front door by her husband George. He wore a solemn expression and seemed eager to get Cissa inside. Did he think she was in danger? More likely he did not wish his neighbors to see the sister of the notorious Sheriff Tarver on his doorstep.

"Oh, my dear, we've been so worried about you," Virginia gushed, taking Cissa's arm and leading her up the stairs. Speaking in more subdued tones, she said, "I'm sure it's all a mistake and they'll get it straightened out soon enough. Uncle Anselm will see to it. He always takes care of family."

"Thank you, Cousin Virginia." Cissa wasn't sure how a United States Senator could help in this situation, but she was grateful for Virginia's expression of sympathy and optimism. "Eli says I should go home at once."

"Yes, of course. I understand. Hattie will bring up some lunch for you and then our boy will bring around the buggy to take you to the station. Oh, I'm so sorry you'll have to travel alone after all you've been through."

Cissa was torn. How could she leave Jackson when her own brother had just been led away in handcuffs, charged with a federal crime? Convicted whitecappers from Burr County were serving time at the state penitentiary. They intended to arrest Eli, too. But what could she do to help? She was powerless. She recalled the shouts she'd heard inside the courtroom after Duncan's name was read. People were angry. She thought of what her father had told her after that first political event of Duncan's that she'd covered: He'd told her not to let her "little job" distract her from her duties to family, by which he meant Mother. But for better or worse, Duncan was family, too. And Mother was being well cared for at Duncan's house in Cowleton. Who else could do what Cissa did as a journalist? *Under the present circumstances,* she told herself, *lots of people.* There were reporters from all the major papers covering this story, including a few she'd heard identify themselves as representing papers from out of state.

When Cissa was fed and packed and on her way in the buggy, she leaned forward and tapped the driver on the shoulder. "Would you please stop by the Western Union office on the way?"

Donna Birdwell

Chapter Thirty-Nine
Shame and Anger

May 4-12, 1905

Minutes before her train was to leave the station, Cissa nabbed a copy of the daily evening Jackson paper from the hands of a very excited newsboy. She tucked it under her arm and boarded, finding a seat next to a window. A stranger helped her secure her suitcase in the rack. She thanked him but wished he hadn't stared with such pitying eyes at her damaged hand.

She settled into her seat and opened the paper. All she could see was the bold banner headline that read: "Indicted 300 Whitecappers - Federal Grand Jury Goes to the Bottom of the Fulton County Labor Troubles - Dr. Tarver Was One of the Indicted." Without meaning to, Cissa slipped down in her seat, embarrassed at seeing her own brother's name broadcast in such terms. She let go a sigh upon reading that Duncan had been released after posting bond of $1,500. "This is the largest batch of true bills ever reported in the southern district of Mississippi and the quickest piece of work ever accomplished by a grand jury in this city." It hadn't seemed quick at all to Cissa. The article claimed that the quick work was due to evidence "so overwhelming that there was no hesitancy in returning true bills against the suspected parties."

Cissa thought about who it was that had been largely responsible for accumulating this overwhelming evidence. Detective Davis's quest for truth had landed Cissa's brother in jail, albeit briefly, and he could face a lengthy prison term if he should be convicted. Cissa also wanted to be on the side of truth, but she was finding that aspiration to be deeply challenging. She knitted her brow and continued reading.

The specific charge against Sheriff Tarver was, the article said, "conspiracy to intimidate government homesteaders." Those were the same words Cissa had used in her message to Mr. Hodges at the *Advocate.* Duncan's was the only name mentioned in the Jackson paper, though the reporter suggested that "a member of the legislature" was on the list of indicted men. Cissa knew this referred to Felix Cortman. She assumed this must be why Gordon and Phillip Cortman had been so eager to distance themselves from him. The article further indicated that "quite a number of the persons whose names are in the true bills are now in the city. They will be taken into custody before night." *Poor Eli*, Cissa thought. But if Duncan had the wherewithal to post his own bond, surely he could do the same for his son.

The report went on to say that the investigation was still in progress, with more true bills likely to be issued next week. Did that mean that Detective Davis might be back in Fulton County? The article also stated that a "posse of deputies from the United States marshal's office" would set out for Fulton County the next morning to bring in the rest of the indicted parties. "The cases, in all likelihood, will be disposed of at this term of court, as the attorneys engaged for the prosecution have expressed opposition to continuances being granted."

Cissa laid the paper in her lap and stared out the window as city gave way to countryside. All this would be over soon, one way or another. By the end of next week she would know whether her brothers and nephews would be going to prison or going home. Her mind swam in confused dismay. Though Cissa had often butted heads with her brother Duncan, she had always seen him as strong and authoritative. How could someone like that be sent to prison? How could the family survive without Monroe and Duncan? Mother would be devastated. And what would Pop have thought about it all?

Pop was the one who had told Cissa she must never be afraid to tell the truth. Surely he must have tried to convey the same guidance to Duncan. She closed her eyes and emitted a soft sigh of regret. Where had Duncan gone astray? If he had indeed done the things that Detective Davis claimed, he ought to be made to pay for his misdeeds. Cissa thought back to the day she'd found Rosie bleeding from a wound inflicted by a whitecapper. She recalled Julia's anger, Julia's certainty that Duncan had been behind the incident, that Duncan was to blame.

As the train wended its way deeper into the countryside, Cissa was grateful for the rain that pelted down, even though it meant windows had to be closed. The raindrops coursing down the panes were the tears she refused to shed. The gloomy sky and oppressive closeness inside the car suited her state of mind.

It was long after dark when the train pulled into the station at Marston. Cissa searched for Lachlan among the crowd waiting under the two kerosene lamps on the platform. There were more people than she would have expected at this hour, especially with the continuing rainfall.

There he was. And there was Monroe, too. With a rush of relief Cissa retrieved her suitcase and made her way out of the car.

Lachlan pulled Cissa into an embrace as soon as she was within reach, almost making her drop her bag. "I'm so glad you made it home safe," he said. "We were worried about you."

"I'm fine," Cissa assured him. The exhaustion of her long day surely accounted for the quivering in her legs and the pounding in her head. She hadn't really been afraid. "Why are there so many people here?"

It was Monroe who answered Cissa's question. "Folks who have heard that they got named in the indictments are headed to Jackson. I'm leaving on the next northbound train myself. Just as well go to them instead of having them come here to haul me up. Albert and Lamar are coming up on Monday."

"I couldn't believe it when they said you'd been indicted," Cissa said. She so wanted to believe that Monroe was innocent of these crimes. "The whole thing was more than I expected."

"Was it you wrote that piece that was in the Marchelle paper?" Monroe said.

"I suppose so. I did send in some information." She blanched, thinking about her quote from an unnamed source. "And I sent in more today, but that won't be printed before Saturday." Marchelle did not have the advantage of a daily paper like Jackson.

"It was a good clear piece," Monroe said. "I'm glad you've come home, little sister. It's not going to be safe in Jackson. These men are angry and they're going armed."

Cissa looked around the platform. The men were a disheveled and rough lot, looking as if they'd been snatched up out of a day's work. There were more guns than suitcases in evidence.

"How is Mother faring?"

"As well as can be expected," Monroe said as he picked up Cissa's bag and led her to where his wagon was waiting. "We haven't told her much about what's going on. Lamar brought her back from Cowleton this afternoon. She's at my house."

Cissa climbed into the wagon, thanking her brother for his help.

"We're family, Cissy," he said. "We look out for each other."

Cissa spent the remainder of that night at Monroe's house. The next morning, after breakfast, Lachlan accompanied her and Susanna back to the big house, which felt much smaller after Cissa's sojourn in Jackson. Cissa felt as if she'd been away for weeks instead of only a few days, but her mother settled into the big chair, the one that used to be Pop's chair, looking as if she'd never left. Elsie showed up at the back door and, without question or comment, went about her tasks.

Cissa tried not to let Mother see how concerned she was over her brothers' and nephews' predicament. As long as the old woman didn't ask, they wouldn't tell her what was going on. She seemed oddly cheerful most of the time, but then Cissa would catch her sitting in her chair in a prayerful attitude with a tear in her eye.

Meanwhile, Cissa's own mind whirled with echoes of the judge's fierce condemnation of whitecappers and with words she'd overheard while waiting in the courthouse hallway. Two of those words that kept being repeated were "conspiracy" and "complicit." Even if her brother Duncan had not personally committed any of the atrocities ascribed to the whitecappers, if he had been part of the planning, the motivation that put the atrocious actions in train, that, apparently, was also a crime. Or if he'd known about it but had done nothing to stop it. The grand jury had been thoroughly convinced that his organization was the hub of the whitecapping activities. How could Duncan not have known? Cissa had tried so hard to avoid acknowledging that Duncan was responsible for the attack on Julia's family three years ago, but now she found her last defenses crumbling. *If I try to excuse him,* Cissa asked herself, *am I complicit as well?*

While Cissa was completing basic preparations for the noon meal on Saturday, she heard a newspaper hit the front porch. She knew it would be the *Beckport Journal.* Like the Marchelle paper, the *Journal* only came out twice a week. When her preparations were finished, Cissa picked up the paper and took it to her father's desk—

she would always think of it as his desk—to read. She spotted an article headlined "Fulton Whitecaps - 300 Indicted." It was no more than a recap of the story she'd read on Thursday evening on her way home from Jackson. She laid the paper aside and stared at the telephone, wishing Duncan or Eli would call, wishing she could call them and find out more about what was happening in Jackson.

Cissa went into the parlor and leaned over to speak to her mother. "I'm going down to the store to get some butter," she said. "I'll be back in an hour." There was no real need for butter, but they could always use extra.

"Make sure you get the butter from McCrays," Mother said. "It's almost as good as the butter we used to make here."

Cissa promised that she would. What Cissa really wanted to do was to see what newspapers had been delivered or if there had been any calls or news from Jackson. As she walked, she struggled to keep her imagination in check.

As Cissa stepped onto the porch in front of the shop she looked up into the face of a young woman who had just exited. "Rosie?" Cissa halted on the step.

Rosie stopped, too, glancing nervously right and left. "Afternoon, Miss Tarver." She fidgeted with a parcel she held pressed under her left arm.

Cissa realized with a start how the arm hung limp, recalling the image of Rosie lying on a bed in a darkened room with a bloody bandage across her left shoulder. She also recalled a small girl who had sat in her lap caressing Cissa's own damaged hand with benign curiosity. "It's nice to see you, Rosie," Cissa said. "How are you and the family keeping?" Cissa wanted to ask so much more than this.

"We keepin' fine, Miss Tarver." Rosie laid a hand on her belly. "You know I be married now." There was pride in her voice.

"Congratulations," Cissa said, trying not to sound too surprised. Rosie was disabled, and yet she was married and soon to become a mother. "And Julia?"

"Mama be fine."

Cissa wanted to ask about Baxter, about whether he was still working at the bank in Tulsa. Instead she asked about Rosie's grandmother. "How is Zolene?" she said.

Rosie's eyes darkened as she stared over Cissa's shoulder.

Cissa felt the weight of Rosie's silence. "Is Zolene unwell?"

"She say she gots a cancer." Rosie's face remained impassive though her eyes glistened with sadness.

"Oh, Rosie, I'm so sorry. Please let me know if there is anything I can do to help. You know how much I care about your family. I never meant..." Cissa stopped.

Rosie had retreated a step from Cissa's onslaught of words. She nodded. "Yes ma'am."

"Well, it was nice seeing you." Cissa reached out with her incomplete right hand to clasp Rosie's limp left hand and for just the tiniest fleeting moment the two women's eyes met in something that Cissa felt might be mutual understanding.

No more words were exchanged. Rosie went her way and Cissa stepped inside the store. "Good afternoon, Mrs. Campbell," she said to the old woman who stood in the doorway scowling.

Mrs. Campbell came closer and, in a low whisper, said, "You be careful, Narcissa, about touching niggers like that. You know they ain't clean. And these insolent ones is the worst."

Cissa was taken aback, but before she could think of anything to say, Mrs. Campbell had bustled out of the shop and down the steps. Cissa thought of the tidy little house where Rosie and Julia lived and bridled at the notion of calling either of them dirty. She wondered who it was that kept Mrs. Campbell's house clean. And as for insolence, well, Julia had never been insolent to Cissa. Except, of course, when she deserved it.

Cissa nodded a greeting to Mr. Barnes the shopkeeper and then turned to the counter where two newspapers lay haphazardly folded. Cissa checked the dates and realized there would be nothing new in them. She read a few headlines—a couple about the rainy weather and its implications for crops, another about some postponed baseball games. She folded the papers back as she'd found them, only a bit more neatly.

"A pound of butter, please," she said. "McCray's if you've got it."

"Right away, Miss Tarver." He wrapped the lump of golden fat in oiled paper. "Anything else?"

"Any more news from Jackson?"

"Folks have been pretty quiet in here. Even the telephone has been quiet. You were there, weren't you? Up in Jackson?"

"Yes," Cissa said as she tucked the parcel containing the butter inside her carry bag. She said no more. She was a reporter. She asked the questions. She collected the news. She didn't give out news freely like some local gossip.

Cissa was on pins and needles all weekend, wondering what would happen on Monday. She wondered why she had submitted to coming home when Duncan told her to. She could have insisted on staying and then she might have known what was happening to her brothers and nephews and the rest of the men of Fulton County. Maybe she could have located Hector Davis and asked him about it. But then she recalled the cool reception Cousin Virginia's husband George had given her when she'd arrived after the indictments had been handed down. No, staying would have been unwise, unacceptable.

Monday afternoon, Cissa decided to walk down to the general store again to see if they'd heard anything or if any newspapers had arrived from Jackson.

"Mother, I'm going to the store to get some butter. I'll be back in a half hour."

"Didn't you just buy butter?"

Why did Mother's memory seem to work perfectly fine just when Cissa wished it wouldn't? "I meant to say lard," Cissa said.

"Oh. Would you pick up a penny of peppermint drops while you're there? My mouth gets so dry sometimes and peppermint drops help."

"Of course." Cissa pulled the coin purse out of her bosom to count up her change. Yes, there was enough to buy lard and peppermint drops and a newspaper if they had one. If they had two, she'd do without the lard.

Cissa inhaled deeply as she stepped out of the house. The air was still heavy from the recent rains, which had turned everything green and propelled the crape myrtles into riotous full bloom.

The only new papers Cissa encountered at the store were local ones and they carried no new information. She hurried back home with a small lump of lard and the peppermint drops for her mother.

When she opened the front door she saw her mother standing in the center of the hallway looking flustered.

"That thing Duncan put in the dining room has been making a dreadful racket," she said. Of course Mother hadn't tried to answer the telephone; she wouldn't even touch it. She refused to believe you could talk back and forth with someone far away by speaking into an object like that.

Cissa handed the peppermints to her mother and seated herself at her father's desk. She stared at the instrument, wishing there were some way she could pick up the receiver and ask the operator who had called.

She almost jumped out of her seat when it finally rang.

"Hello, Dr. Tarver's office." She listened. "This is Narcissa Tarver." She waited. "Yes, I'll hold for the call."

While she waited for the connection to be completed, she took out her notebook and pencil. She sat poised for whatever was to come, her heart pounding ferociously. At last a voice came through on the line, weak and crackling.

"Aunt Cissy?" It was Eli. "Pop wanted me to tell you that the arraignments are being delayed until Thursday."

"Oh," Cissa said, feeling suddenly deflated. "Is there any other news?" Her voice sounded so odd speaking into this contraption.

"They're filing demurrers for the seventeen that were supposed to be ready for trial. It looks like half of Fulton County is here in Jackson." There was an incoherent sound.

"Would you do me a favor and get me a subscription to the Jackson evening paper? I'll pay you for it when you get back."

"Of course," Eli said. "It'll give me something to do. Alright then, that's all. Others are waiting to use the phone."

"Thanks, Eli," Cissa said, but her voice met only stone silence from the instrument. She hung up the earpiece and set the device back in place. She turned and saw a boy standing in the doorway. "Joey! I didn't hear you come in."

"Was that my Pop on the telling-phone?" the boy asked. "Mama sent me to see if there was any news."

Cissa told him that it had been his cousin Eli on the phone. "Eli said your Pop is fine and that he misses you and your brothers."

"And Dee?"

"Yes, your sister, too."

"And Mama?"

"Well, of course he misses her," Cissa said. It was hard for Cissa to believe Monroe's youngest boys were getting so big. Joey must be almost ten now. "Wait a minute and I'll write a note you can take to your mother." She didn't trust Joey to remember words like "arraignments" and "demurrer."

⁂

When the Monday Jackson paper arrived around midday on Tuesday, Cissa read more about the crowds of Fulton County citizens thronging the city and about who Duncan had retained for his defense. The article stated that many of those indicted stood ready to sever all ties with Sheriff Tarver's Farmers' League and might be sent home with a lecture and a nominal fine. It went on to suggest that even if no one else were tried, Sheriff Tarver certainly would be. Cissa took a deep breath and continued reading, her brow knit in consternation. "Dr. Tarver is not hunting a compromise," the reporter wrote, "but continues to be aggressive and defiant of the parties whom he alleges to be his bitter political and personal enemies."

Later that same day, Cissa's copy of the Natchez newspaper arrived. It contained an article flagged "special to the *Natchez Herald*." Cissa skimmed it to see if it contained anything she hadn't seen in the Jackson paper. This piece did mention that it had been "necessary to pretermit the circuit court at Cowleton for the reason that there will not be a sufficient number of men left there to run the court." Cissa's eyes widened when she saw the name of Senator Anselm J. McLaurin listed as a defense lawyer for Duncan.

On Thursday Cissa read that Judge Niles had delayed the arraignments and trials until Saturday. She paced about the house in exasperation. She burned the biscuits so badly that even the chickens refused to eat them. Her next batch didn't rise properly. She went to the store and bought a round steak which she proceeded to beat to a pulp with the meat mallet.

The excitement of her brief adventure in Jackson felt to Cissa like a rich meal that, hours later, leaves you with indigestion and an unpleasant taste in your mouth. Not for the first time, Cissa wished she was not a Tarver, wished she could marry if for no other reason than to change her last name. The name *Mrs. Johnny Welborn* echoed in her mind. But, no, she'd long since rejected that possibility.

Cissa was tired of worrying about whether her unruly brother was going to be thrown into prison or not, weary of the chaos that plagued her mind when she tried to decide for herself whether he was the perpetrator of crimes or only the misguided hero of struggling farmers who were trying to preserve their way of life. Was he Professor Moriarty or Robin Hood?

"What did that piece of steak ever do to you?" It was Lachlan, standing in the kitchen doorway and grinning at Cissa.

Cissa set down the mallet with a sigh and a laugh. "I didn't hear you come in," she said.

"No wonder, with all that racket you were making." Lachlan pulled out a chair and sat, stretching his long legs toward Cissa.

Cissa sprinkled seasoned flour over her very tenderized steak. "Have you heard anything?" she asked.

"That's what I'd come to ask you." Lachlan's expression grew more serious. "You're the one with the telephone and all the papers."

Every day either Sam or Joey had been coming to inquire for news. Cissa was glad Lachlan had come this time. When she told him about reading that there would be a further delay in the trial, he groaned.

"No wonder you're feeling so frustrated," he said.

Cissa draped a cloth over her steak and sat down at the table, wiping her hands on her apron. "Do you think they'll go to jail?" she asked.

"Honestly, Aunt Cissy, I doubt it." Lachlan studied his interlaced fingers.

"But they did send some of the Burr County whitecappers to prison." Cissa tried to scrape some flour from under her fingernails. "And the ones who were officials of one sort or another lost their jobs. Surely Duncan is worried about that."

"All true. But those fellows didn't have a U.S. Senator on their defense team." Lachlan shook his head. "Before he left, Pop was telling me that Uncle Duncan is plenty worried about his job. You saw how he acted when he thought the Law and Order Committee was about to demand his removal."

"I saw," Cissa said.

"Uncle Duncan seems to think this whole thing ties back to a conflict between Governor Vardaman and Anse McLaurin, from the days when Cousin Anse was governor."

Cissa thought that sounded a bit far-fetched. "How exactly is Senator McLaurin our cousin anyway?"

Lachlan shrugged. "For the life of me I can't tell you. A cousin of Grandma's I suppose. Pop did mention that Cousin Anse and

Uncle Duncan weren't always on good terms when Uncle Duncan was running for office as a Populist. The Senator has always been a staunch Democrat."

Cissa thought about how Duncan, during his Populist days, had voted for Anselm McLaurin instead of the Populist candidate the first time Cousin Anse ran for Senate. When politics ran up against family in that instance, it seemed family won out.

Donna Birdwell

Chapter Forty
A Key Witness

May - October 1905

The third time Cissa lifted the telephone receiver on Saturday and had to tell the operator she was not trying to make a call, only checking to see that the instrument was working, the operator sounded decidedly annoyed. "I'm sorry," Cissa said. She hung up.

When the phone finally rang, Cissa jumped as her heart lurched. "Hello. Dr. Tarver's office," she said. "Yes, I'll wait." While the call was being connected, her mind raced through all the possibilities. Duncan had been convicted and was being sent to prison. Or maybe he was being fined some exorbitant amount that he couldn't raise. Or perhaps he had been acquitted and would soon be on his way home.

"Aunt Cissy?"

"Yes, Eli. What happened?"

"They've continued the case until next court term."

Cissa's mind whirled in disbelief. This was the one possibility she hadn't entertained. The prosecuting attorneys had been so adamant about bringing all this to a quick conclusion. "What?" she sputtered. "No trial until...when? The fall?"

"Maybe even next summer. I'm not sure what made Judge Niles change his mind about moving forward, but there it is. Tell Aunt Laura we'll all be home on the early train tomorrow."

Cissa asked a few more questions for which Eli had no answers.

"It will all be in the papers," he said.

Cissa was sitting on the front porch and saw Monroe and then Albert arrive home. They looked somehow two-dimensional, depleted. Her copy of the Jackson paper arrived a couple of hours later and she delved into it, hungry for details of the events that had returned her kin to Hinson and Fulton counties with no resolution of their legal predicament.

"Very much contrary to the expectations of the attorneys for the prosecution," the article began, "Judge Niles has continued the federal grand jury indictments against the alleged Fulton County whitecappers." Cissa already knew that, and she scanned further down in the article for the explanation of why this had happened, pausing briefly to absorb the statement that "the stirring trial and promised exposure of the celebrated Farmers' League is postponed for the present, at the least, and possibly forever, so far as the federal government is concerned." She latched onto the word "forever." Perhaps her kinsmen were home free and not just waiting in some sort of legal purgatory.

There were quotes from Senator McLaurin, who had tried to argue some obscure legal points, even questioning whether the homesteaders who were allegedly threatened had legal right to be on the properties where they resided. As Cissa read on, however, she saw that the continuance was based not on the Senator's contentions, but rather on the argument that the defense was not ready for trial, since "key witnesses were not presently available."

The article went on to detail a "plea in abatement" that had been entered, resulting in a private conference among Sheriff Tarver and his lawyers—including Senator McLaurin—and a signed statement from Duncan that was read in court. The statement charged that Detective Davis had illegally gone into the grand jury room while other witnesses were present. Duncan said he had this on the evidence of a Negro woman who had been waiting to testify about her husband's murder.

The little hairs on the back of Cissa's neck rose to attention as she realized that in fact the evidence Duncan was citing was most likely not from this Negro woman. The "key witness" who was not available was Cissa herself. She knew she had noted the times when individuals entered and departed the grand jury room, just as Duncan had instructed her to do. Her mind raced as she tried to recall whether there might have been overlaps when both witness and detective were in the room simultaneously. She couldn't recall such instances. And surely she would have noticed, wouldn't she?

She went to her bedroom and, tossing the newspaper onto the bed, she pulled out the shorthand notes she'd taken while sitting in the courthouse hallway. She scanned through them, looking at the times she'd noted. Sure enough, in two instances, the time entered for the arrival of Detective Davis and the departure of a witness were the same. And once—was that a three or an eight? Try as she might, however, Cissa could not recall any overlaps inside the grand jury room. It was just that the clock hadn't moved a full minute between the two notations. Or that she might have misread her own notes.

Cissa's hands went cold and clammy. Would Duncan expect her to testify in court about what she'd seen? She dropped onto the bed and lay immobile as a sack of meal while her mind reeled. If she were called to testify, she'd have to take an oath to tell the truth. She could swear to the times she'd entered in her notes. What she could not swear to was Duncan's contention that Hector Davis had been in the grand jury room while witnesses were being interviewed. Her thoughts twisted and turned, peppered with visions of Duncan's anger if she refused to support him, refused to impugn Detective Davis who, to the best of Cissa's recollection, had done nothing wrong. She also didn't want to explain why she'd watched Hector Davis so attentively.

Cissa recalled the oath that members of the Farmers' League took. If she were a member of that organization, she would be expected to support Duncan no matter what. Would she be expected to lie for him? She was reasonably certain that the answer to that was "yes." *But you're not in the Farmers' League,* she told herself.

Yes, but you're a Tarver. And, in a way, wasn't that worse? According to Duncan, family were as good as oath-bound even without signing anything. The very blood in her veins constituted Narcissa Tarver's oath.

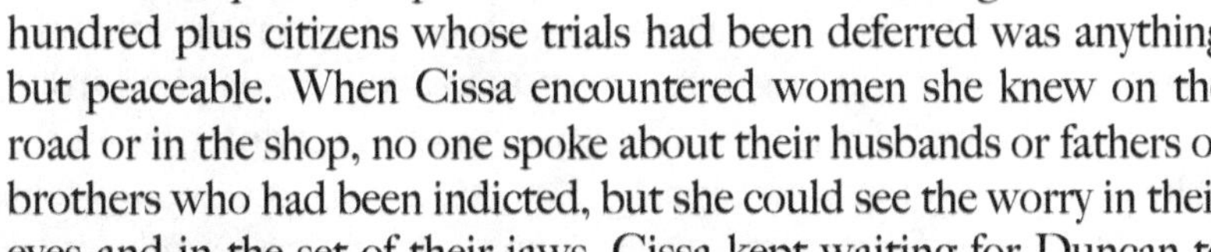

The quiet that prevailed with the homecoming of the three hundred plus citizens whose trials had been deferred was anything but peaceable. When Cissa encountered women she knew on the road or in the shop, no one spoke about their husbands or fathers or brothers who had been indicted, but she could see the worry in their eyes and in the set of their jaws. Cissa kept waiting for Duncan to approach her about testifying at his trial, but for the first few weeks he kept himself busy being sheriff of Fulton County and was rarely seen on Callander Road.

Cissa busied herself writing material for the *Marchelle Advocate.* She wrote obituaries of a couple of elderly folks who passed. She wrote an article about a child who drowned while on a family picnic at the river. She wrote about the state of the crops and about a construction accident in which a couple of men fell from a scaffold and suffered minor injuries.

She read the newspapers that arrived at her home and a few that came to Mr. Barnes's store. She was grateful that people she knew were no longer front-page headlines in Natchez or Vicksburg or Jackson.

As if there wasn't already enough to worry about, news began coming in from New Orleans about an outbreak of yellow fever. The last epidemic of yellow fever had been in 1897, the year that Pop died. That was before anyone had known that mosquitoes were the culprit in its spread. So far, only one case had been reported in Natchez—an Italian who had been working on a riverboat.

Cissa tried not to think about Duncan's upcoming trial and what he might yet expect her to do. Maybe he'd moved on to some other plan of defense that wouldn't entail having his sister testify in court about hastily taken notes and what she remembered seeing in the hallway outside the grand jury room. Or what she remembered not seeing, despite having been acutely aware of Hector Davis's every move.

On one of Cissa's local shopping forays in mid-June, Mr. Barnes greeted her with uncharacteristic enthusiasm. "We got something here I'm sure you'll be interested in, Miss Tarver," he said, pushing a piece of paper and a pencil toward her.

"What's this?" Cissa moved closer. The paper held a lengthy handwritten paragraph followed by a couple of signatures.

Mr. Barnes made no response.

Cissa picked up the document. It was a petition directed to Governor Vardaman that, as best Cissa could ascertain from the somewhat convoluted language, constituted a request that he pardon several of the men from Burr County who were serving time in the state penitentiary for whitecapping. She saw at once the implications of such a pardon for men of Fulton County who were currently under indictment for similar crimes.

"I don't expect a woman's signature would count for much," she said as she laid the piece of paper back on the counter. Cissa was familiar with the trials and convictions of the men in question and felt certain that prison was where they belonged. She committed some of the phrases in the petition to memory to convey later to Mr. Hodges at the *Advocate*. She picked up a copy of the latest Vicksburg newspaper and was paging through it as two men entered the shop.

"This here's the thing I was telling you about."

Cissa recognized the speaker—an older man with a balding sunburnt head and pale gray eyes—as one of the small farmers from over the other side of Callander. He picked up the petition and thrust it in front of his young sandy-haired companion. "I'm certain you agree them boys are bein' treated unfair over in Burr and it's time they git back to they families."

As the young man leaned over the page to examine it, the older one pulled a small black book from his pocket and picked up the pencil that lay next to the petition. "So where is it you want your name writ?" he said, pointing with the pencil toward the petition and then tapping it against the little book.

The younger man took the pencil and signed the petition, mumbling something about not needing any trouble.

He didn't even read it, Cissa thought. Maybe he couldn't read.

After the two men left, Cissa approached Mr. Barnes to make her intended purchase of a spool of thread. "What do you suppose was in that fellow's black book?" she asked as she waited for Mr. Barnes to find the thread.

He placed the thread on the counter and looked at Cissa through narrowed eyelids. "I suppose we can speak freely, since I know where your loyalties lie," he said. "My understanding is the book is where they write down the names of the ones who refuse to sign." He adjusted his spectacles. "Is there anything else you need, Miss Tarver?"

All the way back home Cissa stewed over what she'd seen. She knew full well that there was a long-standing practice whereby gubernatorial pardons were often granted to individuals who had been convicted of crimes. She'd recently read an article critical of the days when Anselm McLaurin had been governor at the same time that one of his brothers was a District Attorney, another brother was a judge, and yet another was warden of the state penitentiary. The implication had been that they could convict and punish and pardon at will. That was no longer the case, if it ever had been. Vardaman was governor now. And given that it was Vardaman who hired the Pinkerton detective who had been instrumental in bringing the Burr County whitecappers to justice and securing indictments on half the men of Fulton County, Cissa had serious doubts as to how amenable he would be to petitions for pardons.

Cissa included a couple of sentences about the petition in her weekly summary of local activities for the *Marchelle Advocate*. From the *Beckport Journal*, she learned that a counter petition was also being circulated, imploring Governor Vardaman *not* to pardon the Burr County whitecappers. Cissa experienced a fleeting moment of sympathy for the governor.

In July, the federal court in Jackson indicted a dozen more Fulton County residents for whitecapping. In the same article that revealed this bit of news, Cissa read that Detective Hector Davis was currently in Texas pursuing an escaped convict on behalf of the city of Dallas. She experienced a twinge of disappointment.

As yellow fever continued to spread, a quarantine was set up in early August along the rail line near Hattiesburg where a case had been diagnosed. Shortly afterward, Monroe showed up at Cissa's house with a load of screening material.

"Duncan says we need to put up screens to keep the mosquitoes out," he said. "It's the mosquitoes that spread the yellow fever. So he says, anyway." Monroe left his two youngest under Lachlan's supervision to install the material.

Town after town began setting up what they called "guard quarantines," in which armed guards were posted to prevent people and goods from entering the quarantined place. It wasn't long before Duncan set up a guard quarantine around Cowleton.

Cissa was in the middle of dinner preparations on a Friday in mid-October when Duncan's telephone began ringing. It didn't ring often—only a handful of times in a week. She wiped her hands on her apron and hurried into the dining room.

To her surprise, the voice on the other end of the line was Ada's. "Cissy, there's been an accident," she said, her voice shrill and unsteady. "Duncan's hurt." She swallowed a sob. "He wanted me to call so that if you heard about it Mother wouldn't worry."

"How bad is it? How did it happen? Is he going to be alright?"

"Lamar says so," Ada said. She paused and there was another sputtering moan. "It's his leg. There was a lot of blood, Cissy."

Cissa had so many questions, but she knew Ada was not going to be the one to answer them. "Is Lamar there? Maybe I could speak with him for a moment." Lamar's medical opinion would be more informative than Ada's whimpering.

"He's still in there with Duncan. I told you, he says Duncan will be fine."

Cissa suspected Ada was repeating this in order to convince herself that it was true. She thanked Ada for the call and hung up.

"Did something happen?" Mother stood in the doorway. How long had she been there listening?

"Duncan's got into a little scrape is all, Mother, and they didn't want us to worry. Ada and Lamar say he'll be fine. Go sit down and rest. Dinner will be ready in a bit."

"Yes, I'm sure he'll be fine." She fidgeted with her handkerchief and glanced toward the front door. "Did you get those crackers I like from the shop?"

"No, they were all out. They're out of a number of things that can't get through the quarantines."

"Quarantines?"

"The yellow fever, remember? No need to worry, though. There haven't been any cases around here." Well, there was that one woman from over past Rundle Springs, but she was from one of those poor white families that didn't mix much.

When Cissa found coverage of Duncan's accident a couple of days later in the *Fulton Gazette*, she better understood Ada's distress. The "accident" had been an exchange of gunfire with a man by the name of Donald Brewer. Brewer had emerged unscathed, but Duncan had been shot in the leg. It occurred to Cissa that she ought to be grateful that her temperamental brother was a poor marksman and that the marksman in the family was her more even-tempered brother Monroe.

The article cited the "facts of the case" as told by Brewer and another witness as these: Brewer and his friend were in a wagon on their way to Cowleton when they passed Sheriff Tarver's buggy on the road and there was a "slight collision" between the two vehicles, which "occasioned some sharp and unpleasant language from Tarver and was returned by Brewer. After passing, Tarver stopped his buggy, got out and again cursed Brewer in a most vile manner.

Brewer then jumped from the wagon and the shooting commenced." The exchange ended only after both men had emptied their guns.

Cissa caught her breath when she read that two of Mr. Brewer's children had been in his wagon at the time of the shooting. *Whatever were you thinking, Duncan?* According to the article, Brewer had been arrested, charged with assault and battery with intent to kill. "Warrants will also be sworn out against Tarver, charging the same offense." The piece suggested that there had long been bad blood between Duncan and Mr. Brewer, though Cissa could not recall having heard this particular individual mentioned as one of Duncan's many enemies.

Cissa felt compelled to ring Duncan's home to inquire after his wellbeing. To her relief, Lamar answered the telephone.

"Ada never said it was a gunshot. That sounds serious," Cissa said. "Would you be so kind as to tell me exactly what his condition is?"

Lamar cleared his throat and then there was silence followed by what sounded like a door closing. "It's worse than we thought, Aunt Cissy," he said. "Pop had bound up the leg himself out there where it happened and kept insisting it was nothing but a small flesh wound. You know how he gets when he's mad. He wouldn't let me even look at it until the next morning. Anyway, it turns out a bit of cloth from his trousers had got caught in the wound and although I got it out, it's become dreadfully inflamed. Dang fool will be lucky if he doesn't lose part of his leg." There was the sound of a deep sigh. "I shouldn't say such things. Please don't repeat what I said, Aunt Cissy. Pop will be even more furious if the papers start saying he's bad hurt. He's already angry enough that they're saying he started it and that it's about politics."

"Wasn't it?" Cissa said.

"Anyway," Lamar continued, ignoring her question, "Eli is trying to help Pop take care of the sheriff business and I'm trying to keep him in bed where he belongs until the swelling and inflammation clears up."

Cissa thanked her nephew for the information. "Please give him my best wishes," Cissa said. "I won't put any of this in the papers." She hung up. She wouldn't tell Mother, either. But she ought to let Albert and Eva know. And Monroe and Laura. Sometimes being the keeper of Duncan's telephone was more trouble than it was worth.

What Cissa really wanted to do was to call Mr. Hodges at the *Advocate*, but she'd given Lamar her word.

When she told Monroe about Duncan's injury he just frowned and shook his head. "I had a feeling it might be worse than they were letting on."

"Why does Duncan do these things?" Cissa said.

Monroe reached for his pipe. "You know he was in a foul mood even before the indictments and now dealing with the yellow fever and enforcing the quarantine he's set up for Cowleton, his fuse has got even shorter." He picked up his tobacco pouch and put it down again. "Something like this was bound to happen, the way he insults folks and sees an enemy behind every bush. And the way he waves that pistol around. Looks like he picked the wrong man to actually shoot the thing at."

Cissa looked away to hide her smirk. "You mean a man who shot back? And who was a better shot than our brother? I'm sorry he was hurt, but I'm doubly glad no one else was. Especially those children."

Chapter Forty-One
Complicity

Winter 1905-06

"There's been another killing down in Fulton," Lachlan said as he handed Cissa the newspaper and a letter that had been misdelivered to his house.

The news came as no shock to Cissa. "Another Negro?" she asked.

"No, a white man this time. Fellow by the name of Jewel Archer."

The name rang a bell in Cissa's mind, but first things first. "How did it happen?" Cissa asked. "Do they know who did it? Or why?"

Lachlan shook his head. "You sound more like a news reporter all the time, Aunt Cissy. I don't have the answers to those questions. I just overheard Pop talking about it with the mailman. He said this Archer had some connection with the post office. I'm sure it'll be in the papers."

It wasn't until after Lachlan left that Cissa remembered with a start where she'd heard the name Jewel. It had been in the cafe in Cowleton. Detective Davis had spoken with a fellow who recommended he look up a man with that name.

She turned her attention to the letter. It was addressed to "Miss N. Tarver, Callander Road," but it wasn't from Johnny or Liz. There was no return address; the handwriting looked somewhat familiar. At her father's desk, she broke the seal and took out a single piece of folded paper. "Dear Miss Tarver," it read. Cissa's eyes skipped to the signature; yes, it was from Hector Davis. With a sharp intake of breath and a glance over her shoulder, she read the message: "I wanted to let you know that I expect to conclude my business in Texas in time to be in Jackson for the trials next summer. I am hopeful that I might see you there. Perhaps we could share updates."

Cissa sat with her eyes wide as she refolded the paper and slipped it back into the envelope. Her mind turned somersaults, thinking about what she might learn from Hector if she went to Jackson, what she might be able to share with him. The Pinkerton detective apparently thought Narcissa Tarver was a person worth speaking to. Maybe she should go to Jackson on her own regardless of what Duncan wanted of her. She took the envelope to her room and hid it away among her things.

When Cissa's copy of the *Beckport Journal* arrived the following day, there was a lengthy article about Jewel Archer's death. It stated that Archer had been carrying the mail from Beckport to McManus Creek, although he was not the usual carrier. He was shot multiple times from more than one gun, and it was unclear whether he'd gotten off any rounds from his own pistol, which had been damaged in the melee. The paper reported that "Jewel Archer was once a member of the whitecap organization of Fulton County, but on discovering its true character, early withdrew from its ranks and took quite an important part by the assistance he rendered Detective Davis." Cissa cringed as she read that Jewel Archer had been one of the key witnesses against the whitecappers in front of the grand jury in Jackson. The *Journal* called the murder a "foul assassination."

With a troubled frown, Cissa continued reading. Family members of the suspected murderers offered a vastly different account of the incident, claiming that "Archer was drunk and started the trouble." This was an excuse Cissa had seen all too often. Three men had given themselves up to Sheriff Tarver and were in jail. Cissa recognized one of the names: It had been on the list of those indicted along with Duncan. Cissa's heart sank with the realization that if Sheriff Tarver was indeed who Detective Davis and Jewel Archer said he was, the three murderers had nothing to fear from him. They were all sworn under the same oath of mutual protection.

Complicity. The word came back to Cissa with a surge of anger. This time it was complicity in a murder that any thinking person could see was politically motivated. Cissa thought again about the upcoming trials in Jackson. Duncan still had not approached her about testifying. She'd begun to hope that maybe he wouldn't.

She was still stewing over all of this when Elsie approached her to say there was a caller at the kitchen door. "She askin' to talk to the newspaper lady."

"Oh," Cissa said, thinking this was highly unusual.

The woman standing on the step outside the kitchen was not anyone Cissa recognized. This, too, was odd, as Cissa knew all of the white citizens of the area at least by sight if not by name.

"May I help you?" Cissa said, holding the screen door open and glancing around to see if there was any conveyance that had brought this woman to her door. She saw none.

The woman stood staring at Cissa with frightened eyes, clutching a folded piece of soiled paper in her hands. She was young, though she looked a bit too old for the girlish garb she wore. Her walnut brown hair was swept back into a single rough plait behind sunburned ears. She thrust the folded paper toward Cissa.

"You need to read that there, Missus," she said.

Cissa unfolded the paper. There wasn't much to read, as the message contained only nine words: "Night has no eyes; dead men tell no tales." There was no signature, only a crudely drawn picture of what looked like a coffin and a figure hanging from a tree alongside a pistol marked "38," which appeared to be riddling the body with bullets. Cissa felt the blood rush to her cheeks and pulse in her temples.

"Where did you get this?" she asked. She tried to keep her voice calm and steady. This woman was scared enough already.

"My pa found it this morning, tacked to our doorpost," the stranger said. "I know you work with them folks at the papers, Miz Tarver. You should tell 'em 'bout this, only don't name no names, you see. My pa don't want no trouble and I know he'd beat me if he knew I told you. But me and my sisters and little brother, we're right scared." She glanced toward the road. "My mama, she died of the fever ..." The girl gulped and then shook her head and turned to go away. "You'll tell 'em, won't you?" she said. "Folks need to know."

When Cissa called Mr. Hodges at the *Advocate*, he assured her that this was not the only such report.

"And all white people?" Cissa had to admit this was the most astonishing part. She wondered if Jewel Archer had received such a notice before he was gunned down.

"Not all of them but most of them," Mr. Hodges told her. "I'll write this piece myself, Cissa. I appreciate you calling this in. Keep watch."

After hanging up the telephone, Cissa remained at her father's desk, staring at the note with its ominous illustration. What had this girl's father done that had caught the attention of whitecappers? He was undoubtedly just a struggling small farmer.

She took out a new envelope and tore a page from a prescription pad. With trembling hand, she wrote, "This was tacked to the door of a poor farmer in Hinson County." She slipped the two notes into the envelope and sealed it, addressing it to "Mr. H. Davis" at the post office box in Jackson whose number she'd memorized from Hector Davis's business card. She affixed a stamp and then stared at the envelope for a moment. *Now who's going to be at risk of attracting the notice of whitecappers?* The next day she slipped the envelope into the mail slot at the general store without being noticed.

Duncan lifted the quarantine in Fulton County just in time for the November session of the circuit court, at which he was eager to participate in the drawing of jurors. "He'll have to go on crutches, but he's determined to go," Lamar said when Cissa rang on the telephone to check on her brother's condition.

Over the next week, Cissa read every account she could get her hands on regarding developments in Cowleton. The lawyer for Donald Brewer who had shot Duncan (and been shot at by him) the previous month filed a motion to quash the grand jury as illegal, arguing that Sheriff Tarver "had no right to draw a jury that he was to be examined before." The judge overruled the motion, and the grand jury proceeded with its work, which included the indictment of three men in the death of Jewel Archer. That case was continued until the next court session and the three alleged murderers were sent to a jail in a neighboring county "for safekeeping."

No indictments were made in the case involving Donald Brewer and Duncan Tarver. Cissa knew Duncan would be relieved to have that case put away, but she couldn't help thinking about the fact that, once again, her brother had gotten away with something for which another man might have paid dearly.

Christmas 1905 was a quiet affair among the Tarvers. Duncan and his family spent the day at the big house on Callander Road rather than in Cowleton, leaving a deputy in charge of things in Fulton County. Duncan was managing to get around with a single crutch now and Cissa almost felt sorry for him. He was usually such an imposing figure, not as tall as his brother, but always managing to appear grander and somehow aloof.

Cissa avoided being alone with Duncan, fearful that he would broach the matter of his defense in the upcoming trial in Jackson and the need for her testimony. He never mentioned it. What he did mention was something the papers were reporting as the "Sandy Bayou case."

"It's the same old politics rearing its head again," he fumed. "Vardaman can't resist an opportunity to try and smear a McLaurin."

Cissa knew that the issue centered on the penitentiary system's practice of leasing private properties that were then worked with prison labor, which was overwhelmingly Negro labor. Duncan's ire was directed at the fact that the one property Vardaman had pursued was Sandy Bayou, a place belonging to Senator Anselm McLaurin. The Senator himself had lashed out in the papers accusing Vardaman of impugning the good name of the Senator's late brother Walter, who had been warden of prisons when the contract leasing the Senator's property had been signed.

"Is it mere coincidence that Vardaman is digging all this up right now when they've got me caught with my tail in a crack? Or so they think." Duncan banged his crutch on the floor for emphasis.

⁂

As 1906 began, Cissa kept her head down. Duncan still hadn't approached her about testifying. And she'd heard nothing further from Hector Davis. Had he followed up on the note she'd sent him? She couldn't help feeling that everything was like a pot of stew on simmer, only needing one more stick in the fire to bring it all to a roaring boil again.

The first issue of a new newspaper in Fulton County came out in early March of 1906. Cissa received a copy special delivery via Monroe's youngest son Joey.

"Pop said you'd want to see this newspaper, Aunt Cissy." The lanky freckle-faced youngster thrust the rolled-up paper into her hands and took off at a zigzag run for home.

The banner on the paper read *Dark Lantern*. Cissa thought that calling it a newspaper was overly generous. It was more like a broadside—a single page printed on one side only. The printing was ragged and looked like they might be using castoff type (certainly not a modern linotype) and a hand press that printed one side of the sheet darker than the other.

The lead article constituted a manifesto of sorts for the publication: "This paper air started to defend the good name of the White Caps, otherwise the Farmers' Protective Union, otherwise the Farmers' League, or any other alias under which they has done business or may perform hereafter, in Fulton and our neighbor counties of Burr and Chahtah. Also to serve as a organ for the good of the order."

The up-front identification of whitecaps with these other organizations in a paper intending to defend them was startling. The low grammar, which was consistent throughout the publication, annoyed and then mystified Cissa. She continued reading: "It will fill a mighty bad felt want; for White Caps hasn't had any organ that half filled the bill before and give the news of the Order to the membership. The ones that was counted on to do this has neglected their job. This was decided at a central meeting of some of our slyest, far-seeing heads."

So they're still holding meetings. Cissa had hoped that after the flood of indictments, men would settle peaceably into running their farms and businesses. But then had come the murder of Jewel Archer and all the threatening notes posted in the dead of night. The *Dark Lantern* was further evidence that whitecappers were not done.

The subscription price for the paper was quoted as "two-bits a year to all members in good and regular standing, who is properly vouched for and every body else will have to pay $1.00, and hard to get at that."

How had Monroe secured a copy? Was he considered a "member in good and regular standing" of their "order"? Cissa had tried to convince herself that his indictment had been a mistake, an overreach. Perhaps she was wrong.

The *Dark Lantern* indicated that its "office will be portable and always run in a mighty shady place as the best insurance policy against J. K. and his prowling detectives." Cissa knew that the "J. K." referred to Governor James K. Vardaman. She reflected wryly on the Natchez article that had attempted to portray Duncan and the governor as the warmest of personal friends. She also recalled Duncan's Christmas dinner diatribe against Vardaman over the Sandy Bayou affair.

The piece continued, "One thing air already settled—we'll make it particularly warm for James K. and every other fellow who wants the law enforced against us, whenever they run for office."

Cissa knitted her brows and read the words again. Apparently, Duncan's Farmers' League folks still thought they had the power to determine election outcomes.

"As some of our papers is bound to fall in the hands of the enemy we will always use very parliamentary language in speakin of our members as the best safeguard against indictments and stripes; but in speakin of our enemies we won't use no gloves nor varnish."

After reading more, Cissa concluded that the bad grammar was intentional, since the vocabulary and spelling of big words indicated a firm grasp of the English language. Was this a joke? A mockery of a certain Jackson paper's description of the indicted Fulton citizens as rough and uncouth? Or was it merely an attempt to obscure the identity of the publishers?

Cissa curled the piece of newsprint back into a roll and crossed over into the parlor where her mother sat with an unidentifiable piece of crochet work in her lap and a cup of cold coffee at her side. "Mother, I'm going down to Monroe's house. Is there anything you need before I go? Will you be alright for a half hour or so?"

"Of course, Narcissa. You fret too much, little girl." Mother reached for the coffee but set it down again without taking a sip.

Cissa had questions about this new publication, but worse than that she had suspicions. As she marched toward her brother's house with purposeful strides, the questions tumbled through her mind, nudged this way and that by the suspicions. She found Monroe sitting on the front steps smoking his pipe. It was almost as if he'd been waiting for her.

Cissa held the paper out toward him. "How exactly did you come into possession of this rag?" she asked, not even attempting to hide the aggravation she felt.

Monroe took a slow drag on his pipe. "It was brought here by a fellow from over in Fulton."

"So does that mean they consider you to be a member in good and regular standing of the whitecaps?"

"I did join up with the Farmers' Protective Union," he said.

"And here I thought they'd made a mistake when you were indicted. You're not from Fulton County and you're not...well, you're not someone who would go around threatening innocent Negroes. That's what I thought, anyway."

Monroe struck a match and attempted to reignite the tobacco in his pipe. After several attempts, during which Cissa stood with folded arms, tapping the rolled-up paper against her right shoulder, he gave up and set the pipe aside. "No, I'm not from Fulton County," he said. "But what I am is the brother of Sheriff Duncan Tarver. So of course when he asked me to..." Monroe paused and tapped his pipe on the step. "Yes, I signed on with his organization. He's my brother, Cissy. I wanted to support him. But surely you understand that. Isn't that why you're going to Jackson with him when he comes to trial so you can testify on his behalf?"

Cissa's eyes widened in astonishment. "What?" she croaked. "Who told you I was..."

"Duncan said..."

Cissa interrupted. "Duncan said? Well, Duncan never said anything to me about it. How dare he assume that I will go without even speaking to me about it." The fire in Cissa's temples threatened to burn right through her skull. "You can tell him for me that I refuse. I will not go, and I will not testify." She threw the rolled-up copy of *Dark Lantern* down at Monroe's feet. "And you can tell him that his little whitecap rag is as transparent as it is disgraceful. His words come through loud and familiar despite the pitiful disguise of low grammar."

Cissa glanced up at Laura who had come to the front door and stood in wide-eyed silence observing her sister-in-law's outburst. Cissa turned on her heel and headed home, her thoughts still in turmoil and her heart thrumming a military cadence. She hadn't even been fully convinced as to who was behind the *Dark Lantern* until the words had come from her mouth. But it had to be Duncan. All that talk of enemies and election losers and the vilification of Vardaman was Duncan through and through. And he had the gall to assume—to assume without even speaking to her—that she would testify on his behalf at his trial in Jackson in another six weeks. This is what loyalty meant to Duncan: It meant everyone doing *his* will and *his* bidding.

By the time Cissa reached home her fury had resolved into a bad case of nerves. She was imagining Duncan's reaction if Monroe told him what she had said. And if Monroe didn't tell him, would she have the fortitude to repeat her accusations to Duncan's face?

Chapter Forty-Two
Hard Truths

Spring 1906

Cissa spent the rest of that day and most of the next on edge. She even snapped at her mother once when all the woman had done was complain that the milk this time of year wasn't nearly as nice as midsummer milk. It was late afternoon when a buggy pulled to a rough halt in front of the house and the voice berating the horse was unmistakably Duncan's.

Cissa's gut twisted. She watched from the parlor window as Duncan labored up the front steps, leaning on the railing and his single crutch. He thumped across the porch and when the screen door slammed behind him, Cissa stepped into the hallway.

Duncan hung his hat on the hall rack without looking at his sister. Then he turned toward her and said, "We need to talk." He gestured toward the dining room where he kept office.

"The parlor will be more comfortable," Cissa said. "Elsie's been doing some spring cleaning in the dining room."

Scowling, Duncan followed Cissa into the parlor.

Cissa took her seat in their mother's favorite chair, which had previously been their father's customary seat. Duncan was left to sit on the couch or in one of the straight side chairs. He took the couch.

"What was it you wanted to talk about?" Cissa was determined to be calm. She'd had plenty of time to let her anger burn hot. It still smoldered.

With a grimace, Duncan stretched his bad leg out in front of him and balanced the crutch against the couch. He cleared his throat. "We need to talk about next month's trial in Jackson."

Cissa said nothing, watching Duncan shift uncomfortably.

He cleared his throat again and continued. "I think you understand the significance of your observations about what went on during grand jury session."

Cissa brushed an imaginary bit of fluff from her skirt. "I thought you were relying on a Negro woman for her observations."

Duncan snorted. "She's long gone. Besides, her testimony wouldn't carry nearly the weight that yours will."

"Testimony?"

Duncan leaned back and took a deep breath. "Yes, Narcissa." His tone was that of a schoolmaster repeating a lesson that should have been obvious. "You need to come to Jackson in May to offer testimony about those notes you took last summer."

Cissa looked at Duncan, savoring his discomfort. He still hadn't *asked* her to come, hadn't asked her if she was willing to testify. Hadn't said *he* needed her. "You have my transcripts of those notes. Surely that will be sufficient," she said.

Duncan shook his head and huffed out an enormous sigh. "They'll likely want you to swear that they really are your notes and that you stand by your observations. And the prosecution lawyers may want to ask questions. All of which I'm sure you'll answer correctly." He glared at her from beneath furrowed brows.

Cissa took a deep breath. Did she stand by her transcript? She recalled the doubts that had arisen in her mind as she'd perused the original shorthand notes. And what exactly did Duncan mean by "answer correctly"? Cissa could see the tension building in her brother's posture. His ears were turning red. Cissa thought about Rosie, and although it didn't calm her nerves it steeled her will. "I don't think I can do that," she said.

Duncan jolted to a standing position, causing his crutch to crash to the floor. His eyes flashed. "You don't think... Miss Tarver," he paused, his lips quivering as he limped toward Cissa. "Little sister, you *will* go, and you will defend our family name and honor." His voice grew louder and his face redder. He leaned toward Cissa and grabbed her by the shoulders and shook her hard. "You will do as I say!"

At that moment, the screen door banged again, and Monroe stood in the parlor doorway. He looked down at his two siblings who appeared to be on the verge of blows. "What's this, little brother?" he said. "I'm sure whatever this is can be sorted out reasonably." He cast an anxious look toward Cissa, whose insides quivered in horror over the audacity of her refusal to do as her brother commanded.

Duncan released his grip on Cissa and gathered his crutch from where it had fallen. He leaned on it and sneered at his two siblings. "You don't reason with women, brother. They have to be told what to do." Monroe stepped aside as Duncan limped toward the hall. In the doorway he turned to face Cissa, who was now also on her feet. "They can pitch a fit if they want, but when they're told what to do, they do it, no questions asked."

Cissa and Monroe stood staring as Duncan made his way down the steps and into his buggy.

The quivering in Cissa's insides hadn't subsided, but at least she'd remained calm outside. She had not pitched a fit. She could still feel how Duncan's fingers had dug into her shoulders. "I assume you're the one who told him that if he expected me to go to Jackson he ought to speak to me about it."

"It seemed necessary. Can you tell me what happened here? Will you go to Jackson?"

"I believe he assumes I will," Cissa said. She raised her eyebrows and crossed her arms. After a moment's silence, she said, "And now if you'll excuse me, I need to fix some supper. Mother is taking a walk in the yard if you wanted to see her before you go."

Monroe left and Cissa went into the kitchen where instead of getting the supper started she sat down at the table to contemplate her future. She sat with her feet tucked back under the chair, her elbows resting on the table, her hands gripping the sides of her head as she stared wide-eyed out the back door where her mother and brother walked quietly, side by side.

Would she do it? Would she defy her brother's expectations and refuse to testify for him in Jackson? What if she went to Jackson but instead of testifying at the trial she met with Hector Davis to share information? What might a personal interview with the Pinkerton detective mean for her as a journalist? In her mind she saw Hector's sparkling dark eyes and rakish smile.

Then Cissa thought about what might happen if Duncan were sent to prison and everyone blamed her for it. She closed her eyes and murmured "Lord help me," which was as close to a prayer as she'd come in quite a while. Somewhere outside, a mockingbird began to sing as Cissa got up to fix supper.

As spring moved toward summer and the anticipated whitecapping trials, Duncan became increasingly defiant in the papers and irritable in person. A Jackson paper quoted him as saying that he was "not at all averse to trial and was willing to confront a jury at any time the prosecution might name."

Meanwhile, the *Dark Lantern* indicated that it was "goin' to keep our off eye on the sneakin' skunks in our own camp that is fixin' to turn state's evidence and give us away." Cissa's heart sank as she remembered the note she'd forwarded to Detective Davis. Cissa remembered Jewel Archer. "Them fellows whats persecutin' good white caps cause we beat 'em out of the offices had better look out!" With better grammar, these words could easily have been uttered by Duncan.

In the next issue, the paper cautioned that "at the last meetin of F. Club it were agreed that captains and members of the order in general ought to be mighty keerful not to send any notises or warnin's to Government witnesses between now and the meetin' of the US Court in Jackson next month... Seein' as how so many of our boys has got they tails in a crack..." The writer admonished Farmers' League members to "play possum," noting that there would be plenty of time to strike back at enemies "when all them Jackson cases is nol prossud for good behavior."

As best Cissa understood that misspelled legal term, it would mean that the indictments would not be brought to trial. In that case, there would be no need for testimony in court. As Cissa was about to grasp at this as the best possible outcome for her, she asked herself: Would it be the best outcome for the county? For people like Julia and Rosie? Surely the lawbreakers ought to be brought to justice for the very real harm they'd inflicted.

The *Dark Lantern* also reported that the petitions that had been circulated in support of pardons for Burr County whitecaps "have fell flat."

It was little more than a week after this that the *Beckport Journal* began publishing what it identified as chapters from a forthcoming book entitled *Whitecapping in the South: A History of the Organization by a Fulton County Man.* The book was purportedly authored by someone who had been a member of said organization. Cissa approached the first installment with avid curiosity and considerable trepidation.

The author began by citing the oath that was given to the members of the Farmers' League. It included the vow that "if ever called upon to sit upon any grand jury, or other jury, to hold out forever against any bill or verdict directed against any member of this organization; also that I will assist in every way directed by the organization to compel Negroes to vacate any and all property owned by merchants and to assist to put out of the way any and all obnoxious Negroes living within the jurisdiction of this club." The penalty for breaking this oath and for "revealing any of the secrets or workings of the organization" was death.

Lachlan had been right about the oath. Cissa had desperately wanted to believe that her brother's Farmers' League had administered an oath no different from the pledges of mutual support that characterized Masonic Lodge or Odd Fellows membership.

There were no names mentioned in the book excerpts, but Cissa knew full well who they meant when they spoke of Democrats who joined the Farmers' Alliance and then the Populist Party. "After they had run completely out of the Democratic party, run the Farmers Alliance into the ground and run the Populist Party to death, these same old disgruntled politicians ran into the Farmers League or White Caps and were elected to office." The author insisted that there could be no disputing the fact that the Farmers' League gave "the orders to do the riding, whereby Negroes were ordered off of merchants' places and some off of homestead entries."

Cissa's blood boiled when she recalled how she had written that article about the Farmers' League based on the papers her brother had given her. According to this former member of the League, those high-sounding purposes and resolutions did not at all reflect the true aims of the organization. Cissa had been duped and she'd been complicit in duping the public. These were not the actions of a responsible journalist; they were the actions of a cowardly woman. A Tarver woman.

Cissa had foolishly clung to the hope that her own family members were not so pitiless as to be involved in the violence ascribed to the whitecaps, even while her mind accumulated all the evidence that should have assured her of the very truths that were printed here in black and white: The Farmers' League and the whitecaps were one and the same. Furthermore, her brother Duncan was not merely involved in the whitecaps. He was their leader.

Chapter Forty-Three
An Unexpected Outcome

Summer 1906

On the same day that the *Beckport Journal* published its final installment of the damning details of the Farmers' League and its lawless and violent exploits in Fulton County, the phone in the Tarvers' dining room rang.

"Hello. Dr. Tarver's office," Cissa said.

"Will you accept a long distance call from Dr. Duncan Tarver?"

Cissa blanched. She wanted to say "no" and hang up, but this was, after all, Duncan's telephone. "Yes," she said. She took a deep breath and waited for the connection to be completed.

Cissa knew that Duncan had gone to Jackson in advance of the expected convening of the federal court. She had tried to prepare herself for what she knew was coming. After reading the material published by the *Journal* she was even more resolute that she could not, would not testify in her brother's defense. She would not lie for him. She hadn't expected to have to tell him this over the telephone, but in a way, wasn't that better? She recalled the sting of Duncan's slap when he lashed out at her after she'd accused him of having a hand in the shooting that wounded Rosie. She could still feel how his fingers had dug into her shoulders when she'd first tried to tell him she wouldn't testify. And then there was his treatment of his wife.

"Narcissa?" It was Duncan.

The pulse thrummed in Cissa's temples, and her hands shook. "Yes."

"Narcissa, Eli will be coming early tomorrow morning to pick you up and bring you on the train to Jackson. He'll arrive before dawn, so be ready. I've arranged with Monroe to take Mother to his house until you return."

The heat rose in Cissa's face, and there was a buzzing in her ears. She took a deep breath. "I'm afraid all that won't be necessary, Duncan. I won't be coming to testify." She held the earpiece in a death grip a few inches away from her head, dreading what came next.

"Won't...?" There was a rough noise from Duncan's end. "Don't be ridiculous," he said. His voice was a low hiss. "Eli will be there. Be ready." A metallic click announced the termination of the call.

Cissa sat holding the earpiece, awash in a torrent of emotions, until the operator's voice came back on to inquire if she desired to make a call. Hastily, Cissa replaced the device on Duncan's desk with the earpiece in its cradle.

You've done it now, Narcissa Tarver. Would her family ever forgive her if Duncan were convicted and sent to prison? And why had she phrased her refusal the way she did? *I won't be coming to testify.* Those had been her words, though she might have said simply, *I won't come to Jackson.* She had often thought that being in the city for the trial could be a wonderful opportunity for her as a journalist. She might even be able to interview Hector Davis. But if she were there, would it be possible for the authorities to force her to testify?

She was still mulling over these things when she heard someone come up the front steps and enter the hallway. "Cissy?" he called softly.

"I'm in here, Monroe." Of course Monroe knew. He'd installed a telephone of his own just last month and Duncan would have informed him of Cissa's disobedient behavior, enlisting him to get their rebellious sister in line. Cissa turned in Pop's desk chair to face her brother. He somehow looked even taller than usual. He looked more troubled than angry.

Monroe pulled out a chair and arranged it to face Cissa. He sat leaning toward her with his clasped hands between his knees. "Duncan tells me..." he began.

Cissa interrupted. "Whatever he told you, the truth is this: I'm not going to testify. I can't swear that his interpretation of my notes is correct, since it doesn't align with my memories of the events there in the courthouse hallway. I won't lie for him, Monroe. He can say whatever he likes about how I'm betraying the family, but it seems to me that he's the one who is the cause of all this trouble, not me." Cissa fought back tears, shocked at the way her words flowed forth once she began. Things she'd barely thought in whispers she now spoke aloud.

Monroe frowned. "I'm supposed to give you a lecture on family loyalty and womanly duty," he said.

Cissa stood up, bracing herself against the desk. "Don't bother," she said. "I've heard it my whole life and I'm sick of it." She raised her gaze to meet Monroe's. "What good has it ever done me? Unmarried at nearly thirty and destined to live out my life caring for our aging mother? She's just as much Duncan's mother and yours as she is mine. But of course she's my responsibility because I'm a woman and I have no husband or children." Cissa held up her right hand. "Sometimes I think when Duncan cut away my fingers he intended to chain me to this family forever. Chained like a slave to work for other people all my life and never for myself." Cissa's composure fractured, and sobs wracked her body. She turned her back on her brother.

"I understand how you must feel," Monroe said as he rose from the chair.

Cissa wheeled to face her brother. "Understand? No. No, you do not understand. You couldn't possibly understand." She glared at him with her arms folded, her feet planted, as silent tears flowed.

Monroe stood. Then he nodded and, with hesitant steps, left the room. The screen door slammed as he departed.

Cissa closed her eyes in relief. After a few moments, she took a deep, unsteady breath and reached into her bosom for a handkerchief.

Mother stood in the doorway with tears in her own eyes. "What's the matter, little girl?" she said. "Did that bad boy pull your pigtails again? You know he didn't mean anything by it."

Cissa almost laughed. "I'm fine, Mother," she said. Cissa had a vague recollection of being teased by an older cousin. She reached up and stroked her mussed hair, wondering how inappropriate it would be to plait it into pigtails once more.

The next morning Eli went to Jackson on his own.

Throughout the day, anger and ambition, resentment and curiosity fought for possession of Cissa's will, and in the end she decided it would be unwise for her to try and go to Jackson on her own. The decision did not sit well. Not going to Jackson was because of Duncan. *When will I be able to do what's best for me?* Cissa fumed.

She was still feeling out of sorts the next day when Lachlan arrived to inform her that the trial in Jackson was over.

"And?" Cissa stared at him, unable to breathe.

"Duncan and his whole crew pled guilty," Lachlan said.

"What? Why?" This was the last thing Cissa expected.

"I'm sure I can't say why for certain, Aunt Cissy. Pop only said..." Lachlan fiddled with his suspenders.

"Yes?" Cissa prompted.

"Apparently Uncle Duncan's lawyers didn't feel like he had sufficient evidence to refute the government's case."

Cissa's entire body went cold. His inability to summon evidence was most likely due to her own refusal to testify. *My refusal to lie for him*, she reminded herself. She looked into Lachlan's eyes, where she saw no accusation, no blame. "What will happen to them?" She was already envisioning her brother in handcuffs and striped pajamas.

"Pop didn't say. I guess we'll get that news tomorrow." Lachlan took a couple of steps and then turned back. "You know this isn't your fault, Aunt Cissy."

"Isn't it?" Her eyes wanted to bore into his very soul, testing his loyalty. "You saw how determined he was to fight this at trial. If I'd testified the way he wanted... I don't see how you can say it wasn't my fault."

"I can say that because you weren't the one who ordered men to terrorize Negro farmers. Because you weren't the one who lured gullible white farmers into signing blood oaths, swearing to lie and perjure themselves to protect one another. To protect Uncle Duncan. That was all his doing. Yes, I read what the Beckport paper published about the Farmers' League and the whitecaps. I can't say much of it surprised me. Only seeing it set out in print shocked me a bit I guess."

"But if it hadn't been for my refusal to do his bidding, Duncan might have gotten away with all of it." Something in Cissa didn't want to let Lachlan deny her role in this, the importance of her own decisions and actions. "Do you think they'll go to prison?"

"I doubt it. They still have friends in high places. Although I understand that our cousin the senator is no longer representing them this time around."

Cissa raised her eyebrows and nodded. Perhaps Senator McLaurin had been convinced by the weight of the evidence as well. Perhaps even he felt that there was a limit to family loyalty. Or maybe he'd decided that Duncan Tarver, the beleaguered sheriff of a backwoods county, wasn't worth his trouble, family or not.

"You'll let me know when you hear more, won't you?" Cissa had a feeling there would be no more calls to her from Duncan or his son on the phone at her own house.

"Yes, of course. And try not to worry, Aunt Cissy."

Cissa watched Lachlan striding back down the road, grateful for his friendship. His loyalty.

When the papers arrived the next day, Cissa learned that Duncan had attempted to get his own case severed from the rest once he understood that many of those indicted were ready to plead guilty. When that failed, he and a few others who also held public offices had tried to plead "no contest," thinking to protect their official standing. The government counsel had refused to compromise and ultimately all had entered guilty pleas, except for a group of seventeen who were "nol prossed," a group that included, Cissa noted, Representative Felix Cortman.

The punishment imposed was what astonished Cissa: Each man was assessed a fine of $25 and sentenced to imprisonment for three months in the county jail, "the latter to be suspended on good behavior." It was the lightest punishment the law allowed. She learned later that the men were also required to pay court expenses, which added a not inconsiderable sum to their fines. The paper noted that Duncan had paid his fine and that of several other men and was on his way home. They still referred to him as Sheriff Tarver.

There was no mention of Detective Hector Davis.

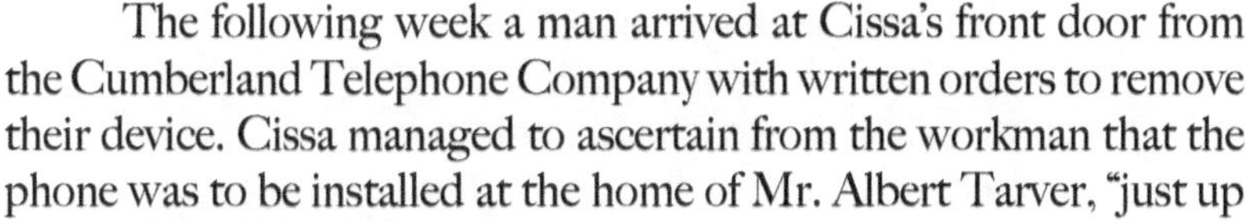

The following week a man arrived at Cissa's front door from the Cumberland Telephone Company with written orders to remove their device. Cissa managed to ascertain from the workman that the phone was to be installed at the home of Mr. Albert Tarver, "just up the road here."

Cissa assumed from this that Duncan intended to set up his Hinson County office in his son's house. No doubt he would soon be around to collect any of his property that remained in the desk. After only a moment's hesitation, Cissa began searching through the desk for items that belonged properly to her father and therefore not exclusively to Duncan. She removed a few books from the shelves, including the copy of *Rob Roy* that she'd read years before. She discovered several bundles of letters that had been stuffed into the back of one of the drawers. She took those, along with a pair of her father's spectacles and the silver letter opener that bore the barely legible initials of her Tarver grandfather.

When Lamar finally came to collect the rest, Cissa voiced no objections.

"Pop and I are going to add an extension onto Albert's house to use as our surgery here," Lamar said. He then fell silent, as if annoyed with himself for having offered any explanation at all to his Aunt Narcissa.

On his way out with a crate overflowing with books and papers and miscellaneous items, Lamar stopped into the kitchen where Cissa was busy at work. "One of the books Pop mentioned that I should get was something called *Rob Roy*, but I didn't find it there. Do you know anything about it? He said he might have lent it to someone once and not gotten it back." Lamar shifted his heavy box from one side to another.

Cissa shrugged. "Looks like you have a heavy load there already." She said nothing more. Lamar left.

So Duncan had read *Rob Roy*, too. She remembered how Johnny had said some poet referred to Rob Roy as a Scottish Robin Hood. She mused over the influence such a character might have had over Duncan's life decisions, over how he thought of himself.

Later that evening, before snuffing out the lantern in her bedroom, Cissa pulled out *Rob Roy* and opened it. There on the first page were a few lines of the poem Johnny had mentioned. It was called "Rob Roy's Grave." The poet was William Wordsworth.

"For why? Because the good old rule
Sufficeth them; the simple plan,
That they should take who have the power,
And they should keep who can."

With a sigh, she closed the book and settled into her bed. Sleep was a long time coming that night for Narcissa, haunted as she was with floods of memories of how her brother Duncan had lived out the "simple plan" sketched in the poem.

From a few brief mentions in the newspapers, Cissa concluded that Duncan's position as Sheriff of Fulton County somehow remained uncompromised by his guilty plea. He was still collecting taxes and making arrests. And, according to Lachlan, he was still as arrogant as ever about his power and influence in Fulton County.

"He's telling folks he pled guilty just to keep the peace. Pop seems pretty sure he's planning to run for some other office soon," Lachlan said. "He's convinced that all the old Farmers' League members will still vote for him."

Old whitecappers, Cissa thought.

Life for Cissa became boring again and this time she told herself she ought to be grateful for it. She experimented with some new recipes that she'd found printed in the papers and shared a few with Elsie. She continued writing for the *Advocate*, focusing once again on the mundane goings-on in Hinson County and avoiding anything that smacked in the slightest of politics. But every time the papers carried articles about important events, she longed for the freedom to cover such stories herself.

She received a brief note from Hector Davis—externally anonymous, of course—stating that he regretted having been unable to speak with her in Jackson. "You're an astute and reliable ally in the quest for truth," he wrote. Cissa was startled at his assumption that they were allies. Were they allies? They had exchanged useful information a few times. She focused on his assessment of her as "astute" and "reliable." Surely those were excellent traits in a newswoman, as was dedication to a "quest for truth."

"I'm off to Texas again and will likely be incommunicado for a while," he wrote. Cissa wondered what he was up to; everything about his life intrigued her. She tucked this letter away with the others.

In late July Cissa received a letter from Johnny, who had been attending a conference in New Orleans. He indicated that he would be visiting his parents soon and would pay a visit to her and Lachlan. She wrote back indicating that she would be pleased to see him. She also offered her good wishes to his wife and their new baby.

As much as Cissa enjoyed receiving letters from Johnny and Hector and Liz, they only accentuated her inertia. Cissa was stuck here on Callander Road. Why couldn't she be the one writing letters from far-flung places like Texas or New Orleans?

Summer had settled in with more intensity than usual that year and afternoons often found Cissa and her mother alongside Elsie, shelling peas or shucking corn on the shady front porch where they could catch a breeze. When Cissa saw the two figures walking down the lane from the direction of Monroe's house, she knew at once who they were. Johnny had filled out and he now sported a much more respectable mustache, but he was still the same Johnny. Was it her imagination or was there a bounce in Lachlan's step as he walked alongside Johnny? She hurried to tidy up the porch, handing the basin of pea pods and the bowl full of shelled peas to Elsie to take to the kitchen. Mother followed Elsie indoors and Cissa offered her a glass of tea in the parlor before shedding her apron and returning to the porch to meet Lachlan and Johnny. Elsie brought out a tray with three more glasses of tea.

Cissa watched, hands on her hips, as the two men strode toward her. "How am I so lucky as to merit a visit from the two best-looking men in Hinson County?" she said with a grin.

Johnny stepped forward and embraced Cissa as she tried her best not to melt into his strong arms and not to think about what it might have been like to experience this every day.

"You're looking pretty fine yourself, Miss Tarver," he said, still holding both her hands in his. His eyes had lost some of their youthful sparkle, but they were still some of the most beautiful eyes Cissa had ever seen. They were not nearly so dark as Hector's.

"Let's sit out here for a bit," she said. "Help yourselves to some tea." Cissa and Johnny settled onto the wooden porch swing while Lachlan sat facing them, leaning against a post.

"I was telling Johnny about your adventures in Jackson, but he seemed to know almost as much about it as I do," Lachlan said.

"Your sister...I mean aunt...writes very informative letters," Johnny said. "But tell me, Cissa, what do you plan to do with your writing now that things have settled down a bit around here?"

"Not much, I'm afraid." She explained about her conflict with Duncan but got the feeling that Lachlan had already caught him up on the latest developments in that story. "I'm back to writing about school activities and church events and the like."

"It's a shame to waste your talent like that," Johnny said. "I'd never presume to give you advice, but these days it seems as if women are finding more and more opportunities to work outside their homes and families. You know, by the time I finished medical school there were two women there, studying to become doctors. You're one of the most intelligent people I know, Cissa Tarver. You're wasted here on Callander Road."

Cissa tried to brush off his flattery, but it attached itself to her heart and wouldn't let go. What might she be capable of doing? She wondered if she would ever have the opportunity or the courage to find out. If it had been only her and Johnny present, Cissa thought she might have mentioned her sporadic correspondence with Detective Davis. She felt certain Johnny would have found it as interesting as she did. But Lachlan was here, and she didn't want to burden Lachlan with information that would be distressing to his Uncle Duncan.

The three friends chatted away for more than an hour. It was one of the most pleasant hours Cissa had enjoyed in a long while. They talked about Johnny's little daughter, whom he adored. They laughed about Monroe and Laura's continuing efforts to find a wife for Lachlan.

"Don't you ever wish for a family, Lachlan?" Johnny asked.

Lachlan was silent for a moment, his eyes drifting back and forth between Johnny and Cissa. "I have a family," he said. "So many sisters and brothers and aunts and uncles and cousins I can hardly keep track of them all. That ought to be enough, oughtn't it?"

The yearning in his eyes as he gazed at Johnny led Cissa to believe that maybe it wasn't. Not for Lachlan. And not for Cissa either.

After they left, Cissa pulled out her most recent letter from Liz. She read again about how Liz had begun attending meetings of a local chapter of the Texas Equal Rights Association. Liz assured Cissa that the push for women's suffrage was stronger in Texas than in Mississippi. Then Cissa read the part about how Liz's husband's printing business was prospering at last and how they might soon be in the position to hire a copy writer. Cissa set the letter down, wondering what life might be like in San Antonio, Texas.

Chapter Forty-Four
Storms of Change

Fall 1906

Cissa awakened in the night to the sound of howling wind and something banging against an upper story window. Monroe and his boys had come over the previous afternoon to secure the shutters, warning that a major storm was coming. Cissa had seen the dark clouds off to the southwest as clearly as anyone, but she'd had to ask, "What makes you think it's going to be such a bad storm?"

"Mr. Clay came by earlier saying that word had come on the wire in Marchelle out of Louisiana saying they were getting a fierce wind along the coast there and that we ought to get ready," Monroe said. Surely it wouldn't be as bad as the storm that hit Galveston, Texas, six years ago, the one that had killed thousands of people.

The wind that began on Wednesday night whistled and howled throughout the dark day on Thursday as Cissa and her mother listened to the shutters rattle and branches and occasionally entire trees crack and snap. Cissa had been through storms before. The one when she was seventeen had been bad, but nothing like this. Pop had been there then, reassuring them with his deep calm voice that everything would be fine.

It wasn't until Friday morning that Cissa dared open the door and peer outside.

"How bad is it?" Mother asked.

"It's bad." Cissa threw the door open. Sunrise illuminated in soft golden tones a landscape strewn with broken trees and debris. "I'm going out to check on the animals," she said, pulling on a pair of old brogans.

The shed looked mostly intact. It had once been the Tarvers' summer kitchen and was sturdily built. A section had blown off the barn roof and lodged up against the smokehouse, but their one cow had come through unscathed. The chickens were another matter. The chicken house had tipped over and two hens lay motionless in a puddle while two others clucked nervously, shaking their muddy feathers. The rooster huddled inside the upturned coop. Cissa picked up the two dead chickens; there would be fried chicken for dinner and a pot of chicken soup for tomorrow.

Cissa found Monroe in the kitchen with Mother. He had the look of a man who had slept in his work clothes. Or perhaps not slept at all.

"This turned out to be even worse than we thought," he said. "I should have had the two of you down at my house."

"We're fine," Cissa said. "Pop built this house strong. Even the outbuildings are hardly damaged." She held up the two muddy hens. "Except for the henhouse. At least we'll eat well."

"Yes, we'll be having chicken today, too," Monroe said. "The telephone is dead, so we haven't heard anything yet from Duncan and his brood. Albert's house looks like it made it through without too much damage. I'll go check on them next. Lachlan has gone out to see about our crops and the hands."

"Do you think the cotton is ruined?" Cissa said.

"Cotton bolls were starting to open. Some fields mostly open. I'm afraid the news there is going to be pretty grim."

Monroe departed by the kitchen door.

Elsie reported for work later that day spattered in mud. After ascertaining that some of the cabins in the Negro community had suffered severe damage, Cissa sent her back home. "You go take care of your own family, Elsie. We'll take care of things here. Come on back in a couple of days."

When the *Beckport Journal* arrived late Saturday, Cissa read reports with some trepidation. The storm had affected not just Louisiana and Mississippi, but Alabama and Florida as well. Electricity was disrupted. Telephone lines were "disarranged," and rail traffic had been halted by washouts, felled trees, and debris, as well as the lack of communication.

The state of the crops turned out to be worse than Monroe had predicted. Corn was flattened to the ground and, according to the *Journal,* "most of the cotton open was blown or beaten from the bolls and the stalks and branches made the playthings of the angry winds." Cissa was impressed by the fact that the editor had gone out into the country to survey the damage for himself.

Perhaps she should go out and survey the Callander Road area and file a report of her own. She knew there was little that she'd be able to learn by walking, and she had no other form of conveyance. With a sigh, she turned back to reheating her chicken soup.

Late that afternoon Cissa was surprised to see Duncan's horse in front of Albert's house. He'd been going about in a buggy of late, in deference to his injured leg, but of course roads were likely impassable for wheeled vehicles of any kind at the moment. It was less than an hour later that both Duncan and Albert mounted the steps on the front porch of the big house.

"Mother," Cissa called, "Duncan and Albert are come calling. Shall I make some coffee?"

"Yes, dear, that would be nice." Mother ambled toward the front door to greet her son and grandson while Cissa busied herself in the kitchen.

The two men entered and, after a brief greeting to Susanna, continued an animated conversation between themselves.

"The children will like the upstairs rooms," Albert said, "and I'm sure Aunt Cissy won't mind sharing space with Grandma for a while."

Cissa's ears pricked up.

"Don't worry about your aunt," Duncan grumbled. "She'll just have to do what's best for the family."

"And what would that be?" Cissa asked, entering the parlor with a tray laden with cups and saucers, a pot of coffee, and a plate of cookies. Despite her effort to sound pleasant, her voice came out a bit shrill. She set the tray down on a side table.

Duncan waited for Cissa to fill a cup with coffee. "There's been some damage to the roof at my old house where Albert is," he said. "So they'll be moving in here."

"Just until we get it repaired," Albert said.

Duncan raised his eyebrows and did not confirm that caveat.

Of course Duncan wants to claim the big house for his eldest son. Cissa told herself she should have expected this, but somehow it always felt as if Duncan had settled in Cowleton where his political life was centered and had lost interest in his patrimony in Hinson County.

The last thing in the world Cissa wanted was to live in a household run by her nephew Albert and—albeit at a distance—by Duncan. But how could she say no to the need for temporary shelter while repairs were made to Albert's own home? "I see," she said. "How serious is the damage at your place, Albert?"

"Just a couple sections of the roof," he said.

"But they're over the kitchen and the children's bedroom," Duncan added. "And we'll of course take the opportunity to complete our planned conversions for office space."

Cissa noted that he hadn't said "addition." Now it was "conversions." Did he ever intend for Albert and his family to move back there? Cissa had always thought that eventually, when this house went to one of her brothers, it would be Monroe. He was the elder brother.

For the time being, Cissa would comply with Duncan's wishes. She would accommodate Eva in her kitchen. But the idea of Albert and Eva taking over her bedroom while she moved in with Mother was galling. She would try and make the best of it. For now.

The cotton harvest that year was less than half of what it would have been without the storm and corn was almost nonexistent. That would mean another sparse Christmas and cutting corners for another entire season.

Elsie came in only twice a week, but barely a month after the storm passed there was a week when she didn't come in at all. Fortunately, Eva's maid was coming in on alternate days, so Cissa made do. Mother didn't seem to notice. When Elsie showed up at last, Cissa had to ask, "Why didn't you come to work last week? You should have sent word, you know." She didn't hide her irritation.

"Mama pass," Elsie said with a sniff as she continued chopping vegetables for the soup.

"What? Zolene..." Cissa recalled that Rosie had mentioned that she was ill. "We didn't know. I'm so sorry, Elsie. Truly I am. Zolene was a fine woman." Cissa knew her words were inadequate as she tried to imagine the grief that Elsie and Julia and all their extensive circle of kin must have felt with the passing of a strong woman like Zolene.

"Yes ma'am," Elsie said.

"Please tell Julia, too. Tell her how sorry I am for her loss. For your family's loss."

"Yes, ma'am," Elsie said. She scraped her chopped vegetables off the cutting board and into the pot. "Julia and her chil'ren be movin' away soon. Goin' up to Tulsa to join up with Baxter." Elsie never turned to face Cissa as she continued. "Baxter, he a big man at that there bank and he be fixin' to get him a loan and open up a shop for Julia so's she can sell dresses."

"Really? Her own shop?" Cissa thought things must be very different in Oklahoma from the way they were in Mississippi. "When will she go?"

"Can't rightly say, Miss. All's she say is 'soon'."

Later that week, Cissa purchased a little leatherbound journal from the general store. She'd been eying it, coveting it for herself, but now she wrote on the first page, in her best script and using the fountain pen that was a gift from Johnny, these words: "To Julia, who cared for me best." She flicked away a tear before it could drop onto the paper, remembering childhood frolics with Julia and how Julia had petted and pampered her when her own parents seemed to find her very presence a nuisance.

She wrapped the little book in a piece of flowered shelf paper and tied it up with a green hair ribbon she hadn't worn in many years. She told Elsie and Mother that she had an errand to take care of and headed out in the direction of Julia's cottage. She wasn't certain Julia would be there.

Cissa was surprised to find the cottage free of the boards that had once covered its windows and door. There were sections of new shingles on the roof and the whole building looked as if it had been freshly whitewashed. It did not look like the home of someone who was about to move away to another state.

The front door stood ajar, but Cissa knocked anyway. She could see people moving about inside.

The woman who answered the door was Rosie. She had a child secured to her hip with a shawl. "Hey, Miss Cissa," she said. She smiled, but it was one of those uncertain smiles that only affects the lips and does not spread to the eyes. "Mama," she called over her shoulder, "come see who come callin'."

Julia was there after all. Her hair was wrapped in a kerchief, and she wore a soiled work apron, which she untied and bundled onto a chair as she greeted Cissa. "It's been a long while, Miss Cissa," she said. "What brings you out here?"

"I wanted to tell you how sorry I was to hear about your mother. You know how much I respected Zolene."

"That's right kindly, Miss. Ain't nothin' the same without Mama Zolene." Julia's eyes glowed with the love of a lifetime.

"Elsie says you're leaving, and I wanted to see you before you go." Cissa held out the little package. "This is for you. A sort of going-away gift."

The two women sat in chairs that almost faced one another. Julia held the gift in her lap as she offered a minimum of details about her mother's funeral and about her own plans. "Rosie be stayin' here in this house with her husband. All the rest goes with me up to Tulsa. Well, Hiram, he be there now. He work at that there bank with Baxter. He fixin' to get married next month."

Cissa's heart yearned for the old informality, familiarity, the playful chatter, the hugs. "That sounds very nice," she said.

Rosie brought glasses of tea and Cissa thanked her. Cissa was impressed at how well she managed with her lame left arm.

Cissa and Julia talked for a while about the storm and Cissa told Julia about her new living arrangements. And then they fell silent, as if there was nothing more to say.

"You can open the package if you like, Julia," Cissa said.

Julia looked down at the little bundle as if she had forgotten it was there. As she began to untie the ribbon, Cissa thought she heard a sigh. When the book emerged from its wrappings and Julia riffled through the pages, finding them blank, she finally looked at Cissa and smiled.

"This a very nice present," she said. "Thank you. I be writin' all in here 'bout my life up there in Tulsa."

"And maybe you could write me a letter sometime, too," Cissa ventured. "And then I could write to you about what goes on around here." Feeling a bit more relaxed, Cissa laughed. "Of course, not much does go on around here. Things have been pretty quiet ever since my brother and his crowd got their come-uppance in Jackson."

Julia laughed, too, but it was a different laugh. A bitter laugh. "Oh, Miss Cissa, you got no notion what go on around here." She shook her head slowly. "Mmmm, mmm. You only know what you reads in them papers you write for." She reached over and picked up a folded newspaper from the side table and handed it to Cissa.

The banner on the paper read *Hinson Chronicle*. Cissa had never heard of the *Hinson Chronicle* and said so.

"That's because this here a Negro paper," Julia said. "Go on, read what it say."

Under a headline "Storm Destroys School," she read about how the Negro school at Rundle Springs had been devastated by the recent winds and how the men working to rebuild it had been harassed, stacks of lumber disappearing overnight. The women from the Cedar Hill African Methodist Episcopal church were raising money for new textbooks, which had been ruined by the rains after the roof of the school was taken off.

"I didn't know about this," Cissa said. She vaguely recalled having heard that some Negro school was damaged, but this sounded much worse.

There was an announcement of a meeting of a fraternal organization Cissa had never heard of and a call for contributions to a poetry magazine. Another article detailed how two men had been detained for a robbery they didn't commit, and three others had been chased down and beaten on the suspicion that they had threatened a white man. "If you don't own a gun, you need to get one," the writer said. "Things will get hot in the lead-up to the next elections."

"This... I thought..." Cissa stared at the paper in confusion.

"You and me, we live in different worlds, Miss Cissa." Julia gazed at her former charge with sad eyes. "Things not quiet at all for us niggers. White folk won't let it be. So we does what we can to make our own place."

Tears welled up in Cissa's eyes. Why did it have to be like this? Why couldn't she and Julia live in the same world? "Could I take this paper home with me?" Cissa asked. "Maybe I could write up something about the school."

"No, ma'am," Julia said. "We don't like our paper in white hands. I lets you read it 'cause I know you likes to hear true facts. But that there paper, it stay right here."

"I understand," Cissa said, although she wasn't at all certain that she did, and she could tell by the look in Julia's eyes that Julia didn't believe she did.

Julia reached into her sewing basket and drew out a small cloth item. She held it out to Cissa. "This here a little something for you, Miss," she said. "So's you remember Julia."

Cissa's eyes widened. "Oh, Julia, you shouldn't..." she began and then stopped herself. Negros were not expected to offer gifts to white people; both of them knew that. Once again, however, Julia was doing it anyway. The first time it had been a doll. This time it was a chair tidy embroidered with roses and narcissus blossoms. "Thank you," Cissa said as her vision blurred with unshed tears. Somehow, this gift from Julia felt like closure.

"You keep on doin' your work, Miss Cissa," Julia said. "You gots a good heart. Jus' don't be poisoned by what other folks says, things they do. You jus' keep on."

On her way home, Cissa let her tears fall for the loss of her beloved Julia. Of course Julia would want to move on now that her mother was gone. Back in the days of slavery, Cissa's mother had owned Julia's mother. But that wasn't what kept them in separate worlds now. The wall that rose up between them now was built by men like Cissa's brother Duncan and their continuing insistence that Negroes were inherently different than whites. That they were less. Cissa recalled things she'd read, things white men had written. Duncan had once compared Negroes to mules, only useful if kept under control. Julia was no mule. Julia was a good person, a good mother, a woman capable of running a successful business, Cissa was sure of that. And wasn't Julia a Negro?

After spreading the embroidered tidy on the back of the big chair in the parlor, Cissa wrote up a brief article about the Rundle Springs Negro school. She based it on what she could recall about the piece she'd read at Julia's house. But the words that haunted her from the *Hinson Chronicle* were these: "If you don't own a gun, you need to get one." She wondered if Julia's young son Chisum owned a gun now.

Having Eva around would have made Cissa's workload considerably lighter if it hadn't been for the fact that her four sons were also there. The oldest was now eleven; the youngest had just turned five and was not yet in school. Eva was pleasant company, but the boys were a rowdy bunch of hooligans. Albert made little effort at disciplining them, chuckling over their antics and even egging them on when the older boys teased and taunted the younger ones. Eva was powerless against them and even Cissa's sternest looks and most severe admonishments had little effect. Albert kept himself busy managing the farm and supervising the construction work going on at his own house.

Mother found the whole state of affairs confusing. She seemed amused by the boys, but then she'd tell one of the noisy youngsters, "I hear your mother calling. Better run along home now." She didn't understand that, for the time being, they were home right here in their great-grandmother's house. She took long naps in her bedroom, which was also now Cissa's bedroom, another thing she didn't understand.

It was near the end of November that Albert received a telephone call about a terrible fire in Marchelle. He didn't tell Cissa and her mother about it until later in the day. The call had been from Albert's banker and was intended to assure him that although the fire had wiped out much of the main street commercial district, the bank's vault remained intact, and their business would continue as usual.

It was Monroe who brought the news that the Hennings' shop—Matilda's husband's family business—had been destroyed and that Matilda was distraught. She begged for Cissa to come and be with her for a few days.

Donna Birdwell

Chapter Forty-Five
Legacy

Winter 1906-07

Cissa was grateful for the opportunity to get away from Callander Road and the house that no longer felt like home. Eva assured her that Mother would be well cared for. As Cissa packed up her belongings for the journey, she ran across the items she'd removed from her father's desk. She hadn't yet had the opportunity to examine the bundles of letters and thought that her time with her sister might afford her that chance. She tucked the bundles into her suitcase and snapped the latches.

The weather was not the best for a ride in an open wagon to Marchelle, but the blanket that Lachlan provided for Cissa helped to dispel the damp and frigid air. "Pop says to expect a freeze tonight," Lachlan said.

"You mean it's not freezing already?" Cissa shivered and pulled the blanket more closely around her neck.

She was grateful for the warm fire that greeted them in Matilda's living room.

"Oh, Cissy, I'm so glad you've come." Matilda grabbed her sister in a tight embrace.

Cissa could tell at once that Matilda was pregnant. She'd had two disappointments since Melba was born and Melba was a big girl now, six years old, nearly seven. Cissa understood better her sister's urgent plea for support. Matilda was now past forty and opportunities for growing her family were fading fast.

"Thank you for bringing Cissy in this frightful weather, Lachlan. Come warm yourselves."

"I can only stay a bit, Aunt Tilly. I've got a whole list of errands to run. Pop figured as long as I was going to be in town he'd put me to good use." Lachlan settled himself with his feet stretched toward the fire as Melba edged close to him and lay her head on his knee.

A young black woman appeared with cups of steaming hot chocolate. After she left, Matilda leaned toward Cissa and, in a low voice, said, "We're letting Doreen go. Frank says until the store gets back up and running we can't afford a maid. She agreed to stay on until you got here."

That was one more reason why Cissa had been called on, a reason she found all too familiar.

"How bad was the damage to your store?" Lachlan asked.

"Frank says our damage was at least two thousand dollars." Matilda's hand went to her belly as she stared into the fire. "We have insurance, but only up to five hundred. Several of the merchants had no insurance at all, so I guess we're luckier than some."

"Smart, Aunt Tilly. Not lucky," Lachlan said. "You'll rebuild, I'm sure. A solid business like Hennings should qualify for a substantial loan."

"Yes, they say the bank was fully insured and will be open again as soon as they find new premises." Matilda assured Cissa that the newspaper offices had been largely spared in the fire. "Only a little water damage," she said.

After Lachlan left, the maid Doreen was sent home, and eleven-year-old Evelyn took charge of getting the two younger children—Irwin and Melba—ready for bed.

"How far along are you?" Cissa asked. She felt as if she should have known that her sister was pregnant again, but with all the disappointments Matilda had suffered, she couldn't be blamed for trying to keep it secret.

"Almost five months now," Matilda said as tears welled in her eyes. "I've been so sick again with this one and was just getting past that when... And the doctor warned me that I was at a fragile time and any upset could make it..." Her hand went to her lips as her shoulders clenched in a suppressed sob.

"Well, I'm here with you now, sister, so you can stop worrying. Mother has been training me well in the art of pampering." Cissa reached over and patted Matilda's arm. "I'll take care of you."

Given the choice, there were many things Narcissa Tarver would rather be doing than taking care of her pregnant and distraught older sister, regardless of how much she loved her and how sincerely she wished for Tilly's happiness. But Narcissa Tarver rarely got choices in life and at least this was better than being stuck in the house with Albert and his band of hooligans. Cissa was determined to make the most of her stay in Marchelle. She let Mr. Hodges at the *Advocate* know she was in town and available for assignments.

"Go out and interview some of the merchants about how the fire is going to impact their lives over the next year," Mr. Hodges suggested. "You seem to have a connection there." He also told her to learn what she could about sentiments on prohibition, since Hinson County was facing a local option election come January.

Cissa's first interview was with her brother-in-law Frank and then Frank introduced her to several of the proprietors of neighboring shops and businesses. Cissa did her interviews when Matilda lay down for her afternoon rest and wrote her material up on an *Advocate* typewriter, returning to her sister's house in time to prepare supper.

As Cissa pulled her third article out of the typewriter, pleased at how her facility with the machine was improving, she saw Mr. Hodges leaning over his desk watching her.

"I don't suppose there's any news about that brother of yours." His statement was clearly more of a question.

"He's keeping pretty quiet these days," Cissa said. She was eager to proof her copy and turn it over to the typesetters.

"I guess there's not much left for that Pinkerton fellow to dig up."

Cissa thought he sounded a bit wistful. "Davis? Oh, he's gone to Texas again."

"Really? I hadn't heard. You have that on good authority?"

"Yes, sir," Cissa said, looking up from her story with a grin. "He told me so himself, though he didn't mention what kind of case he was working this time. Something hush-hush I suppose."

"Oh," Mr. Hodges said. "Well, I...alright then." He returned Cissa's smile, and she thought there may have been a wink, too.

During the first week she was in Marchelle, Cissa had five stories published in the *Advocate*. One of them was about the different viewpoints on prohibition and how being "wet" or "dry" could affect the economic recovery of Marchelle's commercial district. She was delighted when this story was picked up by the Natchez and Vicksburg papers. Remembering Liz's advice, she clipped the articles and stored them away for her stringbook.

Matilda got stronger and calmer. She seemed to relish her late evening chats with her younger sister. They laughed about how they were always at odds when Cissa was a child but got on famously now that they were both adults. The sisterly feeling led Cissa to talk to Matilda about her ongoing correspondence with Johnny and with Liz. She almost mentioned her contacts with Hector Davis, too, but decided against it. Sisters didn't have to share everything.

It was on one such evening that Cissa brought out the bundles of letters she'd found in their father's desk. "Do you want to help me sort through these?" Cissa asked.

Matilda eagerly agreed and so they split up the bundles—two for each of them—and began examining the contents. Many of the envelopes held letters from patients or from distant relatives, some of whose names neither woman recognized.

"Pop always tried to keep in touch with his kinnery down in Fulton," Matilda said. "I think this one is from one of his eldest sister's sons."

Cissa found a few letters that Susanna had sent to Pop when he was away at war and after reading one of them silently she handed it to her sister. "Here, Tilly. You need to read this one."

"Oh, Cissy, I'm going cross-eyed from trying to decipher some of this handwriting. You read it to me."

"It's dated July 1, 1863," Cissa said. "And it begins 'My dearest Joe.' I thought Mother always called him Joseph."

Matilda smiled. "I remember hearing her call him Joe a few times when I was little. Usually when they were hugging and thought no one else was around."

"Oh," Cissa said, trying to recall if she had ever witnessed such affection between her parents. She continued reading the letter:

"I was relieved to receive your letter of the twentieth instant and know that you are still among the living. You could have spared me some of the horrifying details of your daily encounters, though I suspect you have not shared the worst of it with me. I'm grateful for the lives you're able to save though I miss you dreadfully here in our drafty unfinished house. Every day as I walk through it I see in my mind's eye how grand it will be when you're finally able to come home and finish it as you promised.

"We are still mostly spared from any serious conflicts, though we hear rumor and gossip of terrible things around Vicksburg.

Monroe and Duncan are both hale and hearty youngsters and baby Matilda continues to thrive as well. I still give thanks for Zolene's nursing of her when I couldn't. I'm sure Tilly wouldn't have survived without it. Sometimes I think I count on Zolene too much to keep the rest of the servants in line. I've heard folks say that it's a mistake to keep too many servants who were bred local, but I don't think I could bear to sell Zolene. She tells me that we still have enough hands to bring in what's left of our crops and that it should be sufficient to get us through until spring.

"I pray for you daily, my dearest, and for the day this dispute will be ended, and you will be back home where I pine for you."

Cissa laid the letter back in her lap. "She signed it 'Your devoted wife, Susanna.' What do you think, Tilly. Did you know how important Zolene had been to getting Mother through the war years?"

"Well, I knew she'd been responsible for my survival, and I understand now that it was at the expense of her own little boy. She was only able to nurse me because of having a child of her own and then didn't have enough milk for two. But I'd never known Mother had counted on her, as she says here, to keep the servants in line. We've always given Mother all the credit for being so strong through the war."

"You know Zolene passed recently," Cissa said.

"No, I didn't know." Matilda's clasped her hands in front of her face. "Oh, Cissy, you should have told me."

The next evening the two sisters sat with the remaining bundles of letters. Cissa was well into hers when she pulled out an envelope that was still sealed. Her eyes widened and her breath came to a halt as she saw the address: "Miss Narcissa June Tarver." It was unquestionably her father's handwriting.

"Look at this, Tilly," she said, holding up the envelope for her sister to see. "What do you suppose he meant to do with this?"

"Oh, my. That is odd, little sister. But since it's addressed to you, I think you must open it at once."

Cissa sat on the floor next to Matilda and ran her finger under the seal of the envelope. She unfolded a paper that bore the heading of a well-known Marchelle law firm and began to read, her eyes growing wider with every line: "I, Joseph Quinlan Tarver, being of sound mind, do hereby swear and affirm the following as codicil to my previously sworn and registered last will and testament dated December 5, 1886. To wit: I leave my house on Callander Road to my daughter Narcissa June Tarver, provided she continues to reside in said house giving care and succor to her mother Susanna Irene McLaurin Tarver for the remainder of her natural life. To this I set my signature this twelfth day of April, the year of our Lord eighteen hundred and ninety-seven."

Cissa's breathing had gone shallow. She looked up at Matilda. "Does this mean...?"

"I think it means the big house is yours, little sister," Matilda said with a smile. "And, oh, that does feel so right."

A tightness gripped Cissa's throat as tears welled up. All those years feeling so left out of her own family, feeling as if the whole notion of family loyalty didn't apply to Narcissa, all that time her father had been tending toward this. He did appreciate the care she gave to him and to Mother. And this was how he expressed his gratitude. Her mind flooded with images of his gruff kindness when she was growing up, his efforts to instill in her the knowledge she would need to take over the big house when he was gone.

"Do you suppose it's all legal?" Cissa wiped her tears and stared at the signatures at the bottom of the document. There were three of them—Joseph's, a lawyer named Archibald Roberts, and a witness whose name Cissa couldn't decipher.

"You should take it to Mr. Roberts tomorrow and verify it. He lives just across the street from Frank's folks. I think he's a cousin of my mother-in-law."

The next morning Cissa found Mr. Archibald Roberts at home, due to the fact that his law office had suffered smoke and water damage from the fire. He examined the document Cissa handed him and verified that it was indeed authentic and entirely legal. He even remembered having drawn up the document at Joseph Q. Tarver's behest. "He expressed some concern about his health and about his wife's health. And I remember him saying that he wanted to be certain his younger daughter was cared for. That's you, is it? I believe there was land to be inherited by his other children? Anyway, Miss Tarver, according to his wishes expressed in this legal instrument, as long as you continue living in the house with your mother, the house is yours and will be yours free and clear when she is gone."

When Cissa returned to her sister's house with the news, Matilda asked, "What will you do? You told me how Duncan is making moves to take the house for himself. I'm sure that's why he moved Albert into it. Are you going to evict him?" For a moment, Matilda's eyes danced with mischief. Then she sobered. "No, truly. What will you do?"

"I think I'll do nothing for the time being," Cissa said. "Let me discuss it with Monroe when I get home. Then I'll decide." She frowned. "I could never evict my own kin." At the very least, she was pretty sure she shouldn't.

On the following day a letter arrived for Matilda from their niece Janie, imploring Matilda to let her and her young son come and stay for a few weeks while her husband completed a training course in modern telegraphy in Georgia. "He's got a job with the railroad waiting for him in Marston when he gets back, but in the meantime, he thinks it would be best if we let go of our little rent-house here and I and our son stay with kin. And you know I'd rather stay with my own aunt than with any of my sisters-in-law."

"Well, this is perfect," Matilda said. "I was about ready to send you home anyway, since I'm feeling much stronger thanks to your care. Now you can go home and tend to your business while Janie and her little boy come to keep me company."

Cissa was able to secure a spot in a coach going from Marchelle to the Taloa County seat the following day. Due to ongoing road repairs consequent to the October storm, it was temporarily routed down Callander Road and would be able to take Cissa directly to her house.

Her house.

Throughout the journey, Cissa kept turning over and over in her mind the implications of her newly discovered inheritance. A question kept trying to bubble up from the back of her mind: Did she really want to continue living in the big house on Callander Road for the rest of her life? She pushed the thought aside, focusing instead on her newfound sense of ownership and authority.

When she disembarked from the coach at the roadside in front of the house, no one came to aid her. She knew the boys would be in school, all but the youngest. She lugged her suitcase up the steps and into the front hallway.

As soon as she stepped inside, she knew something was wrong. "Mother?" she called out as she set her suitcase down. "Eva? Is anyone home?" She poked her head around the doorway into the parlor and drew back in astonishment. All the furniture had been rearranged. In place of Mother's big chair (which had been Pop's chair) there was a fancy settee. The old rug that had been there ever since Cissa's childhood was gone and a cheap-looking replacement with a garish floral pattern rolled out in its place.

"We didn't expect you so soon," Eva said, her hands stuffed deep into the pockets of her apron.

"What have you done?" Cissa stared at her nephew's wife with unabashed horror. "How dare you do all this without consulting me."

Eva looked as if she were about to cry, prompting Cissa to stifle her anger.

"Albert wanted to let me do some redecorating," Eva whimpered. "He said he was sure you wouldn't mind."

"Where is Mother's chair?" Cissa demanded.

"We took it to her room. She spends most of her time in there anyway," Eva said.

As Cissa started across the parlor toward the door that led to Mother's corner room—Mother and Pop's room—Eva stopped her.

"Not that way. Grandma Tarver's in the other bedroom now. Albert thought..."

"Stop right there," Cissa said, her anger bursting past her best efforts to moderate it. "I don't want to hear it right now. But you can tell Albert for me that he's going to have to put all of my things back the way they were. *My* things. Do you hear me Eva? *My things!* Cissa's mind had flown back to Albert's theft of her essay when they were children. This time Cissa intended to claim what was hers.

Leaving Eva in tears, Cissa went to her bedroom where she found her mother seated in the big chair that had been shoved into a dark corner facing away from the only window.

After spending a few moments speaking with her mother, passing on news of Matilda's family and Janie's plans (though not mentioning Matilda's pregnancy or Pop's codicil), Cissa made her way down the front steps headed toward Monroe's house. The cold had abated somewhat, but she was still shivering when she arrived. She had her father's document tucked into her coat pocket.

Cissa marched up the steps and into her brother's house, closing the door behind her with perhaps unnecessary but decidedly satisfying force.

Laura emerged from the kitchen. "Cissy!" she said, drying her hands on her apron and looking a bit flustered over her sister-in-law's sudden appearance in an agitated state. "Is... Is everything alright?"

Cissa ignored the question. "Is Monroe here?" she asked. She had her coat halfway off when she considered the possibility she might have to seek her brother outdoors. She put it on again.

"I'm here." He stood in the kitchen doorway wiping crumbs from his mustache with his pocket handkerchief.

"We need to talk," Cissa said. She removed her coat and hung it on a peg, reaching into the pocket to retrieve her important piece of paper.

Laura shooed the children out of the sitting room and into the kitchen.

"What's this about, Cissy?" Monroe's voice was calm, but his brow furrowed as he leaned toward his sister.

"I..." Cissa took a deep breath and thrust the paper toward Monroe. "You need to read this," she said. She watched as Monroe unfolded the paper and, holding it at almost arm's length, began to absorb its contents. His head tilted first to one side, then the other. His eyes crinkled in a smile.

"It's all perfectly legal," Cissa said. "I consulted with the lawyer in Marchelle who drew it up."

"It doesn't surprise me," Monroe said. "The house was built on a piece of land Pop bought for that purpose, so he could do with it as he pleased. And it's in line with what he specified in his will about Duncan and me making sure that you and Mother were supported from the farm income."

"What?" Cissa had not known about this provision. She hadn't been present when the will was read, and no one had bothered to tell her that her brothers were legally obligated to support her. She'd thought they were supporting Mother out of the goodness of their hearts and because it was the right thing to do.

There was a commotion in the entryway and Albert stormed into the room, his face scarlet. "How dare you speak to my wife in such a way," he shouted, standing over Cissa with his fists jammed against his hips. "You have no business ordering Eva about like that."

Monroe looked up at Albert, a slight smile still on his face, and said, in a mild voice, "Actually, what happens in that house is all Narcissa's business." He held the codicil up where Albert could see the imprint of the legal firm. "According to this document, the house belongs to her."

Albert turned even redder, anger and shame vying for possession of his countenance. "What do you mean? My pop always said Granddad meant for the house to go to him because of Pop being a doctor like him."

"As it well might have if there wasn't a document saying otherwise. But this one clearly says…" and at this point Monroe began reading.

By the time Monroe had read the entire brief page, Albert's color had gone from scarlet to a mottled gray. "That can't be right," he said. "Granddad would never do that."

"Except he did, Albert. The house belongs to your Aunt Narcissa."

"And to Mother for as long as she lives," Cissa said. "And she deserves to keep her own bedroom and have her chair where she likes it."

Monroe gave Cissa a puzzled look. She hadn't gotten around to explaining the changes Albert had made to the house in her absence.

Albert turned toward the door. "We'll be out by nightfall," he said.

"Albert, wait," Cissa said. "We can talk about this."

But Albert was gone.

Chapter Forty-Six
Tense Times

1907-08

Albert and his family moved back across Callander Road into their own residence. It was Lachlan and his brothers who set the big house back to rights, back to the way Cissa wanted it. Mother smiled as she settled into her favorite chair in the sunny parlor, leaning her head back against the embroidered tidy that only Cissa knew was a gift from Julia.

At first Cissa felt a bit guilty about Eva and her boys having to live in a small house, which was also a part-time physician's office for Duncan and Lamar, while she and Mother had the entire two-story big house for themselves.

"It's what Pop wanted," Monroe assured her. "He didn't want Mother to be put out in any way. And he wanted you cared for, too. Duncan and Albert will be fine."

Cissa began purchasing a few little luxuries for Mother, knowing that Duncan and Monroe were obligated to support her under the provisions of Pop's will. She bought her a set of lace-edged handkerchiefs and a new pair of silk stockings. For herself she bought a supply of better quality writing paper.

After a few weeks, Eva resumed her periodic visits with Cissa, gloating over the modern oil-burning stove that Albert had installed in her refurbished kitchen and the sewing machine he had promised to buy her. "He had no trouble at all getting a loan from the bank," Eva said.

Monroe reported to Cissa that when he'd told Duncan about their father's codicil deeding the big house to her, Duncan had exploded with fury. Cissa was glad she hadn't been there. Monroe also mentioned that Duncan was stewing over the announcement of a new regional Law and Order League covering three counties, including both Hinson and Fulton. "Of course Duncan thinks it's all another plot by his enemies," Monroe said, "since the new league has sworn to cooperate with the existing Fulton County Law and Order League."

When the new group held an organizational meeting in Rundle Springs, Cissa covered it for the *Marchelle Advocate*, incorporating lengthy quotes from the enthusiastic participants. Unlike Duncan's organizations, which had mostly met in the dead of night and far from town, this Law and Order League met in early afternoon in the center of town. Cissa could detect no intention to operate outside the law in their pursuit of order. She liked that they specifically extended their protective efforts to the colored population, which, she was surprised to learn, outnumbered the white population in Hinson County.

Nineteen hundred and seven was an election year and Cissa desperately hoped there would be political events in Rundle Springs that would require a reporter. Although the general election would be held in November, the only races that mattered were the Democratic primaries. Governor Vardaman was contesting for the U.S. Senate, calling for modification of the Fourteenth Amendment to the U.S. Constitution (the one that made citizens of former slaves) and repeal of the Fifteenth (which prohibited denying the vote on account of race). Vardaman's primary opponent was a congressman who agreed with him on most issues, albeit less stridently. Cissa was disappointed, though not surprised, when neither of these candidates visited Rundle Springs.

The Democratic race for governor had six candidates, one of whom was a native son of Hinson County. He held a rousing rally in Rundle Springs, which Cissa reported in vivid prose for the *Marchelle Advocate*. A few other down-ballot candidates also visited, but it was only Cissa's accounts of the gubernatorial rally and another event held by the Prohibitionists that were picked up by other Mississippi newspapers.

Sometimes Cissa permitted herself to consider how she would vote if she were given the chance. Occasionally she even contemplated who Julia or Baxter might vote for if they were here and if they were able to vote. Because the Democratic primaries were so decisive and because the Democrats discouraged Negroes from voting in their party primaries, most of the colored citizens of Mississippi were effectively disfranchised.

As Cissa had anticipated, Duncan was running for office again. He declared himself a candidate in the Democratic primary race for chancery clerk of Fulton County, challenging the long-time incumbent, Donald Griffith. Cissa knew that Griffith had not been among the three hundred plus indicted for whitecapping. This race and a few others in Fulton County grew heated as those still loyal to Duncan's Farmers' League were pitted against opponents allied with the Law and Order Leagues. In the chancery race, the *Fulton Gazette*, still under the editorship of Sam Cortman, refused to endorse either Tarver or Griffith, instead indicating that either man would be a "fine choice."

When all the primary voting was done, Vardaman had lost to the congressman as the Democratic nominee for senate and E. F. Noel had been nominated for governor. Hinson County's favorite son hadn't stood a chance.

Duncan won his county primary for chancery clerk and for once it was a decisive victory: He'd won by more than two hundred votes. Cissa found the result both a disappointment and a relief—a disappointment in that old whitecappers were clearly still supporting old whitecappers, but a relief since it meant that this time Duncan wouldn't be contesting election results.

Supporters of the defeated incumbent Griffith wrote a couple of irate letters to the *Fulton Gazette*, but nothing came of their allegations of election improprieties. Several other men who had been indicted for whitecapping also won their races, although by narrower margins than Duncan's. Representative Felix Cortman even managed to defeat the district's incumbent state senator.

"What do you think it means?" Cissa asked Monroe on one of his visits to Mother.

His bushy mustache twisted in contemplation. "There's still a lot of bad feeling on both sides down in Fulton," he said. "Fierce bad feeling. There may be bloodshed before they manage to sort it all out."

Cissa fervently hoped he was wrong.

The following week, she read in the Beckport paper that Governor Vardaman had pardoned the imprisoned Burr County whitecappers. *Why ever would he do that?* Cissa fumed. The governor had been a major force in pursuing whitecap lawlessness there as well as in Fulton County. And now he was setting them free. What Cissa found even more surprising was the fact that one of the parties who had gone to Jackson to plead with Vardaman for the pardons was none other than the *Beckport Journal* editor, a man who had been a leading figure in the Burr County Law and Order League that had played such a key role in bringing the whitecappers to justice.

Cissa fumed. What was the point in arresting men if they were never brought to trial, in trying them when convictions were unlikely, in convicting them if they were going to be pardoned and released so quickly?

If Cissa had nurtured any hope that Fulton County would amend its ways and turn aside from its support of whitecapping and the men who'd pled guilty to engaging in it, those hopes were dashed. She kept an eye out for any indication of renewed whitecap violence but according to the papers and the gossip she heard from her mother's prayer group and sewing circle, everything was peaceful. It didn't feel much like peace to Cissa. It felt like the tension in the ropes holding a half-felled tree that hadn't yet decided which way it would fall.

Cissa couldn't help but think that in addition to the ongoing hostility between Duncan's faction in the Farmers' League and his "enemies" in the Law and Order Leagues, there might also be something relevant going on in another sector of the population. She recalled her conversation with Julia and wondered if there might be things that the newspapers—the white newspapers—didn't know about or didn't choose to report. How she wished she could get her hands on a copy of the *Hinson Chronicle*. She'd mentioned the paper to Mr. Hodges at the *Advocate* once, but he'd merely scoffed as if to say, *How could Negroes possibly publish anything worth reading?*

In late December, a headline in the *Natchez Herald* caught Cissa's eye: "A Growing Murder Menace." She began to read. "The spread of the pistol toting habit among the Negroes, and the readiness of the toter to commit murder upon the smallest provocation, is a subject of much discussion and serious concern. The Negro with a pistol has become a menace."

Cissa recalled what the colored newspaper at Julia's house had said about the necessity of Negroes acquiring guns. She thought about whitecap attacks with firearms and about the whitecaps' predecessors in the Ku Klux Klan. Invariably they claimed that they were only working to keep the Negro "in his place" and thereby maintain law and order. Julia's angry words came back to her: *Law for them, not for us. And the order they want is order that keep black folk sunk to the bottom.*

In January of 1908 Hinson County became "dry" and Duncan Tarver was sworn in as chancery clerk of Fulton County. He lost no time in placing his stamp on the office. He had all the official records assembled into several leather-bound volumes that almost everyone said were beautiful and so much easier to access, but which some people suspected might be selectively incomplete. At least, that was what one of the ladies at Mother's prayer group said that she'd heard that some people were saying, though of course she didn't believe a word of it.

Cissa wondered what might have been left out and why. The chancery clerk was responsible for documenting and maintaining records of all sessions of chancery court, which dealt with disputes over family matters and wills and such. The clerk was in charge of land records. Cissa hoped that the rumors of impropriety in the chancery clerk's office were wrong, but she knew her brother too well to dismiss the rumors altogether.

Cissa had noticed Duncan's buggy several times passing by the house, going slowly. It was the rare occasion when he stopped, as he did today, pulling his buggy to a halt in the front yard. He still favored his bad leg, limping as he made his way up the steps and in the front door. For the first time, Cissa was annoyed that he didn't feel it necessary to knock.

There was an uneasy equilibrium between Cissa and Duncan now that she was owner of the big house, and he was secure in his new political position in Cowleton. They both felt the uneasiness of it, Duncan perhaps more than Cissa. She couldn't help feeling that Duncan would be looking for some way to restore his ascendancy.

"Where's Mother?" he said as he hung his hat on the hall tree.

"In the parlor." Cissa began removing her apron so she could join them.

"Make me some coffee, would you?" Duncan said. He still hadn't looked at her.

Cissa did as she was bid. *You must be a gracious hostess in your own house,* she told herself. Thinking of it that way calmed her and even made her smile a bit. She added a plate of biscuits spread with fig preserves to the serving tray. As she approached the parlor, she heard Duncan speaking.

"Are you sure you're getting enough to eat? You look thinner to me."

"Oh, I'm fine," Mother said. "I don't get hungry. Narcissa makes me eat anyway."

Cissa set the tray down and handed Mother a cup of coffee laden with cream and a liberal spoonful of sugar. "Help yourself to biscuits, Mother," she said. "You, too, Duncan."

Duncan took one bite of a biscuit, scowled, and set it back on the plate. "Have you taken any more little excursions for the news people, Narcissa?"

Cissa could see full well where this was heading and the annoyance that she'd suppressed earlier threatened her composure. She answered as calmly as she could. "No, there doesn't seem to be much happening around these parts that they're interested in." She paused and took a bite of biscuit. They really were good biscuits. "How are things down in Cowleton?"

Duncan raised his chin slightly. "Splendid," he said. "Things are going smooth as silk now that we've got the right people in office. And you can tell that to your editors."

Cissa wanted more than anything to ask him about the chancery records and why some people were suspicious, but she restrained herself. There was no point in provoking him in front of Mother.

Duncan reached forward and placed a hand on Mother's arm. "I wish you could have been with me earlier this week," he said. "I attended a theatre performance in Beckport that I know you would have enjoyed immensely."

"You know I don't go to the theatre these days, Duncan." Mother took another bite of biscuit.

"Well, I'm sure you would have found this performance well worth the effort. The play was 'The Clansman.' Such an inspiring story, all about the glory days of the Klan and how they brought peace and stability to the South. It was one of this company's final shows before heading off to Europe to perform before the King and Queen of England. Quite the spectacle."

"Which clan would that be, Duncan?" Mother said. "Was it the McLaurins?"

Duncan laughed. "No, Mother. *The* Klan. The Ku Klux Klan. Although there were McLaurins in that clan, too, I suppose. Along with all the Tarvers."

Given what Cissa knew about whitecapping and its relation to the Klan, she was sure she wouldn't have called the Klan's heyday "glory days." Her brow furrowed as a disturbing though occurred to her. "Was Pop in the Klan?" she asked.

"Of course he was," Duncan said. "Everybody was."

After Duncan left, Cissa pottered about the kitchen, feeling thoroughly out of sorts. Her sweet gratitude over Pop's bequest of the house felt threatened. For one thing, her view of her father was shaken by Duncan's assertion that he had been in the Klan. *I shouldn't be surprised,* she told herself. As Duncan had said, "everybody" was in it back in Reconstruction days. Her mind was nudged by a vague memory of men on horseback with lighted torches.

The other threat to her gratitude arose from Duncan's behavior. Going to their father's desk, Cissa drew out the codicil from the drawer where she'd stored it. She wanted to review the wording. Over and over again she read the words that deeded the house to her "provided she continues to reside in said house giving care and succor to her mother Susanna Irene McLaurin Tarver for the remainder of her natural life."

Is that what Duncan was hoping? That Cissa would give inadequate "care and succor" to their mother? That she might once more abandon Susanna to someone else's care in pursuit of her newspaper work? Cissa groaned as she realized that this house, which she had taken as a sign of her father's devotion to her, was in truth a burden, destined to hinder her from pursuing the work she loved. It also threatened to become a symbol of a past she could not defend.

As the year 1908 progressed, Cissa found her involvement in the newspaper business increasingly passive. After she refused two assignments that Mr. Hodges offered her—one in Beckport and another in Cowleton—he stopped asking. Cissa tried to resign herself to writing about the quotidian events in her corner of Hinson County and reading the more momentous stories that others wrote. There was a horrific tornado in the western part of the county that killed nineteen Negroes and destroyed their homes and all Cissa could do was write up a little piece about the collection of relief funds by the

Presbyterian ladies of Rundle Springs. The Beckport paper ran photographs—actual photographs—of the destruction wrought by the tornado.

Cissa received the occasional letter. Johnny's wife had recently given birth to another daughter. Liz's children were well, and her husband's business continued to prosper. There was no letter from Hector Davis; Cissa hoped he hadn't fallen into misfortune over there in Texas.

She learned from Laura that Janie, who had recently given birth to twins and then lost them both in the space of a few months, was increasingly discontent living in Mississippi. "I think the climate is bad for her health, Cissy." That's what Laura had said. Cissa did not say that she, too, felt there was something unwholesome about the climate in Mississippi.

Cissa read about the railroad being extended into Cowleton and the dispute there over the location of the depot. She thought about how she wouldn't be riding that train. She also read about how men and even youths seemed to be carrying guns everywhere these days.

Chapter Forty-Seven
Shootings in Fulton County

January - May 1909

"What do you know about this?" Cissa pointed at the paper to draw Monroe's and Lachlan's attention to an article with a headline that read "Boy Shoots a Young Lady and Her Escort at Cowleton." In the text of the piece it stated that the "escort" was Quinlan Tarver.

"Not much beyond what's printed there," Monroe said. "Our brother is plenty mad about the incident."

The article indicated that Quinlan—Duncan's next-to-youngest, although the paper didn't identify him as such—had been out walking with a young lady when they passed a group of boys. After progressing up the street, one of the boys shot at them.

"A shotgun," Lachlan said. "It says the shot didn't penetrate their clothing, but that means it hit them. That poor girl will never go walking with Quin again."

"But why did the boy shoot at them in the first place?" Cissa had found no indication of motive in the article, the implication being that it was a case of youthful hooliganism. A fourteen-year-old boy had been fined and sentenced to sixty days in jail, but with the expectation that the sentence would be remitted once his father paid the fine and court costs.

Monroe leaned back in his chair with his arms crossed. "Things are tense down there in Cowleton," he said. "Hell, they're tense all over, but worse there. It's like an armed camp with family and clan rallying to Farmers' League or Law and Order League. Somebody's going to end up getting killed if they don't settle down." He reached for his pipe and began packing it with tobacco in pensive silence.

Cissa frowned as she continued staring at the headline. "General tension" seemed to her no better an explanation of the incident than "youthful hooliganism." This was the kind of thing that someone like Duncan brought on himself with his intemperate language and behavior. It was the kind of thing he brought on his family.

Life slunk on at its usual slow pace, which Cissa found increasingly unsettling. A train now ran from Cowleton to Beckport in one direction and on down to New Orleans in the other. There were rumors that the Mississippi Western Railroad might soon run a track through Rundle Springs. More than rumors, really, as the citizens of the town pledged some four thousand dollars toward the project. Cissa wrote about it for the *Advocate*.

And then in March Cissa heard some news that nudged at the slumbering hope in her heart: A gentleman from Taloa County announced plans to start up a newspaper in Rundle Springs.

Could this be Cissa's dream coming true at last? She could stay right here in this house caring for her mother and still—maybe, if they'd have her—work for a newspaper. She should be cautious, though, she told herself. She sent a letter to Mr. Hodges at the *Marchelle Advocate* to ask him what he knew about the planned publication and to indicate her interest in writing material for it.

As she waited to hear back from him, she lectured herself on the perils of optimism. So many times she had felt things were going her way and that she was on the verge of becoming someone who mattered, and then, at the last moment, the rug was pulled out from under her. She mustn't expect too much now. And yet, she couldn't help but fantasize about what it might be like going to work every day—most days anyway—at a newspaper office.

The day after Cissa wrote to Mr. Hodges, an article appeared in the *Advocate* about the planned Rundle Springs paper. The instigator of the project was referred to as a "splendid newspaper man," which Cissa found encouraging. However, the article went on to report "a vague rumor that one of the prime objects of the new publication will be to give publicity to a movement looking to the establishment of a new county, the territory to be taken from Hinson, Burr, Fulton, and Chahtah counties." In an editorial postscript, Mr. Hodges indicated his misgivings about the idea, stating further that "until the new paper is organized we will be glad to be considered the home newspaper of Rundle Springs and vicinity as well as the rest of Hinson County."

Cissa grew apprehensive about how Mr. Hodges would respond to her query. She lectured herself on her habit of always asking permission. If she wanted to do something, shouldn't she just do it? She was a grown woman, turning thirty-three on her next birthday. When a response at last arrived, it was, she decided, optimistically noncommittal. "Of course I have always encouraged you to write for other publications as well as the *Advocate*," Mr. Hodges wrote. "You must do as you think best."

Feeling the need of someone to talk to about her quandary, Cissa went to see Lachlan.

"Since I can't travel about like a proper reporter for the *Advocate*," she said, "I think maybe taking a job at the Rundle Springs paper might be the best for me. If they'll have me, of course. If there really is to be a paper in Rundle Springs."

"Is that what you want?" Lachlan sat down on the porch steps next to Cissa.

Cissa chewed on her lower lip and tucked her hands under her arms. "No," she said with a sigh. "You know I want to be a real reporter. Traveling about and writing stories that matter. But I have to care for Mother. She's my responsibility. Pop is counting on me." Her brow furrowed as her spirits plummeted.

Laura burst through the door, a frantic look on her face. "Lachlan, where's your father? He needs to come to the phone."

"Who's calling?" Lachlan said. "What's the matter?"

"It's just terrible," Laura said, her face contorted in anguish. "Ada is beside herself. Get your pop."

Cissa stood up but didn't know which way to turn.

"I'll find him," Lachlan said. He bounded down the steps toward the barn and in less than a minute Monroe was there mounting those same steps.

Monroe didn't say anything. He went inside with Laura. Cissa and Lachlan could hear him talking on the telephone, but they could only catch a phrase here and there of his conversation.

"Dead?" he said. "Oh, lord. How bad is Duncan hurt?"

Cissa let out the breath she didn't know she'd been holding. Duncan wasn't the one who was dead. She thought she ought to go home to Mother. Or maybe she should learn more about what was going on first. Mother would want to know. And as long as Mother didn't know anything at all about whatever it was, she was fine. Of course she was.

Cissa went inside with Lachlan and waited. She grew impatient, listening to half a conversation, but she was able to determine that there had been gunfire and that several people, including Duncan, were injured and that at least one person had been killed. But who? And how had it happened?

Monroe was not able to answer all of Cissa's questions, but he was able to tell her that Duncan's wound was not serious and that he, along with Albert, Eli, Lamar, and even young Robby—were all in jail in Cowleton. The dead man was Ben Griffith.

"Griffith? Wasn't he the one Duncan ran against for chancery?" Cissa asked. "Is that what this was about?"

"Ben Griffith is one of the old clerk's sons." Monroe picked up his pipe and then set it down again. "I'll have to go to Cowleton to see if I can help straighten things out," he said, his eyes on Laura, who looked close to tears. "Lachlan, go get my horse saddled up. Cissa, you need to get home to Mother. And stay there. Who knows where this will all end?"

As Cissa walked home, her mind was once more overrun with thoughts of Duncan. He'd shot at that fellow Brewer last year but hadn't harmed him. He'd waved his pistol around Lord knows how many times, threatening to shoot someone. Had he had anything to do with Jewel Archer getting killed? Maybe. Probably. And how many other deaths might he have had a hand in? But now he'd shot his gun and a man was dead. And Duncan and four of his five sons were in jail. If any of them were to be found guilty of murder, they might well stay there for a good long time.

The last was a possibility Cissa found unlikely. Duncan knew too many people and had too many loyal friends and oath-bound supporters in Fulton County. If Cissa were a betting woman, she'd be willing to bet her brother and his sons would get off scot-free. She did not find that thought comforting.

Susanna met Cissa in the hallway. "Something's wrong, isn't it?" She drew her right hand from behind her skirt and Cissa saw that she was holding the pistol Lachlan had given them.

"Mother..." Cissa didn't want to startle her. "Mother, everything's alright. You need to hand me the gun."

Mother looked down with an air of surprise at the weapon in her hand and then held it out toward Cissa. She shook her head as Cissa took possession of the gun. "No, it's not alright. Something has happened and you're not telling me."

"Come sit down, Mother," Cissa said. "You're right. There's been an accident and Duncan is injured. But it's not bad. He'll be fine. It was just a little thing." As she spoke, she guided her mother to her chair in the parlor, trying to decide where she should keep the pistol so that Mother wouldn't discover it again. Had she known where it was all along?

"I always know when something's amiss," Susanna murmured. "A mother always knows." Her voice trailed off as she leaned over the side of her chair to stare out the front window.

Cissa took the pistol into the kitchen and found a large crockery jar that had once held saltine crackers. She put the pistol into it and put the jar on the top shelf before returning to the parlor.

Mother's unease was palpable, and it kept Cissa hovering about her all the rest of Monday and through Tuesday morning. Lachlan came by once to see if they were alright and once again to tell them that Duncan had hired a lawyer. "Pop says they have witnesses who will testify that it was Griffith who started the shooting and that Uncle Duncan and his boys were just defending themselves."

Of course he does, Cissa thought. But what she said was, "That's a relief. Perhaps everything will work out." That didn't make Ben Griffith any less dead.

When the Tuesday *Fulton Gazette* arrived, its account of the shooting corroborated Lachlan's optimistic report. It said that Duncan and his sons were riding down the main street of Cowleton when Ben Griffith came out of the drug store with a gun and called out, "God damn you, get your guns and get to shooting!" Of course the paper excised certain letters from the cuss words. The article went on to say that as gunfire commenced, two more Griffith brothers as well as Duncan and his sons joined in the shooting. It was thus far impossible to know whose bullets had hit whom. In addition to Duncan, two bystanders had been wounded. "The trouble has been brewing for some time," the paper said, "there being an old grudge between the participants, having its origin in politics."

Cissa knew that to be true. But why would one of the Griffiths suddenly attack Duncan like that? Men didn't shoot each other just over election results, did they? Surely something more had provoked him.

The Saturday edition of the *Beckport Journal* carried a somewhat different account, supplied to the paper by a pastor who was a relative of the Griffiths and who had been in town to officiate at Ben Griffith's funeral. According to the reverend, the shooting was the result of a dispute over the hiring of a schoolteacher and some debts Duncan owed that one of the Griffith brothers who was a lawyer had attempted to collect on behalf of a client. The lawyer claimed to have been violently assaulted by a Tarver in-law while three Tarver brothers stood guard. There had also been a brief physical encounter between Duncan and one of the Griffiths earlier in the morning on the day the shooting occurred.

"Do you think that's really what it was about, Lachlan?" Cissa asked her nephew when he came by, as had become his habit, to check on his aunt and grandmother.

"Who knows?" Lachlan replied. "All the families hereabouts are so wound up in each other's business and have been for generations that it's pretty near impossible to know what makes things explode like this. If I had to say, I'd say it was likely a little bit of everything. Duncan's trial is set for next week. I guess we'll know more after that."

"Maybe," Cissa said. "I wish we could depend on people to tell the truth once they're giving sworn testimony. Will Monroe stay in Cowleton until the trial is over?"

"That's his plan. I'm the man of the house until he gets back."

As reports on the trial came in, Cissa felt the whole case grow even more murky. There was conflicting testimony, which Cissa found unsurprising. She knew that witnesses would say what was in the best interest of their kinsmen and friends. Did they truly believe what they testified to? Sometimes Cissa thought they must, that they must convince themselves of whatever narrative was most advantageous. And then again, sometimes she thought they just didn't understand the concept of objective truth. In any event, "truth" did not appear to be a commodity held in very high regard in Fulton County. The papers commented on the high level of tension in Cowleton, speculating whether there might yet be another outbreak of violence.

Lachlan relayed reports from Monroe on the final days of the trial. There were rumors that one of the state's witnesses had asked to be called back to the stand so he could refute his previous testimony. And then on the last day, Duncan testified for several hours, never deviating from his insistence that Griffith had shot first and that he and his sons were merely defending themselves. "Pop says there's likely to be a hung jury," Lachlan said.

But there was no hung jury.

"The jury was out for several hours, Aunt Cissy, but they reached a verdict," Lachlan said. "They found Uncle Duncan not guilty. His boys are being fined on minor charges and let go."

There it was. Duncan had gotten away with murder. Cissa knew the self-defense plea carried a lot of weight and she supposed that was just. But it didn't alter the fact that Duncan had killed a man. "How are the Griffiths taking it?" she asked her nephew.

"About how you'd expect."

Monroe returned to Callander Road the following day, stopping by to visit Mother before returning to his own home.

"Oh, I'm so glad they turned you out of jail, Monroe. I knew you didn't belong there," Mother said.

Monroe shot a quizzical look toward Cissa who held up her hands in despair. Where did Mother get these ideas anyway?

"I wasn't in jail, Mother," he said. "Duncan was, but he's free now, so nothing more to worry about. How are you keeping?"

"Better than I deserve," she said. "Maggie babies me. I suppose she means well."

Monroe tried with little success to converse further with Mother. She responded to his questions with unrelated comments when she responded at all. When she started telling him a story about her lost baby daughter Maggie—telling it as if Maggie was nearly grown, telling it as if it had happened recently—Monroe made a polite excuse and left.

Cissa accompanied him to the front porch. "Is there anything I need to know?" she asked.

"Stay close, Cissy. The Griffiths are livid about the trial outcome and would just as soon shoot a Tarver as look at him right now. Duncan's trying to make a brave show of everything being all settled and peaceful but...well, it's not. Not at all."

"I understand," Cissa said, wishing she didn't. "Did they have any trouble coming up with the fines the boys had to pay? Those sounded like pretty hefty fines to me. And for so many."

"Duncan says his lawyer worked it all out. Albert should be home tomorrow. He went to fetch Eva and the children. You know they were with her folks ever since Albert got arrested."

Cissa knew. She wanted to say something about things getting back to normal, but somehow that felt premature. She thanked Monroe and assured him that she and Mother would be fine.

"You still have the pistol?"

"I do." Cissa didn't mention Mother's purloining of the firearm.

"Keep it handy."

Cissa watched as Monroe led his horse the rest of the way home. Laura was on the porch waiting for him.

Chapter Forty-Eight
An End and a Beginning

June - July 1909

The only one who showed up for Mother's prayer circle the next week was old Mrs. Campbell. She brought a plate of chocolate brownies, enough for all the ladies who didn't come, and she insisted on leaving them with Cissa and Susanna. "We shouldn't never be afraid to show up for our Lord Jesus," Mrs. Campbell said. But Cissa understood the fear that kept the other women away.

She knew in her gut that this was different from the worst of the whitecapping outbreaks. Now it was white men gunning for other white men. The papers were using words like "factions" and "feuding."

Cissa tried to follow Monroe's advice, keeping close to the house where she could keep an eye on Mother. She found a better hiding place for the pistol behind some books on the shelf above Pop's desk where it would be safe but readily accessible if she needed it. She hoped to high heaven she wouldn't need it. And yet every time she saw Monroe or Albert, she noted that each of them had a pistol strapped to his hip. Even Lachlan had taken to carrying one. Instead of making Cissa feel safer, all this display of firearms made her more edgy.

It had been like this for several weeks and Cissa told herself she ought to be getting used to it. But she wasn't. It all felt so unresolved. The next morning that Elsie came to the house for a half-day's work, Cissa announced that she was going for a walk.

"Where to?" Elsie inquired in her politely disinterested way.

"Anywhere," Cissa said. She didn't even consider taking the pistol with her. It was one of the things she wanted to get away from.

As she struck out toward the canebrake, a creeping sense of insecurity gathered around her. She wondered if this was how Negroes felt when they stepped outside their communities and into a world that belonged to white people. Now Cissa was afraid of white people, too. Afraid of the ones who weren't her own, anyway. And maybe even afraid of a few of those who were.

Without consciously deciding where she would go, Cissa found herself searching for the old lightning oak. She told herself she was merely curious to see the old tree again, but when she found it, she took the turning that would lead to Nubby's pond.

Nubby. Cissa hadn't thought much about Nubby in years. She still had the red bead Nubby had given her tucked away inside the doll Julia made, a doll that was somewhere in one of her bureau drawers. Sometimes Cissa felt a hard place like that bead inside herself. Or maybe it was more of an emptiness, a yearning for something magical, like the fairies she'd almost believed in, or the bottle tree in Zolene's yard that captured haints, or the Holy Trinity her mother's prayer group invoked, or even a bannee like Nubby, though Mother insisted that bannees were nothing but evil. Cissa found her objective world—this real world—to be quite full enough of evil; she was looking for something else, something uplifting, something powerful and liberating.

There was nothing like that in Narcissa Tarver's world. How she longed to escape the grinding constraints of her life. But she was fettered to her mother and to their house. She had accepted the fact that her father's generosity in leaving the big house to her was in effect another impediment to her ever becoming what she wanted to be.

What did she want to be? For a moment she let her mind wander. She would be a news reporter who went out every day to cover stories about things people wanted to read about, things people needed to know. She would ask questions of important people, and they would answer. She would witness important events and paint pictures with her words that would astound her readers, that would make them feel like they had been there.

The path alongside the little stream was indistinct and yet somehow, all at once, Cissa found herself at the edge of Nubby's pond. There was the big oak tree, the one that sheltered whatever remained of the physical existence of Nubby. Nubby the bannee, the witch. Julia had called her a conjure woman. Cissa remembered sitting under that tree in despair when she was only twelve, wondering how to find her way forward in life. She sat there now, remembering the first time she'd come here and how Nubby had appeared from behind the big rock so suddenly, as if by magic. Cissa half expected her to appear again, but of course she didn't.

Nubby was dead.

Cissa's heart grew heavy with emptiness. Why had she come here anyway? Whatever she was looking for, she felt certain it wasn't to be found here at the edge of a stagnant pond. For a few moments, Cissa thought she would cry. She told herself it would be alright to cry. But the tears didn't come. When your heart is so filled with emptiness, there are no tears.

Cissa rose and brushed the leaves and twigs from her skirt, watching the bits settle onto the surface of the pond. Something caught her eye at the edge of the water, and she reached down to tug at it. It was a scrap of cloth. Dirty and torn, it looked as if it had once been white, with a fine blue stripe. With a sigh, she recalled again her mother's admonition about bannees: You could always see one near a stream or a pond washing clothes and they were always the clothes of someone who was about to die. That was nonsense, of course.

And besides, Nubby was dead.

Cissa walked back home with a heavy heart but a somewhat calmer mind. She was no longer gripped by the anger and frustration that had been eating away at her soul over the past few weeks. She was only very sad.

She found Elsie busy dusting the furniture in the dining room. "Is Mother alright?" Cissa asked.

"Yes, ma'am. She taking tea in the parlor." Elsie turned suddenly. "Oh, I near forgot. There come a letter for you. I puts it there." She gestured toward the hall table.

Cissa's heart leapt. It had been at least two months since she'd had a letter from Johnny. Longer since she'd heard from Hector Davis. Such a letter would be welcome now.

But the letter wasn't from Johnny or from Hector. It was from Liz. Well, that was welcome, too. Cissa had turned to look for her father's silver letter opener when Lachlan came running—literally running—through the yard and up the steps. When Cissa looked into his flushed face, her breath caught in her throat.

"Lachlan?" she said. The pupils of his eyes were unnaturally dilated for such a bright morning, dilated as if they were trying to peer through some darkness. "What is it, Lachlan?" Apprehension crept up Cissa's spine.

"It's Uncle Duncan," he said, trying to catch his breath. "He's been shot." His voice was flat and heavy, and by the way his face contorted as he shook his head, Cissa knew.

Without a thought, she took her favorite nephew—this man she trusted more than any other—into her arms. Standing there in silence, Cissa and Lachlan clung to one another. Her eyes were dry and wide open.

After a while Lachlan pulled away, breathing more calmly. He brushed his sleeve across his eyes.

"I suppose one of the Griffiths killed him," Cissa said, her voice soft but hard-edged. There were still no tears in her eyes, only that emptiness in her heart, an emptiness that suddenly felt almost like a living thing, like something struggling to be born.

"Probably," Lachlan said. He squeezed his eyes shut for a moment. "It was Duncan's youngest called Pop." He took a deep breath, his eyes flitting about the room. "Rob said there was a lot of shooting. Right there on Cowleton main street. Right where Ben Griffith was shot last month. Eli and Lamar are hurt, but I don't know how bad. Other people, too. I think he said..." Lachlan ran his hand through his hair as if trying to arrange his thoughts. "He said Albert and Quin are in jail. They're sending in troops. I think Robby is alright." Lachlan closed his eyes again and set his jaw. In an anguished voice, he said, "Why did this have to happen, Aunt Cissy?"

Something was stirring in Cissa's heart that felt strange and unfamiliar. It felt almost like joy. She shoved it aside. "It didn't *have to* happen, Lachlan." She spoke calmly. "These are all grown men who could have backed off their feuding and fighting long ago if they'd had a mind to. But, no, they had to keep after one another until first one of the Griffiths and now a Tarver is..." Cissa inhaled sharply and looked away from her shaken nephew. "It's come to this: Two men dead," she said. Maybe more. Lachlan hadn't said.

"Pop wanted me to make sure you and Grandma knew to stay quiet indoors. I swear, Aunt Cissy, all this shooting seems like a disease sometimes, with folks catching it from one another." He shook his head, staggering slightly like a man struggling to find his bearings. He glanced toward the big mirror on the wall and then quickly away. "I'd best get back home. Pop will be going down to Cowleton again."

"We'll be fine here," Cissa said. They would have to be. But how was she going to tell her mother that she'd lost another child, this one a grown man, a father and grandfather in his own right? As soon as Lachlan was gone, Cissa reached for the hall mirror and, without looking into it, turned it to face the wall. Then she straightened her shoulders and moved toward the parlor where Mother sat, her body inclined toward the hallway as if she'd been listening.

"Who was at the door?" Mother asked. "Something's wrong..." She looked up at Cissa and there was a sadness in her eyes like one of those deeply overcast days when it seems the sun has ceased to exist.

It was not the first time that Cissa had been grateful for her mother's failing hearing. "It was Lachlan," she said. She took a deep breath. "He had bad news about Duncan. He's been shot." She'd start with that.

"I know," Mother said. "You already told me that. But he's better now." Her eyes had become so small as she got old but now they strained wide. "You told me he's better now." She threw out the words like a challenge as her hands clenched into small fists like knots of hickory wood.

"No, that was before, Mother. He's been shot again. Just this morning he was shot." Cissa would have to be very specific to get through her mother's defenses, her unwillingness to hear what Cissa knew she had to hear. "And this time it's not so good. He's been killed, Mother."

Susanna stared straight ahead and began to shake her head. "No... No, Narcissa. You told me he was getting better. That he'd be fine." She sniffed. "He's going to be fine." There was a choking sound, a stifled sob. "Not my son," she moaned, her voice barely audible. "My boy..."

It was late afternoon verging into evening when the cortege of men from Cowleton came bearing the body of Duncan Quinlan Tarver back to his old house on Callander Road. Cissa walked outside and down the road a piece to watch. As they bore the shrouded body up the steps, one of the men stumbled and an arm slipped from the stretcher as the covering cloth fell away from Duncan's face.

Cissa caught her breath. Lachlan hadn't mentioned that Duncan had been shot in the head. She wouldn't have recognized him. As if killing him wasn't enough, they had to obliterate his identity.

Cissa detested what she'd seen, and yet she was somehow morbidly thankful that she'd seen it. Her arrogant brother had been absolutely brought down, rendered lifeless and faceless.

And then her attention focused on the arm that still hung from the side of the stretcher. Prickles ran up her own arms as she saw, despite the blood stains, that what Duncan was wearing was a white shirt with a fine blue stripe.

No, Narcissa, she told herself. Of course she didn't believe in Mother's old tale about the bannee. It was just a coincidence. Only that. But she couldn't help thinking that somehow Nubby had tried to warn her.

She forced her attention back onto the men crowding around Albert's house, which had been Duncan's house as a young man. There was a muted turmoil among them like a kettle just before it boils. These were Duncan's loyal retinue, his oath-bound friends, and it was clear that they were not taking his death well.

Cissa turned her back and with resolute steps walked back to the big house.

She found her mother still sitting in her chair, still staring out the window. "You said something about Duncan. He's coming over for supper, was that it? Tell Edna to set out the good china."

Cissa sighed deeply. There was no use continuing to press the issue. Mother knew. Didn't she always say that a mother knew when something was wrong among her family? It was only that this time, when the something was so final, she was resisting. Eventually Mother would accept the truth. Pop's death had been such a crisis point in her life, accelerating her mental decline. Cissa wondered how Duncan's death would play out for her.

Cissa went to the front door and looked back down the road toward Albert's house. Robby had broken away from the gathering and was making his way toward the big house. Had Robby witnessed what happened? He'd been there when Ben Griffith was killed last month. As he entered the house, Cissa saw that his eyes were glassy, his hair mussed, and that there was blood on his shirt. Cissa caught a faint whiff of gunpowder.

Their conversation was cursory. Cissa learned that Lamar's injuries were far more serious than Eli's. Both had been taken by train to the sanatorium in Natchez.

Cissa tried to reassure Rob about the quality of medical care in Natchez, but he didn't seem to be listening. He looked so tired, so broken. Wrecked. He pulled himself together enough to inquire as to whether Cissa and his grandmother would be alright there by themselves or whether someone should come and stay with them. "Maybe one of Uncle Monroe's boys," he said. His own family had no one left to offer, with Lamar and Eli injured and Albert and Quin in jail.

The thought passed through Cissa's mind that the Tarver men seemed to be magnets for bullets these days, targets for mishaps and mayhem. Perhaps their absence would best ensure her safety. She refused Rob's offer. But she silently reminded herself of which books she'd stashed the pistol behind.

After Robby left, Cissa watched through the dining room window, thinking about the work going on inside Albert's house where women tended to the aftermath of what their men had done. She watched as her brother Monroe collapsed in tears sitting there on Albert's front porch. Monroe had tried so hard to be loyal to Duncan, even when Duncan tested that loyalty severely.

Cissa snapped the curtains closed. This whole tragic scenario, this tableau of masculine pride, was ludicrous. Laughter wanted to burble out of her and so she let it. It wasn't scornful laughter or bitter laughter. It felt like water shoving its way through a crack in a dam, pushing to find its way. For just a moment, Cissa let it flow.

Composing herself, Cissa moved toward the parlor, where Mother still sat in the big armchair. Cissa couldn't tell if she was asleep or had slipped into some other-worldly dream state. Perhaps she was praying. *Let her be*, Cissa thought. She stood behind the chair for a moment, her hand resting on the embroidered tidy with its intricate flowers embroidered by Julia's expert hand. Pink roses, yellow and white narcissus.

Cissa was master of the Tarver big house, but it was a house full of emptiness. Pop was gone. Julia was gone. Mother was barely there.

Returning to the dining room, Cissa went to the sideboard and pulled out the family Bible. She laid it on her father's desk and opened it to the heavy page between the Old Testament and the New. Picking up her fountain pen, she wrote in a third date next to Duncan's name: June 14, 1909. Her eyes scanned the names and dates. There were so many deaths. Too many. With a deep sigh, she closed the book and restored it to its customary place.

All the turmoil had left Cissa feeling light-headed, so she sat down at Pop's desk to gather herself. Sitting there in the chair where Pop used to sit, where Duncan used to sit, Cissa couldn't help but feel that the solidity, the solidarity of what was left of the Tarver family was disintegrating. A single tear slid down her cheek and fell on the surface of the desk, right next to the letter from Liz. She reached for Pop's silver letter opener, the one that had been her grandfather's, and slid it under the flap of the envelope.

"My dear friend Cissa," the letter began. "I hope this missive finds you well. I was sorry to hear about your brother's mishap. We both know he'll probably skitter out from under it as he always does, but I look forward to hearing the juicy details."

Cissa took in a deep breath as she imagined writing to Liz about her brother's latest mishap. His final mishap. She read on.

"Things have taken a decided turn for the better here with our little printing business. Several organizations have begun hiring us to print their monthly newsletters, which permitted us to acquire new fonts and begin printing fancy things like invitations and calling cards. We've contracted with a local theater to print their programs this season and that will provide even more revenue. Bill and I still dream about publishing a small newspaper for our section of the city and feel it coming closer and closer to realization. Oh, if only you were here to be our star reporter! Come, now, Cissa, wouldn't you like that? But I know you have family obligations, so I won't nag. The twins are growing like topsy, and we now have a nanny most days to look to their care and feeding, giving me more time at the business. Must stop for now, my dear friend! Tempus fugit! I look forward to hearing more news from you soon."

The stirring in Cissa's heart overwhelmed her and her tears now fell in earnest as she began to cry not for her lost brother, but for her own stifled dreams.

Why not? she asked herself. Why not join Liz in Texas and be done with Callander Road and all of the Tarver family drama once and for all? These were her thoughts as she helped her mother to bed and readied two black dresses in preparation for the next day's funeral.

Chapter Forty-Nine
Too Many Ghosts

August 1909

The funeral of Duncan Quinlan Tarver took place under armed guard. Even the men bearing the casket into the sanctuary carried revolvers at their hips. Instead of the quiet dignity that had characterized his father's funeral, Duncan's funeral felt tense and hurried, as men with rifles stood at every door and window. If hearts were broken by Joseph Tarver's death, they were maimed by Duncan's. The father of five sons had only one available to help bear his remains, and young Rob looked as if he might collapse under the weight of it all.

Cissa sat next to her mother on a pew along with Ada and her two daughters and three daughters-in-law who clutched one another's hands in something akin to terror. Cissa wondered what the minister, who had waxed so eloquent in eulogizing Joseph Tarver, would find to say about his son. He announced that his theme would be "the Lord God omnipotent reigneth."

"It is impossible," the reverend intoned, "to draw comfort from any book of human philosophy on an occasion like this, but the above words from the Bible furnish genuine consolation to all who believe them. Paul the Apostle was in expectancy awaiting a violent death. But he knew the Roman ax could not be raised against him unless God willed it."

So that's it, Cissa thought. *We're just going to assign all of this to God's will.* Her fit of laughter from the previous day almost took possession of her again, but she restrained herself for the sake of her mother. She was absolutely confident that Duncan had brought this on himself, requiring no help whatsoever from the Almighty.

As the mourners made their way across the road to the cemetery, Cissa's heart wrenched as she saw Ada stumble, leaning on Milly and Katy. Ada was a mother of five sons, but in this moment she had only her daughters to support her.

Cissa picked up fragments of conversation. "They say the young doctor won't live." "It was one of the Griffiths shot first." "I heard they had a quarrel in the chancery office earlier that morning." "Ain't no need for them troops from Beckport. Cowleton can take care of our own."

After Duncan had been interred, Mother lingered for a while at Pop's graveside. Cissa stood next to her in silence. Then she guided her mother back to where Lachlan waited with a buggy to take them home.

Early the next morning when the sun was barely up and Mother was still sleeping, Cissa was surprised to hear footsteps in the front hallway. She hadn't heard the door open or close.

"Milly!" Cissa reached out a hand to her niece. They'd barely spoken at the funeral, but she knew that Milly had intended to stay overnight at Albert's house, awaiting her husband's arrival.

Milly fell into Cissa's arms sobbing.

Cissa didn't know what to say so she said nothing as she held Milly in her arms, gently kneading her shoulders, listening as her sobs subsided into broken sighs and soft moans. *Duncan was her father,* Cissa thought. *Of course she's distraught.* Finally Cissa said, "Come in the kitchen with me and have some coffee."

Milly hiccupped and nodded.

After she'd had a few sips of coffee, Milly spoke. "I was there in Cowleton, Aunt Cissy. Mother had been so upset ever since Pop's trial, so she sent for me." She took another sip of coffee. The cup clattered as she replaced it in the saucer. "I went with Pop in the buggy that morning to buy a few things in town. He let me off at the grocer. I'd barely gone inside when I heard the first shots."

"Oh, Milly." Cissa leaned across the table toward her niece, beginning to comprehend the magnitude of her distress.

"I haven't talked about it. I didn't want the children to hear." Milly put her hands over her eyes. "It was so awful, Cissy. So much shooting. I couldn't look away." She kept her eyes covered. "There was such a shower of blood when Pop fell. Face down there on the street. And then Lamar. Lamar screamed something awful when he fell. Not like Pop. Pop fell without a sound." Milly shivered slightly and then resumed speaking. "Albert was...I guess he was behind the buggy, shooting. I saw gunfire from somewhere upstairs. A window, a hand holding a pistol. A rifle barrel. Quin was across the street with his rifle. Eli ran out of the courthouse. He had a gun, too. He fell there on the steps. They were all just lying there. My pop and my brothers." Milly emitted a soft moan as she dug the heels of her hands into her eyes. "There was smoke and a terrible stink of gunpowder. Somebody kept yelling at me to get back indoors, but I couldn't go. I was scared, but I had to see. It was my pop. My brothers. None of them saw me. After a while the guns stopped, and I could hear people crying out for help. Albert was standing over Pop. I saw him look over at Quin and I could tell by the way he shook his head... I think Quin had his belt wrapped around Eli's leg. Lamar was still there on the ground, not moving. Everywhere was blood." Milly took her hands away from her eyes, but they were still closed.

"How awful for you, Milly," Cissa said, reaching for Milly's hand.

Her eyes flew open. "For me? I wasn't shot. I'm not dead or in hospital or in jail." Her face contorted into a frown. "*My* husband is fine, and he'll be here soon to take me and the children back home." She picked up a spoon and stirred her cooling coffee. "Do you remember when we were just girls playing fairies and princesses out by the magnolia tree?"

"Of course I remember," Cissa said. "We had some good times."

"Do you remember how you told me that day that the captain of the frog fairies didn't care what color Princess Winifred's dress was because he had powers?"

Cissa laughed nervously, feeling a little ashamed. "Yes, I remember that."

"Well, that was my father. Pop was always so busy being important. Like he had powers. He doted on his boys but barely noticed me or Katy. I've got two sons and a daughter now and I'm determined not to let that happen to her. I loved my pop, Aunt Cissy, but I was never really sure he loved me back." Milly's voice was calm, even as the tears coursed down her cheeks.

Cissa was stunned. She'd always thought of Milly as a bit frivolous and entirely satisfied, even prideful of her life as wife and mother. She felt her heart opening to her niece.

The two women sat and talked a while longer. Then Milly took her leave, but not before giving Cissa a long embrace and whispering,

"Thank you for being here for me. I've always admired you, Aunt Cissy. And I do love you so."

"I love you, too, Milly," Cissa said, and she felt the truth of it in her heart.

When the newspapers finally arrived at the big house that afternoon, Cissa studied them with the images conjured by Milly's words still fresh in her mind. The Beckport paper called Duncan's death an assassination and indicated that the Griffith faction, following a confrontation that morning between one of their lawyers and Duncan in the chancery office, had plotted a surprise assault. Duncan had been fired on from the upstairs windows of the Cortman Building. The paper indicated that it was likely Quin Tarver, shooting from across the street with a repeating rifle, who had fired the rounds that killed one of the Griffith allies and wounded another.

The Beckport paper cited Duncan's recent shooting incident involving Donald Brewer, in which neither man was indicted, but also mentioned that Dr. Duncan Tarver had been indicted some two decades previous in the killing of another man. He'd been acquitted in that case, too, just as he'd been acquitted in the Griffith killing. The Beckport paper went on to note that "Dr. Tarver was also mixed up in the killing of a Negro, but he was never tried for this, nor was anyone. It seems that the Negro was under guard by a posse of citizens, and he tried to make an escape. The Negro had a gun and endeavored to shoot Dr. Tarver and the others. Then the doctor as well as other members of the posse opened fire and the Negro was killed." That one, Cissa thought, sounded for all the world like a lynching.

Why did I never hear about these cases? Cissa put down the paper. She felt increasingly certain that her brother Duncan had never merited the loyalty that he had demanded and that she had mostly failed to give. He was a murderer. He was a whitecapper. Cissa's desire to escape her family and all its chaos and questionable history was escalating by the day.

It was on Thursday that news came of Lamar's death. Another funeral was quickly arranged. Another burial. Milly attended this one on the arm of her husband. It was at Lamar's funeral that Janie told Cissa that she and her husband and son were moving away.

"Where will you go?" Cissa asked.

"Well, you know my health has been poor, and it's said that the climate in Texas is much more healthful. Anyway, Charles has been assured that he can get good work in San Antonio, so that's where we'll be by the end of the year."

Cissa wondered what the climate in Texas might be like, imagining clear blue skies, wide open prairies, and sunshine.

Mother picked at her food at mealtimes and no longer even pretended to knit or sew. She just sat. "When is Maggie going home?" she asked for the second time. Yesterday she had spoken of Eugene and Laura as if they too had been visiting with her, as if they'd come for the funerals. Cissa knew these were the names of some of her lost babies. Sometimes Cissa would find her mother standing in the middle of the floor with a haunted look on her face.

In July, Eli was elected to succeed his father as chancery clerk. Some efforts had been made to discourage him from running in the fear that it would stir things up again. But he had insisted that he owed it to his father to run. "He wouldn't want me to back down. He never backed down." That was true, Cissa thought, and look where it got him.

It was later that same month that Cissa received another letter with no return address. By now she recognized the handwriting and felt an unexpected surge of elation as the face of Hector Davis arose in her mind. She hadn't heard anything from or about him in months.

"My dear Miss Tarver," the letter began. "I read about what happened to your brother Duncan and wish to convey my condolences. He will always remain with me as one of the most unforgettable characters I have ever dealt with. Although he broke the law, I found that many thought of him as a sort of modern day Robin Hood. I know his loss must have been a terrible blow to your entire family. As for myself, I wanted to let you know that I am no longer part of the Pinkertons. Instead, I am starting up my own detective agency in Texas. I have been working with the Texas Rangers on a couple of cases and it seems I will have no shortage of work. I write my new address below so that if you ever feel inclined you can write to me again. I will venture to say that you, too, are one of my most unforgettable characters. I wish you great success as you continue your writing career."

He signed the letter, "Fondly, Hector."

Cissa's sense of elation escalated. Detective Davis—Hector—was not asking for any information or favors from Cissa. He'd reached out as a friend. He seemed to understand what a complicated person Duncan was. And he found Cissa "unforgettable." Her eyes grew wide as she saw the address he had provided: It was for a post office box in San Antonio.

In August, Eli was shot at through a window in his own home. The assailant missed, escaping into the darkness. It was later that same day that Cissa found her mother standing in front of the hall mirror, babbling incoherently with tears streaming down her cheeks.

"Mother?" Cissa started to reach out for her but drew back with a shiver. "Mother, come sit down with me. We'll make some coffee."

Susanna turned toward Cissa with eyes that seemed to look straight through her. "I can't live here anymore, Narcissa," she said. "This house is full of ghosts. I need to go."

Cissa was taken aback. Her mother loved this house. It was the house Pop built for her, the one he started building before the war between the states, and then abandoned as he went off to provide medical care for Confederate soldiers. He'd promised to come back and finish it when the war was over. When he returned, poorer but determined to make the most of his diminished position and take care of his wife and growing family, he had kept his promise. He'd finished the house out smaller than planned but, as best he could manage, the way Susanna wanted it. How could she now say she wanted to leave?

But Cissa wasn't going to argue. "Where will you go, Mother?" she asked.

"Marchelle is nice," she said.

"Well, let me see what I can figure out." Maybe this was one of Mother's whims, a temporary state of mind that would be changed by tomorrow. But maybe it was what Mother needed. She had seemed so haunted lately.

The next day, Cissa went to speak with Monroe. When she told him what their mother had said, his eyebrows shot up. "Are you joking?" he said. "Mother loves that house."

"I know. But can you blame her for thinking the place is full of ghosts and wanting to get away? How many children has she lost now?"

Monroe was silent for a moment. "Seven now that Duncan's gone. It's just you and me and Tilly left."

"And of course she misses Pop, too."

"Of course."

"She mentioned Marchelle. Do you think Tilly would take her in?"

"But what about you, Cissy? Would you want to live in Marchelle?" He paused and chuckled. "Is that what this is about? You want to go work for the newspaper there, don't you."

Cissa bristled. She was only trying to comply with Mother's wishes. She was, wasn't she? It was true that she had once dreamed about moving to Marchelle to work for the *Advocate*. "I don't think that job is available anymore," she said. She got up and walked over to the window, trying to think what to say next. "If Mother could be happily situated with Tilly, we could sell the house, couldn't we? And then I could go wherever I pleased."

Monroe shifted his lanky form and sat up straighter. Cissa noted the gray around his temples and in his mustache. He'd be...what? Fifty-five this year? He was not a young man anymore. His household now consisted of only himself and Laura and their three youngest. Dee was seventeen now, Sam fourteen, and Joey ten. Eleven soon. And of course there was Lachlan who was past thirty. Lachlan would always be here.

"I expect it's not just the ghosts, Cissy. Not that I believe in ghosts. But being a Tarver, being in the Tarver big house in particular...it's become a burden, hasn't it?" He stared out the window in the direction of the big house. "Janie's moving away," he said.

"She told me."

"Well, if you're looking for my blessing with regard to selling the house, Cissy, you've got it. Mine and Duncan's boys have land enough to make a good living without the house, too. Albert may take it badly, but there'll be nothing he can do."

"Albert?"

Monroe huffed quietly. "Duncan had him convinced that he was going to be able to get the house away from you if he could prove your were neglecting Mother. Which of course you weren't. No,

Cissy. Pop left the house to you and if Mother is ready to let it go..."
He shrugged as if it was not important, but Cissa could see the
sadness in his eyes.

Chapter Fifty
A Way Forward

August - September 1909

Cissa's plans came together in a matter of weeks. Matilda said she would be delighted to have Mother come and live with her. "Now that we've no more doctors in the family, I'll feel better about her spending her old age here in town where we can send for doctors when we need them. And Mother always seems to brighten when she's around the children." Matilda's children were quiet and well behaved, just the way Mother liked them.

Liz answered Cissa's telegram with one of her own which read: "Come. We have work for you."

When Cissa told Janie about her plans, she insisted that Cissa come live with her family in San Antonio. "It's only the three of us. You'll be such good company for me. We're going sooner than we'd planned. All this commotion has not helped my health, you know." Their plan now was to arrive in San Antonio in early October.

Monroe promised to take care of negotiating the sale of the house, and Cissa trusted him to handle everything with the utmost integrity. Cissa composed the ad to run in the Marchelle and Beckport papers. She remained unfazed as she read the brief article in the Fulton County paper suggesting that, in order to restore peace to the county, all the Griffiths and Tarvers should move away. The emergence of a petition seeking the same goal troubled her a bit more.

The decision seemed to set well with Mother. She stopped talking about ghosts, though she grew tearful at times as she sorted through the accumulations of a lifetime. She set some items aside to give to this or that grandson or granddaughter, while packing others away to take with her to Matilda's house. Remainders would be given to the Negroes.

Sorting through Pop's things was particularly hard for Mother. "You do it, Narcissa," she said. It was mostly clothing, but some of the clothes still had Pop's distinctive scent about them; perhaps that was what overwhelmed Mother. One item in the inventory stopped Cissa in her tracks: It looked like an old white sack, but when she turned it around she saw where cutouts had been neatly hemmed just where the eyes and mouth would be if someone were to place it over his head. A shiver of memory brought visions of men on horseback, blazing torches, and ghostly faces. With disgust, Cissa threw the item into the stack of discards that were going to be burned. Mother's ghosts were not the only ones that needed to be left behind.

Cissa had to keep a close eye on the trunk she was packing for her own things; Mother kept putting in the oddest items that she was certain Cissa would need—a mismatched set of delicate teacups, a rusty cheese grater, a set of embroidered napkins. Cissa kept the napkins.

Cissa's trunk was a small one and she thought carefully about what belonged in it and what didn't. Of course she packed the little stack of composition books in which she'd written poems and stories over the years. Her stringbook would be essential. The books that Johnny had given her went into the trunk, too. The fountain pen he sent her would be in the carpetbag she'd carry with her on the train.

The doll that Julia made had been crushed in the bottom of a bureau drawer for years now, but it was something Cissa tucked into her trunk without question. There were many memories that she wished to leave behind, but this object did not contain those. Rather, it contained memories of times that came as close to magic as Cissa had ever been. She held the doll for a moment against her breast, feeling the hard bead—Nubby's bead—that nestled inside it.

The book about the commonwealth of fairies that had once belonged to Granny Mag was still among Cissa's things. Should she take it with her? It had meant so much to her in a particular phase of her childhood when she'd desperately wanted to be important, if nowhere else, then at least in an imaginary kingdom. But this was a world she'd left behind and she decided she should leave the book behind as well, there among the things that were going to Monroe's house. Maybe a young great-niece or great-nephew at some point would find the book as enchanting as Cissa had.

The book about Rob Roy would go with her. She slipped it into her carpetbag, thinking maybe she'd read it again on the train.

Thinking of books, she remembered with a start the pistol that she'd hidden behind the remaining books above Pop's desk. She checked to verify that it was still there. No one had yet had the heart to deal with the few books that hadn't been claimed years ago by Duncan.

Should she take the gun with her to Texas? At first she thought, *Yes, I might need it for protection.* But as she held it in her hands, she questioned whether it held such power. Guns were the instruments that had brought her family to its knees, shamed and broken. No, Narcissa Tarver wanted nothing to do with guns of any kind ever again.

When Lachlan came over to help drag some crates down from the attic, Cissa gave the gun back to him. "Thank you for giving me this," she said, "but I don't wish to take it with me."

"Are you sure?" he said. "You never know what might happen."

Cissa stared at him with unwavering gaze, her jaw set.

"I guess I understand, though," he said. "How about this: How about you take it with you on the journey—just in case—and then when you get to Texas you can sell it and buy some books with the money."

Cissa almost laughed. Exchanging the gun for books was a tempting plan. With a sigh, she dropped it into her carpetbag.

There were more boxes in the attic than Cissa had expected. Some of them contained baby clothes with embroidered monograms that made Mother tear up again. There was one whole box of Lester's things that included a wooden toy gun and a yellowed tablet on which he'd struggled to draw letters and numbers. Among the odds and ends was a moth-eaten sweater, which Mother sniffed and then cradled in her arms, murmuring words Cissa didn't catch.

It was after one of these sessions that Mother came into the kitchen where Cissa was preparing supper. She carried something clasped in her hand and wore a distracted expression. "Mother wants you to have this," she said.

Cissa thought it odd that her mother would speak of herself in this way, but she wiped her hands on her apron in preparation to receive whatever oddity might be presented.

Susanna took her daughter's left hand in hers and placed a small item into it, closing her fingers around the object. "Mother brought it from away," she said. "Her mother gave it to her when she left and now she wants you to have it."

"Oh." Cissa exhaled slowly as the import of this little gift impressed itself upon her. This was something that had belonged not just to her own mother, but to her mother's mother. To Granny Mag. And it was Granny Mag's mother who had given it to her. It was something she'd brought with her all the way from Scotland.

Cissa opened her hand and saw a sparkling yellowish stone mounted in silver. It had a loop for hanging. "It's beautiful," she murmured.

Mother frowned and tilted her head as if listening for the echo of a long absent voice. "Mother says it's crystal. A victory stone, she calls it." She looked up and Cissa saw a clarity in her eyes that she hadn't seen in a long while. "Mother's mother Eliza was McLaurin, too, you know."

Cissa hadn't known. "Thank you, Mother," she said as she drew into an embrace this enfeebled woman who had borne her. She still held the stone clasped in her hand and for a fleeting moment she felt a solidarity of generations of women. Not Tarver women, but McLaurin women. It felt like the kind of solidarity that gives more than it demands.

Cissa found a narrow yellow ribbon among the sewing things and strung the victory stone on it so she could wear it around her neck. She wondered where it had been all these years. She'd never seen Mother wear it.

As the work progressed at the Tarver big house, they finally decided to send Mother on to Matilda's. She'd become more hindrance than help, taking things out of one box and putting them into another or back on a shelf or else collecting them up in the middle of the floor.

Monroe came to drive Mother to Marchelle. "Are you ready?" he said after he and Lachlan had loaded two trunks full of her things into the buggy.

"I have to say goodbye first," she said.

Assuming she meant "goodbye to the house," Cissa suggested they leave her alone to wander through the emptying rooms one more time.

Cissa and Monroe and Lachlan sat together on the porch, chatting about plans and avoiding any mention of the upcoming trials of Duncan's boys.

"I'll just check and see if Mother is ready to go," Cissa said, after more time than she thought reasonable had elapsed. She'd expected to find Mother in her favorite chair, which they'd left in its usual spot in the parlor even after other furnishings had been removed and the rug rolled up in a corner. Mother wasn't there.

"Mother?" she called as she went first into the corner bedroom and then into her own room, the dining room, the kitchen. "Mother?" she called more urgently at the foot of the stairs. She hurried up the stairs and looked in both of the upstairs rooms. Becoming frantic, she ran back down and through the kitchen and out the back door.

There she was.

Mother sat under the old cedar tree in the corner of the property that Cissa had always admired because of the profusion of flowers that grew there in the spring and summer. Cissa started to call out, but stopped short as she realized that her mother was speaking. She was too far away for Cissa to hear her words, but her mouth was moving as she swayed back and forth.

As Cissa crept closer, she realized that Mother wasn't speaking; she was singing. Her voice faltered and cracked, but Cissa didn't have to hear the words. She recognized the melody and was overcome by a memory she didn't know she possessed, a memory of being rocked in her mother's arms, her small head tucked beneath her mother's chin in such a way that the song vibrated against her cheek. Mother sang a lullaby filled with nonsense words as little Cissa drowsed into slumber.

With tears welling up, Cissa approached quietly and laid her hand on her mother's shoulder. Susanna looked up at her with surprise and then placed her own hand over her daughter's. "They like playing in the flowers," she said.

"Who?" Cissa looked around in confusion.

"My babies," Susanna said. "Maggie and Laura and Eugene and the ones that came so early we didn't name them."

Cissa shivered. Why had she never known that her lost infant siblings were buried here under this tree? She offered her mother support as the old woman struggled to stand. "I remember that song you were singing."

Mother was breathing heavily as she brushed the leaves from her skirt. "That wasn't me," she said.

Cissa took the arm of this impenetrable mystery that was her mother and guided her back toward the front of the house where Monroe and Lachlan waited. As they made their way, Cissa watched a mockingbird on a fencepost as it sang and periodically leapt into the air with the sheer joy of its song.

"Where had she gotten off to?" Monroe said.

Cissa shook her head. "Just saying her goodbyes."

A week later, Cissa said her own goodbyes to the family she was leaving behind on Callander Road and spent her final night in Marchelle with Matilda and Mother. Lachlan was there, too, as he'd driven her there with her belongings and helped her arrange the shipment of her trunk direct to Liz's address in San Antonio, Texas.

Lachlan and Cissa lingered in the parlor after everyone else had gone to bed.

"I'll miss you more than anyone," Cissa said. "You'll write, won't you?"

"Of course I will," he said. "And I'll let you know how my cousins fare in court." He paused. "You know I envy you, being able to escape all this. You will come back and visit, won't you?"

At first Cissa didn't answer. Would she? "I'll try," she said.

The next morning Lachlan drove Cissa to the station in Marston. Before boarding, she deposited a letter into the letterbox. It was addressed to Hector Davis. She'd signed it, "Unforgettably, Narcissa." Was that too brazen? She'd find out in San Antonio.

As Cissa boarded the train for New Orleans—the first stop on her long journey—she finally permitted herself to feel the giddy excitement of her escape. She was going to live in Texas and work in the newspaper business with Liz. Janie and her family would be there soon. And Hector. He'd be there somewhere. She grinned as she waved to Lachlan from the train window.

Cissa thought about all the things she'd packed into her one trunk and her one bag and about all the things she'd left behind. And she thought about the memories, her memories of a lifetime in the big house on Callander Road. All of those memories would go with her, the unpleasant ones as well as the happier ones, and they would inform her life going forward. Going forward was the only way. Cissa was ready.

She took a deep breath and touched the crystal pendant that hung around her neck as the train pulled out of the station.

—30—

Author's Note

When I interviewed my Mississippi grandmother for a high school assignment on family history, I was eighteen and it was 1966. Emmett Till had been lynched in Mississippi eleven years earlier. Medgar Evers had been murdered in Jackson, Mississippi in 1963. Integration was an issue across the South, though not in Sabinal, Texas, where I lived. There were no Black families in our town, and it was common knowledge that the last Blacks who had attempted to live there had been "run off." On the band bus going to away football games, we sang lusty choruses of "Dixie" and competed to see who had the best rebel yell. Yee-haw. Some of the kids followed up with a shout of "South gon' rise again!" Malcolm X had been assassinated, and Bloody Sunday had happened only a year before I wrote my paper. When I went away to college that fall to Southern Methodist University, I was witness to the Kappa Alpha Order's annual "Old South Ball." The brothers proudly hung a giant Confederate flag across the entrance to their fraternity house. Many a sorority girl was still enchanted by the illusions conjured by *Gone with the Wind.*

Shaking off the vestiges of my myth-laden Southern heritage is an ongoing process, and this book is part of that process.

Just as today's soaring loblolly pines obscure the vision of a Mississippi landscape once blanketed with cotton and corn, so the stories of noble women, heroic men, and loyal "servants" obscure the lives of the real people—more of them black than white—who hewed down the original longleaf pines, mowed through the canebrakes, and drew white wealth from black soil, bundled it into great bales and sent it off to make fine cotton sheets and dainty organdies.

As noted in the Preface, this novel is populated overwhelmingly with my own kin, although the key characters of Narcissa and Julia are entirely fictitious. I have given fictitious names to other characters not to protect their identities or that of their descendants, but only because I have significantly fictionalized the real people. I really know next to nothing about the true personality of my great-grandfather who appears here as Monroe McLaurin Tarver.

Most of the events that shape the plot line of this story are real. I learned about them through newspapers.com, from academic publications, and from the collections of the Historical Natchez

Foundation, the Mississippi Department of Archives and History, and the Ulysses Grant Presidential Library at Mississippi State University in Starkville. I have sometimes reconfigured events and relationships to fit the story, but never in a way that would violate the social and cultural habits of the time and place as I understand them. I have glossed over some of the complexities of political intrigue, while trying to highlight the most powerful through-lines, constantly reminding myself that I was not writing an academic treatise, but rather a story of one woman's struggle to be somebody who mattered in a time and place where everything except her fortuitous whiteness mitigated against her.

The terms "Scotch" and "Scotch-Irish" are used here as they were used at the time, though I am well aware that this violates modern principles of scholarly usage, in which "Scotch" is limited to whisky, people are "Scots," and "Scots-Irish" are people of Scottish origin who settled in Northern Ireland. My grandmother, who proudly self-identified as "Scotch-Irish," descended from inhabitants of Argyll and Bute in Scotland and one direct ancestor is identified as "of Islay," which is one of the islands of the Inner Hebrides. A historical marker in the village my grandmother called home alleges that the community was settled in 1806 "by Scotch Presbyterians, whose Gaelic speech long survived." For the convenience of readers, Scots Gaelic terms used in the text have been anglicized—"bannee" for "bhean nigh" and "shee" for "sìthiche." The importance of Scots heritage must not be underestimated, including the ancient custom of rallying the clans around a fiery cross, as portrayed in its Southern incarnation by artist Arthur I. Keller for Thomas Dixon's romance novel, *The Clansman.*

In telling this story, I found it necessary to place the heinous n-word into the mouths of my characters, though far more sparingly than it was used at the time. It would be unnecessary torture for modern readers to see it used as casually as it was then. White readers may deserve the discomfort, but Black readers certainly do not.

At times I have put indirect quotes from a news article into the mouths of characters, (e.g., Judge Niles) but only when the words were so articulate and well-crafted that I thought the individual in question would not have been offended by the attribution.

Dark Lantern, a newspaper introduced in chapter forty-one, was a real publication. Although I was unable to locate it in the archives that I accessed, other newspapers quoted at length from its pages. I have rendered the grammar and spelling exactly as they did. Whereas *Dark Lantern* is real, the *Hinson Chronicle* is fictional. There were a number of Black newspapers during this time period, but my efforts to track them down came up empty.

Most of the details about court cases are straight out of newspaper reports, supplemented by materials from the B. T. Hobbs archives held at Mississippi State University. Grand jury proceedings are described in close accord with news accounts of the time, even though some of the practices may appear to be in flagrant violation of today's standards.

Shooting incidents and other crimes are also factual as well as the solar eclipse, the ice storm, the hurricane, and the destructive fire in Marchelle. Threading Cissa's story around and through these events, imagining how they would have affected a young woman struggling to become somebody who mattered, was the greatest challenge and greatest pleasure of this project.

Like Cissa, it took me quite a while to come to terms with the character of Duncan Tarver, who is patterned closely after my own great-great-uncle. He was a complicated character, but clearly a white supremacist responsible for inflicting a great deal of harm on Black Mississippians. I am grateful for the numerous letters he wrote to the newspapers. I'm also grateful for the newspaper that printed the text of the eulogy given at his funeral.

I acknowledge having taken liberties with Ian Maclaren's *A Doctor of the Old School,* which I have Narcissa reading in 1891 despite the fact that it wasn't published until 1896.

Further Reading

Censer, Jane Turner. *The Reconstruction of White Southern Womanhood, 1865-1895.* Louisiana State University Press, 2003.

Clawson, Jacob S. "Militias, Manhood, and Citizenship in Reconstruction Mississippi, 1868-1875," *The Journal of Mississippi History,* Vol. LXXVI, Fall/Winter 2014, pp. 157-182.

Coates, TaNehisi. *Between the World and Me.* BCP Literary, 2015.

Cresswell, Stephen.

Multiparty Politics in Mississippi, 1877-1902. University Press of Mississippi, 1995.

Rednecks, Redeemers, and Race: Mississippi after Reconstruction, 1877-1917 (2006, University Press of Mississippi.)

Dixon, Thomas. *The Clansman: A Historical Romance of the Ku Klux Klan.* Arni Books, 2023. Originally published 1905.

Donnelly, Ignatius. *The Collected Works of Ignatius Donnelly.* Halcyon Classics, 2009. Originally published 1882-88.

Garner, James Wilford. *Reconstruction in Mississippi.* Old South Books, 2013. Originally published 1901.

Grafton, C. W. "A Sketch of the Old Scotch Settlement at Union Church," *Publications of the Mississippi Historical Society,* Vol. IX, 1906.

Grant, Richard. *The Deepest South of All: True Stories from Natchez, Mississippi.* Simon & Schuster, 2020.

Huffman, Alan. *Mississippi in Africa: The Saga of the Slaves of Prospect Hill Plantation and Their Legacy in Liberia Today.* Gotham Books, 2004.

Jemison, Elizabeth. *Protestants, Politics, and Power: Race, Gender, and Religion in the Post-Emancipation Mississippi*

River Valley, 1863-1900. Doctoral dissertation, Harvard University, Graduate School of Arts & Sciences, 2015.

Kirk, Robert. *The Secret Commonwealth of Elves, Fauns, and Fairies.* Digireads.com, 2021. Written ca. 1691, first published 1815.

Maclaren, Ian. *A Doctor of the Old School.* CreateSpace, 2016. Originally published 1896.

McMillen, Neil R. *Dark Journey: Black Mississippians in the Age of Jim Crow.* University of Illinois Press, 1989.

Penningroth, Dylan C.

The Claims of Kinfolk: African American Property and Community in the Nineteenth-Century South. (2003. The University of North Carolina Press.)

Before the Movement: The Hidden History of Black Civil Rights. Liveright Kindle Edition, 2023.

Percy, William Alexander. *Lanterns on the Levee: Recollections of a Planter's Son.* Alfred A. Knopf, 1941.

Perry, Imani. *South to America: A Journey Below the Mason-Dixon to Understand the Soul of a Nation.* HarperCollins, 2022.

Smith, Timothy B. *Mississippi in the Civil War: The Home Front.* The University Press of Mississippi, 2010.

Smythe, Ted Curtis. "The Reporter, 1880-1900. Working Conditions and Their Influence on the News," *Journalism History,* Spring 1980; 7, 1.

Stack, Carol. *Call To Home: African Americans Reclaim the Rural South.* Basic Books, 1996.

Scott, Sir Walter. *Rob Roy.* Independently published 2023. Originally published 1817.

Span, Christopher M. *From Cotton Field to School House: African American Education in Mississippi, 1862-1875* Univ. of N. Carolina Press, 2009.

Stewart, Antoinette M. *Property: Both Man and Land, 1828 – 2016, Jefferson County, Mississippi.* Independently published, 2017.

Wells, Ida B. *Southern Horrors: Lynch Law in All Its Phases.* Create Space, 2011. Originally published 1892.

Withycombe, Shannon. *Lost: Miscarriage in Nineteenth-Century America.* Rutgers University Press, 2019.

Woodward, C. Vann. *The Strange Career of Jim Crow: A Commemorative Edition.* Oxford University Press, 2002. Originally published 1955.

Wrem, Lynette Boney, ed. *A Bachelor's Life in Antebellum Mississippi: The Diary of Dr. Elijah Millington Walker 1849-1852.* University of Tennessee Press, 2004.

Acknowledgments

Writing historical fiction, I have learned, is a far more collaborative effort than writing science fiction. Among those who have had a hand in bringing this book to fruition are the following: Mimi Miller, Executive Director Emerita, Historic Natchez Foundation; Nicole deL. Harris, Curator at the Historic Natchez Foundation; Jo Miles-Seely at the Mississippi Department of Archives and History; Jennifer McGillan, Coordinator of Manuscripts, Mississippi State University Libraries; Kate Gregory, Director of Mississippi Political Collections, MSU Libraries; Amanda Carlock, Senior Library Associate, MSU Libraries. I offer my gratitude to each and every one of them, as well as to Jerri Bell, Antoinette Stewart, Deannie Tensley and others on Facebook's Jefferson County History page; retired journalism professor Darwin Payne; and an editor at the *Bluff City Post* whose patience deserves far better than my failure to recall his name.

There were also long phone conversations about family lore with my sister Bonnie Arnett, who had actually traveled as a child to Mississippi with our grandparents. There were the generous Baptists in Union Church who texted around the only photo I had of the old family home until somebody finally recognized it and who also insisted I join them for their Sunday potluck lunch. There was the docent at the Museum of Mississippi History in Jackson who was a retired civil rights lawyer and who warned me not to underestimate the intergenerational trauma of slavery. And there were the staff members at the Natchez Museum of African American History and Culture who endeavored to nudge my research in the right direction. I offer my heartfelt thanks to all of these.

Beta readers Cheryl Rooke, Denman Glober Netherland, and Madelyn Hunt merit special thanks as do all the members of my writing critique group. Their insights and encouragement helped keep me on track. Editor Jenny Quinlan (no relation) was invaluable in wrangling an earlier version of this manuscript.

I know that, despite my best efforts, I have probably gotten some things wrong. None of the above bear any responsibility for that. It's all on me. My hope is that I've gotten enough things right to make this book a worthwhile read.